THE UNCANNY

ALSO BY ANDREW KLAVAN

THE UNCANNY

ANDREW KLAVAN

LITTLE, BROWN AND COMPANY

A *Little, Brown* Book

First published in Great Britain in 1998
by Little, Brown and Company
First published in the United States in 1998
by Crown Publishers Inc

A CIP catalogue record for this book
is available from the British Library.

HARDBACK ISBN 0 316 64415 3
C FORMAT ISBN 0 316 64561 3

Printed and bound in Great Britain by Clays Ltd, St Ives plc

UK companies, institutions and other organisations wishing
to make bulk purchases of this or any other book
published by Little, Brown should contact their local
bookshop or the special sales department at the address below.
Tel 0171 911 8000. Fax 0171 911 8100.

Little, Brown and Company (UK)
Brettenham House
Lancaster Place
London WC2E 7EN

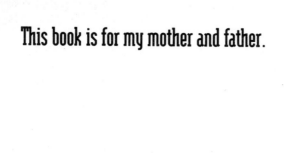
This book is for my mother and father.

"Stay, Illusion!"

—HAMLET

I

PROLOGUE:
BLACK ANNIE

HIS EYES! His eyes were full of fear. And, though I had seen him in London only six months before, he seemed since then to have aged as many decades. A man like myself in his early thirties, he peered at me through the half-open door of Ravenswood Grange with all the tremulous hostility, the white-eyed apprehension, of some ancient anchorite disturbed at his grimmest meditations.

I had already dismissed my trap. I could hear the horse's hoofbeats fading behind me on the Grange's long drive. The autumn darkling was closing around me, the windswept clouds of a lowering sky pressed down on me from above. The house itself, the whole great stone edifice, loomed menacingly before me as with an *adsum* to my *conjuro te*. All this—and the horrid ravens peering blackly at me from the gutters and gables of the place—served to magnify the thrill of dread I felt as I stood on the threshold and stared into the ravaged features of my old schoolmate.

"My God, Quentin!" I managed to expostulate at last. "My God, man, where are the servants?" For he had come to the door himself and, save for the taper guttering in his trembling hand, the hall behind him, the house around him, were all in darkness.

At the sound of my voice, Quentin glanced about, distracted, as if he only now realized he had been forsaken. Slowly, his frightened gaze returned to me— and yet, I felt, it passed right through me. I might have been a spectre, invisible, and he seeing only the empty drive where it stretched into the twilight overhung by gloomy rows of copper beech.

"Gone," he said then, in a high, cracked whisper, an old man's whisper. "All gone. They would not stay. Not one of them would stay with me. No, not one."

The wind rose. The dead leaves swirled and chattered at my feet. From a gable peak came the hoarse cry of a raven, weirdly triumphant, horrible. I shivered. Then, bestirring myself at last from the first shock of seeing my friend in his shattered state, I stepped forward, extending my hand. Quentin merely licked his lips furtively, and faded away from me into the tenebrous front hall.

I followed him, entered. The heavy wooden door swung shut behind me with a melancholy reverberation. I forced myself to ignore it as I ignored the ominous penumbra that quickly gathered round the edges of his solitary flame. Again, and with a soothing word, I came towards him. This time, I was allowed to approach. Taking the poor man by the elbow, I led him gently inside.

I lit a fire in the sitting room, but it could do little to dispel the aura of dejection that had descended over the place. It was a house abandoned. Dust gathered by the wainscoting, cobwebs hung from the rafters. Papers and notebooks were strewn carelessly over the furniture and the floor. Whatever heat and cheer the hearthglow afforded was soon lost, swallowed by the lofty ceilings or transformed into a threatening phantasmagoria by the sombre tapestries hanging on the wall and the thick drapes around the narrow, arched windows.

When I stood from the grate, I found Quentin had sunk into an armchair. Open-mouthed and silent, he sat as if transfixed by the shadows now darting and receding across the complex patterns of the oriental rug. The light from the grate, the light from the candle he still gripped loosely in his hand, dragged at his sallow cheeks like red fingers, like a premonition of hellfire. I removed the taper from his slack grasp and used it to light a lamp on the table beside his chair. Standing over him, I contemplated his macabre transformation with bafflement and with sorrow.

Sorrowful indeed it was and more sorrowful yet for my memories of what he'd been not half a year before. Then, in my rooms in town, we had sat, like the schoolfellows we lately were, casually flung over chair and settee, debating long into the night with all the gay ferocity of old. A churchman with a lucrative Sussex living, Quentin was, as he had ever been, a fervent defender of the faith, an apologist for Newman, a supporter of Pusey, an ardent advocate of the high ritual and the deep *mysterium*. I, a physician with a small but growing practice in Harley Street, was equally determined to ride out upon the lists for science, to preach Reason and Experiment as the keys to comprehending the internal mechanisms of this clockwork life. How well I remembered the passion with which Quentin opposed me, the brightness of his eyes, the vibrancy of his voice as he proclaimed the miraculous and supernatural as our surest guides to the truth.

Now—not a fortnight since he had returned to Ravenswood to settle the affairs appending to the sudden death of his elder brother and sister-in-law—his strong, open face was lined and sunken, his lean, manly frame as much a ruin as the fragments of the old abbey that stood without the Grange's walls. For all my physic, I could think to offer him nothing better than a dash of brandy. This, my hand supporting his wrist, he raised unsteadily to his lips.

The medicine had its effect. Coughing slightly, he set the empty glass beside the lamp, blinked and looked up at me as if for the first time.

"Neville," he said. "Thank Heaven, you've come."

"Of course I've come, old fellow," I responded, as bluffly as I could. "As soon as I got your letter. But what the devil's the matter? You look as if you've been through Hell."

At this, some memory seemed to rekindle the terror in his eyes. He turned from me and stared into the now-blazing fire. "You were wrong, you know, Neville."

"Wrong? In what respect?"

"All of it. All of it," said he, his tone mournful. "There *is* a world beyond the world we know. There is a world beyond, and it's . . . it's . . ." But he did not—could not—finish. Rather, lifting his face once more, he showed to me an expression of such pitiable horror that no further utterance was necessary. "Neville," he whispered then, galvanized suddenly, leaning towards me urgently. "Neville, I have seen it. I have seen *her*."

"Her? Who?" I said sharply. I was moved to irritation by the chill that had begun to edge up my spine. "What the devil are you talking about? Whom have you seen?"

With that, the energy seemed to drain out of him. The poor fellow subsided weakly in his chair, his chin sunk on his chest, his features limp. His voice, when it came again, was as solemn as the echo from an empty tomb.

"Black Annie!" was all he said.

I did not know whether to laugh at this or to recoil at the further evidence of his disturbed senses. In the end, averting my face to hide my reactions from him, I said merely, "I say, do you think there's anything to eat in this mausoleum?"

Fortunately, there was. For it now transpired that not all the servants had entirely deserted the place. One girl, at least—in very pity for her young master, as I suspected—remained. She had agreed to attend to my friend's needs by daylight on the stipulation that she might be well away from the house before the onset of dusk. Thus, on investigation, I found a cold repast had already been laid out in the dining room. No more than a modest portion of mutton, a half loaf of bread and a rather unfortunate claret, still it sufficed. I brought the provisions into the sitting room, where we made a rude feast of them before the hearth.

We ate in silence. To be honest, we drank a good deal more than we ate. Quentin, at my urging, did manage to pick desultorily at his chop. For my own part, however, I mostly sat brooding over my wine, reflecting on what I had so far heard.

Black Annie. The name—uttered in such awful tones by my companion—was not entirely unknown to me. There was, I remembered, a legend attached to the old Grange concerning such a figure. Quentin himself had related the tale to me on one of those evenings at school after lights-out when we attempted to disturb each other's sleep by whispering scare stories across the space between our beds.

I rose from my chair and went to stand before one of the windows on the far wall. Looking out between the dented leaden cames, I saw that night had now drawn down around the place completely. A gibbous moon, sporadically visible in the gaps between the racing clouds, cast a pall of faltering and sickly light over the sere expanse of grassland to the east. In that field, now visible, now vanishing as the moon went once again behind its shifting cover, there stood an ominous and melancholy apparition: the ruins of Ravenswood Abbey—the broken wedge of a chapel wall, the slanting monuments of its ancient churchyard.

In the days before the old religion fell prey to the depredations of our eighth

Henry, the ground where the Grange now stood had been within the abbey confines. It was with this ancient institution that the story of Black Annie was associated. It was hardly an original tale. I don't think there is a ruin such as this in all of England that does not have some deceased monk or other gallivanting about it of a midnight. In this case, so the legend ran, the cowled spectre of a nun—Black Annie—had taken up residence among the decrepit stones. In life, she had been seduced by a canon of the Augustinians—one of the black canons, so called for the colour of their robes. There followed the necessary sequel: the poor woman was soon with child. But before her sin could become evident, she mysteriously vanished. In fact, with the conspiratorial aid of her sister nuns, she had contrived to hide herself within a secret chamber in the nunnery's dorter. There, the sisters brought her food and drink—and kept watch during the frequent visits of her paramour. As her time approached, however, it became clear that the deception could not be continued indefinitely. What was more, the abbey was now under heavy pressure from the minions of the vicar-general, who were then touring the countryside on the king's behalf in search of useful evidence of corruption among the clergy. Terrified of discovery, the canon persuaded his lover to give their child into his charge. He promised her he would remove the infant to some safe and secret place, where it would be well cared for by a local nurse of his acquaintance. But, having taken the babe away, the perfidious canon, hoping to set his crime permanently beyond the investigators' ken, slit the helpless creature's throat and hid its little body somewhere on the abbey grounds. Inevitably, word of this horrible deed found its way to the distracted mother in her hiding hole. When the royal ministers arrived to make their inspection, they were led at once to the secret chamber where—no doubt to their considerable satisfaction—they found the unfortunate woman hanging dead at the end of a stout rope she had secured to the rafters.

This was the gruesome story Quentin had whispered to me one night in our boyhood dormitory. And he added, with appropriately spooky inflections, that the black-cowled spectre of that much-injured sister was said to walk the ruins of the abbey to this very day.

I'm afraid I must have made a soft noise of derision at the recollection of this melodramatic yarn, for Quentin, as if reading my thoughts, said from behind me, "You remember, don't you?"

I gestured from the window. "I remember some nonsense you told me back in school, but . . ."

"True, Neville, all true!" he exclaimed. In a fresh bout of agitation, he leapt from his chair, paced to the centre of the room. He stood there beneath the tapestry of Susanna, whose time-faded flesh the firelight made to seem roseate and alive under the leering gaze of the elders. Quentin's pale, tormented features were also scored by flame and shadow, also given a tortuous life of their own as he lifted a shaking hand to point at the window. "I've *seen* her, I tell you. Out there. By the abbey. And what's more . . ." But his arm dropped to his side and he shook his head.

"What's more?" I prompted.

"Oh!" It was a sound of such hopelessness that all my impatient scepticism was swept away by a tide of compassion. "I knew you would not believe me, Neville. You with your Science and your Reason—your new religion so eager to replace the old. But I tell you, I have seen her and what's more . . . what's more, I have *heard* her." He turned such a sidelong, knowing look then at the chamber's oaken door that, for the first time, I began to suspect he was truly mad. "In the house," he muttered. "She has been in this house."

Shaken—by his expression, by his tone—I tried once more to strike a hearty note of unconcern. "Well, then! It hardly matters whether I believe you or not. If she will appear to you, I hope she will not scruple to appear to me as well. Then I shall have 'the sensible and true avouch of my own eyes,' and I have no doubt," I added in an undertone, "that we can begin to get to the bottom of this whole affair."

Quentin, nodding, only turned and walked heavily back to the blazing hearth. "Be careful what you say, Neville," he remarked. Then he sagged once more into his chair.

"I am not afraid," I told him.

But that was a lie. I was very much afraid, though not for the reasons he might have imagined. It was my friend's sanity I feared for. Whatever vision had appeared to him, it was clear to my physician's understanding that it was no "extravagant and erring spirit," but rather the product of his disordered faculties. What I could not yet discern was whether those faculties were still within reach of treatment or whether Quentin was—and I have seen such cases—spiralling irretrievably into lunacy. I expected—not to say dreaded—that that very night would tell me all.

So we kept vigil, he and I. The fire waned and the oil in the lamp burned away. The shadows wafted slowly down from the rafters and came to enshroud us. The figures on the tapestries blended with the darkness until only a glancing eye, an enigmatic smile, a grasping hand flared into view from time to time with the cracking of an ember.

I had opportunity, in those hours, to think more or less deeply on my friend's situation. My own beliefs notwithstanding, I am, I hope, no enemy to honest faith. Yet I could not help but wonder if it was perhaps Quentin's spiritual studies that had so unnerved him. The civilized religion which we practice in this modern day has still its links to antique creeds and half-forgotten superstitions. Was it these, I asked myself, that haunted the abbey ruins, moulded by my friend's fevered brain into the likeness of Black Annie?

As I meditated thus, the lamp went out. The embers in the grate continued to settle and hiss and a deeper blackness yet enclosed us. I studied my friend surreptitiously, growing even more concerned as the enervated condition in which he had begun our watch slowly gave way to a nervous attitude of growing tension and suspense. Somewhere beyond the room, a clock chimed. It was midnight.

Suddenly, Quentin was on his feet. "This is the hour!" he exclaimed. "She is here!"

Before I could respond, he had rushed across the room to the window, had pressed himself close to the glass. I was fairly at his heels, was peering over his shoulder an instant later.

His breath misted the pane as he cried hoarsely, "Out there!"

"I can't see a thing!" I answered. Beyond a yard away, I could make out nothing but thick, sable night.

And then the wind rose. I heard it in the chimney. I saw it a moment later in the movement of an elm as its naked branches bent and shivered. For as the wind rose, the clouds raced—and the moon appeared behind their wisps and traces. Its eldritch silver glow drew the landscape out of the darkness. Out there, beyond the sinuous silhouette of the elm, stood the abbey ruin, sullen, black and grim. The faltering illumination, laced as it was with the running cloud shadows, gave to the entire scene a floating quality, weird and dreamlike. We seemed to stare through the glass as through a torn curtain at another world revealed.

And as we stared, I saw her. A cloaked and hooded figure—raven-black, so black she seemed less a being than an absence of existence—was moving with slow and awful majesty among the churchyard headstones.

I cannot describe the suffocating horror that swept over me at that uncanny sight. I was unmanned, paralysed, my marrow ice, my sinew water. For long seconds, as the thing glided steadily towards the fragment of the chapel wall, I could not move or speak—I could not breathe—but only gaped unblinking as if I had been petrified on the spot. Death itself would not have seemed as forbidding to me as that ebon wraith who appeared the herald of a realm beyond death, a realm beyond reason, a realm, most terrible of all, beyond the reach of mercy or forgetfulness.

The silent, mournful phantasm proceeded with its lifeless grace to the end of the churchyard, to all that remained of the chapel. There, beside that ruined wall; there—though I write it who can hardly credit his own eyes; there, as I stood watching, frozen and amazed, the jet absence of her seemed to sink at the same stately pace, sink lower and lower into the hard earth, until only the cowled head remained above the surface. And then that too—all, all of her—had vanished.

At almost the same instant, a mass of clouds, propelled before the wailing wind, surged towards us above the ruin. In seconds, it had swept over the moon. The torn curtain closed. Utter darkness pressed once more against the window.

Still, as second after second passed, I could not move, but gazed upon the viewless night as if the extraordinary scene were still before me. It was Quentin's stifled cry that broke the trance. When I turned, I saw that he had fallen into a paroxysm of trembling. Dry, strangled sobs were forcing their way out between his clenched teeth. I feared the onset of an apoplexy. Willing myself to action, I clutched his arm roughly.

"It's all right," I said—shouted, more loudly than I had intended. "It's all right, man, pull yourself together. It's over. She's gone."

"Gone?" The voice that broke from him did nothing to ease my qualms. It sounded choked and high, hollowed by an undertone of barely suppressed hysterical laughter. "Not gone," he said, eyeing me brightly. "You fool. She is not gone. There are tunnels, you see. Out there. Under the abbey. Drains, passages for supplies. Covered over now, yes. They're all covered over. But there's a whole network of drains and tunnels. And one of them . . . one of them leads . . ."

Before he could finish, there came a noise—a noise *from within the house!* Soft, but definite, insistent, it seemed to rise up from below us, to spread through the walls until it filled the darkened sitting room.

Tick-tick. Tick-tick. Tick-tick.

I have heard people say that their hairs stood on end, but I had never before experienced it myself. The sound was like that of a clock's pendulum and yet more resonant; softer, thinner than a knock at the door, and yet as chillingly deliberate. There was a pause as my gaze travelled slowly over the umbral forms and faces on the hanging tapestries. And then again:

Tick-tick. Tick-tick.

I returned my attention to Quentin. He smiled at me, but a smile of such wild misery that I despaired of his reclamation. He leaned forward, whispered almost gleefully:

"One of them leads to the priest's hole."

Tick-tick. Tick-tick. Tick-tick.

There were often, I knew, in abbeys and the neighbouring houses, secret chambers and hideaways built to protect imperilled priests during the Tudor persecutions. It would not have been surprising if these "priest's holes" were connected to the rest of the abbey by the underground passages which King Henry always claimed were employed in the canons' secret amours.

"A priest's hole," I said, as the soft ticking sound repeated yet again, as the febrile gleam in my poor friend's eyes grew brighter. "Where is it? Can we get inside? Come on, out with it, man."

For the second time that night, Quentin cast a queerly knowing look at the door.

Tick-tick. Tick-tick. That infernal noise again. What was it?

"In the study," Quentin said.

I did not hesitate; the slightest hesitation would have done for my resolve. I marched, with more boldness than I felt, across the room to the fireplace. I seized a candle from the mantelpiece, bent to touch the wick to an ember. When the taper ignited, I carried the flame back to where Quentin stood. His face in the wavering glow was stretched and taut with apprehension as he began to understand my intent.

"Neville," he gasped, "we can't, we mustn't . . ."

"We will," I said sternly. "Follow me."

I pulled him from the window, fairly dragged him after me to the door. It was harsh therapy, but effective. As Quentin was torn from his passive terror and offered the prospect of an enterprise, a measure of his former vigor seemed to return to him. His trembling ceased, and by the time we broke from the chamber into the corridor, he was following after me of his own volition.

With every step we took, the sound grew louder, nearer. Yet always, always, it surrounded us, vibrating behind the portraits, beneath the flooring, above the beams.

Tick-tick. Tick-tick.

At my shoulder, Quentin began to protest again, his expression urgent in the trailing candlelight, his words tumbling over one another.

"Neville. Neville, listen . . . For God's sake . . . You don't know what you're dealing with . . . You don't understand . . . Listen to me . . . Listen, before it's too late . . ."

I raced on, ignoring his admonitions, closing my mind to them lest they dissuade me from my purpose. The persistent, rhythmic tapping all around us grew yet louder, nearer. I felt as if it had entered my brain, was rapping at me from within.

Tick-tick. Tick-tick.

"Neville!" Quentin cried again.

"Is this the door?" I said, as we reached the study. Raising my candle high, I grasped the iron handle. At a nod from Quentin, I pushed it down. The door swung slowly inward.

We entered the small room, the candlelight breathing over the veiled windows, the shelves of books, a desk littered, like the sitting room, with documents heaped and strewn about. The flame's unsteady respiration seemed to plunge the place into an element like water. The objects seemed to undulate and swim in and out of view before us.

Tick-tick. Tick-tick.

I stepped forward cautiously, Quentin at my back. It was here, whatever it was—here, or just nearby. The sound seemed to vibrate up out of the very heart of the chamber. I could not help but tense, the flame flickering as my grip on the candle tightened, as the sound came again.

Tick-tick.

"Where is it?" I whispered hoarsely.

"Neville . . ."

"Where is it?"

He inclined his head towards the books on the wall to my left. "That case there," he said reluctantly.

In two strides, I was at the bookcase he indicated, a tall case of some dark wood, its shelves lined with musty leather volumes. Uncertainly, my hand went out to touch the bindings. Quentin continued to protest behind me.

"Neville, let us turn back, let us consider, there is more to say, much more you do not know . . ."

A book—a heavy black book with no lettering on its ribbed spine—shifted inward beneath my fingers. There was the sound of a latch giving way. The entire case seemed to snap free of the wall. With a whining screak, it swung towards me on a hidden hinge.

I pulled the case open as if it were a door to reveal the narrow staircase winding into the blackness below.

Tick-tick. Tick-tick.

Now, at last, as if drawn from the house's timbers, drawn from the air around us, from my own brain, the sound resolved itself upon a single centre, a single source. It ascended in its unceasing, funereal tempo from the dark at the base of the stairs.

Tick-tick.

I started down to meet it.

"No, Neville!"

As I descended, step by slow step, the damp wooden boards groaning thickly beneath my soles, Quentin's gibbered warnings spiralled into a frantic skirl.

"You do not know, you have not understood, you must believe me, I have thought on these things for weeks, I have tried to comprehend . . ."

My own shadow dodged and capered in bizarre shapes on the dripping stone walls around me. My heart was thudding in my chest and there was a thickness in my throat that nearly made me gag.

As my foot touched the bottom step, I felt a clammy draught twine round my legs. The candle flame swelled and, in the broadening glow, I saw before me a door of rotted wood hung in hammered iron bands.

Tick-tick. Tick-tick.

The sound was coming from behind the door. Nervously gnawing my lips, I willed my hand to reach out for the ring that secured it.

"Neville. For the love of God!" Quentin cried. "There were weeks before she died. Weeks when she left her hiding hole, when she wandered the abbey grounds by night. Nights when she used a spade, don't you see! In her distraction, a garden spade, trying to dig through the stone! She was searching . . ."

The door opened heavily, grinding against the floor.

Tick-tick. Tick-tick. Tick . . .

And there was silence. The tapping stopped short. The candlelight faltered, recovered, bathed the priest's hole in its bleak, liquid candescence.

But the place was empty.

Together on the threshold, Quentin and I found ourselves peering into a cramped dungeon with low beams above walls of uneven stone blocks. Nothing moved within and the quiet was so complete it seemed almost unnatural. Not even a rat scrabbled for cover as we two stood baffled, gawking.

Then Quentin blurted, "There! Look!"

I lifted the taper. The light spread over the entire chamber. My gaze, following Quentin's gesture, fell on a small white mound of flakes and powder that had collected on the floor at the base of the wall. It was immediately apparent that the debris had fallen from one of the stones above. I could see where the stone had been chiseled, its edges frayed and chalky as if—just as if someone had been digging at it with the point of a spade.

Before I had time to think, I was moving forward, one hand holding the candle high, the other stretching towards the stone. Quentin shouted my name again, but my fingers were already digging at the jagged edge where the blade had bit into the rock. I gripped it, pulled. The stone shifted easily, wobbled, rolled from its position. It slipped from my grasp and there was a loud crash as it dropped to the floor at my feet. In the same instant, the air seemed to shake. Quentin shouted wildly. I gasped. But these noises were washed away by an indescribably hideous shriek. It flew up around us from everywhere and nowhere at once: a ragged howl full of hellish rage and a grief beyond the soothings of eternity. The entire house seemed to quake and shiver to its foundations as the anguished wail went on and on and on.

For there, in the niche revealed by the displacement of the stone, preserved in that airless cell so that its skin had grown leathery and tight, its mouth had been yanked wide and its eyeless sockets had a stare of endless agony—there, its neck slashed open, lay the body of an infant, which decayed and crumbled to dust even as we gazed upon it.

II

STORM, LIFTING HIS
TRAGICAL EYES

1 A glass shattered across the room and Storm, lifting his tragical eyes, saw, though too late, a woman worth dying for.

The book of ghost stories was still open in his hands. His lips were still parted on the final phrase—*crumbled to dust even as we gazed upon it.* But the phrase, the whole story, had been blown right out of his mind. By the woman, by her beauty. Just the sight of her had brought him from his chair to his feet.

Which was pretty ridiculous when he came to think of it. What was he going to do next? Leap into the air like a cartoon character—his tongue out—his eyes hanging from their sockets on springs—the Valentine shape of his heart boinging through his shirtfront? He was a modern guy, after all, an American guy, a Hollywood guy. A real person with nose hairs and psychiatric problems and an anus. This was life, not the movies. It wasn't possible—was it?—that he had just fallen in love at first sight?

Maybe not, but he went on gawping at her. She was standing in the drawing-room archway, one of the guests who had drifted in when Storm had begun to read aloud. In the sitting room behind her, the great Scotch pine with its colored Christmas lights seemed to him to frame her, to set her in relief. A girl of, say, twenty and some. Not the sort of anorexic starlet he was used to, not one of his usual airheads inflated with silicon and ambition. Hers was a real figure in low-cut black velvet. A waist and hips of substance, womanly in the extreme. A bosom from the days when bosoms were bosoms. A swanlike neck, damask cheeks, skin of ivory, hair of jet. Brown eyes, the palest brown eyes imaginable, bright and snappy and quick. *Woof,* he thought; *Jesus.*

The others around her—all of Bolt's London sophisticates—had begun to laugh now and applaud her. She was still frozen with the hand that had held the glass extended, with her startled gaze on the fragments where they lay. Fragments and glistening slivers on the tan carpet. A spreading, colorless stain. The glass had just slipped from her fingers apparently, must've hit the edge of the butler's tray on the way down.

"Oh," she said finally, "how stupid of me."

Storm reeled inwardly, mentally clutched his chest. What an accent, too, he thought. That real English stuff. Like Julie Andrews in *Mary Poppins.* He could still remember some of his boyhood fantasies about Mary Poppins. The things she would croon to him with that accent. *Oh, Richard. Oh, young master!*

I'm sorry, he was about to say aloud, *sorry if I frightened you. It was just a stupid old ghost story.* But he was already coming to his senses. And Bolt, anyway, was out of his armchair, was going to her, and Bolt was the host.

"Oh, Frederick, let me clean it up, I'm an idiot," she said to him.

"No, no." He took her arm. "I've already dispatched my minions." The two women who had knelt to retrieve the shards glared up at him: a man plummeting into middle age like a bomb, shaped like a bomb, squat-bottomed, potbellied in his green suit and waistcoat. A serpentine, cynical face deeply scored by Bell's and Rothmans. Shaggy gray hair dropping dandruff. Cigarette dropping ash. "And anyway, I rent the place," he said. And he led her gently from the room.

Storm watched—bleakly—as the two of them turned out of sight down the front hall. He could hear their voices receding.

"I am sorry, Frederick, I shouldn't have come, I'm just knackered. I was in Ohio yesterday, and Berlin last week . . ."

"Don't be ridiculous. I live for your visits. I'll save the pieces as a relic. I'll build a shrine on the spot . . ."

Someone clapped Storm on the shoulder. Someone else said, "Well read. Spooky stuff. You put the wind up her anyway."

"Who is she?" Storm murmured, staring at the place where she had stood.

And someone answered: "Oh, that—that's Sophia Endering. Her father owns the Endering Gallery in New Bond Street. Not half bad, eh?"

Storm nodded. Remained on his feet a few moments more, his gaze now wandering aimlessly over the room. A cozy alcove, chairs clustered together, run-of-the-mill pseudo-Victorian prints hung above low shelves of frazzled paperbacks. A wide archway into the long sitting room where the Christmas tree sparkled and the gas fire burbled and recessed lights beamed on bottles of white wine. And where the group that had gathered to hear him read was now dispersing. And the party conversation was resuming.

Above the rising chatter, he heard the front door shut. He could feel it: she was gone. He sank slowly back into his chair.

Sophia Endering, he thought. He sat there with the book held slack on his thigh, his thumb holding the place for no good reason. *Sophia Endering.*

But what difference did it make? It didn't matter now. He was not in love with her. He could not be in love with her. He could not be in love with anyone.

He sat there, silent, slumped, withdrawn again into his unhappy depths.

2

But why? thought Harper Albright. Why should he be so sad?

From her perch among the embroidered cushions of the window seat to Storm's far left, she had seen everything. She had seen Storm rise to his feet with his first look at Sophia. She had seen the ache of passion animate his features, had watched as it drained away again, as his eyes became hollow again, and his expression once more grew distant with despair. It made her think of certain mud crabs who can "throw" their claws, actually detach their claws to break the grip of an enemy. It seemed to her that Storm— she supposed she had to call him by that ridiculous name if only out of respect for the American miracle of self-invention—it seemed to her that Storm had similarly "thrown" his heart, detached his heart to break the grip of life.

And she pondered on this, sitting there, her withered hands clasped over the carved wooden dragon's head that topped her walking stick. She was a grim, peculiar-looking person, this Harper. Not an old woman particularly, sixty perhaps, but dilapidated nonetheless. With lifeless gray hair bobbed on a furrowed brow. Slack, sagging cheeks under deep, gray pouches. And spectacles thick as goggles, through which she blinked intently. A pipe with a meerschaum skull for a bowl was clamped between her yellowing teeth, yellowish smoke trailing out of it. She rested her round chin on the back of her hands. And she wondered:

Why *shouldn't* Richard Storm love Sophia Endering? He was older than she was, certainly—forty at least. But he was youthful and handsome. Rangy, muscular. With a full head of short, sandy hair, and features as rugged as the great western land from which he came. More rugged, probably, seeing as he came from Los Angeles. And Harper knew him to be unmarried; that is, divorced. Humorous and easygoing, and gentle in a lady's presence. She herself was aware of having developed some sentimental feelings for him since he had come to her. Possibly. Some. So why should he disengage himself? From Sophia. From everyone, really. Harper Albright turned the question over and over.

He was, she thought, for all his American amiability, a man of mystery to some extent, of hidden depths at least. A producer, a highly successful producer of Hollywood films, some good ones, some she'd seen, many that were in her line, having to do with horror and the supernatural, ghosts, werewolves, the occasional latex demon or two. And yet, a month ago, he had apparently left this lucrative career behind. He had turned up all unknown in London. He had arrived at her door without introduction and volunteered to serve as an unpaid intern on her little magazine, *Bizarre!* He was tired of making movies about the paranormal, he told her. He wanted to work with her, to get at "the real thing." And that was pretty much all he told her. But uncomplaining—and, again, unpaid—he took to bounding after her like some great red setter, joining her journalistic investigations into claims of haunting, witchcraft, vampirism, alien abductions, and the like. And the question of what he was really after—and why it was he remained, in some way, set apart—had begun to worry at her.

Her reverie was interrupted, however, as Bolt reentered through the archway.

"Well," he growled nastily at Storm. "It was well read anyway, I'll give you that."

This was what had started the incident. The ghost story. About half an hour before. Bolt had been holding forth, pronouncing upon ghost stories in general: Christmas and December gatherings and ghost stories and so on. Storm had said that he had always loved the English variety. *Loved* them, he'd said—that's what had done it—all that Yankee enthusiasm. It wasn't that Bolt disliked Storm in particular, or Americans in general. But there was some vivacious something about both of them that was an insult to his cherished pessimism. Suddenly, anyway, after that, Bolt had felt that he had to play the expert. He'd shifted up a notch from pronouncing to pontificating. And when Storm had said that he thought the Oxford collection was sensational— *Absolutely sensational!* he'd said—it had just been too much for poor Bolt.

"Well, I suppose," the journalist had said. "If you don't mind the fact that they left out 'Thurnley Abbey.' I mean, I don't expect it to be complete, but, after all, it is *The Oxford Book of English Ghost Stories,* which I think entails certain responsibilities. I mean, they left out 'Thurnley Abbey'!"

"Yeah, 'Thurnley Abbey,' that was a good one," said Storm. "I think they put that in the Victorian collection."

"Pff!" said Frederick Bolt.

And Storm, mildly, changed the subject. "Hey, have you ever read 'Black Annie,' by Robert Hughes?"

It was a soft answer, Harper Albright thought, meant to turn away wrath. But it had only made things worse. Because it rapidly became clear that Bolt *hadn't* read "Black Annie," that he'd never even heard of it. Which meant it couldn't possibly be worth considering. And he said so.

"Oh no, no, you're wrong!" cried Storm. Rising from his chair, he went to the shelves. Strolled over, too familiarly, as if it were his flat instead of Bolt's. He plucked out *The Fourteenth Fontana Book of Great Ghost Stories.* "It's in here. You oughta read it, it really is good."

He held the book out to Bolt. Bolt scowled at it. "Fourteenth! They must've been pretty thin on the ground by then." But Storm continued to proffer it. And Bolt's lips curled wickedly. "Why don't *you* read it?" he sneered. "Go on—Christmas by the fireside—a gathering—a ghost story—give us a reading, Storm."

"Oh, for pity's sake," Harper Albright had muttered. Bolt could be intolerable.

Later, though, she wondered whether he hadn't perhaps fallen into the American's trap. Storm took the book back to his chair and began to read "Black Annie" aloud—and Harper was immediately reminded that his father had been an actor; he *had* told her that. He proceeded to deliver a witty and yet genuinely spooky rendition of the piece. And by the time Quentin and Neville were making their candlelit way down the ominous, sombre and melancholy corridors of Ravenswood Grange, most of Bolt's party guests were here in the drawing room and most of them were spellbound. At the last sentence, there were one or two people who actually gasped.

And the lovely Sophia Endering had dropped her glass.

"It was well read, certainly," Bolt conceded now again. "And not without interest. Without originality, or irony or invention—or literate prose. But no one could say it was without interest."

Storm only spread his hands and spoke with such sincerity that Harper Albright thought it would kill Bolt on the spot. "Ah, well, you know. I first read it when I was maybe ten years old. And it just hit me, like: Pow! The English Ghost Story. It got me started in a way. The first film I ever made, twenty years ago, I was, I don't know, twenty-two. *Spectre*, it was called. I'd never even been to England. I wrote it, directed it, shot the whole thing in California. But I set it here, you know, in this total 'Black Annie' world I made up from the story. It just—I don't know—it always stuck with me in this . . ."

His voice trailed off. He shook his head. Well, he was American, Harper reminded herself, and had evolved beyond the need for complete sentences. But what he said— what he was trying to say—did set her thinking again. Chomping on her skull pipe, leaning on her dragon-headed cane, blinking through her goggly spectacles. He certainly *did* love the English Ghost Story, did young Storm, she thought.

And perhaps, she thought, that would ultimately explain everything.

3 Outside, meanwhile, in the bleak city of midwinter, Sophia Endering hurried up the slope of the narrow mews, her heels rapping the cobblestones. The

bosom that Storm had so admired was thrumming with agitation. That story, Sophia thought. That idiotic American and that idiotic story.

She held her handbag pinned to her overcoat with one elbow. Her other arm was swinging freely, march-style. Her face was set resolutely forward. She felt the wind brush her cheeks; flecks of a faint, cool rain.

Tick-tick. Tick-tick.

It was an absurd coincidence, of course. That story, that repeated noise, that race down the corridor of the haunted house. *Tick-tick.* The way it echoed her memories almost perfectly. Her earliest memories. Her worst memories . . .

At the top of the mews, at the brink of the junction, she pulled up, had to breathe in the night chill to calm herself. Above her, a burly sea of clouds, backlit by the full moon, billowed swiftly overhead. It rolled over the impending tree wall, into the cryptic reaches of Holland Park.

Tick-tick. Tick-tick.

Irritated—more upset than she admitted—Sophia scanned the road for a cab. It was unusually quiet here. No cars at all. No people, no sound of footsteps, no sound but her own breathing. It must be late, she thought, after midnight. She checked her watch: in fact, it was after one. She could feel the deserted mews behind her. To her right, there was the unbroken hush, unnerving. She glanced to her left, down the street, down the hill, to the corner. A dreadlocked Jamaican kissed a poxy blonde in the glare of a streetlamp. Some cars rushed by. A group of boys swaggered past, jostling each other. Their laughter reached her and then they were gone and it faded away. She would go down there, to the avenue, she thought. Hail a taxi. She would be sure to find one. She was a woman cabs stopped for.

Tick-tick.

Sophia went rigid. It had almost sounded real that time. Had it been real? A ticking noise on the cobbles behind her? She braced herself. Looked over her shoulder. Brought her body half around and faced the mews.

The passage sloped away from her between old brick walls hung with dead ivy. No. It was empty. Most of the small houses were dark. Even the lighted windows here and there were heavily curtained. Sophia swallowed. This was becoming absurd. The story, her agitation. Dropping that stupid glass in front of everyone. The American with his dramatics . . .

She gave the mews one last look, then turned again. And cried out: "Oh!"

A man was standing directly before her. Close, standing too close, standing over her, his face pressing down on her out of the dark.

Her first instinct was to try to charge past him. Don't talk. Don't engage him. She lowered her head, stepped forward. The man put out his hand. Which made her heart catch. Which made her seriously consider screaming for help.

"Wait," he said. "Miss Endering. Sophia. Don't be afraid."

That stopped her. The fact that he knew her name. His tone of voice. The perfect English, a German accent faint, refined. She pulled up. Examined him. An earnest young man, bundled in a pea jacket, the collar turned up around his cheeks. Very handsome, very young. Incredibly earnest. With wavy blond hair and a warm gaze she could see even in the dark. But a stranger, she was sure of it.

He smiled. "No, no, you don't know me. I am the Resurrection."

The first jolt of surprise was gone. Sophia was in

command of herself again. Still nervous—with him so close, and the shadows so close around them, with him a head taller than she, towering over her, and so close that she felt the heat of him in the cool air. Two minutes ago she had been in the warmth and the light and the crowd of Bolt's party. Surrounded by chattering, laughing people, the taste of wine on her lips. She missed all that pretty badly just now, alone with this man in the cold. The Resurrection.

But she knew she could trust her voice to sound collected, firm. "You're standing too near. It's threatening," she said. "Step back if you want to speak to me."

He did at once, but he didn't seem glad of it. Seemed uncomfortable in the brighter light of the street. He looked in both directions quickly. When a taxi raced down past them towards the avenue, Sophia saw him tuck his chin into his collar to keep his face out of the beams of the headlamps.

"All right," she said then. "Go on. What is it?"

The taxi was gone. The street behind him was quiet again. The moon was hidden in the clouds. The young man lifted his earnest gaze to her. Licked his lips nervously. A lock of his yellow hair stirred on his brow, a brow boyishly smooth. There was something just then so naked in his expression that Sophia felt herself soften, touched.

"I'm going to be murdered tonight," the young man said to her all at once. He gave the breath of a laugh, as if embarrassed by the melodrama. "It is the man who buys *The Magi* who will kill me."

Sophia's mouth opened, but she only nodded, nodded cautiously. She pressed her hands awkwardly into her overcoat pockets, pressed her arms to her sides against the cold. Looked away from the young man, looked at nothing, trying to think.

"Miss Endering, you must—" the young man began.

"Let's walk down to the avenue," Sophia said. "We'll find a coffee shop where we can have a civilized conversation."

The German made a gesture of apology. "I'm sorry. I mustn't be seen. *You* mustn't be seen with me. It would be very dangerous. I am sorry—but I want to be out of the light." He had edged over her again, out of the gray glow of the street. "I do not threaten you, so help me. I only want for you to understand quickly what I say so I can go."

Sophia sighed, looked up at him, her heart beating rapidly, her expression composed. "All right," she said. "Go on. What is it?"

"My name is Jon Bremer. You will remember that?"

"Jon Bremer. Yes?"

"And he will buy *The Magi*."

"You really are serious, aren't you?"

The young man put his hand on her arm. She could feel the urgency of his touch even through the woolen sleeve of her coat. "He is the Devil from Hell," he blurted, lips trembling, like a child's. "All the Resurrection Men are dead. The man who verified the panel: tortured—mutilated—murdered. The couple who found the shop in the east, the same. Tortured, killed. Even the shop owner—his body was pulled out of the Elbe three days after the panel was recovered. His eyes . . . horrible . . . That's five people now—five people have had *The Magi* in their hands, Miss Endering. Four are dead. I am the last."

Sophia murmured, "Good God." She knew that it was true—and yet it made the conversation seem unreal to her, nightmarish. The two of them huddled together like this at the edge of the mews. The words smuggled between them, hurried, secretive, menaced. It was all too ridiculous. The Devil from Hell . . .

"Well, then, you must go to the police," she said decisively.

"No!" The young man's head went back, his eyes went wide, frightened. "His people are there as well. They are everywhere. You are the only one we can trust." His grip on her tightened. She felt his thumb digging into her upper arm. It was painful, but it made her aware of his fear. It made her pity him. She pitied all of them. "It has to be you, Sophia," he said. "It's *The Magi*. You know all the players. You can be there, ask questions, without anyone suspecting. When you see who buys it, when you know—then—carefully—you can approach . . . the authorities . . . your friends in the press . . . someone . . ."

After a moment, she nodded again and he released her. His voice grew softer, the words came faster. "I have arranged for the piece to be auctioned on behalf of a charitable organization—an anonymous donation with good title, all arranged. It will be in Sotheby's mid-January. I've arranged for it to remain in transit until then, so I think it will be safe. That is what I will tell them when . . ." She saw his Adam's apple work between the collars of the jacket. "When they find me," he finished. He went on more slowly. "He will buy it, he will pay anything for it. Do you see? At the auction, he will finally show himself. Do you see?"

The wind whirled. The clouds barreled by. An arc of the full moon shone above their ruffled fringes. The fingery branches of winter trees waved sable against the sky.

"No," Sophia said, staring blankly up at them, frowning. "No, I don't see. Why should he pay anything? Why should he kill for it? The thing isn't worth more than twenty-five thousand pounds, fifty thousand possibly, if you find the other two panels. How can you be so sure this is what he'll do? Your people—"

"Are all dead," said the young man. The naked, urgent earnestness had come into his expression again. "They are all dead. And I am sure. I have come to know him, in a way. He is afraid of nothing; he will let no one else do it for him. He will be there."

Now, at last, he stepped back from her. Sophia felt as if she had been released from a smothering embrace. The young man glanced up and down the street again. Peered at her from what already seemed a great distance. "I don't know why he kills for it, or why he will pay," he said. "But he has killed, and he will pay. He will pay anything, more than anyone. So the one who buys the painting, he is the man. The Devil from Hell. That is what you must remember. Whoever buys the painting . . ."

He seemed to be slipping from her, slipping away into the current of the night. She wanted to stop him, to stop the whole thing. "Look," she said. "You really must go to the police. I can't—"

"Remember," he said—it came out hoarsely, but the word carried to her even as he moved across the street. "Whoever buys the painting has murdered me, has murdered all of us. Whoever buys *The Magi* . . ."

Sophia stood and watched him: stepping up onto the opposite pavement; moving into the shadows of the park wall; grasped by the shadows of branches and drawn into them.

"Whoever buys *The Magi* . . ."

But she could not have heard him whisper it again. He was already gone.

✦

That night—it was a rotten night, if ever there was one. Some of the worst dreams she'd ever had, and she was given to bad dreams. Everything became all jumbled together in her sleeping mind. The cowled figure of Black Annie became the three cowled kings of the Rhinehart *Magi*. The haunted corridor of Ravenswood Grange became an endless labyrinth through Belham. She was wandering, feeling her way. *Tick-tick. Tick-tick. Remember, Sophia. Whoever buys* The Magi . . . She kept waking up, afraid—really terrified—and then sinking back helplessly. *Tick-tick, tick-tick.* The dreams like quicksand, seizing her. The dread seizing her. Corridor after corridor, searching in the dark, and every picture on the walls was the *Magi* panel. *Remember, Sophia* . . .

Finally, with a noise as much of anger as of fear, she wrenched herself out of it. Lay dumbly sullen in her bed, rubbing her arms to keep warm. A blank moment. No memories, a vague hazardous ambience. The familiar shapes of her bedroom congealing: tall frames of exhibition posters, oversized art books on a low case, the curve of her rolltop desk, the friendly bulk of the computer beside it, the towers of books on the floor . . .

The alarm went off. The radio. "This is BBC Radio Four. It's seven o'clock . . ." And the time tones: bing, bing, bing . . .

The Resurrection, Sophia remembered suddenly. Her heart dropped like a hanged man. *I am going to be murdered tonight* . . .

And then the newsreader started speaking: "The body of German antiques dealer Jon Bremer was found floating in the Thames this morning. Police say his murder may have been the work of Satanists. A rising and respected figure in the European antiques world, Bremer was the victim, before he died, of what a police spokesman called 'diabolical torture.' The spokesman said Bremer's eyes were punctured . . ."

Sophia sat up in bed.

". . . and strange symbols carved into his chest."

"Oh," she whispered.

The newsreader moved on to other stories. And Sophia covered her mouth with her hand. She stared into the rising light. Stared at where her desk had been, her books, her computer. At where now she saw only the image of Jon Bremer's youthful, warm and handsome face—his living face. Staring back at her with the gory, running sockets that had been his earnest eyes.

"Who is this Sophia Endering?" said Richard Storm suddenly.

"Shh!" said Harper Albright.

Storm forced a stage whisper: "I was just wondering. Do you know her at all?"

Harper didn't answer, didn't even look at him. So he was still thinking about her, she reflected—and it was almost two weeks since Bolt's party; it was practically the end of December now.

The two of them were standing alone together in a Devon churchyard. At midnight, of course, because that was when the beast was said to prowl. A stabbing, slushy snow had already covered the bracken to the base of the headstones. Worse, it had made a shapeless white mass of the venison sirloin they had placed on top of the churchyard wall: their bait.

Harper herself, this odd little woman, had collected a fair half-inch of ice on both the brim of her Borsalino and the shoulders of her cloak. Leaning staunchly on her stick, she could feel the cloak's gray wool growing heavy as the melt soaked through. She could feel her old flesh growing clammy as the chill began to reach it. And there was no lull in the bitterly thick wind either. It rode to her continuous over hedge and hill. It reached her with a straining, dying note that made her recollect the pixies of the Dart. They were said to have lured a farmboy to his death in the river by crying his name: *Jan Coo! Jan Coo!* She could almost hear them now in the crying of the wind.

Comes the hour, she thought irritably, but not the *thing*.

And yet, cold as she was, cranky as she was, she was still able to stand through the long surveillance stock-still, so still she might have been one of the graveyard's more eccentric monuments—had it not been for her eyes, ferociously quick behind her spectacles' thick lenses.

Storm, on the other hand, was bouncing around like a bottle on the ocean waves. Like a neon-orange bottle: he was dressed in some fantastic downy concoction, some bloated anorak from Ski-Meisters Of Hollywood or someplace, with triangles of bright green and purple scattered chaotically across the front of it. What he really looked like, Harper thought, was a deflated weather balloon. But he had the cameras ready, one hanging in each armpit, both wrapped in blue plastic bags, and their black straps crisscrossing his chest like gun belts. With any luck, the next issue of *Bizarre!* would feature the monster on its cover.

Storm whapped his shoulders with his hands, puffed his scarlet cheeks under his woolly watch cap, kept hopping up and down, up and down to stay warm in the driving snow.

"For pity's sake," Harper muttered. Even her lips were motionless when she spoke.

"Wh-wh-what?" said Storm.

Harper gave another grumpy huff or two. But then she relented. "All right. All right. I know her. I know about her, at any rate," she said softly.

"Sophia? This Endering girl, I mean?"

"I know quite a lot about her, in fact. Does she interest you, young Richard?"

"Me? Nah. She just popped into my mind." He managed to chop the words out between his chattering teeth. "While we were standing here. I was thinking. That's all. Really."

Harper let the lie pass. Her eyes made a slow half-circuit of the scene before her. The toppled steles, the ice-fringed tombs, the castellated tower of the church itself, lopped and moldering at the fringes of the visible. Beyond the graveyard's low stone wall, the snow obliterated her view of the surrounding moor.

"Her grandfather was in trade, as I understand," she said in her gravelly rasp.

"Her grandfather?"

"You wanted to know about her."

"Right, right. Her grandfather. So he was in trade, huh?"

"An antiques dealer. In Surrey, I believe. In a way, it's quite a romantic story. When his son, Michael Endering, fell in love with an archdeacon's daughter, her parents thought him not quite the thing. They forbade the match, and the girl—Ann—was sent off to school in Switzerland. Five years later, however, Michael applied for her hand again. And by then he had become a millionaire many times over."

"What, in five years?" said Storm, chattering, bouncing.

"Yes, and the money did the trick, apparently. He got the girl, her ancestral manse—Belham Grange—a knighthood eventually, plus the blessing and acceptance of an all-forgiving aristocracy. So far as I know, the rumors concerning the Nazis were never even mentioned."

That stopped Storm bopping about, at any rate. He stood flat-footed, panting. Dragged a neon-orange cuff across his dripping nose. "The Nazis? You mean, like, the Nazi Nazis? The evil German guys from World War II?"

"The very ones." She turned her head, faced him—and she'd stood so rigid till then under her gray mantle that it really did give the impression of a statue coming to life. "They had plundered much of the art of Europe, you'll remember, slaughtering many of its rightful owners along the way. Sometime after the war, the stolen masterpieces flooded the black market. England's strict laws concerning ownership made the trade dangerous and difficult here . . ."

"So you're saying Sophia's father was a fence for Nazi loot."

"I'm saying there were rumors to that effect—largely discounted then, and long forgotten now. He married Ann, set up his art gallery in New Bond Street, moved into Belham Grange, and had three children, Sophia being the youngest. His life after that was without any tinge of public scandal. That is, until nineteen years ago, when Ann hanged herself."

Storm's mouth opened. White balls of mist spilled from his lips, whipped away on the howling wind. "She hanged herself?"

"Fortunately, all the children were in London with their grandparents when it happened. Sophia was five at the time."

"Jeez. Nazis and suicide," Storm said.

"Precisely," said Harper.

A long moment passed. The old woman examined her

companion closely. "Young Richard," she said. "If you are planning to approach Miss Endering—"

"No, no, I'm not," he answered at once.

"But if you are, you should know—"

"I'm telling you, it's nothing like that, Harper. I'm not approaching her. I'm not going anywhere near her. Not anywhere. Believe me." He met her gaze almost fiercely, his expression uncharacteristically hard and taut. "I didn't come here for that," he told her.

Behind the dripping lenses of her spectacles, Harper's quick eyes narrowed. She held him then with such a slow, gimlet scrutiny that Storm at last averted his face from her. He frowned miserably into the blizzard.

But when Harper spoke again, her tone had softened. She had long since satisfied herself that there was nothing malevolent in the man. Indeed—she was forced to admit it now—she was developing a definite fondness for him. "All right," she said, more gently. "Why *did* you come here, then?"

Fighting down a violent shiver, he made a clipped gesture before hugging himself tightly again: he was trying to indicate the vista of crumbling stones, the blizzard-whipped church, even the invisible moor around them. The usual—puzzling—melancholy of his eyes was plain to see. And his tone too, Harper thought, had become wistful. "I told you—it's England. I've been making movies about this place my whole life. Places like this. I mean, look at it, the whole country, it's a movie set, I swear."

"Mm. Yes." She followed his gesture with a thin smile. "Some of us rather prefer to think of it as a fortress built by Nature for herself against infection and the hand of war—but yes, a movie set, all right. And so?"

Storm still gazed visionary at the place, with those sad eyes of his. Gazed at a spot where a small elm bent and swayed in what seemed like mourning over the cornice of a decaying crypt. "So, to me, this is where the ghosts live." He murmured it, almost to himself. The snow streaking his face with wet, his watch cap sodden, his anorak sodden, flattened, the puff gone out of it.

Even Harper now, statue that she was, had begun to feel the shivers rising from her depths. And still she stood, her wrinkled hand frozen to the dragon head of her stick, the stick planted in the gathering snow, the snow eating through her boots, through her cape, through her Borsalino. And still she stood motionless, watching the graveyard wall through her streaked lenses, watching the snowy mound that was the venison bait.

"I came here," Storm said, "because I wanted to see—"
"*Shh!*"

He stopped. Harper had gone electric, tensed. The two of them listened, their faces tilted into the blizzard's teeth. There seemed to be something . . . They listened, vying with the storm.

Yes. Suddenly, there it was. Borne to them on the wind, almost a part of the wind's wail. Soft but piercing, a preternatural squall. More than one voice, it seemed. A chorus of voices. A chorus of tormented voices, of subterranean laments breaking free into the swirling air. Now, as they cocked their ears, it strengthened, became one high, screeching yowl, a single, tortured stridor. Rising, blooming, peaking. Then bursting, splintering again into that pitiful choir. It went on and on.

Now am I come where many a plaining voice smites on mine ear, thought Harper Albright, every muscle tight. *There shrieks are heard, there lamentations, moans, and blasphemies . . .*

And even Storm whispered, "Jeepers. It sounds like the damned."

"Yes," she replied aloud. "A very encouraging vocalization."

And then it stopped. It faded into the wind until they couldn't tell it from the wind. Until the wind cried alone, all around them, forlorn. Harper narrowed her eyes behind her streaming glasses, peered intently past crypt and statue, peered and peered at that lump of snow, that hunk of venison, on the wall.

"Do you think . . . ?" Storm began to say.

And the creature took both of them completely by surprise.

There was no warning. A silent enormity of move-ment—a fluid leap, as of the night itself—and it was on the wall. Not where the venison was, not where they'd expected it. It was crouching, poised, to their left, not five yards away, just above their heads. Its carnivore eyes glittered down at them.

Storm threw himself in front of Harper, his arms spread to defend her. It was a lovely gesture. It warmed the cockles of her heart. But this was no time for warm cockles. She'd lifted her stick. Her right hand gripped the dragon head. Her left was wrapped round its shaft. She drew the two apart to reveal a flashing length of stainless blade.

"Never mind me," she growled. "Take pictures!"

She rejoiced to see him go at it. All courage, steely as her sword. Moving at her command on the instant. Snapping the plastic bag from one camera, snapping open its case even as he pulled the strap loose over his shoulder.

Harper felt a moment's anxiety. The cameras—all things mechanical—were as mysterious to her as the White Horse of Uffington. But Storm raised the device expertly, his hand shielding the lens.

There was a flash. It caught the creature. And the creature snarled, glared lightning strokes of white death across the corner of the snowy graveyard, into the camera's single eye.

Harper let fly with her double bark of a laugh: "Ha-ha! Oh, that's our cover art, I think. Well done, well done. 'So one tracks love, whose breath is deadlier . . .' " She had a weakness for quotation.

The beast shifted its panting bulk their way.

"Hoo, boy," Storm breathed. But to Harper's delight, he never wavered, never stopped clicking the shutter, setting off the flash. "What the hell is it?"

"*Felis concolor,* my boy," she cheered, unrestrained. "*Oregonensis,* judging by its size and Bergmann's Rule. The puma, the panther, the cougar—the catamount, I think you call it in your part of the world—which is its natural element, by the way, from Vancouver to Patagonia."

"Swell," said Storm. The thing growled down at him as the flash went off again. "So what's it doing here?"

"I really couldn't say. Probably trying to decide whether to devour the venison—or us."

At which—as the camera flashed once more—the monstrous brown cat reared and snarled, fangs bared to the weather, one claw raised as if to swipe both humans from the face of the earth. It could do it too, they could see that. Even coiled as it was for a muscular spring, it was clearly a long and ponderous thing, and knew its business. It could cut them from the planet like cookies from dough. It would leave nothing but Harper- and Storm-shaped holes in the material of existence.

"Foof," said Storm. "Any wisdom in running away here?"

"I shouldn't think so. Of course, it does prefer a leap of ambush to the running chase."

"Well, there you go . . ."

"But it can leap twelve meters."

"Foof."

"The question is," Harper said, "can it scent the bait in all this weather?"

It could; it did. But it took its own sweet time about it. It stretched the moments to the breaking point. Feinting at the two of them with its claw again. Rearing, looking gigantically down. Only then, finally, leisurely, insolently, did it lengthen itself and arch, did it stride, with one baleful backward glance over one shimmering shoulder, along the top of the wall toward the venison. Storm followed its surefooted progress with his camera, Harper with her bright eyes and throaty chuckle. There was another second of enormous, flowing movement, another huge shift in the snow-lanced dark. As swiftly as that, the white mound on the far wall was ravaged, the venison was plundered—and the creature had leapt away into nothingness.

The camera dropped from Storm's trembling fingers, fell to the limit of the strap around his neck and dangled down around his belly. Harper, her limbs loosening at last, pushed her dragon head and shaft together, sliding the tapered blade back into its oaken sheath. The call of the wind, the patter of the falling slush returned to them—it was as if the volume of the surrounding world had been shut off for the length of the confrontation.

Storm and Harper turned to each other, dazed.

"So," said Harper after a long moment. "You were saying?"

"Huh?"

"You were saying you came to England because you wanted to see . . . To see what?"

Storm stared at her. Then he laughed, a wild, high laugh. "To see if the dead can walk, babe," he told her. "I want to see if the dead can walk."

5 The editorial office of *Bizarre!* was on the second floor of Harper's mansion in World's End. The mansion was, for the most part, a pleasant Edwardian town house of white stone, with elegant, high-ceilinged rooms. But in the office, the character of the place was lost, buried under the magazine's paraphernalia. The yellow-striped walls were almost totally obscured by old covers hung all around. And these were adorned with photographs of outlandish beings never before seen. Alien babies corkscrewed from insectile wombs, human reptiles breasted the banks of Brazilian rivers, translucent wraiths floated in ancestral halls, Momo, Morag, Mokele-Mbembe—even Mothman, in one fuzzy shot—were seen gaping, seething, prancing, escaping into the crannies and caches and swamps of their various habitats.

These grimacing visages presided over a broad square of a room cluttered with memorabilia equally odd. A fishbowl holding a pickled claw. A planter from which some stuffed thing stared. A vase in which a cactus unknown to botany now and then opened, drooling, at the approach of a fly. More prosaic furniture took up the spaces in between. A striped chaise longue by the wall of high sash windows. A computer workstation against a windowless wall. An antique draftsman's table, a few tatty armchairs. Plus, finally, an immense fireplace, its marble mantel supported by a pair of grotesque telamons with hairy faces contorted into expressions of hellish torment. Which Harper found charming.

The magazine had gained in popularity of late—there was always a living to be made in the paranormal, as Harper had sometime remarked, if one could just hold on till the millennium. As a result, anyway, the journal had recently gained a publisher, full color on covers and some pages inside, a more regular monthly schedule, and a circulation soon predicted to rise to over a hundred thousand worldwide. In spite of this, the staff remained what it long had been: two people, Harper and her young factotum, Bernard. There were also several handfuls of eager stringers stationed everywhere around the world. And the occasional unpaid intern—currently Richard Storm.

Storm was brooding by the fireplace this rainy afternoon early in the new year. Harper was lolling on the chaise longue, chomping on her pipe, observing him.

Bernard, as always, was at his computer, his willowy torso curving up out of the strange, backless rocker he used, his shaven head glimmering in the dull light. He tapped away at the keyboard. He studied the screen. He had forced the computer on the business when he'd first started work here five years earlier. It had since become, in spite of Harper's Luddite resistance, the Brain of the operation. To her, it remained inscrutable, vaguely threatening. Yet Bernard seemed able to command the device as easily as a sorceror making dead objects dance. A few runes stroked onto the keys and it would edit like a magic pencil, cut like a razor, paste like a wax mangler—and then fly off like Puck to put a girdle round the earth in search of potential copy from the international press.

Bernard raised his lovely, aesthetic face from the perplexing mechanism now. "A dowager in Lincolnshire is seeking to sell her alien rectal probe," he remarked languidly.

"Is she, by God?" said Harper, round the stem of her pipe.

"'I need the money for my poor cats,' says Mrs. Huddlestone of Theddlethorpe-St.-Helen," Bernard went on. "'Though I hate to part with it, as it's a souvenir of a very memorable experience.'"

"Ha-ha. I daresay," said Harper. "Yes, I think so. 'Notes from All Over.' I think we really must."

Resting a shoulder against one misshapen telamon, staring down morosely into the bluish gas fire, Storm snorted and shook his head.

And Harper watched him. She smoothed her gray schoolgirl skirt down over her swollen knees. Removed a matchstick from the pocket of her white schoolgirl blouse. She struck fire on her blackened thumbnail with what she hoped was regal negligence and held the flame to the crown of the meerschaum skull, drawing smoke. And she watched him.

How could she help but be reminded of the whirligig beetle? With its divided eye, half in the air, half in the water. It sees above and below the surface at the same time—and so she felt she was seeing now. But what was she seeing? Storm's rugged western face, set and withdrawn. His lean figure in jeans and work shirt, relaxed and mopey. And under the surface of those images—what? Some great, roiling tempest of emotion? she wondered. Grief? Loss? Terror? She wasn't sure.

"Did you really come here to hunt for ghosts?" she asked him from the midst of a pearly cloud. "Do you really expect to find one?"

He lifted a broad shoulder, still staring into the flames. "I don't know," he said. "A ghost. A voice from beyond. Something uncanny, you know. Anything. One lousy uncanny thing. You wouldn't think it was so much to ask for."

"Exclusive recent photographs of JFK and Lee Harvey Oswald show them laughing over the hoax that allowed them to consummate their love in secret," drawled Bernard.

"I think not. No," said Harper, waving the smoke away.

Storm pushed off the telamon. It watched him, bellowing in anguish, as he stuffed his hands in his jeans pockets, strolled over the delicate rose pattern of the rug. He paused before the fishbowl, absently considered the pickled claw. "I mean, nowadays, you try to believe in something—in anything—people think you're some kind of idiot. You know? Everything's got to have an explanation, nothing's allowed to be spiritual or mysterious anymore. The scientists—they want to take everything away from you. That DNA guy, Crick. Carl Sagan. Richard Dawkins. All these scientists. They tell you you're just some kind of machine, your body's some kind of machine, even your mind . . . And love is just some kind of pheromone or something. And God turns out to be some kind of mathematical formula. Even if you have a near-death experience—nope, sorry, that's just some mental defense mechanism or a hallucination or . . . I don't know . . ."

Harper shifted her elbow thoughtfully on the chaise's cylindrical pillow. The gray light pouring down on her through the fringes of the silken curtains seemed to age her even more, to burn the last luster from her lifeless cap of hair, deepen the black semicircles under her spectacles, etch the slack flesh of her sagging cheeks with lines. Yet she pointed her pipestem at Storm vigorously. "There is nothing so powerful as an idea whose time has come, Richard—

regardless of whether that idea is true or not. The notion that a scientific explanation somehow negates the mysterious core of a phenomenon—this is a prejudice of the age—no educated person can be free of it. To borrow a page from Lecky, if we believed in ghosts, a hundredth part of the evidence we possess would be enough to convince us. But since we do not believe, a hundred times the evidence would not suffice."

"A gang of Argentinian cannibals were arrested after they sent out for a pizza delivery boy," Bernard remarked. "Authorities discovered a large mushroom and anchovy pizza and a pair of running shoes at the scene."

"Oh, all right, phone the Argies to confirm it," said Harper. "Or E-mail them, or whatever it is you do."

"Lecky," Storm muttered sullenly. "Lecky-shmecky. You're the same way." He flashed a hand at her, at all the monsterly covers on the wall. "I mean, no offense or anything, but I've been here two months now. And everything we do, it turns out to be a phony. We go hunting for the Beast of Dartmoor, it's just an old mountain lion from some shut-down nature park. We get a video of an alien autopsy, you prove it's a guy slicing up a Ken doll with tinfoil on its head. Christ, three independent experts confirmed psychic activity in that basement in Chipping Norton, you go down there with a shovel and dig up a couple of humping badgers. You're as bad as anyone."

"Me? Never. *Alieni nil a me humanum puto.* Ha-ha." But somehow the pun seemed to be lost on him.

"I mean, look at all these covers here," he said. "All these pictures, all these articles you publish. Is it all nonsense? Haven't you ever seen anything really mysterious? Don't you believe in anything?"

"I have seen a great deal, and I believe nothing," said Harper Albright gravely. "Nothing at all, you understand. It's almost a lost art, but I'm a mistress of it."

"Well, then, what do you do it for?"

"History, Richard. History," she announced grandly. "My life has led me to it." The meerschaum skull glowed red as she drew in two puffed cheeks' worth of smoke. Then the smoke flooded out in a coiling rush as she said, "Your trouble, young Richard, is that you confuse these fictional ghost stories you so admire with the genuine article. The English ghost story of fiction had its heyday between 1850 and 1930, a period very much like this one, in that the prodigious leaps made by scientists such as Darwin and Freud promoted materialism and naturalism and shook the foundations of religious belief. The Sea of Faith was receding with its melancholy, long, withdrawing roar, and so spirits rose up in the popular magazines specifically to ask the question, 'Man of the worldly mind, do you believe in me or not?' Ah, but history, Richard, history—that is the province of your true phantom. You've heard of history even in Hollywood, surely. People writing with quill pens, wearing bodices and so on . . ."

"Two Gloucestershire boys were hospitalized for shock last week after they mistook a local constable for a ghost," said Bernard.

"Ha-ha," said Harper. "Cute."

Storm threw up his hands and turned back to the fire.

"The boys had entered the grounds of Belham Abbey on a dare to look for the Grey Lady, who is said to haunt the abbey's ruins, carrying a murdered child in her arms. The boys were terrified when the specter of PC Tim Bayliss rose up to chase them off instead. The none-too-ghostly plod had been summoned by Sir Michael Endering, the owner of the neighboring house, who requested—"

"No, no, no," said Harper quickly. "Forget that one, leave it—"

But it was too late. Storm had swiveled back from the mantelpiece, one hand outstretched. "Wait a minute!" he said.

"Storm, Storm . . ." said Harper.

"Let me see that. Michael Endering. That's him. That's Sophia's father, that girl's father."

He strode across the carpet, barely flinching from his course as the cactus snapped at him. In a moment, he was peering over Bernard's shoulder, reading the screen. He was muttering, "Sir Michael Endering. Sure. And that ghost. In an abbey. With a murdered child . . ."

"It's a White Lady, Richard," Harper cried, overly expansive, waving her pipe about in the air. "A Gray Lady, a Black Lady, whatever you want to call it. We have them all over the country. In my *Island Notions* I link her with the Teutonic goddess Berchta, who was charged with receiving the souls of dead children." Storm did not look up. She continued, louder, "The Christians, you see, demoted her to a witch, used her as a sort of bedtime story bogeyman. It was a natural progression from there to ghost. It's all in my book. Perhaps you should hire someone to read it . . ."

He ignored her completely. "It's Black Annie," he said. "I'll be damned. *That's* why she dropped her glass. That's why she looked so pale that night. I read that story, and right out at her father's house, there's a ghost just like Black Annie . . ."

"Now as for Black Annie, she was no doubt her author's reformulation of the legend of Black Annis," Harper ploughed on desperately, "who was a child-devouring witch of the Dane Hills, more closely tied to the Celtic Anu than to Berchta but perhaps also a folk memory of the anchoress Agnes Scott. History, you see, Richard, hist—"

"I'll bet she's seen it," said Storm, addressing her as if she hadn't spoken at all. "I'll bet anything. You saw the way she acted, Harper. The story really shook her up. She dropped her glass. She went all pale . . ."

It was hopeless. Storm studied the screen again, his expression intent, his face almost level with Bernard's. From Harper's perspective, their profiles overlapped: a cinema cowboy and a Renaissance angel, both in the monitor's white glow. She could only gaze upon them with anxiety—sadly— even grimly. They were all that was left to her in these latter days—all she would ever allow herself—of the cherished company of men.

"Belham Abbey," said Storm. "Belham Grange—that's what you said her house was called, right?"

Heaving a weary sigh, Harper Albright worked her feet to the floor, worked her way up off the chaise longue.

"Richard," she pronounced gently, coming to stand beside him. Her tone made him look at her, look into her thick glasses for a moment. But he couldn't hold her sharp gaze. He turned away. "There is no need to approach her in this fashion, to question her about this." Storm didn't answer. "You could simply ask her for a date."

"It's not about that," he muttered, without any conviction at all. "It's just good journalism, Harper. There might be a connection here. It's a legitimate story . . ." His voice trailed into silence.

Harper sighed again. Placed the pipe in her mouth. "As you like," she said then. She took a brief pace, away from him, back. "But in that case," she said, "in any case, there is something you should know."

Storm bridled, seemed about to object. Harper pushed on regardless.

"Sophia Endering is the product and the proof of her father's ascension to the upper classes," she said. "I know—you may not think that counts for much nowadays, but it counts with him. It counts a good deal. Sophia's education, her social standing, even her appearance—these are the old man's *bona fides*. She has been raised, in a sense, to maintain and protect his position. And she is very, very good at it. The woman is cool, smart, close-mouthed. She has a glance, I'm told, that can turn an intruder to sand. There are no men in her life, despite her beauty. There is no one to whom she entrusts her secrets."

Storm lifted his chin at her. "Yeah. Okay," he said. "So what?"

"So, given her history, it is safe to assume that, if she has a heart at all, it is held in check with considerable force. And if ever she is deprived of her monumental defenses, my guess is you will find her to be as fragile as bliss—and every bit as precious."

✦

"Historeeee, Richard, historrreeee," Bernard mimicked her when Storm had gone. "A historreee cloaked in mistorrreeee."

"Oh, be quiet," Harper grumbled.

She was standing at the window now. Leaning on her dragon stick. Touching her pipe to her lip meditatively. Frowning deeply at the misted panes.

Behind her, Bernard had tilted back from his keyboard,

had folded his arms over his thick woolen jumper. He was regarding her with infuriating drollness, she knew, tongue in his seraphic cheek, one eyebrow cocked.

"You didn't tell him all of it, did you?" he said.

Harper humphed. "I told him what he needed to know."

"Oh, for God's sake, darling," Bernard said.

She humphed again. Stared at the window pane resolutely. Darts of rain on a sheet of condensation. A blurry swatch of the outdoors through one broad runnel. The narrow street below, the brick houses homily lit across the way. The corner entrance to The Sign of the Crane smokily enticing.

Bernard wouldn't stop. "Have you ever seen that first picture of his? *Spectre*? Have you ever watched it?" he asked.

"A long time ago," Harper murmured.

"Well, then, come on. He *just happens* to come five thousand miles to work with you. He *just happens* to read that story on the night she *just happens* to be there. It *just happens* to be her . . ."

"Coincidences do happen, lad."

"Yes, I know," he said, stretching one long leg out before him, rocking one trainer back and forth on its heel. "But they happen more frequently, more profoundly, whenever we get close, whenever the trail gets warm again. Recurring numbers, accidental meetings, unlikely chains of events. They're the spoor of our quarry." Bernard leaned forward, towards her. "There's no way out of it, darling. He's the one we've been waiting for. He has set the thing into motion. And you know it."

"Even if that were true, it wouldn't matter. I don't want him to be hurt. It's not his hunt. It's mine."

"It's ours," said Bernard shirtily. "And you would think,

after more than a quarter of a century, you would be a little bit more eager to see it on again. We can't protect poor Richard from his own destiny."

"Don't talk nonsense," Harper said. "Destiny!" She brought the pipe away from her mouth. Stretched out a hand to the window, stretched out a finger to the glass. Droplets rolled from her fingertip as she slowly sketched a figure in the mist.

"You didn't tell him," her assistant went on behind her, "that before Sophia's mother hanged herself, she opened a vein—"

"Mere rumor. A confused constable's testimony."

"She opened a vein—"

"Never confirmed. The family will not speak of it. We've had a hundred leads far better than that, a thousand—"

"She opened a vein," Bernard insisted, "and made, in blood, upon the wall . . ."

Harper lowered her hand to her side. On the window now, already dissolving in fresh mist and running water, was a symbol something like a horseshoe surrounding something like a figure eight.

"Exactly," said Bernard, lazily triumphant. "She made the mark of Iago."

6   Sometimes the world seemed to come with subtitles, like a foreign film. So help her, sometimes people's hidden motives, their lies, their rationalizations, were so pitifully apparent that Sophia felt she could just sit and read them. Every word they spoke, every gesture they made, revealed them as clearly as words spelled out beneath the scene.

She was at Belham Grange for the weekend. She was having coffee in the morning room with her older brother and sister. It was a small, rich, soft, well-lit room. Windows floor to ceiling which let in the fleeting hour of winter sun. A warm sheen on satinwood dish cupboard and side tables. Paintings of Arcadian dancers amidst Roman ruins on the cream walls.

The seats were in a sort of broad, erratic circle on the rug. She, Sophia, was perched on the lyre-backed Adam chair. In white blouse, tan slacks; her legs crossed at the knee. She was facing the other two. Laura on the cushioned settee to her left. Peter draped over the French armchair to her right. Her father's chair—his enormous Chippendale throne—was empty between them in the falling wedge of sunshine.

Little Simon, Laura's five-year-old, Sophia's nephew, was crawling around under the table. Running his Christmas Batmobile over the rug, battling his Batman figure against the tea table's fierce-looking claw-and-ball leg.

Sophia stirred sugar into her second coffee and observed them. Feeling weary, jaded. Too much work, she thought, too little sleep. *Tick-tick, tick-tick.* Too many worries. Too many bad dreams. The auction was a fortnight away now. *Whoever buys the painting, Sophia . . .* The voice of that poor Resurrection Man was hardly ever out of her hearing. *He is the Devil from Hell.* And then his body in the Thames. *Tick-tick.* His earnest face staring with those gore-drenched sockets—an awful image for her to wake from, alone in bed.

Never exactly the cheeriest soul even at the best of times, Sophia was afraid she was entering one of her really black patches. Which probably accounted for this cynical sense that she was reading life between the lines.

"Darling, do come away from the tea table," said Laura,

for about the third time. A sweet-faced woman with still-silky, still-blond hair. But frantic eyes, and her mouth pinched. "It's Grandpa's antique. You'll scratch the finish. You'll upset the pot. Come away before you break something. Why don't you play over by the window?"

The subtitle: *It kills me that you're enjoying the Batman car Aunt Sophia gave you, when Mummy bought you a perfectly good pirate ship and enough connector sticks to build the Taj Ma Bloody Hal.*

"Oh, for Christ's sake, would you leave the poor boy alone, Laura." This came from Peter. From behind his *Guardian*. Which he was reading with his leg—in jeans—swinging over the arm of his chair so that the antique walnut creaked. The subtitle being: *I'm not afraid of Father.* Which, of course, he was. Sophia, tasting her coffee, thought: And he must've driven five miles before breakfast to buy that paper too. As if having a few opinions and voting Labour made him Danton.

Laura, who could not stand disapproval of any kind, immediately left off Simon—who was ignoring her anyway—and went on the direct attack. "You're looking absolutely beautiful this morning, Sophia. Although how anyone can look beautiful at eight-thirty in the morning, I really don't know. I always tell Spencer that if he wanted me to be spectacular round the clock, he shouldn't have asked for a son and heir."

I have a husband and have produced an offspring—our father's grandson—and you're a frigid, sterile bitch.

Peter lowered his paper, showing a face too old for his haircut. Puffy cheeks and tired eyes under ridiculous curls. "What's keeping the Great Man anyway? It's a small country—how long can it take to suppress every trace of artistic originality?"

And not only are you frigid, but your life's work is absolute crap.

Sophia tucked her silver spoon between cup and saucer. She smiled thinly, her pale eyes lidded, her smooth features serene. Because that was her role in the scenario: to look lofty, to be unassailable, to be the elegant, living proof of her father's ascension to the gentry. Her own subtitle, she supposed, might read: *No matter how many grandchildren you produce, Laura—no matter how bold and independent you pretend to be, Peter—I run the gallery; I'm the one.*

Because for all of them, it was always about Daddy. Novelists make such a mystery of these things, Sophia thought, psychiatrists make a living out of them. But it was amazing to her, as she sat there, how obvious it was, how stupidly plain and inescapable. That chair of his—a Gothic cathedra, practically, carved beechwood with crocketed pinnacles flanking a traceried arch: it stood in the dying sunshine at the center of their circle, and he stood at the center of their lives, and that was that. Why not just come out and say it, she thought, print it plain beneath the picture? Here they are, they revolve around him. They cover the same old traces yearly. Laura cowers and offers the fruit of her womb and knows she's pathetic but can't change. Peter proclaims his leftist politics more and more bitterly, a moral sop to his self-esteem as one after another of his professional ventures fail. And Sophia guards her place at the right hand of power by the simple expedient of being ceaselessly perfect, and frequently depressed. And that's this week's episode of *The Enderings.* Come back next week, and it'll be exactly the same.

"Watch out, Clawface!" said little Simon, under the tea table. "Here comes Batman!"

And then, all at once, he was among them. Sir Michael himself. Charging into the wedge of light, striding from the doorway to his chair. Six-foot-two, ruddy-faced, big-featured, barrel-chested, broad-shouldered in his green country gentleman's tweed jacket and waistcoat. Silver hair in a knife-sharp widow's peak, pointing like an arrow. Chin like a prow. Sophia smiled to see him. The size and power of him made her smile. Sixty-four years old, with the vigor of a bull, with the headway of a ship at sea.

"Morning, all."

Peter had managed to keep his leg draped over the chair all this time. Sophia wondered that it hadn't fallen asleep. Or fallen off. He snapped his paper in half loudly, making sure the *Guardian* logo remained visible. "The day's work all finished?" he asked. "Servants all bullied? Monies gouged? Tendencies to modernism eradicated?"

"And the peasants trod under my horse's hooves, Peter," said Sir Michael, settling into his chair. "It's been a very satisfactory morning."

✦

"Is it me, or has Peter become rather a sad figure?" Sir Michael asked a short while later. He was walking with Sophia in the garden. The two of them treading slowly in step down the flagstone path between scarlet dogwood and robinia. Column fragments, and statues weathered to near-shapeless hulks, stood at intervals in the wild grass, lining the way: the garden had been the abbey cloisters some five hundred years before. "All that moral superiority and outrage," he went on in an undertone. "I suppose it's what one clings to in lieu of success, but still . . ."

"He only does it to provoke you," said Sophia. She took

his arm. Being wifely, on purpose. Because it soothed him. Because it relaxed them both.

"All that talk about the *people*," he said, in his favorite harrumphing lord-of-the-manor style. "Sounds like an American. We the *people*. I mean, it's incredibly sentimental, isn't it? He should be better than that."

Sophia lifted her face to the bracing northern wind. Watched the huge cumulus clouds crossing like a ghostly fleet in the broad blue sky. The red dogwood swayed around her, the robinia swayed. She felt her father's thick bicep under her fingers, under the tweed, and she leaned against him. Life always seemed more tolerable to her out in the garden.

"The *people* have had this century pretty much all their own way, as far as I can see," Sir Michael was going on. "And what have we got for it? More mass slaughter than all the crowned heads of history combined could ever have dreamed of. Gas chambers and cultural revolutions, that's the work of the people. Then, when a Churchill or a Roosevelt sorts things out for them, they start wailing, 'Oh, it was our leaders who did it, our leaders misled us.' Well, who were their leaders? Cobblers and peasants and house painters. What did they expect? The people. Anything they can't murder, they degrade. Television, fast-food restaurants . . ."

Modern art, thought Sophia dreamily.

"Modern art," Sir Michael said. "'The people are turbulent and changing; they seldom judge or determine right.' You know who said that?"

She stroked his sleeve affectionately, thinking, *Alexander Hamilton*.

"Alexander Hamilton," Sir Michael declared. "And he was in the we-the-people business long before Mao Tse-Peter in there."

By the garden's far wall, she drew him up a moment before one piece she found particularly pleasing. It was a small stone Madonna, set under the rose bushes. At least that's what she thought it was. Time and rain had eroded nearly all its features. Only the sweet sweep of the mantle remained around the head, and the graceful gothic S-curve of the figure. Daughter and father stood looking down at it, hand in arm.

"He really must've got under your skin this morning," said Sophia, "if we're going to blame him for both the Chinese and the Americans in one sentence."

The Great Man gravely pressed his great chin against his great chest to suppress a smile. "You probably think I'm an old fart," he said. "Well, I am an old fart. I'm in the very prime of my old fartdom. I've earned it. I won't let it be taken away from me."

Sophia laughed once, laid her head against him. What she thought was: There was more blood and spirit in him than in half a dozen Peters. She thought he was *worth* revolving around.

"You know, I remember standing in London on a bomb site once," he said, and Sophia was glad because she always liked this story. "I couldn't have been more than twenty or so. And there was a real, old-fashioned pea-soup fog on, covering everything. Everywhere, all you could see were just jagged shapes jutting out of the fumes. Hollowed window frames staring like eyes. Skewed doorways opening up onto nothing. Rubble. A moonscape. This acid smell. And this unnatural silence all around, as if the world had simply disappeared."

They turned and began walking slowly back up the path towards the house.

"And I had a vision standing there," Sir Michael said. "And I realized that the world I knew was over, that the best of civilization was done. Europe was sick of itself and done. Its will to greatness was spent. And I thought to myself: There will be no more Raphaels, not ever. No paintings worthy of him, ever again. There'll be no more great operas written or symphonies composed. No odes like Keats's odes, no plays like Shakespeare's. Never. People will forget how to love them, I thought. They're already forgetting. They're learning to love smaller things, baser things, and they're becoming smaller, baser things themselves. One day they'll squat in circles on the ground and hold the relics of the old treasures in their hands and they'll grunt to one another and say, 'What was this? Who thought that this was good?' Like apes gawking at a broken lyre."

The Grange was visible up ahead, beyond the garden wall. Not a stately mansion by any means, but a venerable old manor, set against the Cotswold hills. Long, two-storied. Some of the original fifteenth-century limestone still in place. Those grand, tall windows on the ground floor, two beautiful gabled oriels flanking the pitched roof above. It had been her mother's house, built on what had once been Belham abbey's granary. A double row of copper beeches led away from the broadly arched front door. Through the branches, Sophia could see the ruins of the abbey's chapel. The right triangle of the shattered wall. The churchyard headstones bowing towards the grass.

"I became very depressed and started to walk," Sir Michael continued. "Away from the site, into the City. All through the fog, lost. No idea where I was heading. And then—just like some fairy tale—I heard voices, singing. A choir, singing 'Jerusalem,' the sound coming to me through the fog. I followed it and, sure enough, I came on a church. St. James it was called, I'll always remember. Anyway, I went in and, except for the choir, the place was empty. They were rehearsing—for some big occasion, as I recall, something at St. Paul's. But the place was completely deserted otherwise, and yet there was this choir, still singing to the rafters. A sort of hopeful symbol, I thought. You know—the congregation has departed but the song goes on. By that time, they were singing something else. Something with a lot of hallelujahs. 'Seek thee first the kingdom of God . . .' And one girl stepped forward to do a solo. This lovely creature. With this raven hair, this reverent face. Completely absorbed in the music. Beautiful voice, beautiful. Mezzo-soprano. Timbre like a pearl. 'And all these things shall be given unto you . . .'" He stopped in the path. He patted the back of his daughter's hand. "That was the first time I ever saw your mother."

Sophia tried to smile, but today, somehow, the story turned her heart to lead. She averted her face, looked away, looked off towards the garden shed, just visible through dripping clematis. She was vaguely aware that the caretaker was sitting there. Harry. Straddling the roof. Plucking tacks from between his lips. Tapping them into the side of the rain gutter. *Tick-tick, tick-tick.*

This *was* going to be one of her black patches, she thought. One of the worst of them ever. She didn't know if she was going to be able to endure it.

"By the way, while I'm thinking of it," Sir Michael said. "You know *The Magi* is coming up at Sotheby's in a fortnight. I think we should buy it."

"What?" She turned back to him at once, but she did have time to realize that this was completely normal. Just what he would say, what he should. *The Magi* was German Romantic, right in their period, exactly their kind of thing. They'd be expected to bid on it.

"Yes," she said carefully. "Absolutely. If the price is right. Thirty? Forty, maybe?"

"No." Sir Michael tilted back that impressive head, hoisted that powerful countenance to the heavens. "I don't care if it's twice that. Three times. I don't care. I want it. Buy *The Magi*," he said. "Buy it—no matter what."

✦

Her mother's portrait hung on the wall across from her bed. Her old bed, upstairs at the Grange, her childhood four-poster. As she lay beneath her duvet that night, she could see the painting below the fringe of the canopy.

It had been done shortly after her parents' marriage. Ann must have been almost exactly Sophia's age. In an evening dress of ivory satin. Looking gloriously over one shoulder, her throat bare above the drape neckline. A ludicrous pose nowadays. And the picture was flattering to the point of sycophancy, every individual quirk glossed away. But the likeness to her younger daughter was plain: the same black hair, the same high cheeks, the same brown eyes and pearl complexion. Only in her mother, Sophia thought, it was all warmer somehow, kinder, sweeter. The gaze more gentle, the smile more forgiving and amused. The whole posture seemed to be one of offering . . .

Looking at her, Sophia found the ache of loneliness almost insupportable.

Now, all of a sudden, she was drawing the duvet back. Slipping out of bed. No idea what she was doing or why she was crying. She stepped from the room into the dark of the second-floor corridor. There was a grandfather clock at the far end. *Tick-tick, tick-tick.* The noise was maddening. It clouded her brain. As she went towards the stairway, the worn runner gritty under her bare feet, the landing's perspective seemed to skew. The walls seemed to angle inward overhead. The portraits on them seemed to glare down at her from a great height, as if she were a child. She was afraid. Her heart was beating fast. Her nightgown, so white it seemed to glow, seemed to heave and flow around her; she seemed to be swimming in it as she headed down the stairs.

Tick-tick, tick-tick. Yes, this was exactly how it had happened. She remembered everything now. That's why she felt so small, so frightened. Like a child. She had been a child. Four or five years old. She had gone down the stairs. Like this. *Tick-tick.* Calling for her mother. Following that sound. The house was silent except for that, silent and sleeping as it was now. And she had reached the front hall and turned. Left? Yes. She turned left and kept on walking, swiping her wet cheeks with the heel of her palm, tugging at her running nose.

Another long corridor, a corridor of doors. Paintings and side tables in between; clocks, candlesticks, empty chairs. An arras at the end with a many-headed dragon rampant, its tail up among the stars. *Tick-tick.* She had come calling for her mother. To the last doorway. Her father's study. On her left.

She pushed inside. Closed the door behind her. Turned on the lights. Two dim, yellowish bulbs in shaded wall lamps: they only served to make the place more shadowy, forbidding, gloomy. Shelves of hulking volumes were to her left and right. Before her was her father's desk, stern and mammoth. Its carved mahogany ram's heads brooded at her from the tops of their pilasters. Behind it, the tall leather chair, framed by green velvet drapery, was tilted back slightly from long use. It seemed to regard her suspiciously, as from under lowered lids.

She knew it was stupid, but she really did feel afraid. She wished the curtains had been drawn. She knew the ruined chapel was out there in the darkness. The old graveyard. She stared at her own reflection on the pane, and was half fearful something would drift out of the night, press itself through her own image to the other side of the glass. Black Annie . . .

Tick-tick, tick-tick. It was coming from her right, from behind one of the shelves. That's what had happened. She had heard it. She had called for her mother. She had reached for the secret door. She felt the books beneath her fingers now. The ribbed bindings. Leather, fleshly. There was a click, and the shelves were coming to life beneath her hand. Pivoting from the wall. Swinging outward. *Tick-tick.*

Suddenly, the shelves flew open on a hidden room and there stood her father, covered in blood.

Sophia cried out, "Are you a murderer, Daddy?"

"Yes," he panted hoarsely. "I'm rather afraid I am."

It was only another of her dreams, of course. But it was terrifying, and when she awoke, there was still the sickening memory of her father in the garden. *Buy* The Magi. *Buy it— no matter what.*

She sat up under her mother's tender gaze, trying to blot out the memory, the dream, the whole thing. Lifting her knees beneath the duvet, resting her elbows on them, screwing her palms against her brow.

Whoever buys The Magi, *he is the one who killed me.* The bloody holes that had been Jon Bremer's eyes gaped at her. *Four are dead already. He is the Devil from Hell. He will pay*

anything, more than anyone. Whoever buys The Magi, *Sophia . . .*
Sophia's jaw hurt. She was grinding her teeth together.
Buy The Magi *no matter what.*
She only wished she had been more surprised.

7   On the eve of his approach to Sophia, Richard Storm prepared himself with a meditation on John Wayne.
He had a framed, autographed picture of the cowboy star still enveloped in bubble wrap in a suitcase in the closet. He got it out, unwrapped it, and laid it on the flimsy folding table in his cramped service flat. He sat beside it, in a creaky chair, surrounded by the marbleized yellow wallpaper, the falsely gilded mirror, the matted flower prints that decorated the overpriced motel of a place. He was drinking from a mug of decaf, nibbling at a tasteless Shapers diet sandwich from one of those Boots drugstores: prawn and peach with dill mustard, or some other revolting British concoction. Between bites, he practiced the *prana-patistha*—a sacred form of breathing that this blond babe had taught him at Big Sur. She said it was supposed to infuse an image of your guardian ancestor with life. He also used it to cool his coffee while he sat and studied the photograph.

The picture showed the Duke full-length, striding towards the camera. Squinting from beneath his hat brim, Winchester hanging from his hand. It was a publicity still from *Hondo,* Wayne's favorite of his own films and one of Storm's. All about a rugged rambler who rides out of the horizon to rescue a woman and her boy. Storm had had the photo since he was nine years old, but it was in mint condition. He had always taken extremely good care of it.

Because Wayne *was* a guardian ancestor of sorts. He had given Storm his family name. Storm's father had been Jack Morgenstern when he'd left his old man's Brooklyn haberdashery in the late forties and set out for the West Coast. Shortly after he reached Hollywood, he and his craggy good looks had been rechristened Jack Stern. He had been billed as Jack Stern in his first few walk-ons, as a gangster, a Spanish waiter, and the popcorn vendor who shouts "This way!" in *Strangers on a Train*. But then came his big break. And he traveled down to hell-and-gone Mexico somewhere to play the role of Cade in *Hondo*.

It was James Arness, the co-star of the film, who introduced the newcomer to the Duke. Out there on location amidst dust and scrub, surrounded by mouse-eared cameras and canvas chairs. Wayne—who was in the middle of a wild, hot-blooded divorce at the time—was standing in his fringed Indian scout outfit with a bunch of sweating men in suits. When Arness called him over, Wayne approached Storm's father with that patented swagger, thunderous and balletic at the same time. He sent a truly Duke-like gaze off towards the far horizon, then threw himself side-armed into a big handshake, which the newcomer eagerly joined.

"Duke," said Arness, "this here is Jack Stern."

Wayne's gunfighter squint went up and down the younger man. He spoke—and the voice, the twang, the drop-dead Midwestern syncopation all turned out to be genuine.

"Storm," he drawled slowly, "is the name you want."

And so he had been Jack Storm in *Hondo,* in *Rio Bravo,* and forever after.

And there were many other things—gestures, expressions, phrases—that Storm had inherited from Wayne, through his father, who had imitated them all in developing his persona both onscreen and off. And there was this too, this photograph, that the Duke had presented to Storm personally on his ninth birthday.

Dear Rick, the inscription read, *Live right, shoot straight, walk tall—and have a happy birthday. Your friend, John Wayne.*

All right, *shoot straight*—it was a little hard to know exactly what that meant in a modern context. But the other instructions were clear enough, and tonight Storm felt the burden of them. He was pretty sure he had neither lived right nor walked particularly tall in these last few years since his divorce. There had been some drugs, and some women he'd treated shabbily. And a couple of deals that had cost him more than a couple of friends. He had boasted during that time, "I not only swim with the sharks, I sleep with the piranha." Big man. He wasn't so proud of that anymore.

Because there had come a Reckoning—that awful September morn. A few nights before, he had been coked, tussling in bed with a femme director who thought he would give her work. He had rolled over, fallen, and cracked his head open on the edge of the VCR. There had followed the short, dreadful stay at Cedars-Sinai. And then he had been released, bandaged, gray and visionary, everything changed. He had driven over to Mann's National Theater in Westwood. Gotten out of his Jag and stood beneath the titanic marquee of his latest film. *Hellfire.* With a cutout of Jack Nicholson that must have been two stories tall. A rising billboard of flames. And the words *Produced by Richard Storm* running maybe six feet across, his name as big as his body. And, for the first time, Storm realized that it would all go away. Not just the poster, the credit, the success. But him, Nicholson, the audience—the theater, Westwood—the whole city, Los Angeles, plunked, rootless, in its smoky basin. The far-flung skyline, the Escher-esque coils of freeway, the villas and the slums: the earthquakes would take them, and the ocean waves. In time, America itself would fall, the millennia would make a ruin of it, like Rome. He saw these things: cockroach archaeologists trying to make sense of the rubble of Disneyland—green cows descended from aphids grazing amid the tattered remnants of the St. Louis arch—Charlton Heston pounding the sand next to the fallen Statue of Liberty—he could imagine it all.

And what then would be left of him? Big man. His mother was gone, his father was gone, his graspy bitch of a wife was gone and his house was gone with her. He had no children, no real friends, no relations whom he'd met. He did not even know a line of poetry by heart. He was utterly alone.

Storm set his coffee mug down. Blinked back tears so as not to shame himself before the Duke. Live right, shoot straight, walk tall, he thought. The time had come. Tomorrow, when he met Sophia Endering, he would remember the words with which Harper Albright had described her to him:

If she has a heart at all, it is held in check with considerable force. And if ever she is deprived of her monumental defenses, my guess is you will find her to be as fragile as bliss—and every bit as precious.

Which only underscored what Storm already knew: that love was off-limits to him. Sex, flirtation, even an excess of tenderness were all off-limits, because he would not be able to shield her from the terrible consequences. He wanted to find out if Sophia had seen the ghost of Belham Abbey? Fine. It was to be a purely metaphysical inquiry, that was it, that was all. It might be hard to restrain himself. He might be tempted. It didn't matter.

He rose from his chair, his eyes narrowed to a gunfighter squint. He felt good. He felt strong. He felt prepared for his meeting with Sophia. His meditation had been a success, and he dwelt now within the truth he had been seeking:

A man's got to do what a man's got to do.

8   **Oh, but then** she was so beautiful. The moment he saw her again in the scrumptious flesh, he felt all his resolutions weakening. This was the very next afternoon. He'd been hanging around outside the Endering Gallery for more than an hour. Pretending to study the shirts in a recessed storefront across the street. He didn't know what store it was; he didn't care which shirts. He was just trying and trying to figure out the best way to approach her.

The logistical problems seemed insurmountable. Should he be direct with her? Casual? Sneaky? With her glance that turned men to sand and her heart packed away under pressure, it sure sounded like she had an impressive arsenal against unwanted intrusions. He didn't want to make a mistake.

It was already four o'clock. The winter daylight was already failing. The weather was chill and gray, and Storm was cold, his hands clenched in the pockets of his trench coat, holding it closed. And still, he couldn't make his move.

Then he saw her—her reflection first, in the darkened storefront. Then he turned and saw her in the life, charging through the gallery doors into the deepening indigo of the afternoon. A thrillingly competent stride she had. Swift, unaffected, self-possessed. Marching without hesitation under the bright banners and bay windows of New Bond Street. Despite the cloudy sky, despite the moist wind, she wore only a light cardigan over a blouse unbuttoned at the throat. Her legs were sleek in nylon below the knee and covered with a pleated skirt above that Storm found girlish and adorable. He watched her, thinking, *Oh, oh, oh.* He had forgotten, until that moment, just how crazy he was about her.

He waited until she'd passed, then broke from his cover and followed. Moving quickly to keep up. Dodging between pairs of sharp-suited shoppers. Squeezing past elephantine American tourists. Struggling all the while to belt his flapping trench coat against the steady breeze. He had never tailed anyone before. It turned out to be kind of a strain on the nerves. Out of the corner of his eye, he could see his own image racing over jewelery store windows and he suddenly wondered: What the hell was he doing? What if she saw him, recognized him? What the hell would he say?

Fortunately, the whole thing didn't last that long. The green and gold flag of Sotheby's was just ahead. Sophia was already under it. And then, without breaking step, she had straight-armed the door and disappeared inside.

Storm pulled up a moment. Another new experience: he'd never been in an auction house before. The façade of the place looked pretty daunting. A commissaire dressed like a U.S. Marine patrolled before rose marble entry columns. An obstacle course of reception desks was visible through the glass doors. Past that, there was a formidable pair of sphinxes preening on baize mats, guarding the grand staircase in the front hall. All in all, it seemed very formal and forbidding. Storm wished he'd worn a suit and tie instead of his black jeans and pearl-buttoned hoedown shirt.

But he went in. Tried to look comfortable, confident. Tiptoed clumsily over the Persian rugs spread out before the stairs. Passed between the sphinxes, started up the steps. Now, where had Sophia gotten to?

He reached the landing. He moved off into the viewing galleries. Now he was in a labyrinth of off-white partitions all hung with paintings. Fine paintings, it looked like, though he only caught glimpses of them. Waxy flesh. Golden halos. Feathery wings. Eyes turned heavenward in supplication. He could feel the ecclesiastical chill of old art as he moved down one brief corridor after another, rounded one corner after another.

He scanned the people, searching for the girl. There sure was a lot of money in the place, he could tell that right away. Husky, aggressive Americans with metallic eyes. Dark continentals, with big lips and big lapels. Silver-haired Englishmen in pinstripes that seemed to run down through the core of the earth. They all milled quietly around the maze, gliding slowly before the paintings, studying them with a faintly predatory air. Salespeople danced attendance on some of them—crisp young gentlemen or cardiganed sylphs—but no Sophia.

Storm stepped out into a central aisle and came to a stop with a rosy-toned crucifixion on the wall above him. He cursed silently, looking this way and that. He seemed to have lost her.

And then, there she was. All alone in the farthest corner. Motionless before a single painting there. Perfectly placed . . .

Storm moved up behind her, his hands dangling gawkily at his sides. She'd worn her hair up, and now he saw the downy nape of her neck. And saw that the track lights meant for the paintings brought out a streak of auburn in her black twist. And now he was right up close to her and caught the scent of her and it was like—he didn't know what—like a garden. Heartbreaking. Forbidden. He wanted to turn before she saw him and get the hell out of there.

But now, as his eyes traveled over her, he noticed something else. The painting she was looking at, the lone painting on the off-white wall. His focus shifted, and he saw it clearly.

"Wow!" he whispered aloud.

Sophia whipped around, looked up at him. Let out a quick breath, surprised.

But Storm kept staring over her shoulder at the picture.

It was the very image of Black Annie.

✦

The resemblance seemed incredible to him. The painting showed night falling over blasted trees, the tortured branches drooping over broken stones, the trunks sinking into a deep brown gloom which seemed to rise from the rough earth to swallow them. And there, in that haunted setting, was the ruined chapel. A wedge of wall. A splintered reticulation of a window gaping on a barren sky. And under it, the cowled figure, profoundly somber, moving over the blighted winter ground. Black Annie.

True, there were two other figures in the background, two other cowled phantoms moving in tandem with the first. Maybe it wasn't like the story exactly. Still, thought Storm, what were the odds against the two of them meeting over just such a scene?

"It isn't incredible at all," Sophia said to him curtly, as they walked back along New Bond Street together. It was full dark now. The bays and storefronts were lighted. Glittering jewels and mellow paintings showed behind the glass, warm against the night. Above them, the shop banners, sinking into shadow, made the street seem narrower, more homely than it was. And still, the pavement was crowded with shoppers and tourists, who jostled the two of them on either side. "German Romantic and English Gothic drank pretty freely from the same well, as it were. It was all a sort of reaction to the Enlightenment, all that logic and science and classicism. The German Romantics wanted to bring back a bit of the mystery and religion of the Middle Ages. That's where the ruined abbeys and cathedrals come in: a nostalgia for the days of faith. Your ghost story—'Black Annie,' was it?—that came later, a sort of cheap, commercial version of the idea in which the spirit world is accepted as real, yah? What Rhinehart was trying to show was that the world as we see it is never a thing-in-itself but is always infused, à la Kant, with our own spiritual consciousness."

"Uh-huh," said Storm, whose own spiritual consciousness was infused with the V of creamy flesh beneath the hollow of her throat, and the scent of her on the cold air, and that brittle accent, which absolutely slew him. All the same, he couldn't help noticing that this lecture of hers was rather brisk and distant, dismissive almost. As if she were waving him away. He wanted to ask her, *What about the ghost of Belham Abbey, out by your father's house? What about the fact you dropped your glass when I read the story?* But he sensed that if he did, she would shut him out completely. So he only said, "I don't know. That painting—it sure looked like Black Annie to me."

She brushed this aside, offhanded and yet insistent. " 'Fraid not. It's Rhinehart's romantic version of the Magi, that's all. It's supposed to be the Three Kings bringing their gifts to the infant Christ. We know that because it was part of a Nativity triptych. One of the other panels shows a very folkloric sort of Madonna in the woods, the other's just the babe in the manger. I'm afraid it hasn't anything to do with murdered nuns and that sort of thing."

"Still, isn't it kind of a coincidence? Me coming over, you standing there . . ."

"Not really," she answered at once, very coolly now. "We're considering making a bid at the auction next week. I don't see any sort of coincidence about it." And with that settled, she busied herself straightening the golden brooch pinned to the breast of her cardigan: a design something like a horseshoe enclosing something like a figure eight.

Storm was afraid to press the point. "That's nice," he said, for want of something better. "Nice brooch."

"Oh, thank you. It was my mother's." She went on fussing with it, not even glancing up. "I haven't worn it since I was a child."

They reached the front of her gallery. Stood between two little spruces in cast-iron planters, under the wine-red awning with *Endering Gallery* written in gold letters, and beside the window in which was displayed a landscape of rocky hills and misty distances in a heavy frame. Sophia paused here with her hand on the door, her face turned up to him, her brown eyes remote. He stood over her with his shoulders low, his own hands pressed deep into his trench coat, his own eyes flooded with longing and sadness.

"Would you like to come in?" she said finally—reluctantly, he thought. "We have plenty of works from the period."

She held the door open. Storm went into the gallery.

The place was darkly paneled, dimly lit, a long room hung with paintings all the way down the line. A balcony ran along the wall to his left, with another long gallery of paintings above.

There was a pretty blonde seated at a desk just in front. She was only a bit younger than Sophia, but she smiled up at her deferentially. When she held out a few pink message slips, Sophia took them from her with hardly a glance.

"You see? It's really just the style you're reacting to," Sophia said to Storm. "Look around. You'll find half a dozen paintings in here that remind you of your ghost story."

Then she turned away from him, leaned on the desk, and the two women conferred in low voices as Storm moved deeper into the room. He pretended to look at the paintings on the wall. The tortuous rocks piercing turbulent skies. The crucifixes shooting up among stark, towering pines. Cathedrals draped with ominous gloamings. And moons dying into misty seas. He took in only a sense of their haze and fervor, image fragments and the seething ambience. He was seething himself meanwhile. Struggling with an agony of regret. All this time wasted. All this blather about paintings and theories and whatnot. And now he was going to walk out of here and never see her again.

"That one hung in Carinhall." Sophia was standing behind him suddenly. He found her looking past him at the painting before which he'd stopped: a silhouetted castle on a silhouetted hill.

Storm gazed at her blankly. "Carinhall?"

"It belonged to Hermann Goering during the war," she said. "The Nazis loved this sort of thing. The medieval imagery, all the links to folklore, all the hearkening back to the Holy Roman Empire, it was right up their street. Some people say German Romanticism—the *malaise allemand*—was responsible for the Third Reich. They say the work is tainted with evil . . ."

Storm gave a slow shrug. He remembered what Harper had said about the Nazis and her father. He thought maybe he should say something to reassure her. "Well. Those guys are all dead anyway," he said after a while.

Sophia shifted her attention to him, smiled wryly. "The past is past, you mean."

"Hey. If the past isn't past, what is? Right?"

She seemed about to answer, but said nothing, only shook her head, her lips parted. Then, as if confused, she looked away, fussed with her brooch again. "I think nothing ever dies," she murmured. "It all gets chiseled into the skin of things."

And then, when she lifted her eyes to his again, to Storm's astonishment, everything was different. They had a "moment." That's what they called it in the movie business: a "moment." "We need a moment between the hero and the girl here," Storm would say about a script that wasn't working. "When they first meet, there's gotta be a moment." A "moment" was an exchanged glance, a gesture, a frisson, *something* where emotion or information passed between two people without words. When Sophia lifted her eyes to his, their distance, their flatness, their coolness had fallen away. Her gaze was wide and deep and desperate and there was a "moment" between them, in which Storm thought, *Oh man, she's in trouble. She's afraid.*

But a moment was all it was. It ended so quickly he wasn't even sure it had happened. She sniffed disdainfully, brusquely turned her head. Storm didn't know what to say. He gave a nervous laugh, a nervous gesture.

"Well, I gotta admit, all these paintings all together like this, it does make the place look pretty ghosty," he said. "Don't you ever get nervous when you're here by yourself?"

"Never," she answered at once, facing him again. And the vehemence of what she said next—all in those crystal tones—astonished him.

"I love it here," she told him. "This is where I want to die."

9 A strange feeling came over him now as he wandered home, a thundercloud of foreboding. Nothing felt right to him. Nothing felt good or clear. The sensation rose from the center of him and seeped out into his surroundings. Everything began to seem dead to him and strange.

He traveled back on foot, along the thoroughfares. Piccadilly. Knightsbridge. The wide streets were rushing and rumbling with black cabs and double-decker buses. The sky was roiling, grandiose, over the Wellington arch, over the statue of the Iron Duke mounted, watchful. The dome of Harrod's was lit by little white lights like Christmas, and the sidewalks underneath were bustling and wintry. And yet it all looked flat and dead to him, dead and strange.

On the Fulham Road there was an old hospital, a looming brick Victorian monster, ponderous with history. There was a brick wall beside it, overhung with robinia branches. As Storm passed it, hands in his pockets, shoulders hunched, a black mongrel barked at him. The owner, an old woman, tried to rein the dog in, but it strained against its leash and snarled, backing Storm to the wall. Slowly, the old woman managed to drag the hound away. She called apologies to Storm over her shoulder. He walked on. But the incident upset him. Hounded, that's how he felt.

What was he doing here? he asked himself. In this foreign city, with all these foreign people around him. What had he come here to find? Ghosts? Really? A smart guy like him? Was he really looking for ghosts? Well, it had seemed a reasonable idea at the time. After all those movies he'd made. It had seemed like a logical step. Sort of like what Sophia had said about the Enlightenment and the Romantics: this was his own private quest on behalf of faith and the human spirit, his answer to the relentlessly rational, the implacable scientists, the doctors with their bland, pitiless expressions. It really had struck him as a sensible thing to do.

Now it seemed ridiculous. Ludicrous, useless, stupid. Here he was, five thousand miles from home, hanging around with an eccentric old crazy woman, breaking his heart over a girl half his age, running away, wasting his precious days . . .

He reached his building, a huge block of concrete squatting on the corner like a white toad. He moved, brooding, through its wide automatic doors, past the sleepy woman at reception, past the elevators to the stairs. As he climbed slowly, he felt himself pursued, still. As if something terrible were coming up behind him, its footsteps muffled on the thick green carpet. His legs felt shaky, weak, as he climbed.

He reached the third floor. A long, long hallway. He had to push through heavy fire doors, one pair and then another and then another. His arms began to feel shaky now too. His whole body began to feel heavy and thick.

Midway down the hall, he reached his door. Fumbled with the key. Let himself into the small flat, and punched the lights on with the side of his fist. He slipped out of his trench coat, made to hang it on the edge of the closet door. It fell to the floor instead.

The light on his answering machine was blinking. He ignored it. Trembling, he moved into the kitchen. Ran himself a glass of water. Carried it back into the sitting room, to the sofa. Sank down into the cushions wearily. Only then did he reach out and weakly hit the machine's playback button.

"Hello? Hello? Is it recording now? Damn these things."

Harper. Her voice sounded far away. Hollow. Echoing.

"Richard? I've come across something I think you should see . . . see . . . see . . . ."

The words seemed to him to reverberate foggily. He looked around him at the yellow walls and matted flower prints and the falsely gilded mirror. At the colorless chairs and the orange blocky thing on which he sat. All foreign to him. All dead and strange. What was he doing here anyway?

"It's a little something . . . something . . . something . . . called 'The Alchemist's Castle' . . . ."

He raised the glass to his mouth and the water jerked from it, spilled over his pearl-buttoned shirt, but he still didn't realize what was happening. His hand was shaking violently, but it too seemed foreign, far away, dead, strange. And then the glass slipped from his fingers. Struck the leg of the sofa. Shattered. Fragments and glistening slivers on the carpet. A spreading colorless stain. *Sophia,* he thought. And he looked down blankly and saw another stain spread over the thigh of his jeans. A single razor of pain sliced through his forehead. And, finally, he understood. He clutched his temples with his two hands. He raged—raged—against the relentlessly rational: the implacable scientists, the doctors at

Cedars-Sinai with their bland, pitiless expressions.

"The Alchemist's Castle . . . The Alchemist's Castle . . ."

Six months, you bastards! he cried out in his heart. *You told me I still had six months!*

Then the convulsions struck and he fell to the floor, unconscious.

III

THE ALCHEMIST'S CASTLE

OR

THE VIRGIN'S FATE

1 ANNA HAD LAIN in the moldering family vault this long year past, and her bereaved husband Conrad would not be consoled. Indeed, the villagers had begun to murmur that the hereditary madness which had destroyed Conrad's father had now claimed the son and heir, the last of that illustrious line. Night after night, the young man could be seen sitting at the window of his melancholy, isolated chateau. His ghastly, grief-stricken features made him seem a spectral presence to whatever rude woodsman or peasant passed within sight of the gloomy Gothic manse. Hectic and wild of countenance, he would stare through long hours over the blasted landscape towards the tangled and forbidding recesses of the Black Forest; or betimes would raise a febrile eye towards the crumbling ruin of a nearby tower, which was all that was left of the once-magnificent Castle of Blaustein.

There had been some hope among the local population that Conrad would recover the blithe aspect of former days, especially after the arrival of his cousin Theresa. The child had been given into Conrad's charge after first one, then the other of her parents had succumbed to that plague which had scourged the countryside the year before, sparing neither the great nor the humble.

But alas, the hopes for Conrad's recovery proved as unavailing as they had been fervent. Theresa was a cheerful and lovely child, golden of hair and white of limb. Often, she could be seen playing solitary within the shadows of the chateau battlements, dancing and singing a sweet air to herself even in that tenebrous gloom, or picking whatever flowers had the audacity to grow out of the barren, rocky terrain. And yet, despite the girl's vivacious presence, Conrad, so it was said, continued to appear night after night at the window, gazing in savage despondency at the dismal forest and the tower which stood black and decaying against the turbulent sky.

2 ONE NIGHT, SOON after Theresa had reached her twelfth year, just as her girlish beauty was softening into the more tender loveliness of blossoming womanhood, she awoke suddenly to discover Conrad standing over her bed. It was a night of tempest, thunder resounding through the vaults and corridors of the glowering old mansion, lightning chasing fantastic shapes over the archaic tapestries that draped the mossy walls. It was precisely such an atmospheric clamor that brought the maiden's eyes flying open, whereupon she recoiled at the sight of Conrad's pallid visage hovering above her. A blush swiftly replacing the wonted ivory of her cheeks, Theresa clutched her counterpane to her breast in the first untutored promptings of virginal modesty.

"What is this, cousin," said she, "that you disturb my rest at so unholy an hour, and on so tumultuous a night that my heart nearly fails me for fear?"

Conrad, in a mournful voice fit only for the anguished soliloquies of the sepulcher, would answer only, "You must rise now, child, and come with me."

Accustomed to obeying her guardian in all matters, Theresa asked no further questions for the moment. When Conrad had withdrawn from her chamber, she arose, shying and trembling at the periodic ragings of the storm without. She dressed by the light of a single candle and performed what ablutions she could posthaste; and when she had done, she joined her elder cousin where he paced, brooding, beneath the sinister arches and macabre statuary that decorated the chateau's massive front hall.

To her astonishment, Conrad, himself already wrapped in a greatcoat, now extended to her her own warmest cloak.

"Surely, dearest cousin," Theresa cried, thinking her guardian meant to have some bizarre amusement at her expense, "surely you cannot intend for us to make an excursion in this uproar, for it is as if the heavens themselves were to be swallowed by some terminal maelstrom!"

He replied nothing, but with a second, more insistent gesture, urged the mantle on her so that she had no choice but to receive it from him and clothe herself withal. Then, with an inarticulate groan that sent a tremor of premonitory terror over Theresa's delicate limbs, Conrad hurled open the mansion's ponderous door, and drew her out with him into the storm.

Their heads bowed against the raging gusts, Conrad and Theresa crossed the sere wasteland in a moonless blackness illuminated only by the forked daggers of lightning which at intervals cleft the sky in twain. The furious din of thunder which followed each such incendiary eruption only served to deepen the tremulous foreboding which step by step rose in Theresa's heart, filling her innocent bosom with dread imaginings she knew not how to name.

"Whither go we, my dearest, most trusted guardian?" she ejaculated passionately from time to time. "Oh, in the name of that wife you sometime loved before a good and merciful God found fit to call her to his everlasting peace, ease my foolish virginal fears and tell me whither we go!"

But Conrad, staring into the distance with a disordered mien that did nothing to console his pavid charge, only tightened the grip he held upon her arm and hurried her through the night.

At length, Theresa raised her eyes to find they were approaching the solitary ruined tower of Castle Blaustein. A little gasp, lost in the commotion of the tempest, escaped her full lips as her eye fell on the disintegrating stones, which seemed to be made animate by the violent oscillation of the surrounding trees.

But now the frightened maiden turns her gaze aloft; now for the first time she spies a wavering glow of red light in the highest window of the tower, which was always heretofore plunged in the umbrageous obscurity of abandonment.

"Cousin, oh cousin, what is this?" she cries. "Who is it who can have come to live in this so desolate abode?"

And finally, her guardian directs his burning glance upon her upturned face, and shouts his answer at her above the ferment.

"It is the alchemist!" he shrieks with an intonation of insane joy. "It is the alchemist come at last!"

3 WHAT A PASSION of horror thrilled Theresa's maiden breast as the rotting gate of the tower closed behind her with a reverberant crash.

Her cousin's mysterious and yet strangely appalling words still echoed in her ears as an even more complete darkness than before now enshrouded them; and that sable cerement was made only the more suffocating to Theresa by the weird, flickering tongues of scarlet luminescence which, falling from some unknown chamber above, brought the shape of a stone spiral staircase faintly into view before her. Towards this, Conrad drew her now. And—hark!—as they began to mount the crumbling steps, a faint noise drifted down to them, becoming audible as the howling storm without was muted by the impenetrable thickness of the tower's walls:

Tink-tink, tink-tink.

"Sweet merciful heavens," gasped Theresa, clinging to her cousin in the blackness. "What is that, guardian?"

"It is only the alchemist at work, my child," answered Conrad.

Slowly, he continued to mount the steps, pulling his reluctant ward in his train. The lambent glow above grew brighter; the enigmatic noise grew louder as they climbed.

Tink-tink, tink-tink.

"But what is it, what is it?" Theresa cried out. "What is it, cousin, that makes that sound, for at each repetition of it my heart misgives me?"

"He only hammers the iron rings into the wall," Conrad muttered. "Be still, my child."

Cobwebs brushed against Theresa's soft cheeks, tangled in her silken hair as her cousin continued to drag her up and up and up the spiral staircase. And the flickering light grew brighter above, and the hammering louder.

Tink-tink, tink-tink.

"Oh, what now, what now, my cousin, my trusted guardian?" Theresa babbled in a paroxysm of fear.

"He makes the chains, he only makes the chains," said Conrad, his eyes fixed on the turning path above him. "Have no fear, my child."

On and on, he drew her, up and up. The glimmer of the flames—for such is what they were—now appeared to rise ubiquitous on the walls around her; the noises of the unseen workshop were magnified in Theresa's frenzied imagination until she nearly swooned with affright at each reiteration.

Tink-tink, tink-tink.

"Oh, by the mercy of sweet heaven, what is it?" she whimpered, clutching her guardian's arm with fresh force.

"The fetters now," said he in an eldritch, distant tone. "He forges the fetters, I think. Be of good cheer, my child."

At this intelligence—and at a renewed occurrence of the chilling sound—Theresa fell to her knees on the damp stone of the stairs, clasping at her cousin's hand with quivering fingers, lifting up her beauteous and tear-stained face in blind beseeching. "Oh, my cousin, my guardian, to whom my parents trusted me in their hour of death, in the name of all that you hold dear, take me no farther, do not make me go before this alchemist, for I swear by heaven the thought of him terrifies me exceedingly."

Her fear charged her tender limbs with peculiar strength and for several moments she held Conrad immobile so that he peered down at her through the darkness, confused.

"Not go? Not go?" said he. "When I have sent for him, waited for him all this time? When he has traveled to me all the way from Rome? Not go?"

He knelt before his cousin, took her soft shoulders in his strong hands so that, for an instant, she fancied he might be about to show some familial compassion to assuage her torment of suspense. But Conrad, by a brutal exertion, only lifted her once more to her feet, compelled her once more to rise towards the flames and the hammering.

Tink-tink, tink-tink.

"Not go?" Conrad whispered in Theresa's ear as he carried her all but limp form up another step and another until they neared the top. "When he is known to possess the greatest knowledge of the ancient mysteries of any man alive? Not go to him, my child? When for my sake—nay! for the sake of my beloved Anna, who this bleak, desolate, seemingly endless year past has lain mercilessly imprisoned in her tomb, that flesh which once gave to me my greatest pleasure unpreserved by the tears which I have lavished upon it night after night—when for her sake, I say, he has composed a potion which will restore her to my arms, to my desire—to my love which is so great that it transcends the fear of earthly decay and merely waits for the opportunity to enfold her as in our happy days of yore? Not go? How can you say such a thing, my dear little Theresa? The work is almost complete! The potion of resurrection is freshly prepared!"

And so saying, Conrad brought the girl to the top of the spiral staircase and came before a great door of solid iron, which stood ajar so that the dancing scarlet light of the flame and the repeated metallic percussions seeped out onto the landing where the cousins stood. With a mighty effort of one hand, Conrad oped the door wide, while with the other he dragged the all but insensible Theresa into the room beyond.

And there stands the work table, littered with every macabre, unnameable instrument and beaker of the alchemist's art. There are the chains and manacles bolted into the thick stone of the walls. There the flames soaring and dying in the tower grate and the jet-black pot which holds the unholy potion churning, frothing.

And there, before the poor girl's streaming eyes, stands the alchemist himself, his stare bright beneath his black cowl, his features crimson in the infernal radiance of the fire,—and in his hand—oh, in his hand—one final, most terrible implement of all, its thin, curving blade red and glittering.

"Oh, cousin, cousin!" Theresa shrieked. "Why have you brought me to this dreadful place?"

"Because we need just one ingredient more!" Conrad cried.

And he slammed the door behind her.

4 THE CHATEAU ON the borders of the Black Forest has stood empty of life now, lo, these many years; and the tower of Castle Blaustein has long since fallen to dust. Neither Conrad nor his young cousin Theresa was ever seen after that one tempestuous winter night; and there are some who say they removed themselves to a family villa in the south, while others tell far grimmer tales of what befell them. Whatever the truth of the matter, the villagers rarely go near the old manse, fearing, in their unsophisticated way, that even the sight of its decomposing battlements can portend no good. And yet, there are those informants who report with an air of complete authority that one chamber in the chateau's uppermost story remains occupied, if not peopled; and that anyone temerarious enough to brave the rats and spiders, cobwebs and spectres of the place may see for themselves the antique marriage bed on whose tattered and putrefying sheets lies the skeleton of Conrad—forever entwined with the crumbling bones of Anna, his cherished bride.

IV

SOPHIA,
THE NOOSE AROUND
HER NECK

"Something is terribly wrong," said Harper, tapping the kraken's eyeball.

"What is it?" asked Storm.

"I. Just. Don't. Know," she said, each word a sentence, each sentence punctuated by another tap of her fingernail against the glass. The jar stood on a stone pedestal between them. In the jar—in a clear preservative that filled the jar— lay the carcass of an enormous serpent, its flat, white, gelatinous body rolled into a coil the size of a firehose. Harper Albright leaned in close to the glass and peered through it at Storm. The curve of the jar magnified and distorted her features. The orange torchlight hopped on the lenses of her spectacles. "Every word Sophia said to you, every gesture she made, conveys to me a message of distress."

"No, I mean, what is it?" Storm repeated. "This. In the jar."

He circled around it until he stood beside her. Hands behind his back, he leaned in too. He examined the leviathan's horned proboscis.

Harper, in turn, cocked her head to study him. "The first sighting of such a creature was, I believe, recorded in 1555 by Olaus Magnus, the archbishop-in-exile of Uppsala, Sweden," she murmured thoughtfully. "The occasional reappearance of its kind in northern waters over the next two centuries has led some modern commentators to speculate that they were the prototype of Iormungand, the serpent of Midgard, who encircles the world, and whom Thor might have landed with an oxhead for bait were it not for the cowardice of the giant Hymir."

"Don't tell me, let me guess: it's really, like, a big roll of toilet paper or something." And with a derisive snort, he moved away towards the giant pig of Chalfont St. Giles.

Harper frowned sternly. "A ribbon worm," she said, screwing the point of her stick into the earthen floor. "Phylum *Nemetinea*. And quite rare at this size, actually. Smuggled in from Osaka, where it washed ashore on New Year's Day, 1995. Many Japanese believe that their appearances serve as predictors of earthquake . . . The spike secretes poisonous mucus," she called, in an attempt to hold his interest, but he had already rambled off under the flambeau.

They were in the Secret Museum, a network of medieval vaults beneath a street of warehouses in Southwark. Forgotten, presumed destroyed, the catacombs had been appropriated by a small group of connoisseurs for the display of their bizarreries. Beneath the low stone arches of the underground corridors, jars, aquaria, display cases and picture frames stood on top of pedestals, rested on tables, leaned against derelict sarcophagi, or hung upon the walls. They were lit only by fire—by torches guttering here and there in iron cressets, filling the place with oily smoke. This was an admittedly melodramatic touch, but some of the less scholarly visitors seemed to enjoy it.

As Storm continued away down the corridor, Jorge Swade, the museum's curator and sole cicerone, found himself caught uncomfortably between his most cherished patron and the man he presumed to be her beau. His bloodshot eyes blinked furiously, his buck teeth chattered like a dentist's toy, but he didn't know what to say to ease the tension. He settled for making ridiculous and servile bows in both their directions. Which made his lank hair brush the shoulders of his red sports jacket, leaving an oily stain.

As for Harper, she went on frowning at the retreating Storm for a few moments more. Of all the curios in the place, she really found him the most curious of all. Clearly, he was besotted with the girl—clearly enough to pinch her own antique heart with a twinge or two of jealousy. Why the pretense of indifference then? Why did he insist on it?

With a determined tug at the brim of her Borsalino, with a firmer grip on the dragon head of her stick, she waddled after him now, under the torch, down the corridor, brushing past the cringing Swade.

"A woman like Sophia Endering doesn't just cry out for help," she growled. "Not to a perfect stranger. Not to anyone, I suspect."

Storm had already abandoned the pig. He skirted the pickled rat ring. Passed the mermaid skeleton with only a quick glance. She caught up with him as he headed down a short cul-de-sac lined with framed photographs and lit by a single torch.

"What crying for help?" he muttered, pretending to give his full attention to a picture of Popobawa, the winged cyclopean homosexual dwarf of Zanzibar. "Who says she's crying for help?"

"You know she is." Harper wagged a wrinkled finger at him. "Why else would she adjust her brooch?"

"What?"

"You have a Hollywood producer's eye for detail, Storm. You miss absolutely everything of importance." She shook her head reproachfully. "When you expressed your touchingly ludicrous American belief in the evanescence of history, she adjusted her mother's brooch—which she had never worn before—and disagreed. Which was as much as to say that the issues surrounding her mother's death had arisen in some fresh way to disturb her."

"Harps. Sweetheart. Gimme a break here. I mean, she adjusted her brooch." And barely looking at her, Storm moved on.

"Er . . . the book," whispered Jorge Swade, "the manuscript." He had come scurrying along after them, anxiously grinding his palms together. His nerves simply couldn't stand this dissension. "I've set it out for you. It's all prepared." He gestured hopefully towards a nearby alcove.

"In a moment, my dear," Harper said with a dismissive wave. "Young Richard . . ." He was at the cul-de-sac's far wall now, shaking his head at the latest portrait of Nessie. "You described the conversation to me yourself . . ."

"Described it? You pumped me with questions about it for two hours."

"Sophia adjusted the brooch that belonged to her mother—her mother who committed suicide—and then she told you she wanted to die."

"She didn't tell me she wanted to die, Harper!" he said over his shoulder. "She told me she wanted to die in the gallery."

"Why should she want to die anywhere?"

"Oh, for crying . . ." He lifted his eyes to heaven. "Please!"

Harper rapped the point of her stick impatiently against the earth. It made Jorge jump about a foot behind her, but seemed to have no effect whatsoever on Storm. "What is the matter with you, young Richard? You admitted you sensed it yourself. The woman is asking for your help, crying for your help."

And here, to Harper's surprise—to her dismay—he rounded on her almost ferociously.

"Not my help, Harper," he said between his teeth. "Someone's help maybe—maybe you're right—but not mine."

Harper Albright cocked a gray brow at him. This was decidedly out of character, not at all like the easygoing man she knew. She could see he regretted the outburst immediately. The way he looked down at his shoes, the way he snuffled, annoyed with himself. The way he turned away, averted his face. And yet suddenly Harper wondered whether there might not be an awful logic to it too. An intuition struck her, and she wondered whether all his behavior might not make a terrible kind of sense. Behind her glasses, under her broad-brimmed hat, her eyes narrowed. She frowned again, more deeply.

"Anyway," said Storm in a low, embarrassed tone, "like I told you, we mostly talked about art. She's real smart, she knows a lot about art, and that's what we mostly talked about."

He was now moving back towards her, along the row of photos on the wall to Harper's right. Harper studied his profile, noble brow to heroic nose to cleft chin. She saw for the first time—admitted for the first time that she saw—the new sallowness of his cheeks, the new weariness in his eyes. The way he massaged his left arm from time to time and nursed it. But she pushed her instinct down. She wasn't ready to accept it yet. She drew a breath and launched into him again as if nothing had occurred to her.

"What about the coincidence then? You approached her

just as she was standing before that painting . . ."

"What coincidence?" He was still irritated. "I followed her. There's no coincidence."

"Yes, so she went to great lengths to convince you. There's no coincidence, she said—and that was the other time she touched the brooch. Suggesting that the reason she dropped her glass when you read 'Black Annie,' and the reason she was upset by that painting, and the reason she is contemplating suicide . . ."

"She's not contemplating suicide, Harper. For Christ's sake."

". . . are all connected with the circumstances of her mother's death."

"You're driving me crazy," he said, jutting his face at one photograph after another as he came back towards her. "The whole thing was just a mistake. She just happened to drop her glass. The picture just happened to look like the story. There's no coincidence. There's probably no such thing as coincidence. I read that once. It's just some sort of mathematical deal where stuff sort of falls together and everyone thinks it's this big synchronicity thing and the whole business just doesn't exist. Hey, who the hell is Iago?"

"Ah," Harper Albright said.

He had stopped—he had pulled up short—in front of the photograph just beside the torch. Its glazing was alive with shadows in the flutter and flare of the flames. His face caught the reflected glow as he stared.

Harper's squat form hobbled through the light and shade until she was at his elbow. Little Jorge lagged, fussing, gesturing helplessly at the lectern in the alcove beside him.

Storm and Harper looked at the picture together. "This is one of the reasons I brought you here," she said.

It was an old black-and-white photo, much enlarged, much distorted and blurred by the enlargement. The grain—plus the haze and smoke in the scene itself—gave the setting a poetic, dreamlike quality. So Harper, anyway, had always felt. The photo depicted a compound of wooden barracks in the process of burning to the ground. In the moment at which the shutter had snapped, the flames of the individual buildings were being swept together into a single surging inferno. The smoke was thick. The sky was black with it. The barracks were no more than spectral suggestions at the core of the thing. Only one human figure was visible, there in the forefront: a smallish form charging through the blaze, charging through the tall wooden gate of the compound's entryway, charging, it seemed, to safety, cradling a bundle in the shelter of its arms.

Jorge had written the legend:

THE END OF IAGO

> A female follower of "Saint Iago" carries a baby through the fire that destroyed the cult leader's compound in northeast Argentina. One hundred thirty-three of Iago's followers are thought to have died in the blaze. At least forty-four of the dead were children, many of them believed to have been fathered by the cult leader himself. Aside from this disputed photograph, there is no other evidence that the event took place. The fate of the escaping woman, therefore, remains a mystery. (Cat. 44)

"This . . ." said Storm.

"Yes," said Harper.

He was pressing his finger to the glazing, pointing at the high crossbar of the gate above the escaping figure. Burnt into the crossbar's wood, just visible through the grain and haze, was a symbol: something like a horseshoe enclosing something like a figure eight.

"It's the same as her brooch," said Storm.

"Exactly," said Harper.

She heard him curse under his breath. "What're you trying to tell me? This picture has something to do with Sophia and her mother and everything?"

"I'm telling you it might."

He glowered down at her. "All right," he said. "So who the hell is Iago?"

Harper's gravelly voice, her brusque, marble-mouthed accent, seemed somehow far more suited to the form of narrative than conversation. She never began a long story without a certain hint of relish in the set of her pale lips, a certain glint of it in her eyes.

"His name—or so he pretended—was Jacob Hope," she said up at Storm. "And it is remarkably difficult to discover anything else specific about him. He was probably British, though he seems to have traveled extensively not only through Europe but in Africa, America and the Middle East as well. He appeared on the scene some thirty years ago. A drifter, traveling with other drifters, the new breed of young vagabonds—there were a lot of them at the time." She paced away from Storm, her chin lowered pensively. Her stick bobbed up and down in the air in front of her as her wrist rose and lowered. "Hope claimed to have mystical powers. The power of prophecy, healing. The secret of eternal life as well. He promised eternal life to those who would believe in him, follow him. And many young people did believe him and did follow. Men and women both, but women especially; he had enormous sexual appeal. Women—girls— who had run away from home, who were lost and alone, on drugs some of them, some of them simply confused, gave themselves to him in great numbers, even eventually bearing his children, gladly." She paused, turned, faced Storm again, the lenses of her spectacles awash in reflected flames. "His claims for himself, and his offers to his followers, became more and more inflated, more grandiose. He said he was an oracle. He said he was a son of God. Ultimately, a little over twenty-five years ago, Saint Iago—that's what he was calling himself by then—led his people out of England, on a long pilgrimage. Some of the followers believed the exodus was to climax in the world's final cataclysm. After which, I suppose, their boy was to be crowned king of heaven, his apostles at his right hand. In any case, they followed him. And the great journey took the cult through Spain and Western Africa and finally to South America. There, in the jungles of the Paraná Plateau, Saint Iago made camp, presumably to await the end." She paced back towards Storm again.

He glanced at her, then went on studying the photo. "So how'd it come to this?" he asked her.

"There was one," she said. "In the jungle, in the compound—there was one disciple of this madman who finally—finally—began to guess the truth. Even in the depths of her enslavement to Iago's charisma, there came the glimmer of understanding. She began to suspect that her master's miracles and prophecies, his promised apocalypse, were not simply deceptions—but were deceptions intended to conceal another, more terrible agenda. Children of the camp—Iago's children—had begun to disappear. Their mothers sometimes too. And one woman had gone raving mad and killed herself before anyone could stop her.

"At last, one night, when most of the camp lay sleeping, the Suspicious Disciple noticed certain of the cult's inner circle leaving the compound. She slipped from her bed and followed them into the surrounding jungle."

Now Storm kept his eyes on Harper only, as she drew breath, braced herself, went on. "Trembling with fear, the Suspicious Disciple threaded a narrow path beneath trees so thick they blocked the moonlight and plunged her into a shadowy darkness pierced by terrible animal cries and ominous scrabblings. Finally, the low murmur of voices up ahead led her to the edge of a steamy clearing. Pushing aside the leaves, she peeked through. And there, by the light of a single torch, she saw all her half-formed suspicions confirmed. And worse."

Harper squared her shoulders, blinked through the flame-light on her spectacles. "Iago was standing before a stone altar," she said. "And lying on the altar was a child. One of his own children—a mere toddler—looking up at his father with sleepy, trusting eyes. Around them, a few of the inner circle stood watching, mumbling some arcane chant. And at the clearing's far edge, a young woman was struggling wildly in the grip of two hulking apostles. It was the child's mother, and her wild stare was white above the gag that stifled her screams.

"And then, as the Suspicious Disciple looked on in helpless horror, Iago raised a curved dagger into the air above the child's naked chest. And with a dreamy grin, he—"

"Jesus," said Storm. "Jesus Christ. Don't tell me, all right? Jesus."

Harper went on more quietly. "The scales of a years-long madness fell from the Suspicious Disciple's eyes. She turned to rush back to the compound, to raise the alarm. Unfortunately, in her panic, she fell, gave herself away. She only just managed to evade capture, dashing into the surrounding jungle, working her way back to the camp, where her own infant lay sleeping, as the others hunted for her.

"It was then that Iago—realizing the game was up—set fire to the compound, burning his own followers in their beds, shooting even those of the inner circle who tried to escape."

Storm grimaced. "Like Waco. Like Jonestown."

"But years earlier than both. In fact, one strain of scholarship holds that the Reverend Jones was much inspired by his predecessor."

"Swell. A boy's gotta have someone to look up to."

"No doubt. In any case, no one escaped from Fort Iago alive."

"What about this one?" Storm gestured at the photo with his chin. "The lady with the kid. Is she the—whatchamacallit—the suspicious one?"

"Perhaps. In any case, no one knows what happened to her."

"Well, why not? I mean, all these people dying, someone's gotta know something."

"People disappear all the time, Richard. Especially drifters, runaways."

"Yeah, but I mean, like, how come I've never heard of this? How come it wasn't in the papers or anything? What about this picture—who took the picture?"

"It's said to have been taken by a *Daily Telegraph* photographer named Elton Yarwood. Who subsequently went missing without ever filing a story. In fact, no one ever filed a story. Whatever research has been done on the subject has appeared in such journals as *The Fortean Times, Journal X* in America. And, of course, *Bizarre!* But as far as the mainstream press—as far as any official source—is concerned, Iago never existed and the entire incident never took place."

"So how'd the picture get here?"

"Ah." Harper shrugged, smiled. "One does not inquire too deeply into the acquisitional methods of the Secret Museum, young Richard. Our friend Jorge here is, you will find, a very resourceful man."

Jorge—who respected Harper to the point of idolatry—preened.

Storm, meanwhile, was intent on the photograph again. He had his head up close to it, tilted like a bird's head to bring one eye nearer. "So wait a minute, wait a minute," he said. "This was twenty-five years ago?"

"Approximately, yes."

"And you said Sophia's mother killed herself when Sophia was four or five. Which can't be more than twenty years ago."

"Nineteen," Harper said.

"So how could she have known this Iago guy unless he. . . ?" His mouth still open on the word, he turned to cast an appraising glance at Harper. She had drifted away now to the edge of the torchlight. He studied her there, turned to the photo again, to her again. Then to the photo again, so close now his nose was almost pressed to the glass.

"You know, it's funny," he murmured, "this woman here, this one trying to get out—she looks kind of like you, Harper. Harper. . . ?"

To his surprise, when he looked again, she had vanished.

Only Jorge Swade was there, jogging his oily hair as he bounced up and down inside his red sports jacket.

"If you would . . . Over here, if you could . . . this way . . ." he said, gesturing fitfully towards the recess in the stone wall.

Squinting against the firelight, shielding his face from the heat of the torch with an upraised hand, Storm moved in that direction. And there was his queer old friend. Leaning on her stick in the alcove, in its deep shadow. Waiting for him by the lectern there. With a ceremonial flourish, she motioned to the lectern's slanted surface. There lay a large, thin volume with a brown leather cover. Storm drew nearer. Harper flipped the cover open so that it fell against the lectern with a *whap*.

"This is the other reason I brought you here," she said. "*Tolle, lege,* young Richard." And when he gawped at her clueless, she translated: "Take up, dear boy, and read."

She and Jorge stepped away to murmur together. Storm approached the book, stood over it. Gripped the lectern by its edges like a preacher. Bowed his head over the open page. He traced the illegible script through the darkness, made out that it was in some foreign language. Found the translation printed more neatly beside it. And read:

Anna had lain in the moldering family vault this long year past, and her bereaved husband Conrad would not be consoled . . .

2   There was a man standing on the corner outside The Sign of the Crane, and Harper didn't like the look of him one bit. Big he was, and hunch-shouldered. With piggy eyes under a brutally cut forelock of tawny hair. Plus he had a scar on one side of his mouth that gave him a

permanent sneer. He hung back, out of the glare of the streetlight. Nursed his cigarette in his cupped hand to hide the glow. It was almost nine-thirty now, so he'd been standing there like that for more than twenty minutes. Ever since Harper and Storm had entered the pub, in fact.

Harper remained at the window, eyed him. Gnawed on her pipestem. Stroked the jaw of the meerschaum skull with her tobacco-blackened thumb. She would not have thought so jaded, so scarred a heart as hers still capable of such flutterings, such mixed emotions. But there they were. Fear. Weariness: she felt much older than she was. And excitement too. She had to confess it. Adrenaline tuning her nerves, making her pulse tympanic. Was it possible, after all the blind alleyways, after a quarter-century of faint clues and faded trails—could it really be possible that the hunt was finally beginning in earnest, that she had smoked her adversary out at last?

If so, then Bernard was right—it was Storm who somehow had made it happen. His coming here. Reading that ghost story. Somehow that was what set the whole thing into motion. And this also was a burden to her, a weight of dread and sadness.

She adjusted her vision. The man outside on the streetcorner blurred. Storm, his image reflected on the window, came into focus.

He was sitting at a small, round table behind her. Chin down. His left hand wrapped round a glass of Diet Coke. His right hand massaging his left shoulder. He didn't know she was looking at him and was staring into the fizzy brown surface of his drink with all the grief in his grief-stricken eyes plain to see. Around him, the dark wood tones of the tavern faded into obscurity. Only the brass rail of the bar was gleaming. A couple of older fellows stood propped against it, pints in hand. Talking at times, but mostly staring into the gas fire, which burned high, blue and orange, in the large grate. Except for a video slot machine—sparkling with blithe idiocy in a corner, unused—the place was dim, the yellow lanterns on the wall kept low. The atmosphere was mellow, as usual, quiet.

After a while, Storm stirred where he sat. "All right," he said slowly. "Run this by me again."

Harper had to dredge herself out of her brown study. She answered with a sigh. Not turning. Keeping watch on the scarred man outside as he smoked in the shadows. " 'The Alchemist's Castle,' " she said. "It was published anonymously, in German, sometime around 1798, about a hundred years before the English story 'Black Annie.' When I raised the issue of a possible link between 'Black Annie' and the Belham Abbey ghost, Jorge was reminded of the German work. He located the 'Alchemist' manuscript in a private collection in Dresden. In Dresden, mind. The collector attributed the work to one Hans Baumgarten, who was a member of the artistic circle that included Rhinehart. Baumgarten wrote the story in Dresden, shortly after the turn of the nineteenth century. At the same time and place, in other words, at which Rhinehart painted the triptych of which *The Magi* is the first panel."

"Right. Okay." Storm went on kneading his arm, working his way down from shoulder to elbow. "And all this is stupendously incredible and fantastic because 'The Alchemist's Castle' and *The Magi* have absolutely nothing to do with each other."

"Precisely," said Harper Albright. "*The Magi*—with its cowled figures before a wedge of wall—is reminiscent of

'Black Annie.' But 'Black Annie'—with its foully murdered child and its reiterated sound—reminds us of 'The Alchemist's Castle.' A possible inference is that all three works had a common, earlier source."

"You mean the painting I saw at the auction house with Sophia and the story of Black Annie might actually be based on the same thing."

"So a reading of 'The Alchemist's Castle' would suggest."

Storm thought this over, massaging his arm. "So then I was right—when I saw the painting and said it looked like Black Annie, I was right. And all that stuff Sophia was saying about German Romantics and English ghost stories was—"

"Interesting," said Harper, "but not to the immediate point."

"I'll be damned," Storm said softly. "So what you're saying, you think maybe Sophia was trying to throw me off the trail? But why would she do that?" And then he answered his own question at once: "Because maybe 'Black Annie' and the painting *and* 'The Alchemist's Castle' are all somehow related to the ghost out at Sophia's house. And maybe that's why Sophia dropped her glass when I read the story."

"Ah," said Harper.

"All of which is supposed to have something to do with this cult guy, this Saint Iago."

"I must say your grasp of the implications is admirable."

"My grasp of the . . . Hey, listen, I love it when you talk like that," said Storm with a forlorn laugh. "Only what I'm grasping here is that you think Sophia's in trouble with a dead cult leader who may never have existed and somebody in a cowl going tick-tick who's over two hundred years old."

"Well, it's a ghost you were after," Harper Albright said grimly. "It was a ghost you came here to find." And now she did turn, she did face him. Left the thug on the corner to fend for himself, left her fear and excitement in abeyance, and faced him squarely.

Storm had dropped back against his seat, had stopped nursing his arm. He had started to spread his hands in a comical gesture of confusion. But when their eyes met, when he saw what Harper was thinking, his hands sank down again, and he dropped the comedy.

"Hey," he said.

"You're dying, aren't you, young Richard?" asked Harper Albright.

She felt her spirit grow heavy, felt it fall heavily inside her, as the air rushed out of him, as his hands came to rest on the tabletop and he sagged towards them. "Yeah, pilgrim, yeah," he told her. "It sure looks thataway."

Harper had left her dragon stick leaning in a corner by the fireplace. So she had to hold on to the back of a nearby chair. The old, weary weight of pity again. She had felt it often in her life.

"And this is, I presume, a certainty?" she asked gruffly.

"Yup." Storm winked at her. "It's that old devil brain. Being eaten away apparently. Listen, in my business, it isn't even a liability."

"There's nothing they can do."

He snorted into his Diet Coke. Flicked his wrist and tossed the drink down. Then he set the glass on the table with a bang. "Yeah, well, see, that's the whole thing. That's the whole thing right there. There isn't—but that wasn't gonna stop them. At first, when they found it, they sort of blurted the whole thing out. The tumor's too deep, they said.

Too involved with vital functions. Blah, blah, blah, this and that. Then—you could see it—their fingers started itching for the scalpel. 'Well, we *could* do an exploratory. We *have* got a new technique. We *might* just run a tube into your head and pump the radioactive stuff right on in there.' It wasn't gonna stop me dying, see. They just wanted to make sure I'd be as miserable as possible before I went."

Harper did not want to trouble him with her tears. But the smile at the side of his mouth, the hard glint of humor in his eyes, the courage . . . She turned away from him, back to the window. She glared at the scarred thug on the corner. She felt only a simmering anger for him now.

"So I ran away," Storm said. "They wouldn't stop, you know. They were like Satan or something. Tempting me. A small chance of remission. Good results in a test in Baltimore. I was afraid I would lose my nerve, seize the chance—and then they'd have me, they'd butcher me for no reason, ruin the rest of my life. So I ran away. Came here. I figured, what the hell. I wouldn't have even known I had it if I hadn't cracked my head one night. Had to have a CAT scan, and that showed something. Then they did this magnetic image thing. I wouldn't even have known, if it wasn't for that. Doctors said I might go another six months to a year without even having any symptoms . . ."

Here his voice trailed off in a manner that squeezed Harper's heart. He touched his arm once more, lightly, and she understood that the symptoms were already upon him. Before she could say anything, though, she heard his chair scrape, saw his reflection on the window as he stood up.

"Anyway, now you see the problem. With Sophia, I mean."

Quickly, Harper rounded on him again. Frowned at him.

"I do not. If I'm right, and she needs help . . . if I'm right and she's shown a certain unconscious inclination to confide in you as she's never been known to confide in anyone . . . then I refuse to see the problem. A man and woman should be able to help one another without its becoming . . . overly complicated."

He laughed, working his trench coat off the back of his chair. "They should be, sweetheart, no question," he said. "But they're not. And even if they were, I wouldn't be, not with her. I'm like a tinderbox around her. It's not just her looks, either. I don't know what it is. Every time I see her. I want to kill a rhinoceros for her, or build a castle or something—and then make love to her till the universe turns to clay." Shaking his head, he slid the coat on. Made an ironical expression. Standing there, hands in his pockets. Tall, fit, youthful, lively. It was hard for Harper to tolerate the sight. "Great timing, huh?" he said.

He walked towards the double doors, towards her. Stopped to stand beside her, with his hand resting lightly on one door's brass push-plate.

"Hey—don't look at me like that," he told her. "What can I do?"

"That's not for me to say," Harper answered slowly. "I can only tell you that the young woman seems to me to be in trouble. Judging by the fervor with which she denied it, I would guess it does have something to do with *The Magi*. Perhaps the auction represents some sort of crisis point—"

"Don't, don't, don't," he said. He closed his eyes a moment, held a hand up at her. "Don't. I mean, if you're right, and she took to me for some reason, and she wants my help— and if, like you say, she's fragile, you know, in the emotions department—then it's even worse, Harper. Best-case scenario:

I break her heart. So please. All right? I haven't been a saint. I want to go out clean."

And then he did go out—fled from her, practically, out into the winter's night. And she watched him from the window, sad and afraid.

A terrible moment followed. As Harper looked on. As Storm stepped into the middle of the narrow street, glancing this way and that for a cab. The thug on the corner tossed his latest cigarette into the gutter. Straightened. Two other hulking figures detached themselves from the surrounding darkness and began to close in on Storm. Harper's entire body went rigid. Storm, finding the street empty, had begun to move away to the corner. The scarred thug gave a look to his two massive henchmen, a signal with his eyes.

And they withdrew. As Storm strolled casually past them, they dropped back into the shadows.

Harper relaxed. Nodded to herself. That was as she thought it would be, as she thought it should be too. No matter what mystic role Storm's arrival had played—no matter what role he himself would play—in the events to come, this was not his hunt, not his battle. It was hers.

And she was the one they were after.

3 The siege wore on.

The scarred thug left the corner for a while, but was replaced by one of his mates. A real Frankenstein's monster, this one—cinderblock head and gorilla arms and all. Harper sensed there were still others, standing by, out of sight. She was going to need reinforcements.

She phoned Bernard—twice—from the pay phone at the far end of the bar. He wasn't in, of course. She could hardly have expected him. He lived above the office, in her house right across the street, but he seldom returned there before dawn. His nights, she understood, were spent in the sort of prowling debaucheries she only wished were beyond her wildest imagination. Just in case he should call in, as he sometimes did, she tried to leave a message on his private machine. It being a machine, however, and she being herself, she wasn't quite sure she had succeeded.

So she retired to the fireplace. Sat at a table. Nursed a warm pint of Guinness. Fitfully smoked her pipe, relit it nervously, lay it steaming on the tabletop beside her Borsalino. And prayed that help would somehow arrive.

Shortly before eleven, the two old gentlemen at the bar packed it in and headed for home. Harper was left alone with the barkeep. Robert. A likely lad, sinewy in his paisley shirt, with stand-up hair the color of wheat and a pendulous jade earring in one lobe. But she could no more put him at risk than she could Storm. She was out of options. She finally accepted the fact that she had to call the police.

"Phone's out," Robert told her. She had already picked it up, had already tasted the acid gout of fear at the sound of silence down the line. "Went down about twenty minutes ago."

"You have a house phone," she said.

"That one's out too. Bizarre, isn't it?" He shrugged one shoulder, flipped through the pages of a magazine. "There's another pay phone down on the next corner, you could try that."

"No," said Harper. "That's all right."

"Last call, by the way," said Robert. "We close in ten minutes."

"I'll just finish my pint," she said.

She waddled back to the window. Glanced out. The scarred man had taken up his post again. Was raising his overturned hand to his lips, drawing smoke from the hidden cigarette. He'd grown bold now. He was staring directly at her. His sneer widened when he saw her there.

She showed him her back and hobbled once more to her place by the fire.

The last minutes before closing ticked away. She sat over her stout and brooded. Perhaps it had been a mistake to let Storm leave her here. He would have gladly stayed if she had asked him. He would have wanted to. And he had the courage for it, she had seen that.

But no. This was not his business, not this part. Despite all his talk about ghosts and the paranormal, he was a child of the century. Its prejudices were his, more than he knew. Psychology. Science. Materialism. He could understand only with the understanding of his age. No. It would have been wrong—it would have been sinful under the circumstances of his illness—for her to enlist him against an enemy he could not possibly comprehend. The burden of the Uncanny was hers.

There are few who work the work of wonder. She was one. For others, there could be skepticism or belief; there could be credos, sciences, religions; theories or philosophies; politics; a point of view. For her, there was only ever this slow, steady tramp into the dark, and the narrative trail it left behind. If this should be the end for her—if help did not arrive, if the barkeep should call time and send her out into the street alone—then she would go in the fullness of unknowing. And so she would go whenever time was called. Because unknowing was her nature, the first rule of her game. The burden of the Uncanny was hers.

In the event, however, just as the clock struck eleven, Bernard wafted in. Heavy-lidded, foggy-eyed, he stepped, as if by magic, out of the gent's lavatory. Robert the barkeep started. But Bernard only waggled his fingers at him as his willowy form drifted past like smoke.

He settled into the seat across from Harper. Harper sniffed at him.

"Hmph," she said, so that her Guinness rippled. "You reek of your perversities." She really had been frightened, and her heart was hammering now. "Also you're drunk—or whatever it is you get."

He made a listless gesture of indifference. Sat slumped in his black windbreaker and jeans with his legs splayed under the table, his trainers towards the flames. His shaven head shone in the firelight. "Also, I'm here—which you should be bloody thankful for," he said. "How many of them are there outside—twenty-seven?"

"Three that I've seen so far."

"I had to slither through the toilet window like a snake. No offense, darling, but in your case, I don't think so. What were you planning to do, handbag your way home?"

"All right, all right, I'm glad to see you." Her heartbeat was slowing down again. "If nothing else, I'm gratified by this evidence of our mystic nexus. You seem somehow to have sensed my troubles telepathically . . ."

"Yes, they came to me as in a dream," he said. "I had just called in for my messages, when suddenly I heard a strangled muttering followed by a curse with two old geezers talking football in the background. A mental image formed—I saw before me an idiosyncratic Luddite incompetently attempting to communicate with my answering machine from a local pub. I thought it might be you."

"Ah."

"Time!" called the barman.

Harper tilted her Guinness high, polished off the bottom foam. Set the glass down decisively. "Time," she said. Bernard nodded. They both stood.

The young man fetched her cape from the stand in the corner, helped her shrug into it. He smoothed it down her back as she buttoned the front. Harper then slipped her pipe in her satchel and pulled the strap over her shoulder. Clapped her Borsalino onto her head; adjusted her glasses. Bernard retrieved her stick from the chimney corner and handed it to her. Completely recovered now, she patted his high cheek.

"Thank you for coming, lad. I should not have liked to've been bundled off like washing."

He squeezed her hand. "We'll go as we lived, darling— flailing about."

"Ha-ha."

She lifted the dragon's head to the barman. Walked with Bernard to the double doors. They both paused there, peering through the etching of the crane on the glass. The thug was no longer at his post on the corner. No one else was visible either. The street was empty. It seemed empty, anyway.

"Well," said Bernard under his breath. "It's only thirty steps home."

But they got no more than ten.

She pushed her door open. He shouldered through his. They stepped out onto the corner, under a streetlight. Began to cross the street. Bernard stayed close to Harper's left shoulder. They looked to either side of them. Bernard glanced behind. No one was visible in any direction.

They went across the road diagonally, moving from the streetlight towards their own portico. About midway, they stepped out of the streetlight's glory, into darkness.

And the scarred man came at them as if from nowhere.

He approached them swiftly, without breaking stride. He pointed to his wrist. He smiled, but his scar distorted it into a toothy smirk.

"Have you got the time, darling?" he said.

But he never stopped coming at them, charging at them. And there were other footsteps now, running footsteps, all around them, closing in.

"The time," Harper growled, "is not yet." Her stick was in her left hand, her right was pulling the dragon, pulling the sword's blade free of its sheath. She brought the sharp steel arcing over her head, brought it slicing straight so that the point halted in the air just as the scarred man reached it. He had to brake—hard—on the balls of his feet, and even so, the sword pressed nastily into the hollow of his throat at the place where his overcoat opened.

Bernard, meanwhile, curled around behind her. He set his back to hers—and not a moment too soon. There were four others and they were rushing at him from every side.

Bernard gave a raw, steamy hiss as he pressed out his *ibuki* breath with a tightened abdomen. His right hand described a smooth *shuto-uchi*—the knife-hand stroke—in the air. With that, he slipped into his fighting posture.

"*Oi-ya!*" he added for effect.

It seemed to work: the four men stopped short. They hovered in a semicircle around him. Each glanced at the others, waiting for someone else to break the ring of fear.

The scarred man put his hands up humorously. With the

blade at his throat, he grinned even wider. There was murderous rage in his small, damp eyes.

"There's no need for all this," he said. "Just a word in your ear, darling. That's all I want."

But the other four were edging, dodging around, seeking a chink in Bernard's defenses. Bernard kept his arms in motion before him, kept his head and eyes swinging from this side to that.

"Go on, then!" said Harper—she barked it, too loudly, she was that scared. She cursed herself for a craven old crone. "Go on and say what you have to!"

The Frankenstein monster to Bernard's left faked a lunge. Bernard shouted. This time, his *shuto-uchi* sliced the air so quickly it seemed to whistle. The monster dropped back.

"You're outnumbered, you see," said the scarred man in a shaky voice.

"The first one to reach me wins a wheelchair," Bernard sang back at him over Harper's shoulder.

The four thugs kept dancing, shuffling, feinting. One waggled a box-cutter. One swished a black, mean, flexible cosh. The Frankenstein just balled his fists. Bernard kept shifting, his back to Harper's.

"The game's not worth the candle," said the scarred man. Tilting his head away from the pressing sword that held him at bay, he still managed to fix Harper with his furious, piggy eyes. "I wouldn't kid you, it isn't, I mean it. It's just a small thread you've got hold of, darling. I'm just here to tell you to let it be. Let it be and we all go home happy."

"A small thread," she said to him. "But perhaps I'll pull it and see what unravels."

At which point, the four other thugs attacked.

The box-cutter flashed out, slashed past Bernard's

windbreaker as he drew back. Bernard trapped the attacker's wrist, twisted it. *Snap.* The attacker howled, his cutter clattered to the blacktop; so did he. Now Bernard's body slanted as he drove a *kansetsu* kick into the space just over Frankenstein's shin. The enormous monster staggered, toppled onto his side while, at the same time, Bernard gave a lightning flick of his inverted fist—*uraken*—in the other direction. It drove a third attacker's nose into his face with a splash of cartilage and blood.

But the fourth man's cosh got through. An upward backhand which Bernard only half blocked with his free arm. The weapon glanced off his brow. Bernard saw the sky swim and was suddenly down on one knee. The thug with the cosh moved to stand over him, planted himself just above him. With a grunt of effort, the thug lifted the blackjack high in the air, ready to slam it down with all his might into Bernard's exposed skull.

Still kneeling, still dazed, Bernard drove his open hand up between the man's legs and made a fist.

"Oof," said the man.

He curled up like burning paper and went down to the pavement.

Bernard swayed unsteadily up Harper's back. Regained his feet, leaning against her. Frankenstein and the thug with the splattered nose were already up as well, weaving around in front of him, but not quite ready to attack again. The other two were rolling in the street, clutching wrist and crotch, groaning.

The man with the scarred lip made a move in anger. Harper jabbed—hoisted him onto his tiptoes at the point of her blade.

"You know, I'm just crotchety enough to kill you," she said.

"You stupid old slag," the scarred man spat back. Pinned high at the end of her sword, he let his pink eyes flame down at her. "You know who you're mucking with. He's being good to you, isn't he? For old time's sake. You think he can't finish this whenever he likes? *Whenever* he likes? No fear, bitch."

Terror and fury and excitement all went through Harper in a bolt and she cut him. Jerked him off the point of her sword with a flick that nicked his chin.

The scarred man cried out, staggered backwards, grabbed at the wound with both hands. He looked down at the blood on his fingers. Cursed and stared black death at her.

"Since I am a bitch," she said, "beware my fangs." She had a weakness for paraphrase too.

The scarred man was speechless. Bleeding. All he could do was point at her. Point a threatening finger at her once, twice, three times—but all the while, withdrawing, fading away from her down the street, into the night. The others, seeing him go, were also starting to pull back. The two on the ground, clambering up shakily, joined the retreat. All sent dark warning glances at Bernard where he crouched, panting, with his hands up weakly before him.

And so the circle of men dissolved backwards into the shadows. They grew dimmer and dimmer, the scarred man still pointing his finger at Harper, pointing again and again.

Harper let her sword droop slowly to the blacktop. Tired. She was very tired suddenly. Her eyes, her arm, her whole body. Heavy, tired. And frightened, truly terrified. Trembling violently as the reaction set in. She could hear Bernard gasping for breath behind her. She could feel his narrow back leaning against hers. She had to lean against him as well to stay upright.

For an endless moment more, she could still make out the scarred man, retreating. She could see his pink, piggy glare, his pointing finger. An endless moment more.

Then the two of them, she and Bernard, were alone in the darkness.

 The evening of the auction arrived and—just as Harper had feared—Sophia hanged herself. For her, it was the end of a long, dreamy day.

First thing in the morning, she had burned all her snapshots of her mother. Sitting at home, very businesslike at her escritoire. Dressed in one of the usual uniforms: blue cardigan over white blouse, pleated gray skirt. She glanced sometimes through the balcony doors, out at the gabled roof-scape of South Kensington: chimneys and attic windows, a stone church spire against the solid gray sky, sedate and lovely. One after another, in the ashtray at her fingertips, the photos burned. The char closed in a rough circle over those features so like her own.

Sophia felt cool as she watched this happen. Remote and clear in her mind. Having decided what she would do, there seemed to her a very straight line of perfect clarity between her and the doing of it, an open corridor that proceeded through precise, logical and predictable steps towards the image of her own body, dangling. It was the world surrounding this corridor that appeared hazy, veiled, uncertain. It was that misty periphery which gave the day its dreamlike quality.

When she had done with the pictures, she opened the balcony doors and cleared the air, waved the smoke out over the Little Boltons with the back of her hand. Then she walked down the corridor to the bathroom. Emptied the last load of laundry from the dryer. Folded these clothes in her bedroom, on her bed. Packed them in the suitcase that lay open there. As if she were going on a journey. She felt this would be easier for everyone and would leave less of a mess behind.

She had decided for some reason upon eight o'clock— 8:00 P.M. She thought that was about when the auctioneer would reach *The Magi*. After that, of course, the whole situation would become impossible for her. Her father would acquire the panel, and she would be forced to choose between him and her promise to the murdered Resurrection Man. Which really was no choice at all. Either option was intolerable. How could she betray her own father? And how could she keep the secret that he was involved in something monstrous? *Whoever buys* The Magi . . . *He is the Devil from Hell* . . . Sophia was all for fortitude, but there came a time when to suffer a situation was absurd. That was the time: 8:00 P.M., when they sold *The Magi*, when her father bought it. So she had decided.

She finished with her clothing. Next she packed her CDs into cushioned envelopes, addressed these in her scrupulous hand. Her classical pieces—oceans of Bach mostly and some Mozart—she would send to her sister Laura. The American popular music she sometimes enjoyed—Sinatra, Louis Armstrong, Ella Fitzgerald—would go to her friend Tony; her brother Peter despised it. She would send him her few rock albums instead, plus the Lucian Freud poster she knew he liked.

She tidied her flat, then carried the packages to the post office on Fulham Road. It was farther away than the branch on Earl's Court, but she found the drug dealers and fast-food restaurants near the tube stop depressing. This walk was far nicer. Past whitewashed mansions, under garden walls, through the hanging branches of cherry and chestnut trees. Forsythia that would bloom so yellow come spring. The air was cold and damp and invigorating, refreshing on her cheeks, in her hair.

As she walked, she thought some more about the face in those photographs she had burned. It had been even clearer in these than in the portrait on her wall at the Grange: while her mother's features *had* been very like her own, her manner, her expression had really been quite different. They had been warmer. They had been better, Sophia thought as she walked. That sweet way she would tilt her head to one side. And the way her eyes always looked faintly worried, as if there were some service or kindness she might have neglected. Her smile was so eagerly agreeable too. Even in the Kodachrome square of past time, her generosity made itself known to her daughter. Sophia felt it with a pang. One did wonder sometimes how things might have been different . . .

After she had posted her packages, she took a cab to the gallery.

"Would you be a darling and go to the auction for me tonight?" she said to her assistant, Jessica. "I really don't feel up to it."

"You're not ill or anything?" Jessica asked her. Blinked up at her with her limpid fawn eyes.

"I'll be all right. You're a brick." Sophia squeezed the other girl's shoulder through the soft cashmere cardigan. Very odd—but her mind was so clear now that she felt she could actually look right into Jessica's soul, understand her down to the ground, even see into her future. Blond and cherub-cheeked, vulnerable, deferential and not terribly bright, Jessica would have her pick of the gallery's most opulent clients. She would marry one, would enjoy his luxuries, would suffer his adulteries and would learn to live for her children and her comforts, resigned and only slightly frantic. It really was very odd; Sophia looked into Jessica's big eyes and saw the whole thing right away. She squeezed the girl's shoulder again, with compassion this time. "Sir Michael wants *The Magi*," she went on, and then wittily imitated her father's huffy baritone, "at all costs!" Jessica smiled uncertainly. Gently, Sophia said, "It won't go much past fifty, I'm sure, but he said he would go to three times that, so we have the wherewithal. Just be firm, you know, top the bids quickly, and you'll scare the rest off."

"Yes . . . yes, all right," said Jessica, not very firmly at all. "If you really need me to."

Sophia gave her an encouraging smile. It would be a big moment for her, she thought. Something to remember in her later days. On an impulse, she unclasped the brooch from her own cardigan and pinned it onto Jessica's. "Now listen, if Antonio's there, I want you to flirt with him a little, yah? Especially when the Antwerp lots come up, distract him. Tell him I've got a perfectly good Reubens *Pan* for him and I don't want him spending all his money before I get my hands on some of it. Tell him I was very severe about it. He likes that; it excites him, makes him feel English or something. All right?"

"Isn't this your mother's brooch?"

"It just suits you. The little lapis pieces set off those flecks in your eyes."

"Oh, but I couldn't possibly—"

"No, I want you to wear it," Sophia said. "It looks much

better on you than it ever did on me. I'll consider it yours until I see you again. All right?"

At that, Jessica looked so confused and grateful and admiring that Sophia's heart welled with pity for her and her humiliating future. But she only smiled back, wryly. In her clarity, she understood that what would be, must be. And she continued down her lucid corridor, through her dreamy day.

So she came that night to sit alone in her upstairs office. The gallery closed, dark, quiet below. She swiveling idly in her black chair, only the lamp on her rolltop burning. The electric clock at the corner of the blotter told off the last quarter hour before eight. And, having decided on eight, Sophia waited, nervous now, impatient for the time to pass. She tapped her fingernail twice on the blotter's leatherette border. Twice quickly, then twice again. *Tick-tick, tick-tick.*

She glanced out through the open door, out to where the lamplight died, to where the upper balcony curved along the wall into dusky nothing. She imagined her body hanging there. Hanging, turning. The paintings hanging on the wall above it: the moonstruck mountains, the cryptic glades, the seductive ruins in the grass. The body turned and turned and turned towards her and she imagined its face. The same face that had smiled up at her from the ashtray that morning, that had curled and blackened and crumbled away.

"Your mother cared very deeply about the suffering of others," her father had told her once. "Too deeply, I sometimes thought. She wanted the world to be better than it is. She took on too much of the guilt of things: injustice, poverty and so on. We can only go by our own lights, after all, cover our own patch, you know. We can't solve the troubles of the universe, can we?"

And no, Sophia had answered, we can't. And yet, one did just wonder. If things might have been different. She tapped the blotter with one hand. The other moved slowly across her middle. That face, her mother's face, was so charitable and concerned and responsive and yet so like her own, that one did just think that she, Sophia, might have been more like that herself. Had her mother lived, that is. Had she been around to teach Sophia the trick of it.

This thought only deepened her depression and loneliness, the black well of them inside her. And anyway, it was minutes to eight. She rose, switched off the lamp. Her navy overcoat hung on a stand by the door. She drew the belt from its loops even as she stepped out onto the balcony.

She walked along the balcony slowly. Now one hand slid over the rail and the other held the belt, the belt trailing. The muffled whisk of Bond Street traffic reached her. The glow of headlights rode up over the far wall. Over the paintings, over a desolation of rocks, a sunset, a figure gazing into the vanishing point. Then it was gone. The gallery was dim around her, quiet. Quiet, except for her own footsteps on the hard floor. *Tick-tick, tick-tick.* She thought of how she had heard that sound in her bed, how she had gone downstairs, calling for her mother. Moving to the door at the end of the corridor, the last door . . . After that, she couldn't remember.

She stopped in the middle of the balcony. It seemed a likely place. She tied the belt to the rail, tested it. Made a simple slipknot in the other end and brought the loop down over her black hair. This business and the business of hopping up on the rail, of bringing her legs around to the other side, sitting on the edge of the balcony—this was the worst of the thing, the most depressing bit. It all seemed so shabby finally and miserable. And sitting there, gripping the rail, looking down, she thought unhappily: One should have been taught to love, so that help would come.

Then she looked at her watch. It was just eight, just exactly. They must be auctioning *The Magi* right this minute.

That was the last thought she had before she pushed off the railing.

5 But as it happened, *The Magi* had come up for sale some fourteen minutes earlier. And it was just then—just as the panel was being lifted onto the display easel—that Richard Storm walked into the Sotheby's auction room.

His entrance, in fact, made a lot more of a stir than the display of the panel. The broad, well-lighted room was packed when he came in. The rows of folding chairs were all occupied. Buyers lined up along the white walls, two deep in some places, the aisles blocked. More buyers clustered at the back. There were even some standing behind the phone tables, behind the neat, wealthy-looking young ladies who sat shoulder to shoulder there, waiting for call-in bids. And everywhere, as Storm entered through the double doors at the rear of the room, attention was paid. A subtle effect, but definitely there. The crowd that was gathered before the doors parted slightly to let him through. Heads turned, briefly. Women's eyes went up him in appraisal; men's eyes went down him in critique. All over the room, fine ladies touched the tips of their hair. One egotistical French industrialist unconsciously straightened his posture; an Arab oilman smirked; a Silicon Valley whiz kid snorted derisively and then had to wipe the snot off his lapel. The girls at the phone tables turned like a row of cranes in unison to get a glimpse. The auctioneer himself glanced down from his podium on high, sensing a change in the relative gelt humidity, feeling out the weather.

All because of Storm. And he knew it too. Hey, the man was in battle gear this time, babe. Broad shoulders squared by the slashing planes of an Armani suit. A blinding spit shine on his black Guccis. An elegant splash of gold glinting at his cuffs, and on his tie. Silk at his throat, at his pockets. A hundred and fifty pounds of style on his sandy hair—and we're talking pounds sterling, sweetheart, not the scale kind. There were people in that room who were like computers in judging these things, in assessing potential lovers, customers, rivals. But even to an untutored eye, even to a casual glance, the guy looked like a major tycoon, like an American multi-millionaire at ease with power and glamour and fame. Which, of course, is exactly what he was.

He stepped across the threshold, engine gunning. On a mission, clearly. For Storm felt good again, felt new even, reinvented. The reaction to his seizure had dwindled away. The physical weakness, the gape-faced shock, had dwindled. And his moral strength had returned to him in their wake— a reaction to the reaction. Thus, in the days since his last meeting with Harper—since he had fled from The Sign of the Crane, from the judgment he thought he saw in the old woman's eyes—he had been locked alone in his measly room. He had been warring there with the inner demons of his death. A cast of thousands. An epic, bleak and bloody spectacle, forty years in the making. Day after day, he had flailed in the ravening clutches of his mortality. Night after night, he had scorched his cheeks with tears. Tailor-legged on the carpet. Streaming eyes lifted to the ceiling. Life, oh life, he had cried out to the gods.

And then it had ended. Only hours ago really. As he slumped exhausted just that morning. The answer he sought had suddenly come to him, had suddenly risen before his eyes like a thunderous dawn. And the answer was: Irv Philbin. Or, that is, the immortal words of Irv Philbin, who just happened to be the best goddamned movie publicist between the Canyon and the Coast. It was Irv, seven years ago, who had rescued Storm's worst film, *Castle Misery*, who had slam-dunked the brain-dead spook show down the public's throat with one of the great ad campaigns of all time. And it was the words of that campaign that dawned before Storm at this critical hour, the very words that were once emblazoned across the *Castle* one-sheet in every multiplex lobby in America. These words shone in Storm's mind through the forest of doubt; at the exit of the valley of shadows they shone:

In the battle between Love and Death, there can be only one Survivor!

Storm was here to find Sophia.

Now, at the front of the room, a man in blue overalls was adjusting the easel canvas holders. Now he was stepping back. There was the panel, displayed: the ruined abbey, the broken window, the winter trees, the shadows, the cowled, ghostly figures gliding by the base of the chapel. Hanging from the ceiling above it, an enormous electric toteboard reset itself to zero. Pounds, dollars, deutschmarks, yen—all zero, straight down the column. The glimmer of it caught Storm's eye. He heard the riffle in the seats as the buyers resettled. They crossed their wrists in their laps, focused their blasé regard on the Rhinehart.

"The Magi," announced the auctioneer, up on his platform, behind the wide wooden podium with *Sotheby's* written across it in gold. He was young, tailored, arrow-straight. Prim, thin-lipped, arrogant. A boy whom his colleagues called promising. "Lot ninety-four, a panel of Rhinehart's Nativity triptych, recently rediscovered in the former East Germany and offered as an anonymous donation to the Children's Resource Fund."

It was now thirteen minutes before eight.

Storm scanned the crowd. Still standing amidst the people clustered at the doors, he slowly moved his eyes over the buyers leaning against the white wall to his left. Next he passed his gaze over the audience in their seats, checking off one coiffure after another. Finally he examined the girls at the phone table one by one. No Sophia.

"I'll take an opening bid of twenty-five thousand pounds." The auctioneer went into his practiced drone. Nasal, hypnotic, seemingly slurred, deceptively precise, the words flowed from his thin lips. "Opening at twenty-five thousand, twenty-five, I have twenty-five thousand, do I have thirty? Thirty, thirty thousand from the phone. Thirty-five. I have thirty-five thousand."

It started happening that fast. Storm tried to see where the bids were coming from. He remembered Sophia had said that her gallery might buy the panel. He tried to follow the auctioneer's eyes, but the auctioneer barely moved his eyes. And yet the guy seemed to see everything, everywhere in the room.

"Forty, I have forty thousand from the phone," he said.

From the phone. Storm looked to his right just in time to catch the slightest gesture from the table. A noble swan of a young woman in the regulation cardigan was looking up from her handset to raise one eyebrow, one finger.

"Forty-five thousand," the auctioneer went on. "I have forty-five, forty-five thousand, forty-five, I have fifty . . ."

The green lights of the electric toteboard winked all down the column. Fifty thousand pounds, seventy-five thousand dollars, one hundred ten thousand deutschmarks, incalcuable yen, eight million something. The price of the Rhinehart panel had doubled in just two minutes. It was eleven now before eight o'clock.

The auctioneer massaged his gavel—a heavy disc of wood—as he hummed right along. Now a barely perceptible jut of his chin made Storm turn his attention to the left-hand wall. Yes: another signal. The flutter of a slender white hand, the glint of a gold bracelet, as the price of the panel went up again. Storm nudged his way through the crowd of people around him. He edged along to the right behind the last row of seats. Trying to get a better look at the standing bidder.

Now he could see her in profile. No, it was not Sophia. Some cuddly blonde, hardly twenty. Pouting with effort, her forehead shining too much in the overhead lights.

Storm was about to turn away from her when he remembered who she was. The girl in Sophia's gallery, the receptionist.

"Fifty thousand, do I have sixty, do I have sixty thousand, sixty, sixty . . ." The auctioneer—with that skill for which his friends detested him—had sussed the action, upped the bids. "Sixty, I have sixty from the rear, sixty thousand."

Automatically, Storm glanced back to the rear of the room. Caught the brief wave of a numbered paddle. Another bidder—a man, this one. A tall, slim figure in a white suit. Wearing green gloves, weirdly enough. With black hair flowing to his shoulders. A thin, angular face, almost diamond-shaped, somehow feline, somehow feral. He was standing relaxed as the action popped, his eyes amused, witty. Standing back, out of the glare of the overheads. But even so, Storm took that one look at him and knew he was going to win the auction. He was that type. Storm had been around enough of them to know. Storm had been in auctions for books, for screenplays that had gone into the stratosphere; he understood the psychology. This guy was scorched earth, he was take-no-prisoners. Unless that was the U.S. Treasury on the phone, *The Magi* was as good as his. Sophia's blond friend wasn't even in it.

"Seventy, seventy, eighty thousand, eighty thousand, ninety . . ."

Whoa, thought Storm, getting interested now. The lights on the toteboard couldn't keep up. Even in Hollywood, things didn't move this fast.

By the clock on the wall just behind the board, it was nine minutes to eight.

Storm looked back at the girl against the wall, the blonde from the Endering Gallery. Yeah, as he'd figured, she was beginning to crack. The corners of her lush red lips were turning down, her eyes were frenzied. Every time her bid was trumped, Storm could see her blink, recoil, dismayed.

She fluttered her hand again.

"A hundred thousand pounds," said the auctioneer. And immediately, "One hundred twenty-five thousand from the gentleman in the rear."

That sent a stir through the audience, not quite silence, not quite sound. Several faces surreptitiously came round to get a look at this "gentleman in the rear." And Sophia's assistant—Storm saw her—whipped a stricken look over her shoulder so fast it made her hair fly.

Storm smiled at that. Then he stopped smiling. When she turned that way, he could see the front of her for a moment. He could see she was wearing Sophia's brooch.

The bidding went around the triangle again. The phone table, the blonde, the man in the rear. The auctioneer, with a feel for the atmosphere almost tactile, had sped the bids once more. He was leaning back from his podium with his eyelids lowered as if with passion.

"One-fifty, one-fifty, one-fifty, one-seventy-five, one hundred seventy-five thousand, two hundred. Two hundred thousand . . ."

Wait a minute, thought Storm. This isn't right.

It was seven minutes to eight.

What's she got Sophia's brooch for? he thought. What, were they all part of this evil cult Harper had told him about? That was crazy. It didn't make sense. Her mother's brooch. Which she'd never worn before the other day. She wouldn't have loaned it to this other girl, would she? A cold sweat broke out on the back of his neck. He heard Harper speak to him as if she were standing at his shoulder: *Something is terribly wrong.*

"Two hundred, two hundred, I have two hundred from the rear, do I have two hundred and fifty, do I have two hundred and fifty thousand pounds, two-fifty, two-fifty . . ."

Now the murmur of the crowd was clearly audible. The swanny dame at the phone bank, Storm saw, gave a short, level chop of her hand in the air. The buyer on the line had withdrawn from the fray. It was between the blonde and the weird guy in the white suit now. The blonde's small hand trembled upward like a leaf on the wind.

"I have two hundred fifty thousand—three hundred," the auctioneer said instantly. "Three hundred thousand from the gentleman in the rear."

As the excited murmur of the crowd grew louder, Storm began to move, to edge through the standing buyers, to feel his way behind the backs of the last seats towards the left-hand aisle.

The lights of the toteboard fluttered up front. Three hundred thousand pounds. Four hundred fifty thousand dollars. Nearly seven hundred thousand deutschmarks. Yen beyond imagining. Storm could see the blonde against the wall practically spastic with terrified indecision. Her lips trembling, her eyes filling, her hands hovering before her, unsure.

Then he lost sight of her in the crowd as he moved closer. He heard the auctioneer say, "Three hundred, three hundred, three hundred, three hundred and fif— Four hundred thousand. The bid is four hundred thousand pounds from the gentleman in the rear."

Jesus, thought Storm, as he started pushing down the aisle. This white-suit guy is a killer. He looked over his shoulder and saw him again. Got a closer look at him now. A killer, no question. Something in the brutally cut facets of his face—something in the weirdly smoky depths of his eyes—made Storm shudder, made his collar go clammy. He turned away, glanced up blindly at the toteboard. Noticed the clock instead: five minutes to eight. *Something is terribly wrong.*

Making terse excuses, Storm wedged himself between two people blocking the aisle. Squeezed between two more. Pushed out to see the blonde at the wall just ahead of him. He was near enough now to see her nostrils flare in panic as her hand jerked up again like a marionette's.

"Four hundred fifty thous— Five hundred thousand pounds from the gentleman in the rear."

Storm put his hand on the blond girl's arm. She spun on him with eyes the size of saucers, her lips parted, her skin slick.

"Where's Sophia?" he asked her.

"I . . . I . . . I . . ." she said. And then she seemed to recognize him and whispered harshly, desperately, "She said fifty. I don't know what I'm supposed to do!"

"Five hundred, the bid is five hundred thousand, the bid is at half a million pounds . . ."

Storm nodded, squeezed her arm. "Drop it, honey. You're licked. The guy'd go to a zillion. Where's Sophia?"

"Five hundred, five hundred, five hundred . . ." The auctioneer lifted his gavel. The blonde turned to stare at him with her hand lifted as if to bid again.

"Trust me on this, kid. Drop the potato," said Storm. "Where's Sophia?"

Her face rolled back towards him, she gawped up at him as if from a nightmare. His eyes went to the brooch on her sweater. To the dim-witted terror in her perky, cherubic face.

"I don't know," she said. "She told me to come here instead . . ."

"She told you . . ." said Storm. *The woman is asking for your help,* said Harper Albright in his mind, *crying for your help.*

"*Sold!* For five hundred thousand pounds!" said the auctioneer.

His forearm fell. The gavel hit the podium. *Whack.* Storm felt the blond girl jump in his hand.

Perhaps the auction represents some sort of crisis point . . .

The audience burst into loud applause, loud laughter and conversation. Storm's gaze arced over the room wildly.

Caught a glimpse of the man in the white suit. Holding up his paddle—number 313—in his green-gloved fingers. Grinning, his teeth predatory. And the others in the seats with their hands moving, coming together. The toteboard caught at five hundred thousand.

Sophia saying: *This is where I want to die.*

"Oh my God," said Richard Storm.

It was one minute before eight.

There were some people in the audience who figured he had stolen a purse or a necklace. It was their best guess when they saw him drive back recklessly up the aisle. Wielding his broad shoulders left and right. Shoving people aside without mercy.

But then he was gone, dashing through the rear doorway, and no one was screaming "Thief! Thief!" so it must've been all right. The Rhinehart panel was already being removed from the easel. Another painting was already being lifted into place. The audience turned away and forgot Richard Storm. The business of the auction went on.

Out on New Bond Street, Storm fired through the doors of Sotheby's like a missile. He didn't believe what he was thinking. He didn't dare to. He just ran—the way they'd taught him in high school track: legs stretching, body straight, elbows pistoning. The storefronts whipped by on either side of him, the store banners whipped over his head. People dodged out of his way, looked after him: in his fine suit, in his fine shoes, running as if the devil were on his tail. He didn't think about it. He didn't dare to think anything. He just ran.

He was at the Endering Gallery's door in thirty seconds. Under the port awning, between the two spruces. Plastered to the glass like a bug on the windshield. He probed the dark interior over the fog his breath made on the door. The fog expanded, shrank as he panted. The gallery beyond was still. The front desk empty. The paintings undisturbed on the wall. Everything appropriate, right. He thought it was okay.

Then he lifted his eyes and saw her, seated on the balcony rail. He could make out the line of the belt around her neck.

Storm felt as if gasoline had been thrown on the smoldering coals inside him. Doubt, suspicion, anxiety all flared into a sudden blaze of fear. He grabbed the door handle, yanked. It was locked. He shook it.

"Damn!"

He let the handle go. Once, twice, he slapped the glass with both palms. He felt as if it were he up there with the noose around his neck.

"Sophia! Sophia!"

She didn't hear him, didn't react.

"Sophia!"

Storm clung to the smooth surface, powerless. She sat there another moment. He spun, his mind desperately empty, his eyes looking anywhere, for anything.

The spruce in the cast-iron planter. He bent down, seized the planter, lifted it into the air. It flew up too easily—for a moment he thought it would be too light to break the door's thick glass. But that was the adrenaline: he was so jazzed, he could've lifted the building. He stepped back. Raised the tree, the planter, over his head. Dirt and cigarette butts poured down into his expensive haircut. He hurled the planter into the door and the door shattered.

The black cascade of soil and the white cascade of glass went blue as the gallery's alarm light started flashing, as the siren started shrieking to the sky. Storm charged through the jagged opening. The shards of the door crackled under his feet. The planter was still tumbling to a stop as he leapt over it. He dashed for the stairway, shouting.

"Sophia!"

But she had already dropped off the railing. While he was lifting the planter into the air, she had done it. Her body hung jerking at the end of the belt.

Storm roared and grabbed the curling bannister. He could see her struggling, clawing the rope. His senses burned in electric connection to her as if it were he choking, dying. He vaulted three steps, another three. She was still fighting it, still there. He made the landing. Saw only the flashing blue light, felt only the siren screaming in his head where his thoughts should've been.

"Sophia!"

And he launched himself at her. Up onto the railing, his body stretching out. One hand grabbing hold of the rail, one reaching down. The belt was short. He could reach her. He had her, by the arm. He shouted again wildly. Muscled her up. Tumbled back off the rail under the weight of her.

He fell to the floor, bringing her down with him. Instantly, he scrambled to his knees. Grabbed her. She was gagging. He seized the loop around her neck. Wrenched it over her hair, roughly, with a furious curse. Sophia sank back, coughing, choking.

Storm knelt over her, seething, crazy with rage at what she'd tried to do. He wanted to slap her. His hand flew up over her head. It hung there, trembling. He clenched it, clenched both his hands and shook them at her.

"Oh!" he shouted in his outrage. "Oh!"

Sophia drew a rasping breath. And then another. And then she gave a hoarse, forlorn, animal cry and punched him.

Her fist hit him weakly on the chest. Her hair flew across her face and she punched again, blindly, catching the side of his head. He gave another curse. Snatched at her wrist.

But she was finished. She sagged to the floor, making raw, hacking noises, her hair spilling forward, her beaten figure pulsating with the blue light. As the shriek of the siren rose and fell, Storm heard her sobbing miserably. He reached out with a shaking hand and touched her as gently as he could. But she swept her arm around, knocked him away.

Now people were rushing into the gallery below. There were voices calling. There were figures running to the foot of the stairs. The siren screamed. The blue light flashed and flashed.

Panting, Storm knelt on the floor with his palms braced against his thighs, his head hanging.

Sophia sat there beside him and cried and cried.

V

YOUNG WILLIAM,
A BALLAD

"Who is it who comes knocking there?"
    the widow Annie said.
"And who would come this late round my door
    on a night so dreary?"

Tap-tap. " 'Tis I, your son, Young Will,
    who once around thee played.
Oh, open, mother, and let me in,
    for I'm cold and weary."

"Is it thee, long lost this many a day?
    Is it thee, my darling boy,
who knocks at my door in the dead of night,
    so I feel I fear thee?"

"It is I, it is I, your long-lost child,
    Young William, your pride and joy."
Tap-tap. "Open, mother, and let me in,
    for I'm cold and weary."

"And where have you been this many a day?
    I sought and mourned thee so,
and thought you had left your mother behind
    for some winsome dearie."

"I have been round the old Jew's castle,
    where you warned me never to go."
Tap-tap. "Open, mother, and let me in,
    for I'm cold and weary."

"And what did you do there, my only child,
    my son, my joy, my pride?
And how return after so long a time
    with the night so dreary?"

"Oh, I spoke to the old Jew's daughter,
    and she bid me come inside
with a voice so sweet that I had to obey.
    Oh, I'm cold and weary."

"And what did she do there, my only child,
    long gone this many a day?
For my heart misgives me to hear the tale,
    and my eyes grow teary."

"Oh, she drove her jeweled knife into my heart
    so my dear life bled away
and I lay as cold as a stone in the road,
    so cold and dead and dreary.

"And she used my blood to make her wine,
    and my flesh to make her bread."
Tap-tap. "Open, mother, and let me in
    for I'm cold and weary."

144

And the widow Annie cried out to hear,
  and leapt from her lonesome bed.
And she opened the door but saw nothing there
  save the night so cold and dreary.

And she wandered the village streets alone,
  till at Prime she heard the sound:
Tap-tap, from the earth neath the abbey walls:
  Tap-tap, so lorn and weary.

And they dug at that very spot until
  Young William's bones were found.
And were laid in a grave in the chapel yard
  on a day so sad and dreary.

VI

HARPER ALBRIGHT

AND

THE CLOCKWORK OF

HISTORY

1 **Circle of standing** stones. Murmur of incantation. Dead of night.

This was the crossroad of the Sussex leys, the dowser's crossroad. Subterranean rivers intersected here. Power swirled and vibrated in the very air. Seven spirals of chthonic force were known to snake up from the earth into the tall grass, to coil round the seven mysterious boulders that stood in their ancient ring brimming with intensity.

It was Candlemas Eve, a witch's sabbath, and the old man had brought a sacrifice.

The grass swished, the fallen leaves snickered as he came. Silver light and black shadow raced across the ground in turn. The man traveled with them quickly. He was alone. He was completely naked. His face was puffy, his white breasts pendulous, his belly domed. His phallus was shrunken by the cold.

He murmured to himself as he came:

"Arise, infernal. Hel, Hecate, Goddess of the Crossroad, Gorgo, Mormo, Moon . . ."

The canvas bag hanging from his right fist was writhing. A frightened whimpering could be heard coming from within. The old man's lips were dry, his eyes were glassy. In his left hand he gripped the athame, the sacrificial knife.

Now he arrived at the prehistoric circle, the seven man-sized stones rising beneath the turbulent sky. They were said to be seven maidens who'd been cursed for dancing on a Sunday. Their shapes were undulant. The tortuous rock was animated by the running light from the unbroken passage of clouds over the full moon.

The old man stepped into the circle's center. He could feel the cadence of occult energy, the broadcast of the waters converging underground. He could almost hear the throb of the maidens' music. He knelt before the kindling he had piled up in a small pyramid. He felt pebbles and grit under his bare knee.

The air grew hushed. Leaves, trapped beneath the kindling, chattered softly. The wind haunted the perimeter of the place, seeking ingress, moaning.

"Thou who goest to and fro at night, torch in hand, enemy of the day, friend and lover of darkness. Thou who dost rejoice when the bitches are howling and warm blood is spilled . . ."

He set the bag on the hard earth before him, set the athame on the hard earth, beside the lighter he had left waiting there. He clasped the scruff of the wriggling mass inside the canvas sack. He spread the neck of the sack. Puffing, he worked the shivering animal out into the cold.

The puppy looked up at the old man hopefully. It lapped at his thumb—the thumb that held it fast.

The old man kept the puppy pinned with his left hand, took up the lighter in his right. He worked the strike-wheel, made the flame. Squinted at it, pupils zooming.

The puppy yipped, begging to be set free, to play. The old man leaned across it, held the lighter to the leaves.

"Thou who art walking amidst the phantoms in the place of tombs . . . Come on, come on, flame."

A leaf took, burned. There was a low snigger as the fire spread. A red glow slowly leaked out of the pyramid, spread over the ground.

"Good. Good," the old man said.

The puppy squeaked at him, thumped its tail against the earth.

The old man lifted the athame.

"Now." He hoisted the knife up to the level of his thin, silvery hair. His voice grew louder.

"Thou whose thirst is blood, thou who dost strike chill fear into mortal hearts. Hel, Hecate, Gorgo, Mormo. Cast a propitious eye upon our sacrifice."

With that, he made a heave of effort, his breasts jiggling. The knife went high, went up against the clouds, against the moon.

There was a sudden suction of fumy air. The pyramid of sticks exploded in a mushroom of sparks and fire. Amidst the stone maidens, behind the burgeoning flame, out of the frozen night, there arose a black figure.

The old man cried out in terror.

The figure spoke. It boomed: "Lay not thy hand upon the dog! Neither do thou anything unto it!"

The blade of the athame sang a single note as it slipped from the old man's fingers and hit the stony dirt.

"Harper?" he said.

"Oh, let the poor creature go, Jervis, you stupid old goat." She came humping round the bonfire on her stick. Lowered a demanding hand. "Now."

The old man made a deep frown, mopey, his fun spoiled. But he handed the puppy over to her. Harper held it against the shoulder of her cape. It licked her jowls happily, skewing her specs and Borsalino.

"And snap on a pair of shorts, there's a good fellow," she said. "My virgin heart is all aflutter."

She retreated back behind the fire. She averted her eyes from his nakedness, communing muzzle to muzzle with the little dog.

Jervis, grumbling, towed his wobbly buttocks out of the stone circle, back into the grass to find his clothes.

"Ha-ha!" Harper barked, pleased with the puppy's enthusiasm. It was climbing right up her shoulder to lave the side of her head. "What is it?" she called. "Part retriever?"

Jervis reentered the circle, carrying a bundle of clothes. He held on to the Y-fronts, tossed the rest to the ground. Grumpily, he pulled the shorts on, cracked the elastic band into their groove beneath his overhanging flesh. "How should I know?" In a gruff croak. He unfolded a woolly jumper next. "It was some child's, some girl's." He yanked the jumper over him, popped his head out. "The little idiot left it to wait for her when she went into the news agent. So I borrowed it."

"Oh, Jervis, Jervis," Harper intoned, "you make insult superfluous." But she could only harpoon the old sinner with one eye: her other lens was foaming with puppy spittle. She was busy holding her hat on with her stick hand too. But she went on. "And what's this? Alone on so high a holiday? Where's Granny and Uncle Bob and all the kids? Shouldn't they be gathered round the Black Sabbath tree, singing Black Sabbath carols? Or something."

The fire snapped between them, sinking down. Jervis hawked and shot a gob of phlegm into it. Arched a shrewd eyebrow at her. "Bastards deserted me. All of 'em. I couldn't figure why till now." He plucked his trousers from the foot of a stone. Holding them, he laid a finger against the side of his nose. "You scared them off, didn't you? You warned them you were coming."

"I thought we should have a chat alone. And you can be difficult to find."

He made an animal growl, deep in his throat. Even the puppy paused and glanced at him. "Arrogant, aren't you? Sure of yourself. Aren't you?" He smiled nastily. "Well, what I hear, your days are numbered. You've crossed the line, Harper. Got above yourself. You only walk the earth on his sufferance."

"And you walk free on mine," she said. The dog was growing sleepy, was making a bed of her cape collar, settling in with its chin. Readjusting her Borsalino, blinking behind her smeared spectacles, Harper paced thoughtfully from the fireside towards one of the standing stones. The old man, meanwhile, was jamming his spindly gray legs into the baggy pants. "Imagine my surprise, Jervis, when a charming boy at the Art Loss Register mentioned the name of a mysterious Dr. Mormo, who had been a major figure in the smuggling of wartime plunder. Until then, I had always thought you a harmless conjurer of evil spirits and murderer of children's pets. By the same token, the ladies and gentlemen at Scotland Yard's Bureau of Arts and Antiques have not got my interest in the arcane, and so they have thus far failed to connect you with your alias. But I have done so, haven't I?"

He buckled his belt, battled with his zipper. "Haven't you had enough, you old cow? How many warnings do you think you're going to get?"

Harper moved out of the stone's shadow into the dying firelight. One hand holding the pup at her shoulder, the other the dragon on her stick, her hat half crushed, her glasses lopsided, she was still formidable.

"Why did he want *The Magi*, Jervis?"

"Do you think I'm barmy? You'll get nothing from me."

But Harper smiled thinly. She knew her man. He was half mad, but he was all coward. "Look around you, Jervis," she said. "Your coven's blown. Gone without warning, without even a whispered word. How fast they forsook you when they knew I was coming. Why? I'll hazard a guess. Perhaps it's because daring the powers of Hell is one thing, but facing the inside of Her Majesty's prisons is another and worse. You are old, father Jervis. A word from me, and you'll die on the inside. Let us, therefore, hold high converse with one another. Why did he want *The Magi*?"

She waited, tense. The thrill of the hunt was in her. She had no doubt of it anymore: she was onto her beast. At last. She had him by only a tentacle perhaps, only the tip of a tentacle held between her fingernails, but after all this time it was a true beginning, and she wasn't going to let it go. "It was him, wasn't it?" she couldn't help asking. "At the auction. It was him."

He made no direct answer, but her breath hitched at his reaction. A fearful glance around him; the sign of the cross, the transverse down around his navel, the vertical up to about his chest.

"Come on, then," she said hoarsely. "Out with it, you old fool. For twenty-five years, he lies low. Nothing but little black flashes of him: the body of a child beneath the bogs of northern Finland, another washing up out of the bay in Port-au-Prince; a suicide here and there, a symbol scrawled in blood. Then, suddenly, into the limelight, he steps full-blown before all the world. To buy a painting? Clearly, this was too important a matter to delegate."

The warlock gave her a sullen, sidelong glare. "There are

worse things than to die in prison, Harper." But he was already folding, she could tell. Petulant, with his hands in his pockets, his shoulders up around his hairy ears. "Anyway, it isn't just *The Magi*, is it," he grumbled. "He wants all of it. Of course he does. It's no good without the whole Nativity triptych. *The Magi, The Madonna, The Christ Child*. He wants them all."

He had slunk away from her to the far side of the fire. The puppy stirred and shifted on her shoulder as she stepped after him.

"All right," she said. "Why does he want the triptych, then?"

This brought some of the gleam of nastiness back into his eye. He managed a damp, spiteful smile at her.

"You really don't know, do you? Eh? You're just stumbling in the dark, aren't you? You're walking the same trail he discovered twenty years ago, and you don't even know that it's under your feet."

"Perhaps you could enlighten me," Harper drawled.

"There, that was always your problem," he muttered back at her. "If you ask me, it's the whole flaw in your worldview. You get mired in details. A dead child pops up here, a suicide there, a symbol, a cult in Argentina. You think each thing's just another thing. But they're all one thing, Harper. They were all always one thing."

Harper kept silent, waited. Those who deal in the occult were forever spewing out these grandiose maunderings. She wasn't interested. Little minds think great thoughts, but great minds proceed in the smallest stages. Harper wanted something specific, something she could go forward on.

Her imperturbability seemed to inflame the warlock. He grew insistent.

"Are you blind or just stupid?" he cried. "Do you think he would come out into the open for nothing? *He's onto it, Harper!* He followed the trail and he's onto it."

"Onto what, for heaven's sake?"

"Ach!" He tried again to escape her unbroken gaze. Turned his back on her, waved a hand over his shoulder, walked away. Then whirled on her, cried out angrily, *"The secret, woman! The secret!* Would he show himself at Sotheby's for his health? It's the very secret of the Templars, the secret of the Grail!"

"Oh, come now, Jervis. Really. What's that supposed to mean?"

"Well . . . as for that . . ." he answered darkly. "I know only as much as I'm told."

"And you're told that an eighteenth-century religious triptych contains the secret of the Holy Grail? Really," Harper said again.

"All right. All right. Don't believe me, then. But if you only used your head for two minutes you'd see the sense of it. Do you think Sotheby's puts stolen pictures up on auction? You talked to the Register. They must've run a check on the thing."

Harper gave one of her Zeus-like nods. "They did. The painting had no listed owner. It vanished long before the war."

The warlock clenched his hoary fists at her. "Not vanished, Harper. The coven had it. The Nazi coven."

"Haushofer, you mean? That lot?"

"Yes, yes. Haushofer, of course. But witchcraft ran deep in the Third Reich. High and deep. Right to the top. Don't forget that Haushofer taught Hess. And Hess was imprisoned with Hitler. And Haushofer visited the two men in Lansberg every day they were there." He announced all this proudly. "Haushofer—he knew about the triptych, all right. They all knew there was power in it, anyway. But what? That was the thing. What power? They couldn't crack the code because they didn't know what they were looking for. And then, when the war ended, when the bombers came and the Allied armies and it all came tumbling down around them, Haushofer committed hara-kiri . . ." He opened his hands, spread them. "The triptych was lost."

They were on opposite sides of the fire now. On opposite sides of the stone circle, the light and shadow falling on them from above, racing over them. Harper stood still, frowning, prodigious, the eighth maiden, a boulder of disdain as hushed and hard as the others.

"And you're saying that Iago knows what the Nazis didn't," she said. "He knows what the secret of the triptych is."

"Has done for twenty years," growled Dr. Mormo.

"Then why now? Why has he only come after them now?"

He rolled his eyes at her obtuseness. "Well, he came after them then, of course!" he cried. "He came to me even then. But they were lost behind the Iron Curtain, you see. If any of it had come over on the black market, who would have known it if not me? No, try as he might, he couldn't find them then. It wasn't until the Curtain came down that *The Magi* finally came to light."

"*The Magi*," Harper echoed him. "And the others?"

"The others," said the old man with a shrug. "That's the whole thing, isn't it? That's why he was at the auction, out in the open like that. Whoever has the others, he wanted them to see. To see who they were dealing with. A man who would pay enormous prices for their panels—or who would come and take them by other means." He gave a particularly unpleasant little giggle. "And it's worked, hasn't it," he said. "They're already beginning to nose their way out of the woodwork. Oh yes, they are. They'll all come to Dr. Mormo in the long run, you'll see."

Harper answered nothing, mulling this over. The puppy continued to fidget on her shoulder, started whimpering. It would mess on her cape soon, she thought distantly. And the little girl who'd lost it was probably still awake, still sobbing. No doubt the police would know who she was . . .

"And you say it's all one thing," she said. "Even the cult in Argentina was part of it. Are you suggesting that Iago was searching for these paintings even then?"

"No, no, no," said the warlock sharply. "But it was all part of it, just the same. Part of the secret. Part of the Grail."

The fire clicked and cackled. Jervis, unexpectedly, cackled too. Brought his knuckle to his forehead and rattled it against his skull. "Oh, if you could see your face, Harper. If you could only see your face. You don't think. You don't know. You don't understand what you're dealing with, still. It's not the triptych, or Argentina, or this murder or that. It's not even the Nazis or the war or the Iron Curtain. It's none of it. It's *all* of it." He leaned towards her. The orange flame-glow washed up over his puffy features, his crazy eyes.

"It's the whole clockwork of history," he told her, whispered to her under the moaning of the wind. "That's what you're missing, you blind old woman. The clockwork of history. Tick-tick. Tick-tick!"

2 From time to time, Sophia woke to find life muted, slow, subaqueous. Whatever the doctors were giving her, it had sent her to Atlantis, submerged her in a world beneath the waves. Through this element, reality passed like a dream and dreams like reality. She traced her own footsteps down corridors of Belham Grange, corridors extending into an ominous infinity. She passed her father's portrait on the wall—the eyes followed her—and she passed another portrait, and that was her father too, as was the next and the next . . .

She went on and on. Passages ran off to the left and right of her, ran off to nowhere. On and on. From one such passage a nurse emerged, a pink phantom, silent and deliberate. Then, suddenly, Sophia was in her bed again, her high hospital bed. Looking down the enormous wavering length of her own sheeted form to the figure gliding by beyond the gleaming steel rail.

"Sister?" Her own voice was like a slow recording. Her lips were parched, her throat was terribly sore.

"You're all right. Just try and get some sleep."

"Where am I?"

Beyond the steel rail was the door—not the orange door of the hospital room but the hidden door at the end of the corridor.

"Mother?"

She was drifting towards it, drifting without volition as if she were floating ghostly above the ground. She did not want to go. She cried out against the irresistible tide.

"It's all right, Sophia, it's all right."

Some cool hand was in hers, comforting. She looked up to see her sister. Laura, her real sister. Her small, sweet, worried face made big and blurry with her tears. Her blond hair tied back in a prim style . . . Perfect for a hospital visit, Sophia noted dimly.

"It's all right," Laura whispered again. "No one knows anything. It's all been kept quiet. Daddy's taken care of the whole stupid business for you."

Sophia moved her lips. "There was so much blood."

"Shh, it's all in the past now, darling. No one knows anything."

Sophia tried to smile and nod. Tried to martial her forces, cut through the sea. She wanted to be clear, to be Sophia again. But the warm undertow dragged her down.

"This is a nightmare," she tried to whisper.

Because it was. The dreaded figure waiting for her, cowled, faceless in the dark at the end of the corridor, black, lifting its cloaked arms to receive her, looming larger and larger—she knew that specter—she did not want to see what she knew—she knew she was dreaming and did not want to dream—but she was drawn on and on by the overpowering tide, on and on down the corridor, past tapestries and portraits obscurely perceived, towards the cowled shape, waiting for her, lifting its arms, coming closer and closer until it slowly, slowly raised its face to her, its gory, empty sockets . . .

He will buy The Magi, *Sophia. At any price.*

The shock woke her up with her heart thundering, her eyes wide. There was gray daylight at the windows. Rain dripping from the branches of the plane trees. The cough and grumble of heavy traffic stopped at a light somewhere below. She rolled her head on the pillow as her pulse slowed. The blank screen of the television stared at her moronically from the bureau. And there beside it—to her vague surprise—was her brother Peter. Slouched in a low-slung armchair, his legs crossed at the knee. Brutally flipping through a copy of *Time Out.*

He caught her movement and saw she was awake. Immediately, he slipped into an attitude as if off the rim of a pool. He became insouciant, droll. He tossed the magazine aside.

"You should take it easy with this suicide business, Sophia," he said. "You might hurt yourself."

She licked her lips. Swallowed painfully. The room gave a nauseating roll. She saw the transparent bag above her, the transparent fluid in it, the tube running down to her wrist. She saw the smeary punters in the print of Cambridge on the blue wall. Everything tilting over. And then her brother again. Wearing the bulky white pullover she had brought him back from Dublin. Looking pale and old beneath his curly black hair. Raw and sore.

"Tell them to stop drugging me, Peter," she mumbled.

"Ah . . ."

"I won't throw myself out the window or anything. Promise."

"Yes, well, the worth of your assurances is a bit low on the exchange just at the moment."

"It's making me ill."

"I'll do what I can, darling. The Great Man, as ever, guides these matters with a more or less inflexible will." He smirked, but his smirk looked painful. He pushed from the chair to stand nonchalantly. Strolled nonchalantly to the window. One hand in the pocket of his jeans, the other tossing about at his belt line. He glanced nonchalantly at the traffic below. He was very nonchalant. "You've led him quite a merry chase these last two days, you know. It hasn't been easy on him. Lying to the media, tranquilizing Mr. Plod.

He's been a busy little knight of the realm indeed." A casual look back at her, a raised eyebrow. "You've developed asthma, by the way. That's how we're explaining things. I thought you should know. We're all running around like mad, telling everyone about poor Sophia's asthma. They send their condolences."

"Poor Sophia," she whispered, trying to help him out, trying to catch his ironical tone. But she was getting woozy again, sleepy, sinking. The waves were rising over her as she went down. She made a noise of exasperation, shook her head in an effort to get her chin up above water.

"It's of great importance to the *gallery*," Peter went on. He had his backside propped on the windowsill now. The slate sky, the fingery branches were behind him. His face was eclipsed. He saluted an imaginary general. "Scandal to be avoided at all costs. The good name to be preserved. As if anyone gave a *shit* about us or the gallery or our good name. Though I suppose it would have made an image for the tabloids, you hanging there."

"Yes," she said. The word stretched out like elastic. Her own voice breathed it back to her from somewhere far away.

"Oh, and we're a bit concerned about your American."

"American . . . ?" She closed her eyes for a second. Yes. That stupid, stupid man. That Richard Storm. She was falling into the image of him. She sucked air in sharply through her nose, forced her eyes open. ". . . oh . . ." she said.

"He *says* he'll be quiet, but he won't take our *money*, thank you very much," said Peter. "I told Father, 'Don't be silly. He's an American. Taking money is what they do, for Christ's sake.' I mean, maybe he doesn't understand English. Perhaps we should wave the notes in front of him and shout, 'Lookee, lookee, money, money.' What sort of name is Storm anyhow?"

It was no good. She was losing her grip, going down. "Don't know . . . Don't know him . . . really . . ."

"Well, he saved the old man's arse at the auction, that's certain."

Her eyes shot open one last time. ". . . auction . . . ?"

But she was irresistibly swept under now. She wanted to call out, but she was just too tired and he was too far away. For a while she thought he was pressing his hand to her cheek. She thought she was smiling. And somewhere above her, she thought she heard his voice again, distant, suddenly bitter.

"Don't worry, Sophe. I'll make the bastards stop poisoning you. They're all a lot of bastards anyway. Bastards."

Then it was Richard Storm who had her, his hand in hers. He was pulling her along over a Rhinehart terrain: ground mist and half-discerned crags against an anemic sky, leaning gravestones, looming ruins. Storm drew her towards the moldering fragment of a wall. She didn't want to go with him. She was supposed to be angry with him, she knew. But she found somehow she trusted him, trusted him completely. And he was laughing, urging her to come along, calling back to her gaily over his shoulder, "Tick-tick! Tick-tick!" Cowled figures in the mist moved, like the mist, around them. One raised its head to watch as they passed. Sophia caught a glimpse of eye sockets drooling blood onto decaying flesh. Then Storm pulled her on. She dug in her heels, but lightly, girlishly, laughing too, unable to resist him. "I was never happy like this in real life," she said. He grinned and nodded and tugged at her. "Tick-tick," he called. They were in vaults—a dream transition. They were in an underground passage. There was dazzling brilliance at the exit to her left, but in here there was only the dark. There were effigies of the dead in niches, crawling with spiders, hung with webs. One effigy was Sophia herself—no, her mother; it must have been her mother because she herself was standing there with Storm beside her, with his arm strong and warm around her shoulders, his body so hot it nearly melted into hers. And they went forward together, approaching the hidden cavity behind the stone. "Do we have to do this?" she asked him. "Won't it be dead?" "Tick-tick," he said. It scared her but she trusted him. Then the climax came in a rushed jumble. They removed the stone. A fanged cobra sprung at her, filled her vision.

She gasped, woke, breathless. Looked. And almost gasped again.

There was Richard Storm. In the flesh. Sitting in the armchair where Peter had sat, hunched forward, his elbows on his knees. A cowboy in faded denim and jeans. His face blunt, rocky, handsome.

Sophia shut her eyes tight and opened them again but, no, unfortunately, he was still there.

He lifted his chin to her. "Hiya, kid. How you feeling?"

For another second or two she could tell herself that she was still confused, still caught between sleep and waking. But she noticed that the drip was gone. And time had passed, night had come; the window was dark, the plane tree branches a black latticework against a perse sky. And her mind was getting sharper every second. The drugs had all but worn off.

And she could no longer delay her rising awareness of a richly excruciating sense of embarrassment.

Storm gave her a lopsided smile. "I came for a rematch,"

he said. He pointed to his nose. "Go on. Throw that right again. I bet I could block that right if I was ready for it."

Sophia burst into tears. Which made things even worse. It was all so humiliating. Mortifying. The thought of herself twirling around in the air, gagging, strangling—in front of a near-total stranger. And now crying like this. She felt like an utter fool—which made her hate him—which only confirmed her vague first impression of him as an irksome American jackass.

"Here," he said. He was beside her, holding out a tissue.

She snatched it from him. Blew her nose. But she wouldn't look at him. She didn't like him looming over her like this, his belt buckle at eye level. She was wearing only a nightgown under the sheet.

"Stop . . . looming," she managed to say, waving her hand at him. She went on crying. The man was an idiot.

"Oh. Sorry. Was I looming? I'll go over here." He thumped over to the window. Thumped down on the sill, crossed his arms on his chest. Bigly. That stupid half-smile was still plastered on his enormous face.

"And don't . . ." She had to blow her nose again, blew it angrily.

"What," he said. "What am I doing now?"

"Don't expect me to thank you," Sophia said. "I didn't want you to help me and I'm not glad you did."

"Yeah, well, tough luck."

"It wasn't any of your business. Why couldn't you just leave me alone?"

"Hey. Guess what. I don't need a reason. You do."

She was ferociously wiping her cheeks, her nostrils, trying to stem the flow, but the tears kept on. She hadn't done this in front of anyone since she was ten years old. She detested him.

"A pretty girl like you," said Storm. "Young. Successful. Smart as hell, anyone can see that. Hanging yourself? Hey, I mean, gimme a break. You got some kind of glitch in your inner life, I mean, Jesus Christ, lady, fix it. Don't go . . ." He didn't finish this, just shook his head, glancing out the window as if seeking moral support from the benighted city.

Sophia could only look at him in disbelief. That he would talk to her like that. As if he even knew her. She felt bitterly conscious just then of the fact that her feet were bare, because she would have taken enormous satisfaction in breaking his head open with the heel of her shoe. As it was, she just lay rigid under the sheets, clenching her soggy tissue in her fist, vibrating with rage at his arrogance and his intrusiveness. Snorting and sniffling, trying with all her will to stop.

Finally, when she felt she could work a sufficient amount of venom into her voice, she said, "Is that what you do with your inner lives in America—fix them?"

"Well, yeah," he said with a shrug. "Why, what's the matter? You don't have psychiatrists in this country? Is that, like, in violation of the Stiff-Upper-Lip Laws or something?"

"No, no, I love it, really, it's a charming idea," she said acidly. "Something wrong with your past, just haul it into the shop and have it fixed. Better yet, get rid of your past altogether. I suppose that's how someone like you ends up with a name like Storm."

Which made him throw back his head and whoop like a spotted hyena. Which almost made her despair. Was there no way to hurt the man's feelings?

"All right," he said, chuckling away like a clown. "All right. You can't fix the past. But you don't kill yourself over it either. Like I said, if the past isn't past, what is? I mean, jeez."

She could only roll her eyes. It really was beyond

frustrating now. Her head was getting all stuffy with crying, and her throat hurt and her temples throbbed and he was sitting there with that gigantic self of his, saying, "If the past isn't past, what is?" and at this point even she wasn't sure whether this was pure American cobblers or a nugget of Buddha-like wisdom.

"Well, you tell me," he went on. "What are you supposed to do with your problems if you don't fix them? Put them in a museum, make them a holiday? What am I missing here?" He was off the window again, his voice rising, his hand wagging at her. "I mean, how could you do a stupid thing like that, a girl like you? What're you, nuts or something?"

"Who on *earth* do you think you're talking to?" she finally blustered, appalled. She now saw clearly that she had attempted to hang entirely the wrong person. "Stop . . . doing that with your hand."

He stopped doing that with his hand. He looked at his hand as if he hadn't noticed it was there before. Then he threw it up in the air. "Man!" he said.

"I mean, who on *earth* do you think you are? I'm sure you're not even supposed to be in here."

He nodded. "You're telling me." Turning back to the window, muttering, "You oughta see the security out there. I felt like Obi-wan Kenobi sneaking around the Death Star."

The man was such an idiot, she almost laughed. He glanced over his shoulder at her.

"What was that? Were you just laughing?"

"No, of course not."

"Are you sure? I thought you were laughing."

"Well, I'm not."

"Well, all right."

For a while then, he stood planted there, his back to her.

His back in the denim jacket, hulking, solid, thick. Like his brain.

Sophia had now stopped crying finally. In fact, she was beginning to feel better all around, more like herself. Cool and ferocious.

So she said, "Well, thank you *so* much for coming to see me, Mr. Storm."

And he had the gall to whoop again, to turn to her, grinning. "Yeah, yeah, yeah. I get it. 'Thank you so much for coming to see me.' That's good. That's Brit-speak for 'Get the hell out,' right?"

"I think it's lovely you're learning to speak the language."

And he laughed again. "That's great. I love that. I wish I could say things like that. 'Thank you *so* much . . .' No, that's great, really, I mean it. It's, like, Rex Harrison or something." He swaggered back to her bedside. "All right, I'm going," he said. "But listen up." And he pointed a finger so close to her face that only her impeccable manners kept her from tearing it off with her teeth. "I like you. A lot. Which is Yank-speak for 'I like you. A lot.' Okay? So don't hang yourself anymore. Okay? It really, really bothers me. You hear what I'm—"

"Oh, for God's sake, would you just leave!" she burst out. And she lashed her face away from him. It was the only way she could keep him from seeing her laugh again. *Don't hang yourself anymore.* Christ, he was ridiculous. She heard his footsteps fading across the floor.

Then something occurred to her. Reluctantly, she looked back. He had just reached the door.

"Wait."

He waited. Still with that ludicrous smirk.

"What happened?" she asked him. "At the auction.

About *The Magi*. Peter said . . . What happened?"

"Don't worry," said Richard Storm. "Like I told your father. I got your girl out of it. They were at half a mil with no sign of stopping."

"Half a . . . half a million pounds?"

"You got it, kid, and it would have gone on forever, too. So I called your lady off."

Once more, Sophia's mind began to cloud, to cloud and roll and throb. "Wait . . . You mean, my father . . . the gallery . . . we didn't buy the painting?"

"That's right. But hey, don't bother to thank me again— I'm already leaving."

"Yes, but who . . . ?" she managed to say after a moment. But he had already gone.

3 "The trouble with Americans is that they're so grotesquely forthright about everything, it's impossible to tell what they're really after."

It was her father, Sir Michael, at the window now, framed by the night-dark panes. Bristling and huge in his black suit. With his red silk handkerchief, red silk tie. Clasping his hands behind his back. Frowning a great frown on his great face.

Sophia, propped up on pillows, leaned over the swing-table pushed up before her. She moved a fork around the chunky white mess on her plate. Still thinking about Richard Storm.

She was becoming depressed again, even more painfully than before. The hospital room was getting her down. It was beginning to hang on her like a leaden shawl. It was a private institution, luxurious as a decent hotel. She had cheery blue walls here. Prints of boaters, skaters. A bright pattern of swallows, crowfoot and water lilies on the curtains. Her own bureau, her own TV. But it was drab, really, she thought, just under the surface. The furniture spat out by some machine somewhere, browned with a cursory coat of factory shellac—it filled her with distaste. And she felt hemmed in by the icy metal of the bed rails. And made nervous by the brisk padding of the nurse's soft shoes out in the hall.

But more than anything, she found the place oppressive with the image of her own suicide. The memory—almost the vision—of her own body dangling from the gallery balcony. That picture inhabited the air around her. Her body turning and struggling there. Seconds from dying—dying by mistake—by a terrible mistake. And then Storm had come.

Storm had come. And shattered the door. And run to her. And hauled her up. She still had the bruise on her upper arm from where he'd gripped her.

"What's he think he's up to?" Sir Michael said. Bouncing on his toes. Popping, simmering. "Hanging about. Sneaking into your room like that. We've offered him money. What does he want?"

She went on toying with her food. Funny, but she knew it would never occur to the Great Man that Storm simply liked her. A lot.

Sir Michael began to pace thoughtfully back and forth across the foot of her bed. Chin down, eyebrows gathered like rain clouds. Musing: "Something American. What do they do over there? Sue each other. Go on chat shows. He can't be thinking of suing us—not in a British court. And I've *offered him money.*"

Sophia smiled, thinking of the ridiculous Storm. *Don't*

hang yourself anymore, okay? "He isn't going to sue us."

Sir Michael pulled up right before her. "Good God, you don't think he'd go on a chat show?"

She gave him a look. "No, Daddy."

"I mean, you haven't . . . bared your soul to him or anything."

"Hardly."

"Hm. Good. Still, I don't trust him." He paced back to the window. Stood there, rocking on his heels. Grandly surveying the scene beyond—whatever it was—Sophia didn't know, she hadn't looked. After a moment he said, "He didn't happen to mention the auction by any chance, did he?"

Sophia laid her fork down slowly. She sat back against the pillows. Rolled a tired glance in her father's direction. She saw his face reflected in the pane, a dim, dark, patchy picture of him, the eyes unreadable. And she realized wearily: This was the way they were going to talk about it. This half-spoken, elliptical way. The way they talked about everything. As if the truth were understood between them and need not be spoken aloud. As if the silent subtext were common knowledge. Her whole life she had assumed that this was how people in families did communicate with one another. Yet just now, she found it terribly frustrating. Because she *didn't* know the truth. She didn't understand it at all. She had almost killed herself because she didn't understand it. And she was so tired now. She was tired of subtlety and Endering machinations. She kept thinking about Richard Storm.

"Not really," she answered him thickly. "He said he pulled Jessica off at half a million."

"Yes," he murmured, as if to himself. "Funny he would do that. Impertinent. Funny."

"You didn't want to pay that much for it, did you?"

He only shrugged in answer.

Then there was a long pause. Sophia was so tired of this, so depressed. She did not want to start the whole business again. But it seemed inevitable somehow too. Speaking carefully, she said, "Who finally got it?"

Sir Michael once more lifted his broad shoulders. "Some mystery to it apparently. Fellow delivered a check in the name of some foundation. Children of Hope, I think it was called. The check was perfectly good. But the foundation doesn't seem to exist. No one knows who the man was. No one's ever seen him before."

She looked at him standing there, looked at him a long while. Children of Hope? she thought. And that turned out to be the Devil from Hell? She had almost hanged herself, thinking it was her father, and it was some nonexistent organization? Children of Hope? But then why had Sir Michael wanted *The Magi* so badly? Did he know, had he heard about the murdered Resurrection Men? Why hadn't he spoken to her directly, saved her from what she'd tried to do to herself? Storm had saved her, a stranger. Why hadn't her own father?

"Daddy . . ." she said.

"Anyway, it was just a whim," said Sir Michael. Coming around to face her, cutting her off. "Always liked Rhinehart, thought it would be worth having. Just a whim."

She fell silent, hurt by the lie. He moved to her bedside. Took her hand in his large, spotted paw.

"The important thing is for you to get better. Put all this nonsense out of your mind." He hung over her awkwardly. Touchingly concerned, clumsy, helpless before what he doubtless viewed as her mysteriously feminine inner troubles. "Look," he went on gently, "I don't mean to sound like a thoroughgoing egotist. It's the timing more than anything that suggested it. What I mean is: this ridiculous business at the gallery the other night. It didn't have anything to do with us, did it? With me, I mean?"

Sophia's lips parted and closed several times before she could answer. "You are a thoroughgoing egotist," she said softly then. "No. Don't be ridiculous. It was just one of my bad patches, that's all. It's over now and I feel very silly."

"Ah," he said, straightening at once. Smiling; pleased. "Good. Well. Onward and upward, then." He let her go, clapped his palms together with a hollow report. "Perhaps we'll get the next one."

Called from her own thoughts, she looked up at him distantly. "The next one?"

"Yes. Since the auction, there've been all sorts of rumors that *The Magi* wasn't the only panel of the Rhinehart triptych to turn up in the East. The word is the *Madonna* may be on the market soon."

"The *Madonna*?"

"Yes," said Sir Michael, rubbing his hands. "The rumor is the third bidder—the bidder on the telephone at the auction—has got it, and is looking for a buyer."

"Oh," Sophia said, closing her eyes.

✦

She really was terribly weary of this. And depressed. And alone. *And afraid*—especially as the night wore on towards dawn. It went round and round in her mind. *The Magi*—the *Madonna*—the Resurrection Men—Jon Bremer's butchered eyes . . . She should go to the police—and yet what if that meant her father's arrest—or his ruin? Either one would almost certainly kill him. And she couldn't trust the police anyway. Whoever this Devil from Hell was, Jon Bremer had said he might have contacts on the police. Well, he might have contacts anywhere. She couldn't trust anyone, really, couldn't talk to anyone. Which was nothing new. She never had been able to trust or talk to anyone. She had never confided in a single person her age-old suspicions about Sir Michael, or her childhood memory of that night at Belham Grange. And so it would all just go on and on like this if she didn't stop it. She would be right back in the same nightmare she'd been in for weeks. For years, really. Really, if it came to that, for all her life.

So, as the sky was slowly infused with a tired gray, she rose from her hospital bed. Moved to the window. Divided the curtains with her wrists, reached in between them and lifted the sash. The cold morning air washed in over her, penetrating the thin cotton of her nightgown. She heard tires hissing in rainwater below her. The sough of wind through the plane trees. She raised her eyes to look off down the street.

She was in the old Victorian building's corner turret, the fourth floor. Across the broad intersection, through the branches, over the traffic lights, she could see the Thames glinting dully, seething sluggishly beneath the Chelsea Bridge with an incoming tide. A cormorant flew black over the bridge's white cables, heading towards where the clouds were parting on a feeble dawn.

And she thought: *Yes. The fall from here would do it. That would finish it off for good and all.*

Then there was a *boom* and a *thwack* behind her. The door had flown open, hit the wall. She looked over her shoulder to see Richard Storm amble in, his idiotic smirk screened by a bouquet of roses and freesias, which he held

174

splayed as if he'd just yanked them from a magician's hat.

"Morning, glory," he said. "I'm back—and better than ever. How you feeling?"

"I'm glad you're here, Mr. Storm," said Sophia quietly. "I need your help."

4 *Thump-thump. Thump-thump. Thump-thump.*

Between the demon Asmodeus and a portrait of Ogopogo, the zeuglodon of Lake Okanagan, Storm had found an empty slice of yellow-striped wall against which to bang his forehead repeatedly. He'd been doing it, with pauses to moan Sophia's name, for more than half an hour now, and it was driving Bernard absolutely around the bend. *Bizarre!*'s factotum was on a sort of dream quest through the Internet, following reports of a pixie who had apparently crossed Hudson Bay from Baffin Island and was now said to be traveling downcountry towards Saskatoon. Rocking on his backless workstation chair, dabbling at his keyboard with one hand, Bernard was currently in electronic communication with a copper miner's daughter named Gwen. She, in turn, was feverishly gathering and trans-mitting reports that a four-inch-high green glow wearing a forester's cap was busily baking oatcakes in a fallow wheatfield somewhere to the south of her. The whole business required concentration. And to have Storm doing that on the other side of the office—*thump-thump, thump-thump, Sophia, Sophia*—it was crazy-making.

Finally, lifting his angelic features to whatever gods may be, Bernard gave in, logged off. He swiveled around to face the other. Storm was standing with his back to him, hands in the pockets of his jeans, head down, rocking gently to bring his brow into contact with the wall.

"I sense somehow that you're distressed," Bernard said.

Storm glanced over as if he'd only just noticed the factotum was there. "Anguished," he said. "This is how I do anguished."

But, to Bernard's infinite relief, he left off. He wandered gloomily over to the planter in the corner, the one from which some stuffed something stared with goggly eyes. He stood over it, stared back.

Bernard waited, studied him, wistfully. He had already deduced that his American co-worker was ill. Now, seeing him with his sad eyes ringed and his craggy features somehow blurry, overly pale, he was beginning to feel the situation was even worse than he'd imagined. He didn't like this, not a bit. On top of which, he was given to occasional bouts of hypochondria, and hated to think about such things.

"You know what it's like," said Storm, "when you want to—just—pour a woman into a glass and—just—drink her—just drink her down, one gulp, body and soul?"

Bernard made a bemused frown. "Not really. I'm appalling."

"No, hell," said Storm. "Different strokes . . ."

"No, I mean, I'm a *Pauline:* all things to all people. I have died from time to time, I suppose, and worms have certainly eaten me—but not for love."

Storm, who clearly had no idea what Baldy was talking about, merely shrugged. "Well, you're not missing anything, believe me. I swear to God, I don't understand her."

"I've heard that's part of it."

"No, I mean Harper. I don't understand why she told me

to get involved with this. What did she think would happen?"

The factotum didn't answer. One long leg stretched out, he used the heel of his trainer to shift his chair around. He had his own doubts about Harper's motives, but he thought it best for now to keep his opinions to himself.

Storm lifted his eyes suddenly. Looked over the office as if for the first time: over the magazine covers with their photos of strange creatures, over the strange creatures in the aquaria here and there, over the shrieking telamons supporting the fireplace mantelpiece, and the carnivorous cactus panting against the high windows, against the darkling winter sky above World's End.

"What does she, own this place?" he said. "This whole building? Where does she get the money for this?"

Bernard smiled. That was better. He loved gossip. And this was exactly the sort of pertinent question that the man from Hollywood so frequently neglected to ask.

"Ah," he said, settling in, lifting an exquisite hand, "I see she hasn't told you about her father. Her Magwitch . . ."

"Magwitch? What kind of name is that? How can her father be named Magwitch?"

Bernard sighed. "No, no, her father isn't *named* Magwitch . . ."

But just then there was a noise below. Locks and latches rattled. The ground floor door could be heard to crack open. Bernard placed a finger to his lips.

"Do you think it possible that in the reticula of medieval architecture we are seeing the subconscious reconstruction of shell patterns found in the earliest protista?" Harper shouted up to them from the foyer.

The two men shook their heads at one another. By

following the assorted bangs, creaks, rattles and glubs—not to mention her continued shouting—they could clearly follow Harper's progress into the house. She was hanging up her cape in the foyer. She was thudding to the fireside, where she invariably relit her pipe. She was at the butler's tray, pouring herself a glass of water from the pitcher beside the mounted Tatzelwurm.

"Some claim that one planarian which ingests another can then imitate, without instruction, the behavior learned by the victim during its life," she continued—then paused to swallow. Storm pressed the heels of his palms against his temples. Bernard merely rolled his eyes. Harper's labored footsteps now sounded on the stairs, her voice growing louder as she ascended. "We admit the inheritance of instinct," she called, "but could the substance of a more complex memory have been transmitted by more and more complex means until the smithy of a soul contains not just the conscience of its race . . ." She appeared in the doorway, breathless, propped on her stick, her free hand thoughtfully twisting the mouthpiece of her pipe into her chin. ". . . but of all creation?"

"I shouldn't think so," said Bernard.

"Ah," said Harper. "Well, then perhaps we'll go with the cover story on giant leeches."

Crossing the threshold, she let her stick fall against one screaming telamon. Fished a manila envelope from her satchel and humped across the room to stuff it in a pigeonhole on Bernard's workstation. Humped back to the chaise longue in front of the high windows. And, with an enormous groan, sank down onto it.

Through all this, Storm watched her. Bernard watched her. She took her shoes off, massaged her feet, and they watched her do that. She stretched out on the chaise.

Smoothed down the viny print of her dress—a vomitous mess of green leaves and purple grapes. Storm stood with his hands in his pockets and watched her. Bernard sat. Watched her.

"What?" she cried finally. "What? What?"

Storm shook his head, lifted a hand. "How could you do this to her, Harper?"

"Ah." Her pipe had already gone out. She wagged the dead stem at him. "I take it Miss Endering has turned to you for help."

Still shaking his head, he stepped over to the window beside her. Leaned against the wall with one shoulder, staring out into the dusk. "When I was walking to the hospital this morning, I looked up and saw her standing in this, I don't know, this big brick turret-like part of the building. She looked like a fairy princess up there, captured in a tower."

"Ha-ha," said Harper Albright.

"Then, the minute I walked into the room, she said she wanted to meet with me. Tonight. Secretly. She said she didn't want her father to find out." For a moment he squeezed his eyes shut painfully.

But Harper only said, "Good. She has an important story to relate. She's probably been living with it for ages and needs to get it out. I have no doubt she will tell you everything."

"She hardly knows me, Harper."

"Don't be ridiculous. You saved her life. You were absolutely cinematic about it. If she's a princess in a tower, you're a knight in shining armor. Besides which, I strongly suspect she has no one else to trust."

His hand went up again. His tone was one of fierce complaint. "That's what I'm afraid of."

The last light of day flashed on Harper's spectacles, obscured her eyes. But Bernard could see her lined face soften as she looked up at the man. "She's a big girl, young Richard. A grown woman. Tell her the truth, and she can make her own decisions."

Storm rolled over until his back was against the wall. For a second or two his expression was naked, lost, almost childlike. It was precisely moments like this that made Bernard hanker after debauchery—to take the edge off.

"I don't know if I can tell her," said Storm. "I don't know if I can tell her."

They were all silent after that, and it was sad in the room. Storm gazed up at the pendant toplight. Bernard studied his trainer tips, Harper the skull of her pipe. None of them looked at either of the others.

Then Storm pushed off the wall. He moved to the threshold without a word. Stopped there, hands in pockets. Frowned down at the back of Harper's head.

"How could you do this to me then?" he said quietly. "I mean, I was out of it. You know? I was home, babe, I was gone. The cord was cut. I was, like, sailing away and it was all right. You know? Now . . ."

Bernard waited for Harper's answer, but she made none. She went on studying her pipe. And after another moment, Storm walked out.

✦

Then, though—then, when Storm had gone—Harper was on her feet. Padding back and forth in her stockings over the rose pattern of the rug. Tapping her pipestem to her chin again. Murmuring with grim excitement.

"Getting there, Bernard. We're getting there. Tonight,

one night, with what Richard discovers, with what I might find, who knows, we may understand everything. Everything."

Bernard stood abruptly. Paused to recover his accustomed grace. Then wafted off into a connecting storeroom, just out of Harper's sight. He was agitated, and didn't want her to see it.

The storeroom was small, windowless. There were old copies of the magazine stacked up here. Folders of newspaper clippings. Boxes of pencils, razors, layout sheets; a broken wax mangler. Mostly things that Bernard's computer had rendered obsolete, but that Harper nonetheless insisted on keeping. There was also a basin and a small refrigerator with an electric kettle set on top. And bags and boxes of makings for tea, coffee and hot chocolate. A tin of stale digestive biscuits—Bernard munched on one of these as he filled and started the kettle.

He could still hear Harper pacing in the office proper, muttering to herself. "Arrogant, arrogant, yes. He traipsed after his own ego into the limelight. After all these years. A mistake. Finally. Tonight, we'll get at the truth."

Bernard dropped a teabag into each of two black mugs. He regarded the hissing kettle with hooded eyes.

"How long do you think Richard's got to live?" he called in to her after a while.

He heard her footsteps cease. Steam rose around his face as the kettle's switch clicked off.

"I don't know," she answered gruffly then. "My suspicion is he'll need a doctor's care within a year."

Bernard nodded, his stomach souring. Poured the water into the mugs. "And you don't think there's something just a teeny, tiny bit, oh, say—unforgiveable—in using him in this fashion? To gather information from La Endering, I mean, when he's obviously in love with her?"

As the mugs were filled, images formed on their black sides: the white-domed, hollow-eyed faces of aliens. They were etched there in sensitive ink, and the heat made them visible. The mugs were silly toys that *Bizarre!*'s new publisher gave away to subscribers. For some reason, the trick always delighted Harper.

"Ha-ha!" she said when Bernard carried them in to her, presented her with one. She was sitting on the edge of the chaise longue now, had slipped her feet into her shoes again. As Bernard drifted back to his chair, she held the mug to her lips with both hands, huddled over it, blew softly on the steam as it misted her glasses.

"If he is being used, it is not by me," she said finally, when he had seated himself, when he had swiveled around to her. "You said it yourself. It is Storm's coming here that has set things into motion. He is tied intimately to events, and probably has been from the beginning. That story he read at the party, his connection with the girl, even his nonsensical ghost-hunting—all of it has played a part. A hero is led by destiny, Bernard; everyone else is simply dragged along by it. The only question left for Richard Storm is whether or not he is to be the hero of his own life."

"And Endering?"

Harper wagged her head. "If I were she, I would fall in love with him."

"And have her heart broken."

"Have it broken open, yes."

Bernard could no longer contain himself. "God!" he said, setting his mug down by his keyboard with a careless thud. "Talk about arrogant. You're as arrogant as Iago."

Harper nodded slowly. "He works his work, I mine."

The factotum swung away from her, swung round to his computer. Laid a hand here and there aimlessly about the workstation, looking for something to occupy his attention, to keep him from showing his feelings—which he generally hated to do. That was how he came to hit upon the manila folder that Harper had placed in one of his pigeonholes. He drew it out. Opened the clasp. Pulled a page from within.

"So what's this?"

"Ah. Yes. That is what I meant about tonight." Harper set her mug down on an endtable, rose to her feet. She stretched, gathered her pipe, her satchel. "That is a fourteenth-century ballad called 'Young William,' which I recovered from an anthology in the London Library. I translated it from the Middle English for you, in light of your progressive education."

"Cheers."

"I take it to be evidence that my suspicions were correct and that 'Black Annie,' 'The Alchemist's Castle,' and the *Magi* panel were all inspired by a single earlier source, probably English, and probably predating the thirteenth century. The similarities are too obvious to ignore."

"And this strikes you as interesting somehow?"

She had recovered her stick, had paused beside the mantelpiece. Was regarding him sternly from there, her squat figure not much taller than the grotesque telamon howling beside her. "Bernard," she said, drawing out the syllables reprovingly. "Bernard, Bernard. It strikes me as everything. Reason it out. Iago is after the Rhinehart triptych and he doesn't seem to care who knows it. He *wants* people to know it so that the owners of the other two panels will come forward. What does worry him is that someone might find out *exactly what it is* about the triptych that interests him."

"And the answer is buried in all these stories?"

"Exactly. They are the trail, at least—the trail our warlock friend Dr. Mormo kept raving about—a trail of ghost stories, which I suspect led Iago to the triptych in the first place, and which now may lead us to the answer as well."

Bernard examined the ballad, frowned at it.

"That must be it," Harper continued. "You'll notice: Iago did not become concerned with us until I had Jorge unearth 'The Alchemist's Castle'—the one story that forms an essential bridge connecting the tales to the paintings. When I discovered that, he sent his thugs to attack us. Now, if I can continue to follow the story trail to the common source of all these works . . ."

"Then perhaps he'll send his thugs to kill us."

"Hm, well . . . That is what I'm going to find out right now. An oblique note in the anthology said the ballad was connected with a work by none other than the greatest of ghost story writers, M. R. James. So I am going to see Mrs. Ponsonby. And if she can supply me with another link in the chain, and if young Richard can work his way through Miss Endering's defenses . . . who can say?"

With some effort, Bernard had recovered his best languorous manner and was tilted back, stretched out in his chair again, his long lashes veiling his eyes.

"So what do you suppose it is, this secret?" he drawled as Harper turned to go. "This thing that Iago wants, is it some sort of weapony business, you reckon? The key to world domination and suchlike? Has he got some political agenda or something? One of those blueprints for the greater good that are bound in actual practice to make the world a living hell? Because, I mean, if that's all he wants, he may as well break out the champagne: we're already there."

Harper paused long enough on her way to the door to cock an eyebrow at him. "You are too young to be so cynical," she said. "And I am too old and wise. No, I'm certain we're beyond politics now. There are only two things Iago and I have in common. And one is a richly sustaining indifference to the question of personal philosophy. It is completely irrelevant to either of us whether one tortures and kills in the name of racism or brotherhood, oppression or liberty, the devil or God. History is not written by the hand of intent. It's the deeds alone that matter."

"Do you really believe that?"

"I believe nothing."

"Oh."

"Well, then. I'm off."

"A trifle peculiar, perhaps."

"Ha-ha."

"What's the other thing you and Iago have in common?" Bernard murmured wryly—but by the time he murmured it wryly, he had already heard the front door shut, and her stick rapping away over the pavement into the night.

5 Shortly thereafter, Harper grew terribly afraid. She was in a cab. Squeezing up Drayton Gardens from Fulham Road. Lost in thought. Rubbing her wrinkled chin with a wrinkled hand. Gazing vacantly out past the driver's head through the windscreen, at the headlamps coming towards her through the dark.

Gradually, a phenomenon began to work its way into her consciousness. The taxi was stopping and stitching along the narrow strip of road between parked cars, dodging in slow motion through the oncoming traffic. And it occurred to Harper that a disproportionate amount of that traffic bore weirdly similar license plates. Some combination of the numerals one, three and three kept recurring: 133, 313, 331—two digits, three permutations, over and over.

She knit her brows, sat up, took notice. Her cab was just now reaching Priory Walk. A sprawling brick and stucco building was to her left, an automobile dealership to her right. There were arc lights over the dealership, and streetlamps all along the pavement; the scene was quite well lit. It was perhaps two hundred yards from here to the junction with Old Brompton Road. Not that far. Harper started counting.

Nine cars went by in the time it took her to reach the traffic light on the corner. Of those, four—a Rover, a Volks, a BMW and a Volvo—had the numbers on their plates: 133, 313, 331 and 133 again.

Harper told herself it was only a mild case of synchronicity. Happens all the time, to everyone. And yet, an intuition brought the goosebumps out in force on her arms.

Coincidences happen more frequently, more profoundly, whenever we get close, whenever the trail gets warm again. That was how Bernard had put it. *Recurring numbers, accidental meetings, unlikely chains of events. They're like the spoor of our quarry.*

Now she was watching for it—which complicated matters. Were the number combinations actually appearing more often, or was her attention picking them out, excluding others?

In either case, as the cab wove through the backroads of South Kensington, the phenomenon abated for a while. Harper began to relax, began to shrug it off.

Then the taxi broke out onto Kensington High Street. A

newsie near Marks and Spencers hawked the late edition of the *Standard:* "1:33 to Nottingham Derails." The taxi climbed up Kensington Church Street, and the price tag of a brass curfew seemed to stand out from the window of an antique shop: £313. The cab began traveling faster now, traveling farther north into Notting Hill. Harper looked up at the spotlit charity thermometer under the steeple of St. Peter's . . .

She found herself shuddering, found herself thinking against her will: *Near. He is very near.*

A few moments later, the cab slid over to the curb. Stopped.

"Here we are," said the driver, smiling round at her. "One-three-three Portobello Road."

✦

Rose Ponsonby lowered her ninety-year-old frame into the purple pillows on the settee, and her cats swarmed over her. They mewed and nuzzled her, flexed and purred. Rose had to hold her cup and saucer well above their heads as she took a dainty nibble of her biscuit.

"I myself believe the severing of the jugular to be decidedly orgasmic," she said sweetly. Her voice was high and tremulous and creaky. "But the other ladies fell out over the use of teeth, you see. Margaret was very disagreeable and insisted they were entirely phallic, while Joan—who is getting on and can no longer hear quite as well as she used to—was shouting terribly loudly that their phallic qualities were a mere screen to protect the vulgar mind from the obviously vaginal threat of the fanged mouth." She chuckled happily. "I do so love discussing *theories,* don't you? Pointless hostility is such a wonderful stimulant, I find."

"Yes, yes, charming, charming," Harper muttered—but her mind was elsewhere. The tea in her blue willow cup was untouched, the biscuit on her plate untasted. She had been alternately tamping and lighting the tobacco in her meerschaum skull for the last ten minutes, but she hadn't actually smoked the pipe at all. She was perched on the edge of an ancient pink sewing chair, a black Manx glued around one of her veiny ankles. Her eyes were darting nervously, continuously about the small parlor.

It was a room filled with books, shelves of books, stacks of books, clogging the fireplace, overflowing from the mantelpiece. And with the bay window covered by heavy green drapes, and the round tea table and its mismatched cushioned chairs virtually filling whatever floor space was left, Harper was beginning to feel closed in, clammy, claustrophobic. Because she kept hitting on little occurrences, dangerous little events. The miniature mantelpiece clock, for instance, was stopped at 3:31. A disordered pile of library books among the tea things were all from the section on the supernatural, all bearing the index numbers 133. A little bust of Constantine stood in one corner of the floor beside a sleeping Persian. And why on earth Constantine? Harper couldn't help wondering. And she couldn't help noticing that its inscription read, *In Hoc Signo Vinces,* part of the vision that the emperor saw in 312 A.D., and that caused him to take the cross a year later.

"But you wanted to talk about Monty," said Rose Ponsonby. "Get off there, you naughty things," she added, as a tiger and a tortoiseshell leapt up on the table and butted heads over the teapot. "He's upstairs, you know—Monty—but I doubt he'll come down. He hasn't, I'm afraid, since Julia Fitzroy-Leeman-St. John insulted him last autumn.

She asked him why he hasn't been more malevolent since he died—because the revenants in his own stories were always such horrid pills, you know. As if dear Monty could be malevolent if he tried." She cooed this, stroking a Maltese curled up in her lap. "The truth is Julia has always been jealous of his fondness for me."

"Yes, hm, ha-ha," Harper murmured, lifting her teacup, touching the cold tea to her lips. A newspaper wedged between two books in a tall stack displayed its browning folio line: *Friday, March 13, 1992*. Harper felt a cool sheen of sweat at her temples. She half expected Iago's minions to burst right through the door, to kidnap her where she sat.

Rose Ponsonby loosed an elaborate sigh. Pensively touched the silver bun at the back of her head. A long tabby stretched up the shapeless front of her, blinked a greeting into her face. "We were just reminiscing about the old days, Monty and I, the days before the Great War, before the Great War swept the world away. I was barely born, of course, but Monty remembers. He was Dean of Kings College Cambridge, as you know, and I was getting him to talk about the Christmases there, the famous Christmas Eves."

Harper frowned and grumbled impatiently as the old woman went off into a fugue state: smiling to herself, rocking slightly in her chair, stroking the cats that all but covered her. Harper, meanwhile, noticed an apparent phone number scrawled on a piece of paper atop a lamp stand: 313- . . . and the rest covered over with flotsam.

"There would be services first in the beautiful chapel," Rose Ponsonby said. "Then dinner and hot spiced beer and a game of cards. And then a select group would retire to Monty's rooms. And there, finally, finally," she went on, leaning forward over the cats in her lap with brightening eyes, "Monty would go into his bedroom and come out with his latest manuscript. And he would blow out all the candles except for one. And he would sit in his great wing chair with that one candle beside him and his manuscript in his hand—and he would begin to read. Oh, imagine, Harper, imagine—to be the first to hear those great stories. 'The Ash Tree' or 'Abbot Thomas.' Or 'Whistle and I'll Come to You, My Lad.' Those great ghost stories. The greatest ever written, I believe. And now to be a ghost himself, poor dear . . ." She shook her head, sighed again, another elaborate sigh.

Harper's cup rattled against her saucer as she set them down on the table. She seized her pipe and began once more to tamp it furiously. But she knew her friend could not be rushed.

Rose Ponsonby poured herself just another splash of tea. Gave it a speculative taste. Said: "Ah!" Then: "Robert Hughes was at several of those readings, you know."

Harper stopped tamping her pipe. Stopped casting anxious glances here and there. She gave all her attention to the other woman, to the slack, sagging face in the yellow light of the fringed lantern above them.

"Robert Hughes," Harper said slowly. "The author of 'Black Annie'?"

"Well, yes, dear, you wanted to know about the 'Young William' ballad, didn't you? It was Hughes who brought Monty the illuminated manuscript on which the ballad was based. A very nice young chap he was too, Monty says. And even at the time, of course, not without literary ambitions of his own. Anyway, this illuminated manuscript. It was done by one of the monks at Belham Abbey in Buckinghamshire apparently, and had somehow found its way to Germany after the Dissolution of the monasteries. A friend of Hughes's had only recently rediscovered it there and brought it back to England and so Hughes showed it to Monty, who was, of course, one of the great medieval scholars of his age. Oh, Monty can still be very cross on the subject of the Dissolution, let me tell you. Especially in regards to the frightful carelessness about the books, you see. Aside from the most cursory listing by Leland, King Henry took absolutely no care whatsoever to preserve the monastery books! Isn't that awful? All those lovely illustrated manuscripts that the dear monks took such pains over—lost, just lost. It upsets Monty quite terribly; I don't even like to mention it in front of him."

"No doubt," Harper murmured, chewing her pipestem with great vigor. "And so you say Hughes somehow came into possession of this illuminated manuscript. And gave it to James. And James based a ghost story on it?"

"Oh, no, no, no, no!" cried Rose Ponsonby in her high screak. "*Mr. Hughes* based his dear little ghost story on it. That one you mentioned: 'Black Annie.' That was inspired by the medieval manuscript. All Monty did was translate the manuscript itself. From the Latin, you know. He had thought to publish his translation in the *Cambridge Antiquary Society Publication,* but doubts about its provenance prevented him. And, of course, he considered it far too shocking for his Western Railway guide to the abbeys. So it was never published at all."

Harper had now leaned so far to the edge of her sewing chair that she was in danger of slipping off. She peered eagerly through her glasses at Rose Ponsonby. "Rose. My love. What happened to this manuscript? The one written by the dear monk and so forth. The one from Belham Abbey."

"Yes," said Rose, wistfully lifting her chin. "It was put in the British Museum."

"Ah."

"And destroyed, I'm afraid, on the tenth of May, 1941. German bombs, you know. It was burned along with two hundred and fifty thousand other books. A terrible loss."

Harper felt her throat going dry. "Yes. No doubt. And what about James's translation?"

"Oh, that was in the library at Kings."

"But . . ."

"But it was stolen, apparently, some twenty years ago."

"I see." Harper swallowed—which was getting to be hard work. She reached under her spectacles, rubbed her eyes. "So—as I understand it—this manuscript from Belham Abbey no longer exists. There is now no copy of either the original or of James's translation."

"Well, except for this one, of course," said Rose Ponsonby. And she leaned forward—three cats falling from her to plop onto the carpet. She tugged a manila envelope out from under a stack of books by her feet. Lifted it. And presented it to Harper across the tea table.

Harper seized it with a trembling hand. "This is a copy of James's translation?"

"Well, no, not exactly," said Rose. "Monty was kind enough to dictate this to me some time ago when I expressed an interest in it during one of our conversations. But you can be sure I wrote it all down quite faithfully."

Harper closed one eye, examined her friend. "The ghost of M. R. James dictated this to you."

"Oh, it's all right," said Rose Ponsonby. "His memory is quite, quite prodigious, you know. And anyway," she added with a naughty little hoist of her shoulders, "I checked it against the original, many years ago at Kings, before the manuscript was stolen. And what do you think? It was exactly right. Why, it was absolutely word for word."

✦

Had Harper been less excited, she would probably have been more alert to the danger she already knew was pressing in around her. But as tense as she'd been, as wary, every other thought was now pushed aside by the realization of what she had in her possession: the source; the last ghost story. Secreted in a hidden pouch within her cape was the translation of the document she believed had inspired 'Black Annie,' 'The Alchemist's Castle,' the ballad of 'Young William,' and the Rhinehart triptych itself. This, she believed, was what Iago had discovered twenty years ago, what had started him on the triptych's trail. And now, all at once, it had simply been placed into her hands. She could think of nothing else but getting home to read it.

Hunched against the night chill, she trundled down the short path in front of Rose Ponsonby's dainty little house. A cortege of cats danced attendance on her as far as the picket gate. Rose waved from the doorway. Then the cats disbanded and Rose Ponsonby withdrew. The door closed and Harper was alone on the Portobello Road.

Her head bent in contemplation, her hat pulled low across her brows, her stick rapping the pavement, she walked beside the empty, narrow street. A grim brick housing estate hulked in the shadows to one side of her, a row of modest houses stood on the other. A streetlamp passed over her head. She passed through its glow—and then out of it into darkness.

And a cab pulled up slowly behind her.

If she had been less excited, if she had been more alert, she would have noticed. That it had been following her, moving along with her. That it sidled up to her now only as she stepped into an all-but-deserted stretch of shuttered antique shops and abandoned stores.

As it was, she was brought out of her meditation when the beams of the taxi's headlamps entered her peripheral vision. Turning to discover the cab, she smiled at her luck and raised her hand to hail it.

The cab moved to the curb alongside her and stopped. The front window came down. Harper leaned into it. The driver, on the other side of the car, tilted back so that his face was obscured by the night.

"World's End," Harper said.

"Absolutely right, darling," said the driver.

She climbed into the back, settled into the seat. Set the tip of her stick against the floor between her feet, rested both her hands atop the carved dragon's head, rested her chin upon her knuckles. And she sank deep into thought again as the cab pulled away.

Her thought was so deep, in fact, that it was many minutes before she realized what was happening. By that time the taxi had strayed from any possible route into her neighborhood. Instead, through a series of sharp jolts and turns, it had veered off into the backstreets of Kensington. And Harper, furiously discussing with herself the long and complex history of Anglo-German cultural exchanges—from the Celtic migrations to the dropping of bombs on the British Museum—glanced up in complete astonishment to find herself passing eastward under the Royal Albert Hall.

She straightened. Her eyes went quickly to the plaque fastened on the seat in front of her: *The number of this cab is*

331. Suddenly more frightened than she had been since she could well remember, she lifted her gaze directly to the rearview mirror.

And she saw the burning malice of the driver's reflected stare. Saw his scarred mouth twisted into a grin of jeering bitterness and cruelty.

Harper could only gape another long moment at that face—the face of the man who had attacked her outside The Sign of the Crane.

The taxi's doors and windows—as she discovered a moment later—were all securely locked.

6 Not far away, on Waterloo Bridge, went Richard Storm, his heart leaden. The city; the city—the Big Smoke, the gray lady, London—so beautiful all around him: it was tearing him apart. *Look, look at it!* he thought. The dome of St. Paul's blossoming into a haze of spotlight to the east. A flock of birds wheeling and diving in perfect harmony around it, brushing their balletic patterns on the dew of night. The Houses of Parliament at his other shoulder—the clock tower, finials, spires and fletch spearing and doodling on the dark. And the bridges launching themselves over the river. And the lights hung like bunting above the riverside walk. The ships, towers, domes, theaters and temples—all this crushed him as he barged south across the water, his hands in his trench-coat pockets, his soul racked with longing.

Because he wanted to be here a lifetime and he didn't have a lifetime left. Because he wanted to be here with Sophia, wanted the churches and the bridges and the spires to be the backdrop for their kisses and intimate conversations.

And he couldn't even run the movie of it in his mind because it was so impossible, because the impossibility hurt too much. He kicked the pavement as he went, butted the cold, damp air. He had been free! he kept telling himself. He had been out of it. He had cut himself loose from life and desire. He'd been Buddha. He'd been Humphrey Bogart in *Casablanca*. The Goodbye Guy. He had been ready to go. Now this.

Trolls, he thought. That's what it was. Religious people believed God ran the world. Atheists figured it was indifferent nature. But it was trolls. Sadistic little homunculi in leather jackets with lots of zippers. Hiding behind the scrim of being. Working the machinery to maximize human suffering for their own amusement. Thumbing their noses, wagging their puds. He could almost hear them laughing at him.

Yeah, and they were good, sweetheart. They were real good at their jobs. When he'd crossed the bridge, when he reached the southern embankment, when he saw Sophia there—the exquisite arrow of pain that went through him: it was a masterpiece of natural cruelty. Fucking trolls.

She was leaning against the stone balustrade, under a string of lights. Looking quietly down at the muddy banks of the Thames. She straightened and turned as he approached her. Her cheeks were pink with cold above the lifted collar of her navy coat. A kiss-me curl was blowing from beneath the silken kerchief on her hair. She was as he'd seen her first, cool and superior. Her stance relaxed but straight. The line of her mouth firm, faintly ironic, faintly smiling. A ball of white vapor broke from his lips as the full effect struck him.

He reached her. They stood at a loss for words. Then she extended a small, delicate hand and shook his briskly.

"Thank you for coming, Mr. Storm," she said.

They walked in silence together above the Thames. The gulls crying, sailing, landing. The efficient, imperial skyline of Whitehall across the way. The jagged concrete wedges of the theater complex hanging over them. Storm's mind raced, searching for something to say. But he had only one thing to say and he couldn't bring himself to say it. He could no more speak of his illness to her than a married man, feeling as he did, could have mentioned his wife; it would have killed the illusion of possibility.

So they strolled and he stole glances at her, watching her organize her thoughts. Then, finally, she stopped. He stopped. She looked up at him.

"I'm afraid . . ." she said. And all at once, she started laughing.

Bewildered, Storm smiled, waited.

She tried again. "I'm afraid I . . ." She covered her mouth with her hand. Her shoulders shook. She fought the laughter off. "I'm afraid I . . ." But it broke out again, high, musical peals. She waved quickly at the air as if to erase them. "I'm afraid . . ." She was overcome with laughter. She veered away from him, staggered towards the balustrade. Storm, still puzzled, still smiling dopily, scratched his head. Sophia hugged herself, giggling. Glanced her apologies at him but was laughing too hard to speak. She hid her face behind her arms, struggled to compose herself again. Lowered her arms. Said, "I'm afraid I've made rather a bad first impression . . ." But that was as far as she got. The laughter crippled her. She fell back against the balustrade, slapped the top of it. Her whole body quaked as she laughed.

Storm went on grinning blankly, went on waiting. Watched her laughing, his hands in his trench-coat pockets.

Life, sex, money, springtime, his own skin—he had never loved anything so much. He had never really even understood that it could happen. Like this, like a song. Like a really bad, clichéd song. One of those songs that went: *I never kneeeeew—that love could be so truuuuue—until I met yooooooou . . .* That kind of thing. And what was worse—what was potentially disastrous—was that if she went on leaning there, against the balustrade, against the background of the city, went on leaning there, laughing, red-cheeked, he was actually going to start singing that song, or one very much like it, right there, right then, out loud. Oh, that would be a bad, bad thing, he knew. But the urge was strong upon him, almost irresistible. And he suddenly realized: here he was, Richard Storm, of Hollywood, of America, of the twentieth century's end, of the planet Earth—and there was poverty and race hatred and terrorism and those horrible nose rings girls were wearing and Western culture was probably in free fall and people said words like *fart* on network television— and here he was, standing in his own sad body—his own rapidly decaying body—*and there was a song in his heart!*

Good Christ, if he didn't kiss this woman soon, he was going to explode.

"Oh!" said Sophia Endering finally—finally exhausted, finally tapped out. Holding her cheeks between her palms, rocking her head wearily. "Oh. I don't know why every time I'm around you I'm reduced to such absolute *imbecility!*" She wiped her eyes. She stared at her feet, at the concrete under her feet. She shivered. The laughter had all blown out of her. "The very first time I saw you I spilled my wine all over the place. And the next thing you know I'm jumping off a balcony with a belt around my neck. And then I punch you, and then I'm in hospital, crying like a baby. And now I'm laughing like a complete idiot. A bad impression! You must think I'm stark, staring mad."

She raised her face to his for an answer, but he said nothing; he could think of no verbal equivalent to lifting her in his arms and carrying her away to a castle in the clouds.

"But you see, the thing of it is," she went on helplessly, "that that's exactly why . . ." She narrowed her eyes, trying to catch the idea, phrase it. "That's exactly why I wanted to talk to you, I think. To see you. So badly. Really. Because everyone else—yah?—well, I don't know how to put it without sounding terribly egotistical, but everyone else thinks . . . I don't *do* those sorts of things. Everyone else thinks I've got everything under complete control. All the time. And when I lose control, when I do do something irrational, everyone just ignores it. So it's as if I hadn't done it at all. And now here you are, and you must think at this point that I never do anything else. You must think: Oh yes, Sophia Endering, she's that absolutely insane girl who's always throwing herself off balconies and so forth. Crazy old Sophia, you must think—I don't know what you must think of me, actually. But here you are, you know? And there you were in hospital. And you said . . . you liked me . . ." She averted her eyes, embarrassed. "I know it's absurd—it sounds absurd even to me as I say it—but you said you liked me and it just seems rather remarkable to me at this point that you should. That anyone should." She drew a long breath of the damp air, held it; braced herself. "And so I wanted to see you. To talk to you. It's all got so confusing that I wanted to explain things to somebody who won't . . . hate me for them afterwards. Is that . . . is that all right? Do you mind?"

Storm started singing.

"Yooooou dooooo something to meeeee," he sang,

"something that simply mystifiiiies meee."

Sophia's jaw dropped. She stared at him.

"Tell meeee why should it beeeee," sang Storm. "You have the power to hypnotiiiiize meeeee. Let meeeeee live 'neath your spell. Do do that voodoo that you do so well. 'Cause yoooou. Doooo. Something to meeee—that noooobody else can dooo. 'Cept you," he added as a jazzy little flourish of his own and then brought it on home with, "That noooo-body else can doooo."

"I . . . Well . . . I . . ." said Sophia. And then she smiled at him.

Storm stepped forward, took her by the shoulders, and kissed her.

He hadn't been in the movie business for nothing.

✦

"Look, I'm no good at sex," Sophia said. "I suppose that's very important to you, being a man and everything."

Sex? Storm thought. Sex? Here they were. Here they actually were, walking back across Waterloo Bridge. With St. Paul's behind her, and the wheeling birds and the backdrop of London. And her eyes were hectic with his kisses, and he could feel her body tense and then yield every time he took her to him, and her face was turned up to his, confused and appealing.

"Couldn't I just look at you for now?" he said. "Like that, against the dome, with those birds?"

She glanced over at them vaguely. "Dome?" Which presented her cheek to him, so he brushed it with his lips. "It's just . . ." She turned back, bringing her lips to his. She held him off gently, her fingertips on his face. So he kissed her fingertips. "It's just that people think . . . Men are always . . . There are just all these *things* I have to tell someone. About me. I have to . . ."

He gathered her up again, felt her tense again, yield again, and kissed her a long time, deeply. He was having an insight. An erection and an insight, both profound. No, no, his insight was saying, no, no. Not *trolls*. You idiot. How could you ever have thought it was trolls? This incredible, this resplendent city; this cathedral in the mists of night; this bracing winter breeze, those stars; this flesh, this flesh—this vehicle for bringing two souls together at the mouth, at the loins: it's the work of fucking Santa Claus, Jackson! Even Death; even Death was sweet in that it made a moment out of this, which was too fabulous to last for more. That Claus, what a man, you could count on him to get the whole thing perfect.

"Then tell me," he said, breaking away, coming up for air. She was hankering after him now, following after his lips with hers. "Tell me everything. Tell me why you tried to kill yourself. How could you? How could you do it, Sophie? I was so mad, I was so crazy. I wanted to slug you. I *would've* slugged you if you hadn't slugged me first."

She laughed at him, patted his cheek. They let each other go. She moved to the bridge railing, looked down into the streak of glimmering light on the black water. She shuddered once, so that he wanted to hold her again, but he restrained himself, waited.

"I have these black patches," she said. She made a face. "That's what we call them. In my family. Sophia's black patches. It's the oddest feeling. Everything gets very heavy and sort of brown and I feel thoroughly detached from it all and superior and miserable at the same time. I know everything's the same as it was before, but it's all just—*blah* somehow suddenly, yah? I feel funny telling you this. We never talk about it."

Storm sniffed. His nose was beginning to run with the cold. "Who never talks about it?"

"We . . . you know, my family. They'd be horrified if they knew I was telling you. An outsider." She smiled, as if at a fond memory. "Once I even ran my father's car off the hard shoulder of the M4 at about ninety miles an hour. There was a dreadful row. The police came . . . Daddy was browned off something chronic. We *never* talk about that!"

Distracted, Storm took a quick, secret swipe at his nostril. He didn't want her to see him streaming. He wanted to be perfect in her sight. "Is that all it was? You got depressed?"

"No," she said, after a moment. "There was something else." She studied the water again and he studied her, surprised at how hard it was for her simply to speak to him, to tell, wondering at it. "There are these people. They call themselves resurrectionists. Most of them are just professors and dealers and so on. But some of them operate more like . . . like spies and suchlike, in secret. Basically, they try to find the artworks that were plundered during the war. They try to recover them, get them back to their rightful owners. There are still thousands of them, masterpieces, missing, lost. It can be dangerous getting at them, you know, because the people who deal in them tend to be . . . unsavory, of course. Fascists, neo-Nazis. Or just thieves." She looked at him directly, forcefully. As if it were an effort for her to do that too. And Storm kept wondering at it, thinking about it, how hard it was for her. "That night, after the party where you read that . . . that ghost story. One of them approached me. Outside. A man named Jon Bremer. He said that people had been killed because someone was trying to get *The Magi*—the Rhinehart panel, the one—"

"Yeah, yeah."

"And that he had arranged to have it auctioned, here, in

England, with the idea that it might draw the murderer out into the open."

Jacob Hope, Storm thought. The Iago guy. The resurrectionist had obviously been right. But he waited to hear what she would say.

"And then he was killed, Bremer, that same night. They found his body in the river." She inclined her head towards the water below. "And then my father told me we should buy the painting and I was in one of my black patches and I thought maybe he was responsible . . . for Bremer . . . for something. I don't know what I thought now."

Storm, pressing his arms close to himself against the cold, dug his hands deep in his pockets. Found, to his great relief, a crumpled Kleenex. Wiped his nose.

"Poor thing, you're freezing," said Sophia.

Shivering, he waved this off. "But did you know this guy, this Bremer?"

"No. I'd never met him before."

"And he just came to you? Out of nowhere like that? Because you're, like, a Rhinehart expert? What."

He knew at once it was the right question—he almost began to understand. He saw how she looked down, began to walk off, along the bridge, so that he had to follow behind her.

"No," she said. "No, the thing is . . ." She stopped. They stood in the wind face to face, hands in pockets, both shivering now. "The thing is, I've done a few favors for the resurrectionists before. They're so awfully . . . decent, you know. Germans mostly. Very earnest, idealistic. Trying to set things right about it all. They like to bring works into England, because the laws on ownership here are much more stringent. Most countries, if you buy something in good faith, it's more or less yours, but here, if the work is stolen, the original owner has the stronger claim. So sometimes, when things were difficult for them, I've offered to help because . . . well, because . . ."

And Storm finally got it. Spoke it without thinking, "Because you're trying to make up for your father," he said.

She made a noise. Looked up with her lips parted in surprise and her head faintly shaking. Made a whispery "Oh," of such relief and gratitude that it went right through him. He reached for her. Drew her to him, drew her head against his chest.

"You're right," he said. "I am freezing."

✦

"There's been nothing for years," she told him. "Nothing definite. But I've always known."

They were in the American Bar now, at the Savoy Hotel. Shoulder to shoulder in a corner banquette. He aching towards her, muzzy with her scent, with the light in her hair. In a confusion of guilt and desire: He had to tell her, to tell her the truth before it went too far. But he was still listening, thinking, trying to work it out, his Diet Coke undrunk before him.

The piano man was hammering out "If Love Were All" as if it were a march. But the piano was on the other side of the large room. It was quiet in their little section. The lights were soft. The waiters, the other diners were far away among the neat laquered tables and the huge stuffed chairs.

Sophia was gazing at nothing. Rolling a G&T between her palms, the ice melting. She seemed almost dazed, resigned to the flow of her story.

"I don't even know when I first heard them—the rumors," she said. "I can't remember anyone ever saying a word to me.

Not directly. It was just always in the air somehow. That Daddy had got rich off black-market art from the war. That everything we had was somehow . . . tainted, you know." She looked at him, added quickly: "There's never been anything dodgy on my watch. Not ever." Storm didn't let his gaze waver or darken. So she went on: "It's just . . . now and then . . . I don't know. I'd find an entry in some account I don't control and I'd start to wonder. Or . . ." He saw her mouth twist with distaste. "Once or twice, someone's approached me. At the gallery. Someone not quite . . . savory. Sometimes someone like that would speak to me . . . *familiarly,* if you see what I mean. As if they expected me to do something for them, as if it were understood." She pulled into herself as if a spider had walked across her hand. "No one's ever done it twice, though. No one." She glanced at him. He breathed her in. He loved her eyes: besieged, alone, unyielding. He thought he saw almost everything now. "You probably think I should have done something, said something. But one doesn't. In my family. And anyway . . ." It hurt him to see her face pull down, her mouth pull down convulsively. "It would've killed him. Any hint of scandal. Even just to know for certain that I knew . . . it would've killed him. I couldn't have stood it." She closed her eyes a moment. "I always took care of him, you see. After my mother died. My sister got married and my brother . . . well, of course, he wasn't interested. And Daddy was always so helpless about the little things. 'Where have I left my diary, Sophia?' 'Where is my dinner jacket?' I think it was the one area in which we could communicate, really. And then at the gallery . . ." She let her drink go, drummed the surface of the table softly with her fist. "It's all so long ago. The war. What does it matter now? I mean, at the end of the day—at the end of the day, it's only *art,* isn't it? It's only paintings he's dealing in. It isn't as if he ever killed anyone."

"Then why were you so ready to believe he was the guy the resurrectionists were looking for?" said Storm at once.

"I . . . Well, it was just . . ." She looked at him, pleading.

"Tell me what happened to your mom," he said.

Sophia covered her face with her hands.

✦

" 'My heart swims in blood because my legion of sins has made a monster of me in God's holy eyes,' " she said wistfully. "How did you know it was my favorite?"

"Hey, with catchy lyrics like that, how could I go wrong?" he said.

He had put the CD of Bach cantatas on her stereo. Had selected it from between the oversized art books on the tall shelves. Sophia sat on the sofa and watched him, her smile ironical, her eyes defenseless. Now, as the soprano sang the lilting recitative—*Mein herze schwimmt im blut weil mich der sunden brut in Gottes heilgen augen zum ungeheuer macht*—he was moving from window to window, drawing the curtains closed. Despite her smile, he understood that she was in his hands now, had given herself over to him. He moved around her flat as if he owned it. Crossing the airy room to the fireplace. Kneeling to work the cock, to touch a match to the gas nozzle, bringing a low flame up between the panels of William Morris tiles. And she sat still, watched. Defenseless.

"It's just like Laura—my sister—it's just like her to have put them all back," she said dryly, only a faint quaver of suppressed hysteria in her voice. "The CDs. I posted them to her before I . . . before I went to the gallery that night. She couldn't just return them, you know. Everything had to be just as it was, so we wouldn't have to talk about it."

"You want a drink, you want another gin?"

He was at the little cherrywood cabinet in the corner now. Trying to figure out the latchwork hidden in the Asian-style carvings.

"No. No, I've had enough," she said.

"Good. I can't figure out how to open this thing anyway."

The cushioned armchair was by the fire, across from the sofa, facing it. He went to it, sat there, to put some distance between them, to keep his mind as clear as he could. Still, she suddenly seemed awfully small and forlorn, all alone there on the sofa. Under the wide white wall between the windows. There was a large framed exhibition poster over her head. Two men looking off towards the moon, from a Berlin show of Caspar Friedrich. He thought of her picking the poster out, framing it, hanging it carefully. It made him sad for her, for her lonely life.

He leaned forward uncomfortably, working his hands together between his knees. "So . . ." he said.

"So she killed herself," said Sophia, and laughed. "Which was a bit of a bore."

"Ah, come on!" He went off so loudly, sat back so roughly in his chair that she winced. " 'A bit of a bore about dear Mother.' Gimme a break here, Sophie-girl. Christ."

"I'm sorry." She tried to regroup, re-present herself, but only managed to look so lost to him that he wanted to fling himself at her feet. "It's just we don't . . . I've never really spoken to anyone about it."

"Well, speak to me," he said, more gently. "Just tell me. Okay?"

Apparently it was—okay—because Sophie-girl did. Drifting into that dazy passivity again. Speaking as from a dream, the long-dammed current of the tale flowing out of her, seeming more alive than she.

"I hardly remember her. Except her smiling. Sitting in a chair, watching me play with Nanny in the garden. I know she loved the Grange, our house. Her family, her family history. It was very important to her. Fulfilling her responsibilities, you know. To our tenants, the community and so on. Everyone says she was just wonderful. Very warm, very charitable, kind. And fun—she liked shows and music. Oh, and the cinema—she adored Hollywood films. She had a wonderful sense of humor . . . You get left with that, traits like that, words . . . They don't really tell one very much, do they? But I have . . . I used to have photographs. And she seemed . . . There was something lovely there, generous. People say she balanced my father. I can imagine that. He's so definite about everything. Very old guard, very conservative. Peter—my brother—says Mother used to tease him about it, bring him out of it. I've tried to do that sometimes, but . . ." She shook her head, shook this off, still gazing away. She tried again to adopt a more businesslike tone, her usual tone. "Apparently people say she got very depressed after each of the children was born. What we would call post-natal depression nowadays. But back then . . . I don't know. I don't know why she did it, really. Killed herself. Sometimes I feel quite cross with her about it. I suppose that's awful of me."

She betrayed herself with a quick glance at him—a glance to see if he thought it was awful too.

"It's just natural, kid," he said. "It's just one of those things people feel."

The blood rushed to her cheeks. *Auf diese schmerzensreu fallt mir alsdenn dies trostwort bei,* the soprano sang on the stereo.

"As I say, no one will ever talk about it," Sophia went on. "Certainly not my father, and he's the only one who might know."

Storm rested his head on his hand, between thumb and forefinger, his elbow on the arm of his chair. He was growing careful now. He composed his expression carefully. He knew—he sensed at least—how exposed to him she was, how delicate. *If ever she is deprived of her monumental defenses, you will find her to be as fragile as bliss—and every bit as precious.* Storm even breathed carefully, tense. "But—what?" he said. "You think your mother's suicide might have had something to do with your father's . . . with his business dealings."

"No," she said quickly. Then, vaguely, she waved her hand. "I don't know. I really don't."

"But something made you think your father might be involved in the murder of the resurrection guy. Something about your mother's death. Is that right?"

She made a show of pulling herself together, straightening where she sat, straightening even her long neck, folding her hands calmly in her skirt. In a precise, clipped voice, she announced to him as from a height: "Well, I do have this memory. It sometimes gives me bad dreams."

He waited. Listened.

"When I was four or five," Sophia said. "Sometime before my mother died. I woke up one night in bed. Something woke me. I heard a noise. A ticking sound in the walls. *Tick-tick. Tick-tick.* Like that."

Storm's hand fell slowly away from his face, his arm sank slowly to the armrest.

"I called to my mother, but she didn't come," Sophia went on. "So I got up and went to find her. My parents' bedroom must have been empty. I don't remember. I just know I went downstairs, down a corridor, calling my mother, following that sound in the walls."

"Jesus," said Storm.

"Yes," she said. "It's just like the story you read, isn't it?" She continued in the same steady tone. "I'm rather confused about what happened next. I seem to remember I came to the last door, which is my father's study. When you read the story, I could almost see the book-lined room. But in my memory—I'm not sure—I also seem to remember furniture all around, old boxes, chairs, a big something-or-other in the middle of the room—just like a storeroom or something. And that ticking sound, getting louder. And as I came down the hall, the door to this storeroom opened, and there . . ." Her voice hitched. It seemed to annoy her—her eyes flashed. She pushed on. "And there—it's all very confusing. Sometimes I think it's not a memory at all, but just a dream. Or maybe I read the story once and remember that. But I think I saw my father, crouching over my mother, struggling with her. He was struggling with her—and then he stood up. And there he was, standing up over my mother, holding something in his hand, some kind of weapon. A knife, I think. And my mother . . . she was lying there, curled up on the floor. And they were both . . . covered . . . covered in blood."

She looked into his eyes so coolly then that he almost bought it, almost believed she was that far above things, that tough, that hard.

He shook his head. "But she hanged herself, didn't she?"

"That's what I'm told, that's what everyone says. But I don't remember anything after that night. My father saw me right away, sent me back to bed. I only had a glimpse and I'm not even sure of that. Nanny came and sat with me, I think.

I suppose it was all explained away somehow. I suppose I went back to sleep. I don't remember."

They sat silently. The music went on. *Ich, dein betrubtes kind, werf alle mein sund . . . in deinetiefe wunden . . .* Sophia sat as she had, erect, gazing at him, almost looking a challenge at him now that her story was finished. The gas fire bubbled. The windows bucked and rattled with the wind outside and the curtains stirred. To Storm, the room felt isolated, floating: they were in space, they were the last two people left anywhere.

He remained quiet. Instinct told him he couldn't take her too much farther. Even if he could, he didn't think he could stand that look she was giving him. Everything marbelized on the outside, everything immolated within.

But there was something wrong with her story, he knew. Something off, something missing.

"Have you ever heard of a man named Jacob Hope?" he asked after a while. "Or Iago? Or Saint Iago? Or anything like that?"

She thought, shook her head curtly. "No. What a strange name. No, never."

"That brooch, your mother's brooch. You know where she got it?"

A shrug. "I always assumed it was an heirloom. It's supposed to be some Norse symbol, I think. As I say, the family history was very important to her, and the Abingdons like to believe they have Viking blood. I think the symbol is meant to represent the secret word of hope that Odin whispered in the dead Baldr's ear."

"Yeah. Yeah, that was my first guess."

She smiled only faintly.

Storm slapped his hands down on his knees. "Well," he

said. "I guess now I know why you dropped that glass of wine, huh?"

"Yes, I suppose so," said Sophia. And she began to cry. "I'm sorry, I'm sorry," she said, trying to brush it away.

But he was over her, had her by the shoulders. Lifted her to her feet, held her. She squeezed her eyes shut, pressing her face to his shirt. "I remember thinking, just before I jumped off the railing in the gallery, I remember thinking how shabby it all seemed. My life, me. Everything. Just so shabby and miserable."

Und mir nach reu und leid nicht mehr die seligkeit noch auch sein herz verschliefst.

"Nothing about you is shabby and miserable," said Richard Storm. "Not to me."

✦

She was right: she was no good at sex. Stiff as a board, dry as a bone. And frantic and apologetic and distrustful of him all at the same time, which tended to make things worse and worse.

But by the happiest coincidence, this precise situation seemed to bring out two of Richard Storm's most appealing character traits. For one thing, he was capable of displaying almost boundless patience and good nature with people he truly liked, women especially. He'd been born like that probably, but formative years of dealing with a fractious, theatrical and yet adorable mother had honed this feature of his personality to a skill. Of course, even for him, patience wasn't particularly easy just then. Sophia was even better looking with her clothes off. Lying on her bed on her back, with her breasts spilling wide. Her face turned up to him, her eyes panicky and entreating. Her skin may have felt frosty to her, but it was burning under his hand, burning. And she had one white knee bent, parting her legs to him, a sight that made him so hard he was afraid he might go off like a rocket and end up three blocks away. He had been dreaming of taking her—against a wall, on the floor, over a chair—a little knockabout passion, a little ripping of clothes, a little Brando action from *Last Tango in Paris*. He wanted to send her richocheting off the stars like a pinball. *It's never been like that for me before, Richard!* He'd had the whole thing pretty well worked out in his mind.

But that was the other thing about him: his nature, his business, a not altogether inattentive eye on the world, had combined long ago to convince him of the important fact that things almost never shake out the way they do in the movies. He scoped the real lie of the land pretty quickly. He held her, stroked her, kissed her. He cooed to her long after the inner powers were shrieking for him to morph into a human jackhammer. And in the end, with jazzman fingers and a serpent's tongue—and with a little bit of the gunk from a diaphragm that looked like it hadn't been used since 1947—he was delighted just to slip inside her with a semblance of sweetness and ease. Which is where he wanted to be when he told her he loved her. Which he did, kissing her panicky eyes till they softened, letting great handfuls of that raven black hair cascade from his grip onto her valentine cheeks. Drawing from her, finally, some small signs, at least, of spontaneous pleasure. Which would serve for now. Which was enough.

✦

Spent, of course, he was almost instantly appalled. He was still in her, still on her. She was clinging to him. He was caressing her face. There was light in her brown eyes and she was smiling as if she thought she had done something exceptionally clever. She was even glancing coyly at him. Mata Hari suddenly. Marilyn Monroe. The femme fatale of the universe. He adored her.

And he was appalled that he had let things come this far without confessing to her, without telling her how short, how terrible their time was bound to be.

Storm buried his face in Sophia's hair, sick with himself and sick with love. He closed his eyes and breathed in her scent and wanted this to be what the world was like forever. Maybe it would turn out all right somehow, he thought. Maybe the doctors had been wrong. It could've been one of those farcical mistakes. Like *Send Me No Flowers,* with Rock Hudson and Doris Day. He felt fine. He felt good, in fact. Since that one night all those weeks ago. There'd been nothing. Some headaches. Which anyone could have. A little weakness in his left arm—but only sometimes, only off and on. And other than that, he was terrific. Great. Excellente, Clemente. Life wouldn't make sense otherwise. God wasn't going to teach him to feel like this for someone, make someone so dear to him, and then just snuff him out. Was He? Come on. Not a swell guy like God.

Sophia let her arms fall to the mattress on either side of him. "Gosh, I'm so *hungry*," she said. She clasped him again. Hummed. "Was that all right? Was it all right for you? Gosh, I've never felt so *hungry*."

His heart swam in blood because his legion of sins had made him a monster in God's holy eyes.

Or, as he put it to himself, *Oh, Magoo, you are such a shmuck.*

7 Now at about the same time Storm and Sophia were starting back across Waterloo Bridge, as they were heading for their drink in the Savoy Hotel bar, the taxi numbered 331 was driving down the Strand past the hotel's entrance. With the scarred man squinting his piggy eyes at the windscreen, the cab chugged along in the thick traffic without stopping. Just ahead, teeth bared, the city's griffin loomed rampant on its pedestal. Harper Albright looked out at it from the cab's backseat.

She clutched her dragon stick tighter with both hands. Pressed her lips against her knuckles, her lips trembling, her knuckles white. Here, where the West End became the City, where the flash and flicker of theaters gave way to the dimmer, narrower canyons of Fleet Street, she had her last notion of escape. She might rap on the cab's windows, she thought. She might gesticulate at the thinning crowds of passersby, or at the other drivers edging along the clogged thoroughfare. It would be a long shot, given the noise of traffic, given the nature of cities. And it would be a risky business, given the death-rays of vengeance beaming out of the eyes that now and then glanced at her in the cab's rearview mirror. She had no doubt the driver remembered that notch she had made upon his chin with her sword. He was just looking for an excuse to even the score.

But once they left the crowds behind, once they entered the deserted City streets, her last chance would be over. She would be at the mercy of her enemies. She knew it was now or never.

And she just sat there. Hunched over her stick. Lip-gnawing her knuckles. Afraid—melting inside with fear—but silent, unresisting.

The cab went on, towards the canyons.

What a stubborn old woman she was. She could've kicked herself for it. But the fact was she had to satisfy her curiosity. It was that more than anything that held her there. She had to know what was going to happen next.

Of all the questions left unanswered about Iago—of all the thousand questions—the greatest was this: Why hadn't he killed her yet? Out of pique if nothing else. Or in his determination to keep her from finding the very manuscript she now had hidden inside her cape. Why the warnings, why the threats? Why not just snuff her out? Her own uncomfortable suspicions on the matter tantalized her. The desire to confirm or disprove them—the desire to discover any answer at all—the desire simply to know more—were such powerful drives in her that she felt there was no overcoming them. This imprisonment in a London cab, this drive to nowhere, to somewhere: it felt to her almost like fate.

An aggravating business. It angered her. Here she was, being sucked into a vortex, being carried down and down into certain danger, and her most powerful emotion—aside from this liquifying fear—her most powerful emotion was *anticipation*. Which was confused in her mind with that other, hateful anticipation: the anticipation she had felt in the old days at the prospect of seeing him again.

What a foolish old woman. She really could have kicked herself. She clutched her stick, gnawed her knuckles, angry. Afraid. Excited.

Then, to her surprise, the cab pulled over. Stopped. Just on the far side of the griffin, still within sight of the West End crowds behind it. The movement wrenched her from so deep a study that for a moment she didn't recognize the place. She saw the scarred driver give a glance to the heavyset newsie standing just outside on the pavement. The newsie, in turn, glanced at two ancient and enormous iron doors set in the wall behind him, shut tight.

The driver turned in his seat. Leered at her.

"Here you go, darling. Just what you asked for. The end of the world."

The newsie darted forward. Yanked the door open. Stuck his horny hand in at her. "Right this way, love." He was leering too, leering down at her.

"And none of that Smith and Sons nonsense," said the driver with a rueful nod at her stick. "It won't help you anyway. It's too late for all that now."

"I should've pinned you like a bug when I had the chance," Harper grumbled. But she slid across the seat towards the open door.

She'd be damned if she'd take the newsie's hand. She worked her way out herself. And when he touched her shoulder, she sloughed him off with a vehement shrug. Out in the open air, she smoothed and straightened herself. The newsie hovered near her. Tried to take her elbow. She glowered him back. "I'll break those sausagy fingers if they touch me again."

He scowled, but kept away. Contented himself with a rough gesture at the iron doors.

"All right, all right," she groused.

Hoisting her satchel strap over her shoulder, she waddled, muttering, towards the wall. Slowly, as if magically, the doors opened inward at her approach.

Harper's teeth clamped, her breath caught as the corridor beyond was revealed to her. She saw a downward slope through a constricted close. She had a glimpse through windblown sycamore branches of the west porch entry to the church of the Knights Templar. She knew where she was now. The entrance to the Inner Temple Court.

The newsie dropped back behind her. She passed under the entryway. The great doors swung shut.

She was alone in the dark alley with the damp night wind.

She halted. Harrumphed. Looked around her. Sneered angrily at the descending passage. But this was all bravado, in case anyone was watching. If she'd been melting with fear in the cab, she was practically a puddle now. It was another long moment before she could bring herself to head down the slope to whatever lay below.

The wind rose higher, a hoarse moan of warning between the walls on either side of her. Just what she needed, just what the scene required to feel really terrifying. But she moved on, regardless, her squat figure pulled into itself, her stick stabbing the pavement as if she would drive it right through the stone, her Borsalino bowed against the cold.

When she glanced up, she saw the Temple Church slowly moving into view from behind the alley's corner, through the trees.

The Knights Templar—guardians of Jerusalem after the Crusaders took it, after they slaughtered its paynims and established the rule of the armies of the Prince of Peace; protectors, in legend, of the Holy Grail; pattern of the Teutonic Knights of Germany and rival of the Knights Hospitalers; soldiers, bankers, politicians; and finally, outcasts accused of Satanism and infanticide; disbanded, tortured, burned at the stake: they had built this church in 1185, some sixty-five years after their inception. Its round tower—one of only five round church towers in England—was modeled on Jerusalem's Church of the Holy Sepulchre.

Its castellated crown lowered blackly against the dull sky as Harper moved under it.

And there was more of the eerie wind business—the tree branches whispering and chattering all around her. And there were the ancient coffins oddly shimmering at the tower's base. And there was the western porch of the church right before her, its obscure entryway: a chiseled Norman tympanum receding to the shut door. That recessive shape seemed to her to give a tide to the darkness, a tide that was dragging her in. She had again that irritating sense that she had come to this place helplessly, in answer to an over-powering summons. She had an awful feeling that everything to come was expected, had been expected for a long time, forever.

She felt sickened—but not surprised—when she heard a muffled thud as of a body dropping, and the heavy church door began to swing open.

She stopped before the archway. Steeled herself, squared her shoulders. The door continued to swing back until the interior of the church—or, that is, the utterly lightless murk of its interior—was displayed before her.

"You always did love an effect," she muttered to no one between her teeth.

Then, her stick clicking on the stone, she stepped under the arch. Staring blankly ahead, she hobbled under the tympanum. She entered the church.

At once, the door swung to behind her, shut with an echoing boom. She'd been expecting that, but it didn't matter, she couldn't help herself: her whole body went so tense it thrummed. Now the dark was complete. It surrounded her. She could see absolutely nothing. Could only feel the church's dank and stony atmosphere. Could only smell—

what was it?—something fetid and hot, something panting, dangerous, close. He was there. With her. She knew it. Circling her, predatory. She was so frightened she began to shiver. She wanted to shout out in fury: *This is unworthy of you!* But she didn't. She wouldn't give him the satisfaction. And anyway, it was nonsense: this was right in his line.

"You know, you remind me, in some ways, of the Pacific salmon," he said from directly behind her.

Again, she couldn't help it—she gasped, startled. She spun towards his voice.

"I think I must've taught you about the Pacific salmon. I always took great pains over your education, as I'm sure you remember." He was already moving on, moving along the circular walls. Harper turned where she stood, trying to follow the sound of his voice. "Really, it's an amazing creature. The salmon. It smells its way out of the ocean, upriver. Smells its way hundreds of miles, against the tide, against all obstacles. Finally comes back to its home waters, its headwaters, the place where it was spawned. And there it mates—and then it dies."

His voice ceased. Harper was still turning in her place to follow him. But he was playing with her. When he spoke again, he was once more behind her.

"What I mean is, it's an awfully long way to travel for love—and then death. Isn't it? But then the salmon can't help itself. I think an instinct for self-destruction must be built into the nature of its desire. That's what I'm getting at: some people are like that too. Maybe most people. You, for instance, come after me and after me because you can't resist me, can you? Even knowing that I'm going to kill you. Is that a labored metaphor? It just popped into my mind."

"A little. It's a little labored." Harper had to moisten her lips before she could say any more. "But since we're in it, I do seem to recall that the salmon, just before it dies, grows fangs to fight with."

He laughed happily. "You do remember." And he lit a match.

An explosion of red blindness. Her hand flew up. Then, shadowy vision came seeping in from the edges . . . Grotesque stone heads sculpted on the encircling arcade. A demon, a satyr, a dead-eyed king. Staring at her from between the arches' columns. A tortured soul with a beast's jaws clamped to him. A twisted nose-picker, a grieving peasant. Head after Gothic head. And now, the light dwindling, Harper, lowering her eyes against the glare, saw the effigies of dead crusaders at her feet.

And then she looked up at Iago.

He was holding the match to a candle wick now, looking from the flame to her, smiling wryly. And the moment she saw his face in the yellow glow, she remembered what it was about him.

He was not only a handsome man, with his slim, straight figure in the white suit, his long black hair, his sharply faceted face and those smoky, hypnotic eyes. There was something else. A certain unbridled, animal vitality, a pent energy in every movement he made; a kind of ease and confidence; a fluid comfort in his own skin. He was all alive, and the world sat so lightly on him.

It was an attractive quality. Standing there in the respiring flame light, Harper had to fight to remember what he'd looked like when she'd seen him last. That night after she'd crept from her bed in the cult's compound. After she'd pushed the branches aside and peered into the clearing.

There he'd stood. In the mists of the Argentine jungle, in the flare of the bonfire. His acolytes chanting. The mother shrieking through her gag. His own face mad, exalted, as he lifted the curved blade. And the child lying trustingly on the altar before him. His own child.

Twenty-five years she had hunted him for that. She had to remember it now.

The candle caught. He held it up. He held it out to her with one green-gloved hand, drawing his long hair clear of his cheek with the other. He moved the flame to and fro slowly in front of her, examining her minutely, as if she were some statue he had discovered in a cave. She stood like a statue, clutching her stick—so tightly that the ears of the dragon bit into her hand. But she shrank inwardly, wishing to hide herself under her hat, behind her glasses. She knew what he was seeing—every sag, every wrinkle, every premature, flaccid pouch of flesh.

"Oh, Harper," he said at last. "You've grown so old."

And it stung her. In spite of everything. Still, she managed to answer him with a frown like granite thunder. "It's been twenty-five years."

"Oh yes, I know, but really." He pursed his lips. "You've gotten all . . . grim and wrinkly."

"Ah. Well."

"That wasn't necessary."

"I'm afraid it was."

He laughed. "Because of me, you mean."

"Yes."

"Poor baby. All because I showed you who you are."

"You showed me who I could be, Jacob, who I might be," Harper said. "You showed me who *you* are."

He laughed again. And stretched, spreading his arms like

Christ. The candle in his hand lifted a dim, yellow dome of light over the church's round: the gaping sculpted heads; the effigies in their tormented postures on the floor.

Stretched like that, he resumed pacing gracefully around her, looking her up and down, his tongue in his cheek.

"Who I am," he repeated slowly. "But really, darling— you always knew who I was."

"No," she tried to say, but the word caught in her throat.

"You did," he said. "You knew. And yet I seem to recall I was your lover."

Harper forced herself to stand still as he circled. The glow of the candle passed and faded from before her. He was behind her now, out of sight. It made the skin prickle on the back of her neck. She had to fight to keep her exterior steady and stern as her insides churned, molten.

"I—was—your—lover," he insisted.

"If that's what you call love," she shot back.

He stopped at last, beside her. Just beside her. She felt his breath on her cheek. Hot, wet, rank. A panther's breath. He went on in the same easy, ironical tone.

"You're right," he said. "Let's not mince words. I was your master. Wasn't I?"

Harper's lips worked as she tried to swallow her distaste.

"I mastered you, Harper," he continued softly. "I mastered you, and then you begged me to master you again. I remember the sound of your voice as you begged me."

The words burst from her. "I was young."

"Not that young."

"And half insane."

"Only half."

"It was a long time ago, Jacob."

"Not that long, really. You remember it too. I can see you

do. You remember it in your flesh. Don't you?"

She barely turned her head towards him. Barely lifted one corner of her mouth. She was afraid she would start to quake. "I remember. Yes."

"And that's why you can't stay away from me. Even if it's only to feel my hands on your throat."

"You know why I've come after you," she said.

He rolled his eyes. "Oh yeah. I forgot. The children. The dear, dead little children. Tell yourself that's the reason."

"That is the reason."

"For this obsession? For this compulsion to irritate me?"

"To destroy you, Jacob, actually. Yes."

He let out a breath, threw up a hand. She flinched away from it. But it was only a gesture of mild frustration, the gesture of a teacher with a dense student. "You know, dear, I really did teach you to be more honest with yourself than that. I showed you how to plumb the ugly depths, didn't I?"

"Yes."

"But you're going to stand there looking like my maiden aunt and tell me that you gave your life, you wasted your prime, you wore away your beauty, trailing after me—all because you cared so very, very deeply for a few armloads of dead babies?

"Yes."

"Oh, I don't think so, sweetie."

She couldn't hold it down any longer: a painful shudder went through her, head to toe. She had forgotten the weakness—the limp, physical weakness—that invaded her whenever he came this close.

No, she had not forgotten. She had fought to believe it was a thing of the past.

"Look at you," he whispered. "Harper. Trembling. Look at you."

She made a gulping noise. Rapped her stick convulsively upon the stone. "I . . ." she said. She took a breath. "I am not the woman I was, Jacob."

"Oh no? Really? Then why are you here?"

He came swinging around in front of her. She could see him in the candlelight with his head tilted to one side, his smile gleeful, his black eyes smoky and seductive. He looked so vital to her, so relaxed, that she began to feel like a fusty old crone just standing there, frowning at him like this.

But she stood there. Frowned at him. And swallowed hard. "What do you want me to say?" she asked hoarsely. "You're the philosopher, Jacob, not me. I only know . . ." She shook her head.

"What?" he said, smiling. "What do you know?"

"I know my spirit opposes you."

"Your spirit! Oh my!"

"And not just my spirit."

"Dear, dear. What more?"

"All of it," she barked. "All of it opposes you. The . . ." She groped for words. "Oh, all right. The Everlasting Thing."

Jacob Hope guffawed at her. Threw back his head, one hand on his belly, the other—the one holding the candle—held to his brow. Laughed and laughed, staggering where he stood, his feet among the dead crusaders. Then he shook his head. He daubed the corner of his eye. He wound down to a low chuckle.

And then—suddenly—he roared at her: *"For Christ's sake, woman—look!"*

The curtain of his black hair crackled and fizzed as he

held the candle up to his own face. The flame seemed to rise along his skin in a caress. The murky depths of his eyes seemed to turn like slow Catherine wheels. Her own image in them seemed to turn like Catherine.

She looked. And she saw that what she feared was true. What she had suspected since Storm had described him to her. It was impossible to deny it now.

He was a man of thirty—of thirty-five at most. As he had always been. As he had been the day she met him.

In all these years, he had not aged a single hour.

"I *am* the Everlasting Thing," he said. "I feed on the marrow of time. I was here before the oceans turned black with life, and when the deserts are white with death I will remain. And you're really starting to get up my nose, Harper," he went on in his normal tone. "So maybe you ought to reconsider your position."

Whoosh —he blew out the candle. Harper hissed, recoiling, as the inky air clamped over her. There was only his voice again now; that harsh breath; that feral smell. The dark.

"Oh, Harper, Harper, Harper. You really can piss me off at times. I swear, after Argentina, I wanted to kill you. Oh . . ."

In that blackness, he made a noise, a low growly hum, a sound of such sensual hunger that she felt certain he was going to kill her right now.

But he went on: "That's just the sort of debilitating woman you are, you know. You made me doubt my own destiny. Almost. But—but, but—I still had the Grail. The blue flower, the blue stone. I still had more than enough of it, and that's what brought me to my senses. I mean, when a fellow just buys something like that—just picks it up wandering through a Moroccan bazaar—that's not just chance, that can't just be chance. Whatever you say. 'There will arise one who will become the eternal creature.' That was the prophecy. So, in spite of what you managed to do to me, I knew I'd been chosen. I *knew* that. And I lay low." A tone of self-congratulation had entered his voice. He was bragging to her, Harper realized. "I lay low. Patience, patience. And sure enough, just five years later, in a little place off the Edgware Road—on the road to Damascus, Harper—like a flash: a spilled soda, and the next stage was given to me. The trail of stories. Oh, I know you know. Well, let me tell you, darling, it's been twenty years. I had to wait twenty years before I could follow that trail to its end. Patience, patience, though my time ran short. And just when things were getting desperate, just at the brink of disaster, the wall came tumbling down and my destiny was all before me again. All before me. And now—again—*you* . . . !"

She was scorched by the word. He must've leaned within inches of her. Even in darkness so complete, she thought she could make out the glint of his stare. "I can see how far you've come on the same slender thread. And well, why not? I taught you everything you know, didn't I? I'm proud of you, old girl. I admire you for it. In fact, I admire you so much that if I thought for a second one chance remained, that even one copy of the final text was still in existence, so help me, so help me, I would give myself the pleasure: I would grind your bones to make my bread."

Again, his breath burned her. Her hand spasmed, jerked, her stick tip ticking twice on the stone. *Why didn't he? Why didn't he just do it?* In spite of everything, her curiosity almost made her ask aloud. But she mustn't. It might tempt him. It might give him ideas. For the sake of her life, she must force herself to keep silent.

It seemed to provoke him. He snarled: "You think I can't?"

"Why don't you?" she blurted out. What a foolish, foolish old woman. "Why don't you just do it? Why don't you just kill me?"

He drew away. The heat of his breath diminished, at least. But no, he had retreated from her, she could feel it. She stood where she was, staring after him, seeing nothing. She tried to swallow, but her throat was dry as dust.

"It's the boy, isn't it?" she said softly. "You want the boy. Our boy. You need him somehow. Not just his life. You need him with you, you need him on your side. That's it, isn't it? Isn't it, Jacob?" He made no answer. Where was he? She couldn't tell. She took an unsteady step forward, called after him in the darkness. "If you killed me, he would know. He would know it was you. If I were hit by a car, by lightning, drowned in the Thames—if I died in my sleep— he would still know who was to blame. And it's the one thing he would never forgive you for. It's the one thing that would keep him away from you forever. You don't want to make me a martyr to him. You need him on your side. Isn't that it? Isn't it?"

But aside from her own frightened wheezing, there was no noise in the round, in the church anywhere.

"Jacob?"

Nothing. Nothing she could hear or see. And yet . . . And yet, the silence had a quality of motion. The emptiness, the blackness had a life. She could feel it, in the prickpoints of her skin, in the warp of her nerves. He was still there. He was stalking, circling around her. Closing in on her. There were shuffling footfalls on the stone—she could hear them. Coming towards her. He was closer with every moment.

Gripping that curved knife she had seen in the jungle. Lifting it. She could hear the swishing upswing of the blade.

"Jacob!" she cried again, in terror this time, her voice trembling. The dragon stick fell from her slack fingers. It clattered on the stones. She grabbed her satchel, yanked it open. Drove her hand in, fumbling around. What a mess. She felt her glasses case. Her compact. A lipstick. Some tissues. Some receipts. Her keys. Half a Twix bar. Then her matches—she found them—she seized the box. Drew it out, the satchel dropping free on its strap. She heard herself panting as she fumbled for a stick. She struck it on her thumb. Again, there was the blinding flame. The shadows scrambling like rats. The round of the church. The staring heads on every side. The stone bodies of the knights at her feet. The long nave. The far altar, the faint glow of stained glass above . . .

But empty, all of it, otherwise. The entire place. Utterly empty. Except for her.

"Crikey," she whispered.

And she grabbed her stick and got the hell out of there.

8   Weary, weary, weary, she reached home. Hung up her hat, her cape. Climbed the stairs. She had to rest halfway, her hand upon the banister, her head against the wall. Then she climbed on.

She reached the third floor landing. Paused again. Peeked in through Bernard's half-opened door. She watched the factotum sleeping for a moment. She allowed an unwonted expression of tenderness to cross her face.

Bernard had placed a bottle of Gilbey's by his bed. He

had filled his room with marijuana smoke and left a pile of snuffed-out roaches in the ashtray. It was childish of him; he confessed as much to himself. But it was such a rare thing for him to sleep in his own bed that he feared it would betray how worried he had been for her, how frightened he had been.

So he had set the scene. Too much alcohol, too much dope. The television on at the foot of the bed, the sound off, the images glimmering. And he positioned himself like Chatterton in the painting: lying atop the covers fully dressed, one arm dangling decadently over the side. His mouth was open, his eyes were closed, his faint snore was almost convincing. Through slightly parted lids, he watched Harper as she paused, as she watched him. He saw the uncharacteristic emotion in her expression. Saw the heaviness too, the savage work of gravity on her exhausted features. Without stirring from where he lay, but with an undeniable little thrill of terror and excitement, he thought, *She's seen him!*

Then Harper passed on, out of his view.

She went up the stairs again, to her own room. An attic cell. A cupboard, stacked with books, littered with loose papers, pictures. A bed, a rocking chair. One small window on the night sky. Divested of her stick, her satchel, she stooped, grunting, to light the gas fire. Sighing, she sank into her rocker before the feeble blue flame.

She set the chair into motion. She had had some vague idea of sobbing her heart out once she'd reached the privacy of her home. Sobbing for her sins, for her weakness, for her misspent life. But she found she couldn't be bothered. She was too tired. The grief was too deep for tears. And anyway, she had work to do before she could get to sleep.

She bent to drag her satchel to her. Brought out her pipe,

her baccy. Brought out the envelope that she had transferred from the pocket of her cape. Brought out the manuscript and placed it on her skirted lap.

Well, at least he wasn't infallible, she thought with some small satisfaction. He had reckoned every copy was destroyed. He hadn't counted on the ghost of M. R. James.

She adjusted her glasses. She chomped her pipe. Torched the skulltop. Primed the flame. Rocked and smoked awhile, Iago's words reverberating in her mind. *I was here before the oceans turned black with life, and when the deserts are white with death I will remain.* Strange words. Overwrought. Silly. And yet eerily familiar somehow.

The room was quiet but for the rhythmic shifting of the rocker's joins: *tick-tick, tick-tick.*

The clockwork of history, Harper thought.

And she began to read.

VII

THE MONK'S
CONFESSION

I AM DYING. There can be no mistake. The same lines of discoloration that heralded the demise of the others have now appeared on me, running from my knuckles to my wrist on my right side, from my knuckles all the way to my elbow on my left. On both sides, they are creeping slowly up my arms. Having witnessed the end of my two companions in this undertaking, I can have little doubt of what is waiting for me: the torment, the living decay, the insanity of remorse. For William and Anselm, the terrible process overtook them within five years of the beginning of our venture. Simple arithmetic killed them, as a little consideration might have told us that it would. I only am escaped alone to tell this because of a talent for deceit and a practiced way with women, and through the complicity of one who shall remain nameless lest his body be exhumed and cast out of holy ground.

It is all one now, however. What I had thought was deliverance has only been delay. It will not be long before the thing is fully upon me. There is no time left to satisfy the hunger of the stone. There would be no time, even if I had the spirit for it, which I no longer have.

Nor can I pray. I cannot unburden myself before the Lord. So great is the love of Christ that I fear He might forgive me. I could not abide that: it will take an eternity of damnation to cleanse my soul of these sins.

Instead, I make this addendum to my chronicle of Belham Abbey. I record what I cannot confess.

✦

It is now almost forty years since the people of Belham burned the town's Jews. It was done in the time of the first King Henry. The Jews had taken refuge in the abbey's infirmary chapel as they had once before in past troubles. This time, however, the people were so enraged against them that even the law of sanctuary could not restrain them. Leaders of the mob bolted the chapel's doors and hurled brands in through the windows, setting the building on fire.

Though most of the monks were at supper on the far side of the grounds, we were well aware of the disturbance. As the flames rose, I myself could hear the shouts of the men trapped within, the shrieking of the women, the children crying. It was, however, a long time before Anselm sent a novice to beat the board and summon us to help.

By then, the fire was raging so fiercely that the infirmary's iron doors glowed red at the edges. Many of us ran to fetch water from the rain tank and even from the clock. But when the cold water hit the burning building, the very stones cracked and collapsed so that, in the end, no more was left of the structure than a single scorched and crumbling wedge of wall. The bodies within had been reduced to charred flesh and bones; skulls that seemed frozen in their death cries.

And all this occurred because I had told a story, a tale I invented in my desperation to save my own life. I had spread it among the people that it was the Jews who had murdered the infant, that it was they who were responsible for the little body that had recently been discovered near the abbey grounds. I said the Jews had sacrificed the babe. I concocted an arcane rite, invented enough details to make it sound convincing. I said the Jews had stabbed the child and used his blood to make their Paschal bread: an abominably distorted version of the mass. I made it all very believable.

And the story slowly spread until the people rose up in a mob and took their vengeance in the chapel.

By then, of course, poor Annie was too far gone in madness to convince anyone of the truth.

✦

For weeks before the child was found, Annie had wandered the streets, babbling about the murder. She said she heard the baby tapping at the earth above his secret grave, tapping and tapping night and day. She would roam the village in her rags, her hair hanging down around her face in filthy tangles. Her eyes had a wide, white, almost mystical aspect. She would seize the arm of any passerby who would stop for her.

"Listen!" she would whisper. "Tick-tick. Tick-tick. Hear him? Hear him? He is trying to get out. He is trying to come back to me."

Anselm, William and I suffered agonies of suspense for fear that someone might actually pay heed to her.

In the end, as it will, disaster came like a thief in the night. We monks departed mass one morning shortly after Easter, to find a large crowd had gathered just beyond the cemetery garth, where the walls had been undergoing repair. I was sent to investigate—in what state of guilty tension I cannot describe—and there found many of the local farmhands clustered in a murmuring circle. I pushed my way through and what I saw brought my heart into my mouth.

There was Annie, lying on the ground half naked. She had torn her rags from her body with her clawed hands. Her long nails were black with dirt. Her fingertips were bleeding.

She had dug up the infant's body.

Because the builders had been mixing mortar there, the earth was rich with lime. The child was thus in an advanced state of decay. And yet, Annie clutched the rotting thing to her bare bosom as if it still lived and might take nourishment.

"You see? You see?" she cried up at the horrified farmers. "He was trying to get out. Tick-tick, tick-tick. I heard him. He was trying to come back to me all along."

As I looked from her wild face to the faces staring down at her, I knew I must act at once. Thus I began to spread my story about the plot of the Jews.

✦

It was some months prior to this that the murder of the child was first proposed to me. Anselm himself summoned me from my bed in the hour after Lauds and led me without a word across the silent cloisters to his lodging. There, seated at a table in one corner, was a man I had never seen before. He was outfitted as a brother of the

Knights Templar, of whom I had then only heard reports from the pilgrims returning from outremer. But I recognized the red mantle and the gules cross blazoned on his robe.

Before him, on the abbot's table, was a small brazier with a cauldron set upon it. The steam from the boiling liquid within wreathed the templar's face in mist, the glow of the coals gave a fiery cast to his long, melancholy features. This was my first view of William, who had but lately returned from Jerusalem.

As I make no confession, I make no excuses either. The moment the three of us were seated at the table, I knew it was a dark business. The fact was revealed by our lowered voices and huddled postures, our faces leaning together over the steaming cauldron. The mist with its thick, sour smell and the unholy glow rising around us seemed to me even then the visible token—the aura—of a bloody conspiracy.

The blacks of William's eyes were gleaming as he pressed in towards me. "Tell me," he murmured in his low, oily tone. "Why did you become a monk?"

I explained briefly that I had been brought to the abbey in my eighth year, had been raised and schooled there and had known little else.

"And yet you received the tonsure as a man," he said. "You freely took the vows of poverty and of obedience."

"I did," I said.

"And of chastity," said he.

I averted my eyes from him. "Of chastity too."

"A life dedicated to labor and prayer. In the hope surely of an eternal life of joy hereafter."

"It is written that whosoever believeth in Him should not perish but have everlasting life," I replied cautiously.

At this, William only nodded.

Using a pair of tongs, the Templar now lifted the cauldron from the brazier and set it aside on the table to cool. For the first time, I noticed that a length of twine had been dipped into the cauldron, one end submerged in the bubbling liquid, the other hanging over the lip of the pot. From time to time, William pinched one end of the string in his fingers and tugged on it gently, as if bobbing a line to tempt a fish.

"You dedicate your life on earth to Christ because he offers you an endless life hereafter," he said. "That is the chief reason, is it not?" He toyed with the twine as the cauldron cooled. He smiled at me. "But what if I myself could promise you as much—not on faith but in truth, not hereafter but here and now?"

I glanced from William to Anselm, who watched us eagerly. "Promise me . . . ?" I asked.

"That you should not perish, but have life everlasting," the crusader said softly. "If I should offer you the power of Christ's Sangreal and, as I believe, the secret of his resurrection, for your own use. If there were no prayers required, no sacrifice, if you need not wake to Matins and toil to Vespers and Compline. If I offered you an eternal joy not of hosannas but of the rich, round women of the earth, its wine, its powers, its free fresh air. Whom then would you serve, brother?"

I looked again from him to the abbot, from Anselm back to him. I was about to recite on the subject of the Last Judgement, which is to all men no matter how long their earthly lives.

But it was clear that this was no place for such hypocrisy. I said nothing. Indeed, my tongue felt as if it had turned to sand as I realized for a fact what I had until then only suspected: that my own corruption was but a dram of the poison that had eaten into the abbey's very heart.

When he saw that I would make no answer, William smiled again. Again, he lifted the twine that ran into the cauldron. He lifted it this time until it came clear of the boiling mixture. He held it up before my eyes and I saw, through the mist, that a chain of bluish crystal had formed around it, and clung to it. Its facets grew out on every side like the petals of a blossom.

"This is the 'blue flower,'" he said. "The blue stone: the sangreal. The formula for the making of it was given to me by a paynim magician in the Holy City. It was the ransom for his life. First, the ingredients are heated together, and then allowed to cool and crystallize. Then, a bit of the crystal is dissolved again in water—just the littlest bit. And this creates a medicinal fluid. Immersion in that fluid once every six months so restores the natural substances of the flesh that it forestalls the process of ageing. The body—this body—your body—can be made essentially . . . deathless."

I stood up with such violence that the bench I had been sitting on overbalanced and fell to the floor behind me. Even in the cold of night, I felt the sweat break out all over my skin. I felt my heart beating powerfully against my ribs.

"This is the devil's work," I said. "Why have you brought this to me?" My mind raced in search of an answer, found none. "Why have you brought this to me?"

"Sit down, sit down," Anselm muttered. He leaned over, righted the bench that had fallen.

Slowly I sank into my seat again.

The red light of the coals seemed to grow brighter on William's features as he smiled. His eyes shifted to Anselm once and Anselm nodded.

"The stone is only part of the elixir," William said, so softly I had to lean closer to hear him. "In order for us to test its efficacy—we require one ingredient more."

✦

One ingredient more.

I will not attempt to mitigate my crime by detailing the struggle with my conscience that followed that conversation. The truth is, no matter what pangs I suffered, no matter what qualms arose, one thought from the beginning burned uppermost in my mind. Life! Eternal life! Eternal youth! With such a gift on offer, what did conscience matter? What was conscience in any event but the fear of punishment after death? The threat of death removed, the threat of Hell postponed forever, what power had conscience? What power had God? With life and youth guaranteed, I would be as a God myself, able to shrug off the petty fears and limitations of humanity. I would be free to indulge whatever desires, seize whatever prizes appealed to me, without terror or remorse.

All this—an eternity of pleasure—in exchange for just one ingredient more.

And so I went to see mad Annie.

It was painfully easy to bring her in on the scheme. Even then the woman was so simple and deranged that she was really little better than an animal. Often, in the days of my passion for her, she would present herself to me exactly as an animal would: dropping to all fours the moment I approached her, hiking her shift to her waist, grunting, drooling. On her, I had satisfied the cravings so long denied, content that she was too debased to feel an ordinary woman's affection or shame, assured that she would never be believed if she decided to reveal the truth. It seemed a perfect arrangement.

Until, one day, I realized she was with child.

Fearing that her condition would betray me, that her chants and babblings would reveal what it was becoming impossible to deny, I decided to take precautions. I had arranged for her to be secreted in the forest, in the home of a cunning woman with whom I had had some previous dealings. It was there I went to see her now.

By this time, Annie was very near being brought to bed, yet I suspect she still only half understood what was happening to her. When I explained what was to be done, she agreed to it instantly—distantly, as one speaking from a dream.

It was a distasteful meeting, but necessary. This is why Anselm and William had come to me in the first place. Because the stone needed to be tested. Because they were childless and Annie was close to term.

Because they needed this one ingredient more.

✦

And so we conspirators met again soon after, met again in the night, in the woods this time, beyond the farmland. The elements of the crystal were once more mixed together, placed in a small cauldron over burning coals and finally cooled and allowed to crystallize. The formula had by then been made known to me. I record it here for him who has eyes to see with, and no fear of damnation or no soul to save.

The crystal was carried to an iron tub. A bath was drawn from the river. A small piece of the crystal was broken off and dissolved again in the water. It bubbled furiously as it dissolved.

Then, at the appointed hour, Annie arrived. She was carrying our newborn infant in her arms.

That scene will be before me when I die. It is before me now, has been before me ever since. I have no doubt it will be before me always and will add the torture of conscience to the torture of the everlasting flames.

We three stood cowled and waiting. The trees around us seemed to bow together as if to screen us from the eyes of the angels. In what little I could see of the sky above, there was no moon, no stars. Only the low scarlet glow of the coals illuminated the overhanging branches, and that with so hellish an illumination that there could be little question into whose care we had commended our spirits. The red branches stretched down towards us like grasping hands.

A damp, cold breeze was blowing. The woods groaned with it. The trees seemed to whisper one to another. No birds sang, and the chatter of night creatures was so low and consistent that it was only another kind of silence.

Annie stepped forth from the darkness of the forest. I felt my breath catch, and a fever spread through my blood like a stain. It was clear from the way she supported her burden, from the wordless tune she murmured to it, that even in her befuddled state an animal tenderness had been excited in her by the birth of her cub. On reflection, I do not think she truly understood what we were about to do.

She handed the baby to me. I did not have the courage to look down at it. I looked only at Annie as William took the bundle from my arms. The poor raggedy creature stood unprotesting while William spoke the portentous paynim incantations. The slackness of her face, the deadness of her eyes reflected, I felt, the slackness, the deadness that seemed now to have invaded my entire soul. I felt as if I were floating in a sea of space, with every sensation muffled, every thought as still as the woods around.

Chanting, William laid the infant down on the flat rock that was to be our altar.

The chanting went on—a long time. It rose slowly until it reached a climax, filled the quiet wood. Even as I averted my face, I saw in the corner of my eyes the gleam of the gold-handled knife as William lifted it above his head, as the blade caught the red light of the coals.

There was a single, inquiring syllable from the babe. A single noise from Annie—a dumb, despairing moan—as the knife came plunging down.

Then, Anselm was stepping forward with a silver chalice to catch the gushing blood.

I let my robes fall to the ground and stood naked in the night air. I stepped forward and submerged myself into the chilly bath.

There was silence. There was the wind. Anselm came towards me, bearing the chalice.

Something in me even now, degraded as I am, hardened as I am, damned as I surely am, cries out at the memory, wails, weeps. But I will resist. It would be foul of me to argue a case for mercy now, to make a pretense of humanity now, to make a pretense of repentance. The will of man is free and the love of Christ is boundless. And I in that wood, on that night, made my decision.

And in despair of Heaven, and in the sight of those present, I was washed in the blood of the lamb.

✦

So I have written it here that it may be known. I have put it down so that it shall not die with me. I have lived for almost forty years since that day. I have seen one and then the other of my companions perish, as some accident or failure left them short of the blood they needed, that precious ingredient more without which the stone is useless. I have seen the flesh curdle and rot then on their living frames, have heard them shrieking with the pain of it. I have seen the light of a terrible realization enter into their helpless eyes, too late, too late. I have seen that light finally, mercifully extinguished.

And yet I hear them shrieking still in the pit of their eternal master.

But I have gone on. I have been a wanderer on the face of the earth. I have crept among my fellow men and hidden. I have seduced their women and slaughtered each of my own offspring even as it drew breath. I have libeled and condemned the innocent in order to protect myself. I have lived as the fox lives, hunted. Men cross themselves when they mutter my name. Children cry when their mothers invoke me. Priests deny my existence, and the bravest knights fear my presence in the woods. I have made myself their nightmares.

This is the life everlasting that was promised to me.

And yet—and yet I must say it—the promise has held good. I am dying now, but I have lived these forty years. I have lived—and I have not grown old. My body is the same today as it was those decades hence. Others have aged and crumbled, others have died, but I am as I was. I am unchanged.

This is what I feel compelled to declare. I feel compelled to proclaim it, knowing not even now whether I write the words in horror or in joy: the grail is real! The legend of the stone is true! I am the living testament to its powers, the dying testament. He who has eyes to see, let him see.

I conclude with a prophecy, and a warning. This is what I believe.

I believe that, in the days to come, there will arise one stronger in courage than I, more replete with cunning, one who will realize all the potential of this thing which has been heretofore hidden from us, and become the eternal creature that I sought to be.

But two things he must remember, two things he must keep in mind always.

The first thing: the blood must be found; every six months, the blood must be made available or all is lost. It was a failure to accomplish this which has killed first my companions and now me.

But there is a second thing as well: the stone dissolves. Only a little bit is needed each time, but once it is dissolved it cannot be reconstituted. The exact formula for its creation must therefore be always remembered, always preserved. For this reason, as I say, I have recorded that formula here.

Always remember: If he is deprived of either the blood or the stone—either one—his death, the most horrible death imaginable, is a certainty.

And contrariwise, if he—this future man—if he can find the blood, if he can maintain his supply of the blue flower—then it is all before him as it was once before me. Then—ah, then—what power will accrue to him, what endless power. If men worship Christ for the mere promise of immortality, what will they give to him who possesses it in living truth? If Kings kneel before the cross, what will they not lay at the feet of an actual presence? In him, I have my hope that the coming death, this awful death, will not be in vain. To him, I leave this document, this formula, these words.

And from the depths of Hell, where I soon shall surely be, I salute him across time.

VIII

THE NIGHT
OF IAGO

1 The day's light faded. Rain swept against the high windows of the mansion in World's End. Blasts of wind plastered the panes with water. An observer looking up from the street would have seen only a blur of yellow lampglow within, the suggestion of a fire in the grate, a dancing orange shimmer. Even in the moments when the storm subsided, when the rain on the glass drew into streaks and droplets, the editorial office of *Bizarre!* was hidden from the world by clouds of roiling smoke, an interior fog that also obscured the squat figure standing in there, made of it no more than a dim, dark outline.

Harper Albright puffed another gout from the meerschaum skull and watched night fall. The others were behind her, no one speaking. Bernard was playing solitaire on his computer, the repeated click of the mouse sounding curt, violent, agitated. Storm was brooding on the high stool, drumming his fingers atop the draftsman's table or sometimes, absently, massaging his left arm. Sophia, by the fire, hugged herself, rubbed her shoulders, nervously eyed the grotesqueries staring from the covers on the wall, from the jars and aquaria around the office.

And Harper stood, smoking without surcease. She could see the others, all of them, in wavery reflections on the rain-washed glass. For the most part, however, she let them fade from her consciousness, melt from her focus.

She was thinking about the trail of stories. About what it had revealed to her. About how it had led her to this dangerous night.

It had been ten days now since her meeting with Iago. It had been enough time to work out her understanding of the thing. The chronology, anyway, was more or less clear to her.

Some thirty or forty years ago, before Harper had met him, Jacob Hope had chanced to purchase a supply of a blue crystalline stone at a bazaar in Morocco. That much he had revealed to her himself. The merchant who had sold him the stone must have told him some version of the Belham monk's confession—some legend, anyway, of the stone's power to grant eternal life. Obviously, either Iago had believed the tale at once, or he had tried out the powers of the stone for himself and found the story to be true. In any case, Harper had no doubt that the pleasure of killing an infant would have been motive enough for him to proceed.

After that, he had returned to Europe. There, he had begun to collect his followers. At a time when cults were springing up everywhere, he had invented a cult of his own. But the cult, of course—as the warlock Dr. Mormo had suggested—the cult was merely an excuse. What Iago was really after were the women. The women, and the children he could sire off them. The children—and their blood. The cult was a perfect system for creating a steady supply of that "precious ingredient more without which the stone is useless."

And so, in the compound in Argentina, he had carried out his experiments in the jungle. Dissolving bits of the blue stone in water, completing the elixir by murdering his children for their blood. In this mixture, he had bathed himself every six months. Indeed, judging by the looks of him, he had somehow continued to feed the hungry stone, even after Harper had discovered him and he had burned the compound—and his children—to the ground. Using charisma and cunning, Iago had somehow kept the children's blood flowing for the last twenty-five years.

But finding the blood he needed—that was only half his problem, wasn't it? There was still the difficulty of the stone itself, the crystal. As the monk had warned, the stone would not last forever. Each application required a bit of it to be dissolved. Iago knew he would eventually use up his Moroccan supply. And so far, apparently, he had been unable to analyze the components of the thing or reproduce the process by which it was made. Ultimately he was going to have to figure out how to create the stone for himself. And he would have to do it before the lines of discoloration began to appear on the backs of his own hands, before he, like William and Anselm and the monk of Belham Abbey, suffered the agonies of living decay.

And that's where the trail of ghost stories had come in. Twenty years ago. After the destruction of the compound in Argentina. After five years in exile. "In a little place off the Edgware Road," as he had told her. Somehow, something had led Iago to "Black Annie." Something had led him to connect that story with "The Alchemist's Castle," which linked it to the Rhinehart triptych, and with "Young William," which linked all the others to the monk's confession.

And it was the confession, it was surely that, which had begun his twenty-year search for the triptych itself.

Because when he read the monk's confession, he had

noticed—as Harper had noticed—the monk's claim that he had recorded the formula for the stone in his document. But if that was true, then where had he recorded it? It was not in the words. It appeared nowhere in M. R. James's translation. Therefore the scribe must have encoded the formula into the illuminations, the pictures. Which were destroyed when the British Library was bombed in 1941.

But which—possibly, even probably—had served as the inspiration for the Rhinehart triptych.

This was the ultimate message of the story trail, of its convoluted chain connecting the Belham monk's confession to the Rhinehart work. Because if the Rhinehart work was based on the confession, then the triptych was not—as Iago clearly believed it was not—a depiction of the three magi visiting the Madonna and child. No. It showed instead the three conspirators meeting Annie in the woods to perform their sacrifice.

And if Rhinehart had copied the pictures from the Belham manuscript, he might also, knowingly or unknowingly, have copied the coded instructions for the making of the crystal.

He who has eyes to see, let him see.

For years, anyway, an oral legend of some kind had surrounded the triptych with an aura of mystery. The Nazi magicians—those mad black artists who hung around with all the other madmen of the Third Reich—had clearly known there was some sort of power in the paintings, some valuable secret that needed to be brought out. They had been unable to find it, unable to crack the code, because no one had known what to look for.

Until Iago. Until now.

What had led him to it? she wondered, as the darkness drew in before her. What had happened in his "little place off the Edgware Road," that had led him to "Black Annie" and the other tales? The connections weren't obvious, they weren't easy to make. How had he found them, how had he even known to look? They were important questions because—from the moment Storm had read the story at the party—she had become aware of the uncanny aura of coincidence and destiny that hung over the whole affair. And if she could figure out how it had got started, she might be able to deduce the shape of it. She might be able to seize control of events, or at least outrace Iago to their conclusion.

Already, some possible answers were beginning to form in her mind. But for now . . .

For now, she had a plan to draw Iago into the open once again. A plan she had formulated when she was out by the standing stones with Dr. Mormo. She knew there was only one way to do it. There was only one piece of bait that was certain to work. And this time, if he rose to that bait, she would be ready for him. She would bring her quarter-century hunt to a close right away.

She continued to stand there, continued to send up plumes and tendrils of smoke from her skull pipe. Bernard went on clicking away at his computer solitaire. Storm went on drumming his fingers on the draftsman's table. Sophia went on fidgeting nervously by the fire.

And then the phone rang.

Harper turned around. The others froze. The double chirp of the phone sounded again as Harper hobbled across the carpet to the stand beside Bernard's desk.

She lifted the receiver.

"Yes?"

"Harper." She recognized the harsh croak at once, the warlock's voice. "It's Mormo."

"Jervis," she said dryly. "How good of you to ring."

"Never mind that. I've got it."

Harper felt her heart hitch. She swallowed, said nothing.

"It wasn't easy either, let me tell you. The competition's stiff."

"But you've got it in your possession now?" said Harper.

"Come after full dark," the warlock went on. "And make bloody well sure you're not followed."

There was a click, and he was gone.

Harper laid the receiver down slowly. She raised her eyes to the steady gazes of the others.

"He's got it," she said.

She heard Storm and Bernard and Sophia all let their breath out at once. She tipped the stem of her pipe at them.

"Tonight, after full dark, Bernard and I will go to Lonsdale Square."

Storm curled his fingers into a fist, thumped it softly on the tabletop. "What about me?" he said.

Harper turned her head to look first at him, then at Sophia.

"You have another job," she said. She sighed. "Before we can get to the end of this business, it's necessary for us to get to the beginning of it. And I have reason to believe that that involves the suicide of Ann Endering."

"My mother?" Sophia said. "What has she got to do with it?"

"That's what I don't know," Harper told her. "But it's possible your father does."

Sophia drew back, drew erect, stared at her.

"My friends," said Harper slowly, "I'm afraid I must ask you to go out to Belham Grange."

2 **Dr. Mormo hung** up the phone. He sat there on the floor, disgruntled. His round, bloated face was pale. His round, bloated belly, under a sweat-stained shirt of shiny gold, was gurgling ominously. The trouble with working for the devil, he reflected bitterly, is that you get paid the wages of sin.

He sat cross-legged. His black pentagram banner was spread out on the carpet before him. His black candles were lit, the low flames wavery. A stuffed goat's head sat to one side of him, its glass eyes flickering with the light.

And between them, in the center of the pentagram, sat the *Madonna.*

The panel was in a box, the box was standing open. The candlelight played over the features of the virgin, spread into Rhinehart's tangled brown background and breathed it to tenebrous life. The tubby warlock brooded over the picture gloomily.

Mary was in the winter woods. She was down on one knee, clasping her hands together. She was clothed in drapery of royal blue, which set her off from the stark snarl of lifeless branchwork all around her, and from the great, twisted dead oak that hung over her, like threatening doom. Her face was round, fleshy, Bavarian, a peasant's face, but with pale eyes mystic and tender. She had a lovely, distant smile.

Looked more like a fairy-tale princess than the Queen of Heaven, Mormo thought. Looked more like Snow White in the Disney movie than anything.

He could hardly wait to get the holy bitch out of here.

He reached up, grabbed hold of the bedstead. Grunting, he hoisted himself off the floor. "Too old for this," he grumbled miserably. His bare feet white beneath the cuffs of his dirty corduroys, he padded to the bedroom door and out into the hall.

The house was dark around him, all the windows shuttered against the rain and the fading light. But Mormo knew the place, one of his more familiar hideaways. He trudged surely through the shadows to the top of the stairs. The floorboards creaking in the surrounding silence. The old man grumbling. All this intrigue. All this danger, he thought. He was way too old. It was way past time to get out of the business, retire, settle down. Get himself a place in Cornwall by the sea. Gather a cozy little coven about him. Spend his declining years in quiet contemplation and blood sacrifice, appeasing the dark powers in hope of the life to come.

He started heavily down the stairs. Well, he thought, tonight should pave the way, provide him with a nice little nest egg. Assuming it didn't kill him first.

He came slowly down into the foyer. Caught an obscure glimpse of himself in the mirror there. Poor old bloke with not a true friend left to him, he thought. Hard done by. Everyone on him and on him. Difficult to know who to be most afraid of at this point, really. The old Nazi who'd passed him the panel, there was a right spooky loon if ever there was one. Going on and on about death and culture. "It takes a mountain of corpses to make a Madonna," he'd said. His eyes all shiny. Mormo could hardly wait to get the hell away from the lunatic.

But the Nazi had been more terrified even than he was. He knew he'd put his tit in the wringer when he'd phoned Sotheby's to bid on *The Magi*. He knew Iago would cotton onto him, come after him double quick and no mistake. And now poor old Dr. M had that to worry about too, didn't he? Iago. He shivered.

He continued his trek, through the darkened sitting room towards the kitchen. No noise anywhere besides his footsteps and his sighs.

He didn't want to think about what Iago would do to him if he caught him at this. He didn't want to think about it for a minute. But the truth was: Iago—he would do for him sooner or later anyway, wouldn't he? At the end of the day, there was no percentage at all in dealing with a man like that.

Which left him with Harper, the devil forgive him. Fancy him making arrangements with that sanctimonious old cow after all these years. It was against his religion, no question. But there he was at the end of the day. When he'd balanced all, she was his safest bet. He could evade Iago if he had to. Been doing it on and off for years, hadn't he? Master of shrouding himself in darkness, that's what he was. Enough safe houses to become an estate agent and all the powers of Hell on his side.

But Harper. Now she had connections. She seemed to be able to find him wherever he was. Turn up right in front of him like Hecate herself, she did. And she'd set the Yard on him too. She'd said so. At the kitchen doorway, he shivered again, grumbled again: "Too old." Too old for prison, that was for bloody sure.

He switched on the kitchen light. The fluorescents crackled, flickered on. The old warlock blinked against the sudden brightness. The linoleum tiles felt cold against his bare soles.

This was why he'd always favored this house: the kitchen. A nice big one. Nice big larder behind the door to his left. Nice big fridge, lots of worktop space round the basin. Dr. Mormo liked to cook. It relaxed him. And he could do with a bit of relaxation just now.

He opened the fridge and stuck his head in. American-made—you could practically walk right into it if you had a mind. It was comforting just to hear the hum of it. The place was too quiet, almost creepy here all by himself.

He gathered up the onions, tomatoes, scallions, prosciutto. Brought the whole armload to the worktop and laid it out beside the cutting board.

He rummaged through the cutlery drawer, removed a formidable cook's knife. Lifted it, held it expertly to the light to make sure it was clean. It was plenty clean. The stainless steel was gleaming.

Iago's grinning face was reflected on the blade.

Mormo saw it, let out a weak mewl of terror. The knife fell from his slack fingers as he spun to face the open larder door. He felt his legs turning to water, his bowels turning to water. He felt the front of his corduroys going hot and damp.

The shiny knife fell down and down to the floor, turning and turning in the air as it fell. The reflected wedge of that cruel, leering countenance flashed on the blade, disappeared, and flashed again as the knife spun.

The thud of the steel on the linoleum was very loud in the silent house.

3   "I won't do it!"
Sophia had, when she meant to, a voice that slashed like a saber. She had seen men, at the sound of it, look down appalled as if to find themselves cut off at the knees. It was that voice she used now on Richard Storm, who was crouching in her kitchen, rummaging through her small refrigerator.

"I've never heard of anything so ridiculous. It's unnecessary. It's cruel and stupid. And, in any case, it isn't going to happen. I won't go."

"Let me ask you something," Storm said, not looking up. "Is there, like, some big warehouse or something in this country where you guys keep the other halves of all your refrigerators?"

Sophia felt the flush of anger in her cheeks. "Don't do that. Don't just dismiss what I say to you."

"I'm not dismissing you," Storm answered mildly, reaching in deep. "I'm ignoring you. Which is hard because you're so beautiful and I love you like music. And I only want to do things that make you sing tra-la and dance around in the fields throwing daisies everywhere. But you asked me to help you, and I think you ought to reconsider."

"Well, I won't," she said. She crossed her arms on her chest.

"Can I eat this?" He had found a plate of cold chicken, brought it out.

She had swung away, and barely glanced at him. "Go ahead."

Storm stood up, flinching, working out the kinks in his knees. He came out through the open doorway into the dining room, out to the long table. She was standing on the other side of it, against the curtained doors to the balcony. Seething, flashing her anger at him.

"I mean it," she said. "I won't."

"Hey, what do you expect me to do?" he said. "Throw you over my shoulder and carry you out there? It'd be fun, but I don't need the hernia." He set the plate down, started to undo the plastic wrap that covered it.

"I think your friend Harper is a nutter," said Sophia.

Storm laughed.

"I think she's playing some sort of ridiculous game.

Whatever conspiracy theory she's come up with, I'm sure my mother could have had nothing to do with it."

"Yeah, Harper's a kook all right, no question. Except everything she says always turns out to be true. You don't have any Coke or anything . . . ?"

The question broke her chain of thought. She massaged her forehead. "I don't know. No. There's some sparkling water in the cabinet left of the basin."

But Storm remained where he was another second or two, rubbing his arm, puffing his cheeks. Tired. She noticed now he looked terribly tired. The rings deep under his melancholy eyes. The rugged face puffy and slack. She felt herself softening towards him—which was irritating, because she found that kept on happening: whatever he said, she was always feeling herself soften towards him sooner or later. It was all that naked affection he threw at her. The goofy American earnestness. Even the fact that he did not react to her wrath in the manner to which she was accustomed was bizarrely endearing.

"Are you feeling all right?" she found herself asking as he wandered back into the kitchen. "You look tired."

He didn't answer her. He was opening the cabinet.

"You mustn't let that old woman run you ragged with her nonsense."

"At my advanced age, you mean." He was reaching up for the water bottle now. "Hey, maybe you're just embarrassed to have your dad see you're dating an old man."

"Don't be stupid. You're not an old man. I like how old you are."

"Or that I have no culture."

"Well. Never mind," said Sophia. "You have many other lovely qualities."

Storm laughed again, shaking his head. Looked at her like . . . like she didn't know what. The man had absolutely no rein on his warmth at all. "I really do love you," he told her. "I think you're the greatest."

She forced herself not to smile. "Well, you do. And I'd be proud to introduce you to anyone."

"Gah."

"Well, I would. You know perfectly well it isn't that."

"I need an opener for this."

"It's in the—"

"Oh, wait, I got it," he said, pulling a drawer open. "Somebody ought to break the good news to these jokers about the twist-off cap."

She watched him as he ambled back towards her, swigging from the bottle. Watched him with the first, faint, frightening realization of what he meant to her, of the power she had somehow given him. At first she had thought him just silly—a shallow American. And, well, he was. But she had come to understand that that American shallowness ran very deep. He knew how to overlook things. Like her history. Like her problems in bed. Like all her terrible character flaws. And she saw now that she had come to rely on that.

She was thoroughly dismayed to hear the tone of appeal in her voice when she spoke again.

"My mother didn't do anything wrong, Richard," she said.

Storm only shrugged, which made her go sour inside. He sat down at the table. Pulled the plate to him. Didn't look at her. Pulled the salt shaker to him.

"Oh, you can't eat that with your fingers," she muttered. She came around the table to the tall sideboard, pulled a knife and fork from one drawer, a linen napkin from another.

Storm was already tearing into a slice of breast, wrestling

the meat off with tooth and claw. But he took the silverware from her without a word. Silently put the napkin on his lap. Salted the chicken again and attacked it this time with the fork and knife.

Sophia stood behind him, looking down into his sandy hair.

"Stop doing that," she said finally.

"What?" he said. "I'm eating. This is the way we do it."

"I mean stop thinking that. What you're thinking."

He set the knife and fork down. Scratched his head.

"My mother was a . . . sweet, liberal, charitable woman. Everyone says so. Everyone. I'm sure she didn't have anything to do with any of your friend's imaginary villains, or with anything. And to go out to Belham Grange and interrogate my father over a twenty-year-old tragedy . . . Maybe he hasn't been perfect. Maybe he was once involved in some dubious business. I don't even know that for sure . . ."

"Yeah, well, that's the thing," said Storm. He shifted in his seat to look up at her—to gaze up at her. Chewing his food, choosing his words. "You don't know. You see?"

Sophia was turning away from him when he caught her hand. He held it, stroked the back of it.

"You don't know, and it's eating you all up," he said. "You can't think about it and you can't think about anything else, so you can't think about anything. You don't know, so you can't forget about it—you can't forget about what you don't know. See? That's why I think you ought to do it. Because it's got you all . . . bunged up and frozen."

She drew her hand away, hugged herself with it. "That's just . . . You're just . . . talking about sex. It's just not that important to me."

He balled his napkin in his fist, set it on the table. Stood up, stood beside her, stood close. "I'm talking about you being depressed all the time. And having black patches. And being crazy, doing crazy things."

She faced him and his power occurred to her again, more clearly, more frightening this time.

"I don't want to do it, Richard." She could not believe it: she was pleading with him now. "Asking my father about this, confronting him. It would be . . . too painful."

"Painful?" He touched her hair gently. "Excuse me, but aren't you the girl I saw throwing herself off a balcony? How painful was that?"

"I meant painful for my father," she said up into his eyes. "He's an old man. He's not as strong as he looks, as he thinks he is. He's not as independent. He lives . . ." *In my good opinion,* she was about to say. But she stopped when the thought came to her that she now lived in Storm's, that she had allowed herself to live in Storm's. And she was scared of what was going to happen, what he was going to make her do. "Stirring things up," was what she said when she went on. "Making trouble over all this old business. What's the point?"

He had his fingers deep in her hair now, combing them through, holding her arm with his other hand.

"The point is for you to have a life," he said.

"I have a life."

"Have a big life. Have a real life, Sophie. With, like, musical numbers and chariot races. Even just inside, even just a Fred and Ginger dancing around in your head. It's important. Trust me on this, kid. I know about this." He seemed about to say something else, something more. His eyes had grown deep and hot—and mournful; they were so sad. " 'Cause it's short," he said after a moment. "It really is.

We don't stay long. You gotta do it big-time."

She lifted her chin curtly. "I haven't the faintest idea what you're talking about."

His lips pulled back, his teeth bared, as he seemed to look about the room for the words he wanted. His glance rested finally on the table.

"Look . . ." he said. He let her go, picked up the salt shaker. Unscrewed the metal top. He licked the tip of his index finger and dipped it in, brought it out with a circle of white crystals clinging to the tip. He set the shaker down and returned to her. "Here," he said. He moved his finger towards her lips.

Sophia blinked, recoiled. "What . . . ?"

"Shh," he said. He took her elbow. "Here."

He brought his finger closer. Closer until it touched her lips. He moved it gently through, gently into her mouth until her lips encircled it, until the salt was on her tongue. Instinctively, Sophia sucked on his finger, unable to break the hold of his gaze. Frightened by the sudden intensity of it.

Then his finger drew away. She licked her lips, the flavor still spreading over her palate. Storm's face stayed close to hers. His eyes stayed on her eyes.

"What," she said helplessly. "It's salt."

"It's *salt*!" he told her softly, urgently. "Salt! See? It's like . . . *Close Encounters*, you know? When the mother ship comes down out of the sky and it's the size of, like, a city? Like *Die Hard*, when the whole building just goes *bang*, just explodes and the fountain's all going. It's *salt*."

Sophia shook her head, afraid. Tears swam into her eyes.

"Here. Here," he said. "Let me taste."

He took her face in his two hands, drew her to him.

Pressed his lips to hers and then slid his tongue into her mouth, over her tongue.

Sophia tasted the salt and the chicken he'd eaten and the warmth and the size of his tongue. She was confused, her thoughts hectic. And, as his tongue went on moving over hers, she realized—realized with a sinking weight of fear and depression—that she was going to do whatever he wanted. They were going to talk about it, on and on, into the night. And then she was going to go out with him to Belham Grange.

Storm drew back, drew his tongue out of her. But he went on holding her face, holding her close to him. His eyes, she saw, were swimming too.

"Salt," he whispered hoarsely. "Live. Live, Sophia. It's the only thing I'll ever ask you to do for me."

4 Bernard's Morris Minor, meanwhile, was gunning wildly round the corners of Chelsea's backstreets. The rain walloped the windscreen, covered it, spit, slippery, out from under the tires on either side. The night was now so dark, the streets so sparsely lit, that it was all but impossible for Bernard to see much ahead. Still, the car darted through the tempest like a minnow as he worked the stick and wheel in the same languid, offhanded way in which he noodled his computer. He checked the rearview mirror frequently. He was trying to make certain there was no one on his trail.

The automobile, like all machines, was a complete mystery to Harper Albright. But she was so used to her factotum's mastery of such things that she was thoroughly unconcerned.

Slicing dodges between other cars, rugby-player dives under amber traffic lights, explosions of speed over abbreviated straightaways rendered invisible by the rain: she took no notice of any of them. Her stick propped on the car's damp floor, her hands crossed over the stick's dragon head, her chin resting on the backs of her hands, she cogitated quietly.

"I think," she murmured after a while, "that we had better discuss arithmetic."

The Morris skidded out onto the embankment, sped along the river, spangled bridges whipping by.

"It was simple arithmetic," Harper went on, "which, according to the Belham scribe, led to the death of his two partners in the enterprise of the stone, whereas he himself was saved by the complicity—that was his word—the complicity of one who remained nameless. Do you understand what I'm getting at?"

"Would anyone?" Bernard asked, casting a glance in the rearview as he swept in and out of oncoming traffic to overtake a van.

"It's the underpinning of the whole business," Harper insisted. "The very reason the scribe was brought into the conspiracy in the first place was that he had already impregnated the town's madwoman; she was close to term. You see, in order for the crystal's properties to be effective, one must apparently dissolve them in a bath of blood and water and then be baptized in the mixture once every six months. Without the constant repetition of the treatment, the fatal reaction sets in, beginning with the lines of discoloration which the Belham monk described. In the case of William and Anselm, such a reaction did set in within five years of the first experiment. Because of arithmetic. You see?"

The Morris flashed under the raised sword of King

Alfred, past the twin towers of Westminster Abbey. Shot like a cannonball into the enormous roundabout of Parliament Square. The place was ablaze with racing headlights, loud with horns, streaked and foggy with the angling rain. The car plunged into the melee. The cannonball became a sewing needle: the Morris stitched its way neatly through the chaos, Bernard rapidly steering, rapidly shifting gears. They were through—and speeding away into the broad canyons between the granite monoliths of Whitehall.

"There is a clear inference—so clear that the monk didn't even think to spell it out: in order for the stone to work, the blood must come from one's own child," Harper continued calmly. "That was the mathematical problem Iago was trying to solve when he gathered his cult around him. It takes, as you may have heard, nine months to produce a baby. The amount of blood required for the bath is clearly enough to kill the infant. Given the time of gestation—not to mention the occasional female resistance to any of various stages in the proceeding—how does one produce enough of the priceless stuff to bathe in it every six months?"

"You know, I think I had that problem on my last maths exam."

Harper, with rigid dignity, ignored this. Went on, "But what if mad Annie's child was not the scribe's first? What if he also had a child already grown? It might be possible to take the necessary amount of blood from an adult without killing him—often enough, at least, to fill in the gap between new births."

Bernard pondered these matters in silence as two huge double-decker buses converged on either side of him, threatening to crush the Morris to cinders. He downshifted nimbly, causing his car to spurt forward. The buses lumbered after him like two elephants in the slipstream of a jet.

"Which brings us back to that word—*complicity*," Harper said. "It would require complicity on the part of the adult offspring. No reasonable scenario can be imagined in which the blood is continually taken by force. Even if you locked your victim away, you would be hard pressed to keep him alive for very long. And in Iago's case, for all his powers, his own nature would work against him. Because any offspring of his would likely inherit at least a measure of his strength of will. Such a captive would almost certainly commit suicide rather than be a toad and live upon the vapor of a dungeon."

"Iago has obviously managed to produce all the offspring he needed this last quarter-century," Bernard said.

"Perhaps," said Harper. "But perhaps only just. Who knows how many times he's come close to the limit? And all the while leaving no child behind who could grow to adulthood, who could offer him a steady supply of what he needs."

Bernard gave a slight shake of his head. "Well, why didn't he think of that before?"

"I believe he has been thinking about it these last twenty-five years."

"Tell me something, darling," said Bernard suddenly—and speaking suddenly with peculiar sincerity. "We enjoy our little subtleties, you and I, but—"

"Stop the car!"

They had reached Lonsdale Square.

They had reached Lonsdale Square—and Harper had noticed something peculiar about the house on the corner. This was in spite of the fact that Bernard, at her command, had hit the brakes so hard that the Morris had gone into an hellacious skid. They were corkscrewing insanely through the narrow strip between parked cars. Bernard was wrestling desperately with the steering wheel. Harper was craning her neck to keep the house in sight.

"Interesting," she said.

There was a gap at the curb beside the garden. The Morris slid into it, bumped up onto the pavement, headed for the garden's iron gate—then stopped, as Bernard, downshifting, braking, used the concussion to bring the machine under control. It came to rest with two tires up on the curb, two in the street. He gave his companion a glance of mild exasperation.

"Look," she said to him. "Turn off the headlamps and look."

Bernard sighed. Killed the lights. Bent his head to peer up through the windscreen at the narrow, gabled building in front of them.

The square was quiet, dark. A claustrophobic crunch of buildings round a tangled winter garden. The narrow façades of the townhouses lanced the sky, irregular, looming, Gothic. The sharp points of their gables seemed to close like teeth on the purple clouds above.

The rain was softening again, a thin fog drifting in over the garden's branches. A streetlamp threw a halo of pink light into the weather, but the façade of the corner house seemed to shrink back from it into the folds of night. Every window was shuttered. No light shone through the gaps, no sign of light or life at all.

"What . . . ?"

"Wait for it," said Harper.

Then there it was. As the two watched through the windscreen, through the broad, clear arcs left by the ticking wipers. A white spot appeared through the slats of an upstairs shutter. It lengthened to a white line, angled off. It was gone. Then it appeared again, moving. Glaring for an instant at the point where the shutters joined. Then it vanished.

"A torch," said Bernard.

"Yes," Harper said.

A few moments later, it went on again—on and off at a window lower down. Whoever held the flashlight was descending through the house.

"Why would he be using a torch?" said Bernard.

"Exactly my point," said Harper Albright.

She had her Borsalino resting on her lap. She lifted it now, put it on, pulled it low on her brow. She clutched her stick, her eyes alive behind her spectacles. She watched, her nerves electric. She did not stir.

The light flickered again; the outer edge of its nimbus touched the slats of a shutter on the ground floor.

"He's coming out," Bernard said softly.

Thirty seconds went by like an hour. They watched. The wipers ticked.

Then the door to the corner house came open, closed. There was an obscure movement in the recessed entryway. Harper could hear her pulse in her ears, could hear Bernard breathing beside her.

A hunched, stocky figure emerged from the recess, stepped out onto the pavement. He stood. Looked left and right along the deserted street. The rain dampened the slash of his tawny hair. The lamplight glinted in his pink, piggy eyes; it drew his features out of the shadows.

It was the scarred man.

"Turn off the wipers," Harper hissed. "Quickly."

Bernard did, and the windscreen misted over. The Morris's engine popped and hummed.

The scarred man stepped to a hulking black car parked at

the curb. He pulled the door open, ducked inside.

"He'll see us if he comes this way," Bernard said.

"Shh. No. Maybe not. He's in a hurry."

The black car started up, moved out into the street, came towards them. Harper heard Bernard's breathing stop. Her own breathing stopped. They sat absolutely still.

The black car roared, accelerated swiftly. Swiftly, it was past them. Out of the square.

Harper threw open her door. She was in the street in a second, heading for the house.

"I'll go after him," Bernard shouted, and he threw the car into gear.

Harper took another step before she realized what he'd said. She stopped dead, turned in the fog and rain, her eyes widening with fear.

"No, no!" she shouted.

But it was too late. The Morris was already twisting off the pavement, spinning in the road. Its headlamps flashed on as it swiped by her, caught her with one hand outstretched, her mouth open on her cry.

But Bernard either didn't see this or ignored it. The Morris kept spinning. The engine gave a hoarse rumble. The Morris darted forward—and then was gone after the black car. A moment later, and the noise of both their motors faded away, leaving the square humming softly with city noises, pattering with rain.

Harper's hand sank back to her side. She stood, gazing at the place where the cars had gone out of sight, her heart thumping heavily.

Then a wrenching, tormented scream sounded above her.

Startled—frightened—she lifted her eyes just in time to see an enormous black shape launch itself from the corner house's gable top. A raven—its wingspan enormous—soared off above her head. A vast, outreaching blot against the sky. Then it was past her, over the dead garden trees. Out of sight. Another shriek, fading into the distance. And the street was quiet around her once again.

Harper let out a breath, raised a hand to her thundering chest. She looked at the dark door of the house, from the house back to the corner where the cars had gone. She knew an evil omen when she saw one, and she felt dread in her belly like a weight of stone.

Her shoulders slumped, her steps weary, she headed towards the house.

 She did not ring. She pushed the door. It came open— she expected that—but it made her swallow hard just the same.

She stepped across the threshold. The foyer was dark, but there was a light on somewhere in the back of the house. In the misty fluorescent glow of it, she could make out the objects strewn about her feet. An overturned umbrella stand. A flimsy lowboy under a mirror to her right, pulled open, emptied. Umbrellas, drawers, papers scattered everywhere. She stepped gingerly through the mess into the sitting room.

The light was brighter here, filtering in directly through an open doorway. Harper could see the upended sofa. A standing lamp lying lengthwise. The peaks of books that had been cast from their shelves to the carpet. The carpet was slashed into strips. The entire place had been ransacked.

Her breath came out unsteadily. She shifted her grip on her stick. She hobbled forward, kicking the books aside. She reached the lighted door. Her eyes, behind the thick spectacles, peered into the kitchen.

In the purplish glare of the fluorescents, she saw at once the cook's knife gleaming on the kitchen tiles. There was a small puddle beside it. Harper moved to the puddle. Her knees cracked as she knelt down over it. She sniffed. Wrinkled her nose. Urine. The weight of dread inside her grew heavier still. Poor old Jervis, she thought. He must have been very scared when they came for him. And no doubt, he had good reason.

She went back—through the ransacked sitting room, to the foyer, to the foot of the stairs. She looked up grimly where they rose before her into blackness.

She moved to the foot of them. Started up.

She climbed slowly, step by hesitant step, almost blind, her stick probing before her. She could not help but picture the scene as if she were watching it from the front row of a cinema. Richard Storm himself might have filmed something exactly like it. The apparently deserted house, throbbing with danger. The old woman climbing the steps into a threatening gloom. *You idiot*, she would be thinking to herself as she munched her popcorn. *Don't go. Get out. Run to a phone. Call the police.*

Which was pretty much exactly what she *was* thinking to herself.

She reached the top, stepped up onto the landing. Shadows and darkness. Blackness, down the hallway to her right. To her left, a low, orange, wavering glow: candlelight. She forced herself to head towards it.

She shuffled unsteadily over the runner, one hand reaching out to guide herself along the wall. She expected the sudden onslaught of Iago's minions any moment.

But the onslaught didn't come. She reached the glowing doorway and looked in.

The candle was on the floor at the foot of a four-poster bed. A single black candle, burned nearly down. Its orange glow danced, reflected, in the glass eyes of a stuffed goat's head. The thing was staring up at her from atop a black silk banner with a silver pentagram in its center.

A box sat on the pentagram. Its lid was open. Harper had to step closer before she could see what was inside.

She stepped closer. She saw. And her whole body went acid with fear.

There was a photograph in the box. A black-and-white snapshot of a woman holding a baby in her arms. Harper could not remember whether she had ever seen the photograph before. But she knew the woman's face well enough. She recalled the desperate eagerness of her eyes, the tremulous misery of her smile. She recognized the beauty of her youth though she had watched it decay and crumble in the mirror with unnatural speed, almost overnight.

The photograph was scarred and partly covered by a mark drawn over it in black ink. Something like a horseshoe enclosing something like a figure eight.

The mark of Iago.

Harper gripped her stick, trembling. The acid of fear within her turned to the acid of anger. She cursed herself. He was still smarter than she was. Still. Smarter and quicker and more cunning by half. She had meant to acquire the *Madonna* and set a trap for him. Well, he had got there first. And now he had set a trap for her.

No, not for her. He had set a trap for Bernard.

And Bernard was headed straight into it.

6 As it will in England, the rain ceased suddenly. The clouds blew out of London to the northeast, and Bernard trailed his quarry through clear weather.

The scarred man's black car—a Mercedes, Bernard determined—tooled smoothly over the glistening roads ahead of him. Down the back ways and closes to avoid the traffic, over switchbacks to anticipate the complex system of one-way streets. Slithering like a silverfish through caulk, seeming sometimes to meander. But south ultimately, Bernard noticed, always south. And faster, probably, than by the main roads.

It was a cabbie's route, he thought, a Knowledge run. The scarred man definitely knew his way through town.

It made it difficult for Bernard to keep out of sight. To lose track of the Mercedes' red taillights even for a moment on those twists and turns might be to lose track of the car entirely. But to stay on it, to stay after it on the short spurs, round corner after corner, Bernard had to stay close behind. Sometimes the Morris's front end was no more than a few meters behind the Mercedes' boot. Sometimes the two cars were alone together on an empty stretch of road. And twice—once in Finsbury and once as they descended together through Clerkenwell—Bernard thought he saw the scarred driver lift his pink eyes to the rearview and stare directly back at him with piercing intensity. Bernard braked and slipped back into the night then. But it didn't reassure him much. His heart was beginning to rap against his ribs like a fist. He had to tighten his abdomen, practice his *nogare* breathing by force of will to keep himself steady at the wheel. Had he been spotted? He wasn't sure.

The Mercedes went on—and the Morris followed—into the dense and suffocating alleyways beneath the Barbican.

Moment by moment now, Bernard had very little idea where he was. Modern offices, warehouses crowded close on either side of him, moldering homes and faceless blocks of stone replaced them and hemmed him in. Boarded pubs, empty bakeries and restaurants, an open construction site, all dark, all deserted, were before him, then past. The Mercedes kept winding round, turning, avoiding the thoroughfares, hiding from the traffic.

And Bernard trailed along. His angelic face was tense, his eyes ached with staring at the red taillights before him. Despite the smooth movements of his hands upon the stick and the wheel, his body felt brittle, his muscles throbbed. Ahead, the Mercedes' pace remained even, unhurried.

Was it possible, he wondered after a while, was it possible that he was being drawn in?

Oh, Harper, he thought. You old witch. He had seen her back in the square. With her hand outstretched, with her mouth open. She had been trying to stop him, hadn't she? And he had ignored her. Because he was always tailing after her and she was always telling him what was what and she was always right about everything and, well, it rankled from time to time. So he had ignored her, and driven on as he thought best.

Was it possible, he wondered now, licking his dry lips, was it possible that she had been trying to save him from exactly this?

The Mercedes turned again, headed now along a curving street so narrow that the crumbling Tudor bays to the left and right seemed to hang directly over them. Then, all at once, with a harsh splash through a gutter puddle, the black car dashed out of sight, down an alley.

This was too much. In so tight a space, Bernard would be

a fool to follow. He let the Morris glide past the corner. Glanced over as he went by, just in time to see the black car's taillights wink out.

The Morris rolled on another short distance. Then Bernard pulled it to the curb beside an overflowing skip.

He switched off the engine. Flumped against the seat, his head falling back wearily. He shut his eyes.

He'd had a glimpse of the street in which the Mercedes had parked: a dead end, a walled close with barely a hand's breadth of space on either side of the car. Trail the scarred man into that and he would come out with his head under his arm. And here he had been so looking forward to a ripe old age of moral degeneracy and exquisite perversion.

He cursed aloud, and then shouldered the Morris's door open.

His long figure unfolded from the car. He was all in black. Only the shaven dome of his head shone under the single streetlight. He moved swiftly, with his willowy lope, back along the housefronts to the alley entrance. He pressed himself to the corner wall—feeling like a right idiot, feeling like a cinema spy—and peeked around the edge.

It was a forbidding prospect, worse than he'd expected. The alley was thick with night. The oppressive walls seemed to angle towards each other as they went in. The hulking form of the Mercedes rose between them. And beyond that rose another shape, big, dark: a rearing hump of stone, a silhouetted spire. A church, sinister, against all that was visible of the sky. With this, the alley abruptly ended.

Bernard hesitated. There was, he saw, a weird blue glow coming from the place, and a vertical line of yellow light—as would appear at the edge of a shrouded window. He licked his lips again. His heartbeat was fierce and loud. His palms, pressed to the wall behind him, were clammy.

He peeled off the building and started into the alley.

Crouched, his hands lifted, held before him, he moved with predatory grace. He was now, he decided, absolutely terrified. His eyes darted here and there. To crannies of blackness. Clutters of bins and boxes. To the hump of the Mercedes, which seemed to him ready to rear up at any moment and spring. The alleyway closed over him, the dark closed over him. Yes, *absolutely terrified*—that was the phrase he wanted.

He came up behind the waiting car. Peered, as well as he could, through the rear window into the unlit interior. It was quiet in there. There was no movement. But he couldn't make out the floor in back, and beyond the front seats he could see nothing at all.

Yet he began to squeeze around it. A tight squeeze. The brick wall scraped the back of his black windbreaker. The door handles plucked at the buckle of his belt. He could be fairly certain now that the car was empty. He edged past it, around to the front, under the rising church.

He crept on, towards the end of the alley. The church's spire pierced the blowing clouds above him. The small domed hexagon of an apse grew huskier and more imposing as he neared. His senses were all electrified, his nerve ends naked and snaking like live wires. He could smell things— not just ordinary things, but everything. Not just the rotting garbage and the grainy sting of old exhaust, but the dirt of shoe soles and cigarettes ground into the pavement over time, the edge of seawater in the southwestern breeze—and something else, some citrusy smell, which was mighty like the aroma of his own fear. And he could hear—the sussurus of the city, a burst of laughter from far away, a baby crying—

but also, he was almost certain of it, a portentous undertone of voices through the heavy stones of the church walls, the burr of a conversation within. And the weird blue glow—he could see now: it was light filtering out through a stained-glass window. He could even make out the figures on it and guessed they were Christ with Lazarus rising. And he could see that the thin line of yellow light did not come through a shrouded window but through a fissure in the apse. Its narrow panes were clear and, though the light was faint, his eyes were so wide, so receptive, that the glare of it seemed to scorch his pupils. And to draw him on.

He was stopped. He had reached an iron railing close against the church wall. He grimaced, intensely aware that the wisest course was to turn and run for it. Instead, he grasped the heads of two spikes and vaulted his long legs over the rail with a single, swinging motion. He landed on the opposite strip of pavement without a sound.

Now the spire stretched up out of sight above his head. One angle—two sides—of the apse pushed in towards him. He reached out and his fingertips touched the damp stone, glided over it as he stepped around the angle's point to the lit fissure. Slowly, he stretched his body up to peer through the window's bottom half.

The murmur of conversation still reached him, not much louder than before, no clearer. But he couldn't find the source of it at first. He was looking slantwise across a vault in the end of a stunted transept. Whatever the source of the light was, it was out of sight. All he saw was the dim yellow glow of it, spreading from somewhere up the aisles, dying within his field of vision. By pressing far to one side, he could take in some of the front pews running up to the altar. But the scene was mostly in shadow.

After another moment or two, he began to make things out. The spiral staircase leading up to a simple pulpit. An enormous crucifix sunk back into the dark behind it. The gnarled shape of the figure hanging on the cross. He saw the muted colors, the faint glimmer of a stained-glass window on the wall above. But, beyond that, there were only half-delineated forms hunkered before invisible recesses. The hollow reaches of the church seemed to drift with a sort of smoke of gray darkness. Then a movement caught his eye . . .

And he saw three men. The featureless figures of three men. They were gathered together on the far side of the chancel rail. They were standing in a tight cluster. They were talking almost in whispers. One of them laughed, a deep chuckle. Another nodded, the black shape of his head bobbing.

Bernard strained to hear, strained to see. Raised now on tiptoe. His neck hurting as he craned it to keep the men in view.

And, as he looked, he heard another noise—a dreadful noise—a faint, low, agonized sob from somewhere in the shadows.

Bernard's eyes moved to the sound. His mouth opened. The air came out of him in a long, unbroken gasp.

The body on the crucifix was moving.

It shifted weakly. It moaned again. "Don't know. Don't know." Bernard saw the dark liquid lines trailing down from the palms. Saw the arms straining against the ropes that held them. Feebly, the crucified figure lifted its head.

Bernard gaped. The man's eyes were gone. Pools of gore were spilling out of his sockets, running down his cheeks. His head dropped forward.

Shocked, Bernard lost his grip on the fissure. He fell away, took a step away from the church. He whispered harshly, "Jesus Christ!"

And at once, he heard another laugh, another deep chuckle. Only this time, it came from directly beside him.

"Not exactly, mate," the scarred man said.

Bernard was fast. Jumped back even as he spun to face his attacker. But he was still so staggered by what he'd seen, so fazed by the first jolt of it—and much too surprised by the ambush to fend it off. Even as he leapt, even as he dropped into a semblance of a fighting stance, even as he lifted his hands in an attempt at self-protection, the small, burning eyes, the disfigured mouth of the scarred man completely filled his field of vision, completely overwhelmed him.

The sap was falling before he knew it. It struck him on the side of the head full force.

Bernard saw the sky, saw the spire, spinning, wheeling. And then he pitched over, onto the railing, clung to it, hung from it—and finally slid senseless to the ground.

7 Sir Michael Endering sat erect behind his huge mahogany desk. Sat pressed into his high-backed leather chair like the statue of a man enthroned. The lights in the study were off, all of them. The green velvet curtains were drawn. The walls of bookshelves were only faintly visible.

Belham Grange was silent all around him, silent everywhere.

The great man sat stalwart. The prow-like chin was raised, the mighty head upheld. He seemed unaware that his features had collapsed over the last several hours, had thinned amazingly and grown old. His lips were parted and flecked with white drops of spittle. His cheeks were suddenly hollowed and pale, the ruddiness gone from them. His silver hair was in frantic disarray.

His eyes, glinting in the dark, were shifting, quick, afraid.

This was how they were going to get at him, he thought. In the cruelest way. Through his daughter.

Long minutes passed. Sir Michael stirred. He reached into his waistcoat pocket and brought out a ring of keys. He gazed down at them lying in his big hand as if he was not sure what they were. He murmured wordlessly. Swiveled slightly. And bent down to unlock the desk's bottom drawer.

He brought out an elegant box topped with studded green leather. He set it on the blotter before him. Unlocked it, opened it.

On a tray in the box lay a line of Havana cigars and a sterling silver lighter. The tray lifted out to reveal a swatch of velvet underneath.

Underneath the swatch of velvet was an ugly and brutal-looking revolver.

It was a snub-nosed .38, American, Smith & Wesson. So compact he could nearly swallow it in his enormous palm. A cardboard box of bullets lay beside it.

Sir Michael lifted the pistol out, cracked the cylinder. Spun the chambers once to assure himself the gun was oiled. His long fingers were unsteady on the bullet box, but he got it open, removed a bullet, two. He sniffed once, as if disdainfully, but then his whole body shuddered.

His daughter was coming to the house tomorrow. His daughter—and Richard Storm.

It seemed to Sir Michael now that he had been dreading this day for twenty years, that he had been watching for it, ever since his wife died. But the fact was, for much of that time, he hadn't believed the warnings were real. He had thought they were all a figment of Ann's final madness. He hadn't known enough. He hadn't got sufficient information. All he'd had to go on were his wife's ravings, the things she had said to him that terrible night when she lay on the floor, the blood gushing from her. *Get the Rhinehart triptych. Don't let him have it, no matter what. Iago. He'll kill you for it. He'll kill everyone.* And on and on in the same vein. *Don't speak to anyone. Don't trust anyone. Everything depends on it. He'll kill you. He'll kill anyone.* Well, what on earth was he supposed to have understood from that?

All the same, he had done what he could. Then and now, out of loyalty to her, he had done what he could. But he was stumbling blind; he had never been certain what it was he was dealing with. When *The Magi* came up for auction—out of loyalty to his wife—he had sent Sophia to make a strong offer for it, more than strong enough, he thought, to secure the thing. It was only when poor Jessica was outbid, when the price skyrocketed as high as it did, that he began to believe—to believe truly—that Ann's hysterical gibberish might have been grounded in fact.

And now, tonight, there came the rumors from the street. That the *Madonna* was in play. That that crazy old bastard Jervis Ramsbottom had vanished, might even be dead. And now, tonight, the real fear, the terror, had struck him like a blow. And he had begun to think: Yes. Yes, it's all happening, just as she said it would. *Iago. He'll kill everyone.* And Sir Michael had finally thought, *Good God. I'm next. They're going to come for me next.*

Then—even as he'd thought it—Sophia phoned. She was coming here to the Grange tomorrow, she said. She was coming with Richard Storm.

And everything fell into place. He had been suspicious of Storm from the very beginning. Calling Jessica off at the auction like that. Weaseling his way into Sophia's life like that. Now he was certain: if Storm was not this Iago fellow himself, he was surely working as his agent. This was how they were going to get at him. Through the American. Through Sophia. By corrupting the daughter he loved more than anything in life. By stealing the one thing he loved best—just as they had before.

His broad shoulders straightened. His weary features set. Well, if they thought he was going to lie down and take it this time, they had another think coming. Another think entirely.

Richard Storm, is it? Sir Michael thought angrily, sitting there. *Richard Storm indeed.*

And then, slowly, he began to load the revolver.

IX

SPECTRE

130   INT. THE CRYPT OF ST. JAMES

The repeated CLANG-CLANG continues and DR. PRENDERGAST, with the faithful HEDLEY trailing after, rushes in, following the sound.

They stand for a moment at a loss. Then, again: CLANG-CLANG.

> DR. PRENDERGAST
> This way, Hedley!

> HEDLEY
> But there's nothing here . . .

Ignoring him, PRENDERGAST rushes to a large sarcophagus in the center of the crypt. He seizes the stone lid.

> DR. PRENDERGAST
> Lend a hand, Hedley!

Baffled, HEDLEY joins the doctor. With a massive effort, the two men manage to push the lid off. It falls to the floor, breaking into pieces.

> HEDLEY
> By Jove, Prendergast: a stairway!

The CLANG-CLANG sounds again from beneath the crypt, much louder now.

> DR. PRENDERGAST
> Follow me!

First DR. PRENDERGAST, then HEDLEY, climb into the sarcophagus.

131   INT. HIDDEN STAIRWAY

DR. PRENDERGAST and HEDLEY descend into utter darkness.

Again: CLANG-CLANG.

> DR. PRENDERGAST
> Quick, Hedley, a torch!

HEDLEY produces a flashlight and the beam plays eerily over the mossy walls, suddenly illuminating . . .

The flayed body of SERGEANT ANDERSON, hanging in chains.

They examine the corpse grimly.

> DR. PRENDERGAST
> (continuing)
> Poor devil.

CLANG-CLANG.

> DR. PRENDERGAST
> (continuing)
> Come on, Hedley, there's no time to waste!

DR. PRENDERGAST continues his descent. After another moment confronting the body, HEDLEY follows.

132   INT. UNDERGROUND PASSAGE

DR. PRENDERGAST and HEDLEY reach the bottom of the stairs and enter an underground passage. An ominous RED GLOW is visible at the far end.

DR. PRENDERGAST touches HEDLEY's arm and nods at the flashlight. HEDLEY turns it off.

They move slowly, cautiously, down the passage as the CLANG-CLANG sounds again.

The RED GLOW grows brighter as they near the end of the passage. Their faces tense, they round the bend into . . .

133   INT. THE GREAT VAULT

The whole scene lies before them. JACOBUS, in the full evil splendor of his miter and pentagram robe, stands triumphant before an altar on which lies a purple blanket.

ANNIE, her clothes torn, is chained to the wall, writhing in her bonds.

As the CLANG-CLANG sounds again, we see . . .

The hunchbacked GORGE hammering out the blade of the jeweled SWORD OF THE SEIRIZZIM.

JACOBUS looks up at DR. PRENDERGAST with a calm smile, as if he had been expecting him.

> JACOBUS
> Why, Dr. Prendergast, I'm so glad you could make it. I left Sergeant Anderson to show you the way.

HEDLEY starts forward angrily, but DR. PRENDERGAST restrains him.

> JACOBUS
> (continuing)
> You're just in time to bear witness to my final apotheosis.

GORGE, his work finished, now shuffles forward, bearing the SWORD to his master.

ANNIE struggles on the wall, crying out through her gag.

JACOBUS handles the SWORD lovingly, then lifts it into the air.

> JACOBUS
> (continuing)
> Poor Prendergast. That you ever thought to defeat me. Could you not see that I am the agent of an immortal power? In such incarnations as this, I travel through the centuries. I feed on the marrow of time. I was here before the oceans turned black with life, and when the deserts are white with death I will remain. The petty hindrances you have put in my way have only served to amuse me. But that's all over now.

He raises the SWORD higher. And then . . .

Then, with bright eyes and an eager grin, GORGE steps to the altar. With a swift movement, he pulls the purple blanket away to reveal . . .

ANNIE'S BABY, *lying naked on the altar!*

ANNIE shrieks behind her gag, struggling on the wall.

JACOBUS raises the SWORD above his head, ready to drive it into the infant's breast.

But DR. PRENDERGAST only smiles with grim calm.

DR. PRENDERGAST
Not so fast, Jacobus . . .

X

BLACK ANNIE II:
THIS TIME,
IT'S PERSONAL

	His eyes! His eyes *were full of fear. And, though we had*
1	*seen him in London only two weeks before, he seemed*
	since then to have aged as many decades. A man in his

middle sixties, he peered at us through the half-open door of Belham Grange with all the tremulous hostility, the white-eyed apprehension, of some ancient anchorite disturbed at his grimmest meditations.

No shit, thought Richard Storm, as the withered, hostile, white-eyed face of Sir Michael peered out at them.

We had already dismissed our cab. We could hear the car's engine fading behind us on the Grange's long drive. The winter afternoon was closing around us, the windswept clouds of a lowering sky pressed down on us from above. The house itself, the whole great stone edifice, loomed menacingly before us as with an adsum *to our* conjuro te.

Well, all right, the house didn't loom exactly. It was a neat, pretty old mansion, a long stone structure with lots of windows, light and airy. And there were no "horrid ravens peering blackly from the gutters and gables of the place" either. But Storm did feel a "thrill of dread" sure enough at the sight of Sir Michael's "ravaged features"—his pale, sunken cheeks, his watchful eyes glaring out through the crack in the door. He felt a thrill of dread and a whirling, dreamy, febrile sense of swimming distances and unreality. He had a faint headache too, which had been bothering him all morning.

Sophia stepped from beside him to kiss her father's sagging cheek.

Storm took a last glance over his shoulder. Back up the empty drive, "where it stretched into the distance overhung by gloomy rows of copper beech." The clouds barreling in over the hills were thunderheads, great and threatening. The February wind was wet and chill, and the day was darkening to a false twilight.

And through that dark, through the dead, dangling branches intermingling above the drive, he could just make out the ruin of the abbey in the distance: "the broken wedge of a chapel wall, the slanting monuments of its ancient churchyard."

Storm straightened and took a breath, trying to clear his head. He turned to the house again.

Sophia had crossed the threshold. Sir Michael was holding the door open for him.

Well, he thought, he had come to England to find a ghost story, hadn't he?

And, forcing a smile, he walked into Belham Grange.

2 Detective Inspector William Pullod stood in the church round and watched the old woman. She was moving slowly among the stone effigies of dead crusaders. Prodding them with that freaky dragon stick of hers as if she half expected them to come to life. Frowning and muttering under her wide-brimmed hat, darting glances here and there from behind her goggly spectacles.

DI Pullod sluiced the air from one cheek to another, rolled his eyes.

He was a small, quick, sinewy man, a balding weightlifter with shoulders that seemed ready to burst the seams of his raincoat. He hated wasting time and he hated dead ends. And he hated churches too, if it came to that. He found them creepy, lonesome and yet weirdly alive—like a house where all the clocks have suddenly stopped ticking.

This one, the Temple Church, was bright enough with its big doors open to the noonday sunlight. Busy enough with a group of Japanese tourists chattering as they examined the stained-glass windows down at the other end. Here in the round, though, there were disturbing, distorted faces sculpted on the columns of the arches. They stared down from every side at the stone knights lying twisted on the floor. And it was creepy. Like the old darling herself.

Still, Pullod thought, there was definitely something about her. Nutter that she was. With her Saint Iago who never lived, and her Argentinian cult that never existed. Supernatural conspiracy theories. Little gray men and such. She ought to work for ITV, he thought. Still. Her eyes were sharp as a needle, smart. And she looked like she'd been alive forever. Sounded like it too with her gruff, grave voice. Not to mention the fact that she'd identified Lester Benbow from his photofit, and Pullod would've given his teeth to catch up with that scar-lipped assassin.

He strolled over to the woman now, his hands in his overcoat pockets.

"Everything look in order, love?" he asked her. He kept his voice low. Churches had that effect on him.

"Yes," murmured Harper Albright after a moment. "Yes." She went on prodding the dead crusaders with her stick.

Pullod ran his eyes over the gibbering faces on the walls. He could not restrain a weary sigh. "You're sure this is where you saw him last, this Iago fellow?"

Harper only nodded. "I didn't expect him to return, but it seemed worth trying. It was something he said about being chosen. I have a sense, you see, that he is not only following this trail of stories, but attempting somehow to inhabit them. As if he thought they were all about him in some way, as if he thought he were their ongoing protagonist. It makes one think he might seek out locations that bore some relation to them. That he might use them as the base for his operations."

"Aha," said Pullod. He put his tongue in his cheek to keep from smiling.

Harper Albright looked up at him sharply. "I don't expect you to believe me, Inspector. All I ask of you and your people is that you let me know the moment you locate Bernard's car."

Pullod, caught out, lost the smile and nodded briskly. "Morris Minor. We're keeping our eyes peeled."

She studied him through those goggles of hers for a long, uncomfortable moment. Then she sniffed.

"Please do," she said. "Because whether you believe me or not, the truth of the matter is: We haven't got very much time."

3 Then a church bell tolled some unknown hour and Bernard began to come around. He had no idea where he'd been, where he was, no notion of what had happened to him. For a long time the only thing he knew for certain was that the business of living had turned dimly dreadful.

Then, after a while, his eyes came open. Slowly. Breaking

the dried crust that had held them shut. He looked.

Nothing. Blackness. Darkness more complete, more empty than any he had ever known. He became aware now too that he was deeply uncomfortable. Lying on his back, inert, twisted. Knees to one side, one hand flung up by his face. The reek of the air was foul. There was a stench of vomit that made him want to vomit. He could feel the stuff soaking his shoulder through his shirt, viscid, lumpy. There was the smell of urine as well: his crotch and thighs were stinging with the drying damp.

A steady throb in his forehead was fast becoming intolerable. The taste in his mouth defied description.

Well, he'd woken up in a similar condition any number of times. But no, this wasn't an ordinary hangover. He was remembering now. The church. The crucifix. That moan; that man. His head lifting. His eyes . . .

Bernard made a weak, shuddering noise, a sound he'd never heard himself make before. The blackness seemed to be growing heavier, thicker. Closing in around him. Smothering him. Entombing him.

Entombing him. The thought started a stain of panic spreading up towards his chest from his loins. He could feel now the rough stone beneath his shaven pate. He moved his hand—felt a wall of the same rough stone to the right of him, another to his left. Rough stone was at his feet when he tried to extend his legs. And then, slowly, fearfully—*prayerfully*—he upstretched his fingers.

There was a slab of rough stone right above him, not six inches above his nose.

Buried alive. The panic swarmed up over him like rats. A chill sweat bathed him from head to toe. His breath grew short, shallow, his pulsebeat quick. A whispery voice spoke over and over in his head: *buried alive they've buried me alive I'm buried alive . . .*

He had to get the hell out of here.

With a choked cry, he thrust both hands up through the blackness. Instantly, the pain in his skull became excruciating, the veins bulging against his temples like spiked balloons. He pushed against the slab that covered him—pushed and pushed—struggling with all his sinewy might against that unyielding weight.

It was still unyielding. The breath stuttered from him in intermittent grunts. Then he gasped out the rest of it, and his arms collapsed on top of him.

"Help!" he shouted wildly. "Help!"

Then he retched, turning onto his side as best he could to keep the acid spittle off him. Then he plumped onto his back again, staring into the blackness.

Then he began to weep.

Buried alive. Christ, Christ, he didn't want to die like this.

"Christ," he whispered, sobbing. "Christ."

He worked his arm around in the cramped space, reached his trembling hand to his cheek to swipe away the hot tears.

And his heart seized in him like a dry engine.

There was something lying beside him in the blackness.

He had touched it with his knuckles. He could feel it there, an inch from his face. He could feel the smooth, yielding surface of moldering bone. The empty eye sockets. The image formed in his head as if he could see it: a human skull. Gaping at him, grinning at him. He was in a stone coffin—a sarcophagus—with a rotted corpse.

His body bucking with wild terror, he drove his hands against the coffin lid again. The pain was even worse this time. White pinpoints danced before his eyes. He almost lost consciousness. But he poured his strength into his arms, his soul into his arms, a high screek tearing from his throat as he fought to move the slab even a millimeter, even the width of an eyelash.

It was no good. The stone wouldn't budge. Bernard lay gasping, sobbing, trembling. *Buried alive I'm in the earth in a grave I'm buried alive* . . . He could feel his mind trying to tear free of its tether, trying to careen out of his control. He was about to start shrieking . . .

No. He set his teeth. No, no. He pressed his fists against his mouth, gnawed at the skin on his knuckles to force the scream down into his throat. Once he started that, there would be no end of it. He had to hold on. Hold on—by main force—there was no other way.

He summoned his will. He shoved the whispery voice of panic down, down. His breath. He focused all his concentration on his abdomen, on his breath.

He lay still. There was the dark, and the inner frenzy of his helplessness, the smell, the damp, the terrible pain. And yet he lay still, focusing on his breath.

He came down from the panic in notches, bit by bit. After a time—he didn't know how long—he became aware that he was whimpering, and forced himself to stop. His muscles began to relax. His fists sank down from his mouth, sank slowly over the length of him. He kept his hands directly above him, kept his elbows pressed close to his side to avoid touching that horror just next to him, that gaping horror.

"Help! Help me! Help!" Bernard shouted, not wildly this time, but as loudly as he could.

Then he lay very still, trying to control his breath so he

could hear. Lay with his eyes wide against the impenetrable blackness. Listening, listening.

"Help!"

Each time his voice ceased, the silence that followed seemed deeper than the silence before. It seemed to flutter down over him like a shroud and swaddle him round. A man could suffocate in such a silence. He could almost hear the worms crawling in it. He could almost hear the skull beside him speaking, whispering, *buried alive buried alive buried alive* . . .

"Help! Help!"

A high note of hysteria entered his voice and he clamped his mouth shut, clamped his eyes shut. Clamped his hands together over his belly, clamped his elbows to his sides. Hearing his breath, hearing his heartbeat, hearing the whispering skull beside him: *buried alive* . . .

And then—possibly—he heard something else. A noise. Possibly. Outside.

Bernard's eyes sprang open. His body, taut as it was, went tauter still. He stopped breathing altogether, and there was only the throb of his pulse, the throb of his head.

And, yes, something else. Definitely now. Rattle, crank, creak, thud. The sound of a door, he thought. A heavy door with a metal latch. Opening, then swinging shut again.

"Oh!" he said. Fresh tears surged from his eyes, tears of relief and gratitude. He wasn't under the earth, not buried, not yet.

"Help me!" he shouted.

Painfully rigid, he listened, yearning upward towards the coffin lid, beyond it.

And there were footsteps. Footsteps on stone. Steady, echoic. Coming nearer.

They stopped.

Bernard, crying, hardly dared to speak again. He stared upward, ached and prayed upward into the darkness. Someone was standing there, just over him, just on the other side of the stone, just on the other side of the blackness. He could feel the presence. Standing there. In the light, in the open air. Looking down at him.

Bernard licked the mucus from his upper lip. Swallowed it. Sniffled. Spoke through his tears in a tremulous whisper.

"Help me. Would you please."

There was another moment's silence. And then the presence spoke. A voice distinct and mellifluous. Casual, gentle, even kind. Strange and yet strangely familiar.

At the sound of it, some warm, potent emotion he couldn't name bubbled out of Bernard like blood from a wound, ran like blood all over him.

"I'm here, son," the presence said. "I'm here."

4 The silence was oppressive. The chink of cutlery on china. The slow crunching of cold food. Sir Michael sat at the head of the long table, swirling the wine in his crystal. Staring before him. Not speaking. Storm found the old man's sunken features, his disheveled hair, his wild glare painful to look upon. He kept his own head down, picking at the roast beef and carrots on his plate.

The dining room was narrow, but trim and pleasant enough. The lunch was laid out in gleaming plates and servers, blue and white. The crystal chandelier sent dancing rainbows over them and onto the flocked paisley on the long walls. Low sideboards and a serving table ran along one of those walls. And above these, there hung a gilt-framed painting of shepherds on sunlit hills. The landscape was almost a reflection of the landscape visible through the tall windows on the wall opposite, the wall Storm was facing. Out there, though, through the port-red curtains tied back with golden cords, he could see the hills stretching away under gathering clouds, a roiling black mass of them. A hem of thunder sounded from time to time, distant at first, but growing closer.

Sophia sat with her back to the scene. Her black hair, her pale valentine face were etched sharply against the sallow, murky light of the afternoon. Storm glanced up at her. Her figure was softened by a fuzzy tannish sweater with snow-flakes all over it. But she held herself very straight and he could feel the tension in her. He tried to catch her eye, to telegraph his question: When would she speak out? When would they begin?

She seemed not to look at him. Her head moved almost imperceptibly. A little forbidding shake of it: not now, not yet.

He went on eating, impatient, nervous. His head aching; thick; foggy. He did not feel well.

More thunder sounded, a longer grumble this time, and closer. Storm thought he caught a bland silver flash over the far horizon. The yellow light outside grew thicker, dimmer. He could see isolated trees bending here and there before the wind. He could feel the heat of Sir Michael's feverish eyes.

Let's cut to the damned chase, he thought. But he glanced at Sophia again, got that look again, that shake of the head.

"I'll make coffee, shall I?" she said softly.

And before either of the men could answer, she had risen and left the room.

Storm and Sir Michael sat in silence and listened to her footsteps fading down the corridor.

"I'm going to kill you, Mr. Storm," Sir Michael said then.

Storm was spearing his last piece of beef. He heard another roll of thunder. He took this in a full second before he comprehended Sir Michael's words. Then he raised his eyes to the other man. His lips parted, but he couldn't think of a thing to say.

Sir Michael had placed his glass down on the table now. He sat relaxed in his chair, with his hands folded over the belly of his vest. The great head seemed almost to have caved in upon itself. It reminded Storm of corpses he had seen in museums, half preserved, the skin clinging to the skull. Except for those eyes. Those eyes were alive enough, boiling, almost bulging out at him. Storm felt his stomach curdle, felt a point of pain stab at his temple.

"What?" he said.

"I'm going to kill you," Sir Michael repeated quietly, hoarsely. "Do you think I care what happens to me? Do you think I'm going to sit back and let you or your people do this to me again? Good Christ, whom do you think you're dealing with?"

"Whoa!" said Storm.

"You should be more careful, Mr. Storm. You should learn to leave a man something worth living for. I only have Sophia, and I won't let you use her to get at me, to get what you want."

"Hey, hold on a minute . . ." said Storm.

But Sir Michael plowed on irresistibly. "I've made inquiries. Do you understand? I'm not without contacts, here or in the States. I should hear back at any time, perhaps even today, perhaps within the hour. And the moment I'm certain you're who I think you are, I'm going to put a bullet in your head."

"Hey, listen up here a minute . . ." said Storm.

"No, you listen up. I'm going to blow your brains out,

boy, with pleasure. In my wife's memory and for Sophia's sake, and the consequences be damned." With a short, sharp motion, he snapped up his wine again. "I strongly suggest you run for your life."

Storm opened his hands, opened his mouth. He found himself utterly at a loss for words. His heart was racing. His mind was racing. Was Sir Michael making some kind of mistake? Or did he know why Storm was here and mean exactly what he said? Storm didn't know where to begin to answer him.

"Lookit . . ."

Hurried footsteps in the corridor stopped him, stopped them both. Sophia came back in. Pale, her lips working, she moved at once to Storm's chair, put her hands firmly on his shoulders. Even in his confusion, he heard the pitiful urgency in her voice.

"Come on, Richard," she said quickly. "While the coffee's brewing. I'll show you around the place before it rains."

"Sophia . . ." he said.

"Come *on!*"

5   The open-air market on the Edgware Road was in full swing. Harper Albright threaded slowly through the crowd. The pavements were still wet with rain but the London skies were clearer. The people were out in force, filling the spaces between stalls and bazaars, paging through racks of tie-dyed and heavy-metal T-shirts, milling past open boxes of vegetables, tables of pottery, jewelery, antiques, junk. Loud, tuneless music blasted from speakers under the canvas that covered some of the stalls. The shouts of hawkers

blasted back from their uncovered stands. "Cabbages! Lettuce! Tomatoes five a quid!" The tide of the crowd came on against her, but Harper pressed into it steadily. Her shoulders hunched, her stick jabbing at the concrete, her head uplifted grumpily and her quick eyes peering out from under her hatbrim, taking in the scene.

She took in everything. A young man pierced and bedizened at the ears and nose and eyebrows. A young woman holding a baby under one arm, examining a Grateful Dead shirt with the other. A John Bull toby mug on a table. A Chelsea football strip fluttering from a hook in the wind . . .

She took in everything. But what exactly she was looking for she did not know. She didn't even know exactly why she had come. She supposed it was enough at this point that a nagging instinct summoned her. She supposed it had to be enough; it was all there was.

And Bernard was out there—still alive. Captive, but still alive, she was certain of it. She could feel that much, she could feel him living. Feel it in the termites of anxiety gnawing steadily at her innards. Iago had no reason to kill the lad yet. Not yet. It wasn't his life he wanted. He wanted his blood. An endless supply of it. And for that, he would need to win over the factotum's will. He would have to poison his mind, gain his complicity. In other words, he would have to steal his soul.

And that would take some time. Bernard's soul was strong. It would take some time, but it would not take forever. She had to find him—soon.

And she had to find him on her own.

She had seen the look on the inspector's face. She had seen that look before in her dealings with the police. She had seen even worse looks than that sometimes; she knew Iago had his minions on the force. She could not trust the police to help her. She could not trust anyone. She had no clue to go on, no direction to follow, no spot to search in the wide world that seemed more likely to her than any other. Her enemies were legion, and she was only three. She had nowhere to turn, no one to turn to.

The time had come for her to catch the current of the Uncanny.

That was why she was here, really, she supposed. Shopping in the open market for inspiration. Peering down the aisles between the clothing racks. Running her eyes over the heads of lettuce. Watching the faces of the shoppers, the bopping rhythms of their youthful strides. She was seeking for coincidence, the pawprint of her adversary.

A little place off the Edgware Road. That's what Iago had said to her. *On the road to Damascus,* he'd said. That was where he had had his own inspiration twenty years ago. Whatever had happened then, somewhere near here, it had started him down the trail of stories. From "Black Annie" to the Belham Chronicle. Everything that had followed radiated from that one instant. Ann Endering's suicide. The hunt for the Rhinehart triptych. Even, perhaps, Richard Storm's arrival. From Iago's instant of revelation off the Edgware Road had come everything that had led them to this hour.

So she pushed through the crowds in the Edgware market. Her eyes moving. The anxiety gnawing away. Searching, she supposed, for the mystic spark that would put her inside Iago's mind. That would lead her to Bernard.

Her chance of making such a connection, in ordinary terms, was almost nil. And in one sense, ordinary terms were all she had. There is no life but life, she knew. There is no world but this one. If the Uncanny operates at all, it does not operate above the laws of nature but through them. The unseen moves forever in the manifest, the spirit speaks in the language of material; the soul lives in the interplay of neurons; and God, if He is anywhere, is in the details. Even coincidence—the spoor she was seeking—could be shown to exist within the rules of probability. But it did exist, the hidden tides and patterns of it. The trick was to find them when you needed them most.

And the trick to that—as always—was to believe nothing. To believe nothing lest the pattern of your beliefs be imposed upon the pattern of events. To believe nothing, and keep your eyes open. In wise passivity, to strive, to seek . . . and not to yield . . .

She reached the corner. The light was with her, but she paused, uncertain. Across the street, the market ended. The crowd thinned. Litter blew along the pavement, between whitewashed walls, past lampposts, under traffic signals, off down the avenue into the piebald sky. To her left, a man was selling sports caps. To her right, an Englishwoman dressed like a gypsy fortuneteller sat sullenly behind a table of used books. A tinker with a baby carriage held her hand out to the passersby.

Harper, for comfort, worked her fingers over the ears of the dragon head. The anxiety was seething now all through her. She felt like an empty sack full of racketing nerves.

And a voice spoke in her ear: "Oh, hey, look here. Look at this."

Without thinking, she glanced over, towards the speaker, to her right. There was just a boy there, in his late teens. A pale, pimply face pocked with red spots under a wisp of beard. A dull-eyed girl beside him, her arm in his, her nose and eyes and lips so full of studs and rings she seemed to be held together by them.

The boy had lifted a book from the table. Was holding it up to her.

"Look at this. Do we have this one?"

Harper did look. And as the lad rotated the book in his hand to study it, she saw the cover of *The Fourteenth Fontana Book of Great Ghost Stories*. The book Storm had read from at Bolt's Christmas party.

Harper stood and gazed at it. She felt a slow change begin to take place inside her. Her nerves continued racketing around, but now, instead of eating at her, they began to fuel her, to energize her. Anxiety was changing to excitement. She had found what she was looking for.

A little place off the Edgware Road, she thought.

The hunt was on.

6

"Do you know who I am?"

The voice came down into the sarcophagus like a tendril of smoke. It mingled like a smell with the smell of vomit and urine and sweat and fear. It coiled around Bernard's body where he lay with the tears still streaming down his cheeks, with his nose still running, with the agonizing pulse still beating in his head. He was aware now that there was blood at the pulsing spot, a stain half-dried, half-sticky where the sap had caught him. He was feeling woozy again and weak and sick. And the voice in the utter blackness came to him as with the cool of the open air, with the light of day. That first passion he had felt at the sound of it still coursed through him.

"Yes," he said, his own voice trembling. He cleared his throat. "Yes. I know who you are."

"Good. It's about time we became acquainted with one another."

Bernard could feel the coffin's stone lid pressing down on him, the rancid air growing more rancid yet. He could feel that skull beside him, not inches from his face, staring, grinning.

"I've never stopped keeping watch over you," said the voice. "You might know that."

Bernard closed his eyes, opened them. It made no difference; there was only the dark.

"Yes," he whispered.

"Some of the people you've met on your night excursions. Some of the people you've . . . played with, been intimate with . . ."

"Yes."

"You've known that."

Bernard cried quietly.

"In fact, I feel I already know you fairly well," said the voice. "In fact, I feel you already know me, but . . . But the truth is, I don't feel that you know you know me. If that makes any sense. I don't feel that you admit to yourself that you know me as well as you actually do."

"Let me out." The plea broke from Bernard before he could stop it. He screwed up his face, furious with himself for his weakness. But when he tried to slow his crying, he only produced a loud and humiliating sob.

"That's why I'm here," the cool voice went on, went on like smoke, filling the sarcophagus like smoke. And the worst thing about it, Bernard thought, was that it was so much better than nothing. He could feel how desperately he was holding on to the sound of it, holding on to the power of the presence above him, the power to set him free. He had to hang on to it. Where there was life . . . he thought. "I want to let you out," the speaker went on. "That's all I want. It's as much to my benefit as it is to yours. Maybe more. But I have to make sure you hear first what I have to say. So the bargain is: you promise to listen, I promise to set you free. Is that fair enough?"

Bernard shuddered, trying to control his breathing, to fight his panic. He didn't want to answer. It was degrading to agree where he had no choice.

But the voice insisted: "Isn't that fair enough?"

"Yes, yes," he said angrily, his own voice full of tears.

"Because everything you know about me, every single thing, has been told to you by one person, one person only. And that one person—I tell you this in all honesty—that one person has every reason to hate me. Isn't that true? Even from what you already know, wouldn't you agree that she's not an objective observer? Wouldn't you agree with that?"

Bernard hugged himself. "I don't know," he said wearily. "I don't know."

"Well, if you don't know," said the voice, "then it's because she hasn't told you everything. It's because she hasn't been as honest with you as I'm being right now."

Christ, thought Bernard. *Christ, Christ.* Hugging his shoulders more tightly, arms crossed like a corpse. He didn't know how to answer this, even within himself. He had always thought that it didn't matter, that he never minded. That he even enjoyed the unspoken knowledge, the tacit understanding between himself and Harper. He had been raised by a sturdy innkeeping family up in the lakes. Educated at a boarding school outside London. But Harper's visits to him had been frequent even in his childhood. Her conversations with him had always been intimate and pointed. She had explained her mission to him so thoroughly, so steadily, with such maternal assurance, that he had understood, from the earliest age, that it was his mission too, by birth, by right. Was it dishonesty for her not to speak aloud the fact he already knew?

"I can't breathe!" he screamed. His hands flew up, scrabbled at the rough slab. The flesh at his fingers tore and the blood ran down over them. Then his hands fell back again. He lay there, crying. "I can't breathe."

"When I first found her," the voice went on, unmoved. Cool, smoky. "When I first found her, she was in ruins. Her mother gone, her father in prison. Her own life a round of the worst kind of self-abuse: your life, believe me, is a poor imitation. It was she who attached herself to me, Bernard, not the other way around."

"I know that," Bernard said, under his breath so it wouldn't be heard.

"Good," said the voice. "I'm glad she told you that, at least. Because the rest was the same. If I degraded her, if I hurt her, it was because she wanted me to. Begged me to. Crawled to me on her knees, Bernard, and demanded it. On her knees, Bernard."

Bernard felt he was going to be sick again, sick unto death this time. He felt he was going to vomit up everything inside him, blood and guts, the very tinkerbell-flicker of life itself. The smell and the worsening air had all been displaced by the miasma of that voice. It seeped into his skin, cool and vital and refreshing. His own weird passion met it, and he felt sick and poisoned unto death.

"And now," the voice went on. "Now the memory of that

disturbs her, and she puts it all onto me. Her own desires are off the hook and I become the villain of the piece. And that's . . . distorted. It isn't the truth. It not only deprives me of the right to defend myself—but it deprives you too. It deprives you of that part of yourself that is just like me. Because you are like me, Bernard. And that makes you afraid. You suppress it. It becomes anathema to you. You indulge in petty, humiliating perversions to—how can I put it?—to *stave off* the real urges, the real *impetus* of your nature. She's made you like that. She taught you to despise yourself, that part of yourself that's like me. And why? Because she's peddling a worldview in which she has no responsibility, in which I work like some sort of . . . grand puppeteer on the world stage and she just dances. All I'm asking you to accept, Bernard, is the possibility—just the possibility—that there's another worldview. A worldview in which you can live freely as what you really are."

Bernard covered his face with his bleeding hands. Felt the damp, sticky surface of his flesh beneath his fingers. He was experiencing a remarkable floating sensation now, as if he were detaching from his own body. As if some part of him were being drawn up out through his pores and into the smoke, becoming part and parcel of the smoke. He could feel himself striving to float with it, float on, float up through the coffin's stone, float up into the freedom of the presence above him.

"I'm sorry, Bernard," the voice said calmly. "But there comes a time—it comes for all of us—when you have to consider the possibility that everything you've been taught is a lie; when you have to entertain the idea that the people you love best have in fact deceived you."

Bernard floated in the smoke. The smoke caressed him.

"I am who you want to be, Bernard. And you contain me within you," said the voice. "We are, both of us, Saint Iago."

7 The sky above Belham Grange churned with black rainclouds. The wind that carried them in from the south rattled the naked branches of the trees overhanging the front drive. It made mysterious trails in the grass, swift, swirling strips of lighter green as the blades bent over before it. These swaths appeared in front of Storm and curled around him and vanished. They appeared again as the wind picked up, moving off into the hills like ghostly footprints.

Sophia was marching quickly into the darkening day, charging angrily away from the house, away from the drive and off into the field. Storm had to take long strides to keep up with her, hurriedly belting his trench coat against the cold.

There was thunder above, and Sophia's eyes were flashing. Her own overcoat was open. It blew back around her. The wind swept over her hair and sent wisps of it across her face, into her mouth. She snatched at them, pulled them back.

"We can't go through with it," she said. "We can't. He's sick. You can see that. He's ill, Richard, something's wrong with him."

"You're telling me," said Storm. He rubbed his aching brow. "He just threatened to kill me in there."

"What?" She barely broke stride, barely glanced at him. "Don't be ridiculous."

"He did, honey! He said he was going to blow my head off. Really."

She snorted. "I'm sure he was making some kind of joke."

"Hey, ha, ha, ha," said Storm. "The guy's a comic genius."

She stopped. Faced him fiercely with the swaying beeches behind her and one stone wing of the house with the gathering clouds on its dark windows. She crossed her arms beneath her breasts. Oh boy, he thought, pulling up short. He'd seen *that* look before. He'd had to have a couple of them surgically removed from his neck. Jesus, there were moments with women when it seemed a man was born two apologies behind.

"I cannot believe I let you talk me into coming here," Sophia said. "I can't *believe* you expect me to interrogate and . . . and torment that man about a . . . a tragic, tragic thing in his life that happened twenty years ago. Especially now, especially when he looks like this. He's sick, Richard."

It was a tragic, tragic thing in your life too, Storm wanted to say. But he was a mite too experienced for that. Go head to head with a girl in this state and you wound up explaining to the judge why you should be allowed to keep the clothes on your back. This called for a little Relationship Judo.

Sophia kept glaring at him. The first jagged fork of lightning fired off clear of the horizon. Storm flinched, but not because of the lightning. The cold wind carried the thunder to them, long and low.

"So why don't you ask him what's wrong with him?" Storm said finally.

"What?"

"You come home, your dad looks like the cat dragged him in, how come you don't say, 'What's the matter, Pops? Should I call the doctor?' How come you don't ask him that, okay?"

The glare faltered. Thank God. "Well, I . . . I don't know, I . . ."

"I mean, like you said, Sophie—look at him."

She shifted from foot to foot. Glanced away. "Well, if he doesn't want to talk about it . . . I mean, if he's . . . reluctant . . ."

"He wants to talk about something, that's for sure. The man threatened to shoot me."

"Oh, he did not."

Pain raked through the fog in his head. He said, "Yes, the hell he did." It came out rougher than he'd meant, and he was sorry at once. But he saw too that it made her believe him. Suddenly uncertain, she ran her hand up through her hair. Her eyes grew frantic. Her lips trembled. Which was worse than the glare. "Something really is wrong here, Sophia," he said more gently. "I think you have to find out what it is."

"Oh, I don't know what's what anymore," she whispered. "You've got me all confused."

"Look." He stepped closer to her. "Harper didn't send us out here for nothing."

"Oh, I don't give a *tinker's damn* . . ."

"Awright, awright. But . . ." He lifted his hand to calm her. "She thinks that finding out about your mother might help her figure where Iago is headed."

"Oh, *Iago!*"

"Awright. But these guys . . . these bad guys who killed your friends . . ."

"They *weren't* my friends . . ."

"Awright, awright. But the thing is . . . I think they're closing in somehow. That must be what your father's afraid of, see. That's my guess. He must think that I'm the one they've sent."

The way she frowned at him then—it burned into his chest like a brand. "Well, maybe you are," she said. "I mean, how do I know?"

It was so dark now, the clouds so heavy, that the air seemed thick between them. There were no birds singing. And though Storm could see a small highway off in the hills by a distant church steeple, there was no sound of traffic, no noise louder than the wind.

"You don't believe that," he told her. "You'd just rather say something like that than find out about your mother's death, than come right out and talk with your father about how she died and what you remember. And it's no good, Sophia." He let out a breath, lifting his face. The answering wind was damp on his skin. Cooled his forehead, cleared his mind. "Everything with you and him depends on these secrets," he said. "It's all what you don't tell each other, what you don't ask. I don't think you have time to go on like this anymore, to keep doing this."

Sophia brought both hands up to her hair now, clutched it. And Storm, watching her, just felt terribly lonely. It only took an instant of her anger to remind him that her affection was his only comfort just now, might be his last comfort forever. It only took an instant of her confusion and simmering panic to remind him of how much stood between him and what he needed from her. How much dead life would have to be cleared away before they could really be together.

These were not the sort of ghosts he had wanted to find.

"Why are you doing this to me?" she said softly, in a voice that was not like hers at all. "If I can't handle this, well, then I can't. Why do you keep pushing and pushing me? Why does it matter so much to you? Why is it so important to you, Richard?"

As if she had spoken into his thoughts. And Storm knew that his misery showed in his eyes for an answer. His failure.

His hypocrisy. All this talk about honesty, about airing secrets. And he had never even found the courage to tell her that most basic truth. To say to her: I'm dying. My love is as selfish as anyone's. I need you to be free in your mind so you can give yourself to me and I won't be alone for this. I need you to break out of your past so I can feel I've done something for you, so I can feel I've left a life I love behind.

He reached out and put his hand against her cheek. And she—to his surprise—closed her eyes and leaned into it, took hold of it with her own. It just about broke his heart.

"All right," he said, swallowing hard. "Listen. Listen. There's something I have to tell you . . ."

"Sophia!"

In the rising wind, the call seemed to come from a great distance. But, looking back across the field, Storm could see movement through the screen of beeches. Sir Michael was standing at the door of the house.

"Sophia!"

Calling her.

She glanced up at Storm. Their eyes met quickly. He tried to speak again, but couldn't. She patted his hand and drew away without a word.

Storm stood alone under the low clouds with the wind trails appearing in the grass all around him. He stood with his hands in his trench-coat pockets. He watched as Sophia ran off towards the house.

Then, with a sigh, he turned away. Turned away, and confronted, for the first time, what had been behind him all this while.

There, beyond the sinuous silhouette of an elm, stood the abbey ruin, sullen, black and grim. An ominous and melancholy apparition: the broken wedge of a chapel wall, the slanting monuments of its ancient churchyard. The faltering illumination, laced as it was with the running cloud shadows, gave to the entire scene a floating quality, weird and dreamlike.

Eesh, thought Storm, his heart like a stone.

And, as if compelled, as if driven by the wind, he began to move across the field.

Towards the abbey. Towards its ancient graves.

8 **A ghost story.** "A Little Place off the Edgware Road" was the name of a ghost story. A fine one, in fact, by Graham Greene. It was included, with "Black Annie," in the collection from which Storm had read. It was this, no doubt, that had brought the particular phrase into Iago's mind when he was speaking of his inspiration.

Harper spent the next several hours in the basement of the London Library. Paging slowly through the bound volumes of newspapers twenty years old. She knew now what she was looking for. She suspected, at least, what she was going to find. But she couldn't afford to rely *too* much on coincidence. To make a mistake now would be to lose what little time she had. She had to make certain she was right before she proceeded. So she went on, page after slow page.

Outside, the short winter's day edged on towards evening. Within, the fluorescents shone their misty bluish light down on the tall shelves, the long wooden tables. It shone down on Harper's bowed head, on her short, dull gray hair. On the stick propped against her chair, and on the hat set beside the open volume.

Her eyes scanned the newspaper columns slowly. And when, finally, she came upon the advertisement she wanted, she had a feeling inside her like a long, slow sigh. She wasn't yet sure how this was going to help her. But the confirmation of her suspicions was encouraging. It indicated, at least, that Iago was like everyone else in one respect: whenever he spoke, he gave away much more than he intended.

The phrase that formed the ghost story's title had no doubt come into his head unbidden as he thought back on the revelatory event. There was no reason it should have stuck with Harper, no reason she should have worried at it. But now, as she sat alone in the windowless basement under the fluorescents' grainy glare, she understood why she had.

Because the little place off the Edgware Road was, in the Greene story, a cinema. Iago had been in a cinema twenty years ago when he'd had the revelation that started him down the story trail. And the newspaper advert before her was for the Odeon Cinema, on Church Street, just off the Edgware Road. The advert told her what, all this time, she had really known. That the inspiration that had led Iago to "Black Annie"—and the other stories and the monk's confession at last—had been a film.

One day, twenty years ago, Jacob Hope had gone to see *Spectre*. Written, produced and directed by Richard Storm.

9   From time to time, Bernard still sobbed weakly, but there were no tears anymore. They seemed to have all dried up. Everything inside him seemed to have dried up so that it felt as if even his sweat had stopped flowing, even his blood had stopped flowing. Even his swarming panic had become a motionless thing, a weight of dread, squatting on his chest like a gargoyle.

Only his mind . . . Only his mind kept drifting, floating, losing itself within the fumy substance of that voice. Iago's voice.

"Let me ask you something, Bernard. Have I ever hurt you? Before this, I mean, when my hand has been forced by circumstance? Have I ever done you personally any harm?"

"That man . . ." Bernard could barely move his lips to speak. "You . . . crucified that man."

"Ach," Iago said. He laughed pleasantly. "I've killed hundreds of people. Tortured lots of them. And laughed? Let me tell you, for comic relief? There is nothing quite so hilarious as other people's suffering. When they're bouncing around like pachinko balls, screaming, begging . . . Oh. Well. One day, you'll see what I mean. No, no, no, that's not what I'm asking. You have to listen, Bernard."

It seemed now that he leaned in close, that he must have pressed his lips right to the sarcophagus lid. The cool voice seemed to pour down over Bernard's face, queerly refreshing with its tincture of power and freedom. A memory came into the prisoner's drifting mind of a lover who smoked cigarettes, who kissed him with a lungful of smoke, and released it into his mouth so that he breathed it in while they kissed. Sickening, exhilarating, beautiful.

"I'm just talking about you," said that voice. "All right? Have I ever done anything personally harmful or painful to you? Or to Harper, for that matter? Or to any of your friends?"

Bernard lay silent under the weight of dread and stone and smoke and pain.

"Nothing of you or yours has been harmed by me in any way," Iago continued casually. "Not a thing. And if that's true—if that's true, Bernard—then all your objections to me, all your fear of me, all your loathing even, is purely abstract, purely philosophical. You hate and fear me because you have an idea—an abstract idea—that the things I do are somehow wrong. That they're nasty. That one is not *supposed* to do them. And who taught you that idea, Bernard? Who told you that they were wrong? Hm? I mean, I know that everyone says that it's wrong to kill, wrong to cause pain, but who cares what everyone says? Everyone is frequently wrong, more frequently than not. No, I mean, who taught *you*, who tells you every day that what I do is wrong in the abstract?"

Bernard could almost feel his floating mind beginning to work apart from him, to think and answer on its own as it drifted and swirled about the darkness. His mind seemed only to be using his body as a vehicle for speech. "Harper," it answered—he answered—hoarsely.

"Harper, that's right," said Iago, well pleased. "Harper, who was mine, who begged to be mine at the cost of any degradation. Who begged for the degradation to prove to me that she was mine. And who now can't stand the thought of herself as she was with me and so takes her revenge by trying to destroy what there is of me in you. Because that's what it's all about, really. These abstract ideas of hers— wrong, right, good, evil—where do they exist? If you can show them to me, I'll bow down to them, I swear. If you can hand them to me, Christ, I'll eat them. All right? But they exist nowhere. Except in Harper's vengeful mind. So what are her notions of good and evil but just her way of training you to repress the part of you she's afraid of? I mean, I see this every day, Bernard. The weak teach the strong to be afraid of their own strength—why? So that the weak won't have to suffer at the hands of the strong—more than that, so that they won't have to face their own natural propensity for suffering. You, Bernard, have to walk through the world repressed and stunted and twisted inside so that Harper can be free of the memory of her own desire, so that Harper doesn't have to face herself. If you want to talk about truth— that's the truth. And it isn't fair. I mean, I asked you if I've hurt you, and you know I haven't. Now I ask you: Has *she* hurt you? Harper. Has she hurt you personally? Not abstractly, but really." He didn't wait for an answer. "I think she has," he said. "I've shut you in a box, in a coffin. But she's turned your whole world into a coffin. She shuts you—your true self—inside it every single day. I'm not only offering to set you free from *this* box, Bernard. I'm offering to set you free from the box she's put you in, the cage of Harper's ideas that has your true nature crouching like an animal inside. Because you're more like me than you are like her. You're more my son than hers."

Dimly now, Bernard became conscious of the fact that he was losing himself. Truly losing control of his own mental functions, of his own responses. His own thoughts and the insinuating voice were becoming fused together. And he lay there in his woozy agony, watching it happen, as if from a restful far. It was a strange feeling, dreamy, even sweet, even sensual. So sweet, in fact, so sensual that he could not think of a single rational reason to make it stop. All he had to do was listen, after all, lie there and listen and go along, and eventually he would be let out of this place, which was all in the world he wanted. The lid would come off and he would be welcome—with smiles, with open arms—into the help and comfort of the daylight. All he had to do was stop fretting, stop trying to hold on, stop muddying the sweetness with his will, and the worst of this would soon be over.

Who had taught him, anyway, that he should do otherwise?

"And I'm offering you even more," said the voice above him, around him, within him. "I'm offering you life, Bernard. I'm offering you free, unfettered, unending life. Come out of this coffin—come out to me—and you will be free of the prospect of burial forever. Free of decay, of the fate of that hideous thing in there beside you. Forever, Bernard."

"I won't!" The shout went off in the coffin like a bomb, like a flash of light, before Bernard even realized it had come from his own mouth. *"I won't listen anymore!"* He felt as if he had awakened suddenly—had awakened from a deep sleep to find a thief making off with his most prized possession. His mind. He wanted his mind *back*. And his hands were up against the lid again, his raw fingers bleeding again as he pushed and scrabbled violently at the stone. The hot, filthy air filled his lungs. The nausea wrung his stomach. His movement brought a fresh sense of how tightly enclosed he was and with that came fresh panic and terror.

And, at last, he was overwhelmed by all this, by his own efforts. He was exhausted by his own helplessness. His hands fluttered down on top of him. "I won't listen," he said. Coughing. Sobbing.

There followed a long, an excruciating, pause. Bernard tried uselessly to shift onto his side. He coughed and dry-retched. He felt that he was gagging on the very air and on his self-disgust. How little physical pain it takes to make a man nothing; nothing.

Then Iago spoke again: "All right."

Panting, Bernard forced himself to stop coughing. Swallowed a hot gout of his own vomit. Gasped, gagged. Tried to listen.

He heard a sound that caused a tremendous solid sphere of icy cold to form itself in his abdomen. He tensed, swallowed again, held his breath. Listened.

Footsteps on stone. Moving away. Fading away.

Bernard started screaming. *"No! Don't leave! Don't leave me here! Don't leave me! Please!"* Babbling in a high, wild, raggedy voice that hardly seemed to belong to him. "Come back! *Please! Please!"*

He stopped. Lay shivering, his face contorted as he willed the speaker to return, as he strained and strained to hear.

He heard.

Clank, rattle, creak, thud. The door opening, closing.

And then silence.

"Don't leave me," he murmured. "Father."

And he lay weeping in the dark alone.

10   At that moment, Richard Storm suddenly realized he had arrived.

He was standing in the shadow of the abbey wall, the clouds lowering. He was standing amidst slanting headstones worn faceless with weather and time. The afternoon was roiling, black. The wind was damp and biting. Lightning dashed fiery from the meridian to the vanishing point, and thunder followed hard on, loud, enormous. Around him, broken steles lay crushed upon the grass. A single crypt sat crumbling. The streaking shadows on the ruined wedge of wall made it seem animate, wraith-washed.

He had come upon the living soundstage of his imagination.

He remembered a ghost story he had heard once. A

woman dreams she's standing outside a house. Every night, in her sleep, she's there, staring at this same house. She becomes so troubled by the dream she decides to take a vacation. Driving into the countryside, she comes upon the very house of her dreams. Unable to resist, she gets out of her car and approaches. The front door opens. A butler stands in her way.

"This house," the woman says. "I have to see inside this house."

"Of course, madam," says the butler. "But I should warn you: the house is haunted."

"Haunted?" says the woman. "Haunted by whom?"

And the butler replies, "By you."

Storm looked around him at the ruins of Belham Abbey.

How often, he wondered, had he had this place put on film? Some place like this. He couldn't count how many times he had dreamed it up as if new, filled it with fresh vampires and ghouls and monsters. *Spectre* featured a ruined church like this one. So had *Castle Misery*. So had *Hellfire*. But it wasn't until he had come to stand here that he fully understood that they had all been this, this very site.

Because this was the setting of "Black Annie," which he had read when he was ten years old. Which had made him what he was.

He could remember—not which day, but the way the day felt—when he had read the story first. The palmy Santa Monica breezes, smelling of oranges and the sea. The lush greenery at his window, and the whitewashed wall of his neighbor's house, the ruddy slate of its roof. Birds were twittering. Bees were humming among the oversized flowers whose names he didn't know. He could hear the plash of someone swimming in his backyard pool. His mother. And he lay alone, in his room, on his bed. Little California Rick in shorts and T-shirt. With the Aurora monster models on their shelves above him staring benignly down. Franken-stein, Godzilla, the Creature from the Black Lagoon with genuine green scales. Dracula, on whose black plastic chin he had hand-painted a line of red. And he held the book of ghost stories on his stomach. *Spooks and Phantoms.* The book his father had given him, resigned to the fact that the boy would read it with more pleasure than his gifts of westerns, Jack Schaefer, Louis Lamour. Young Richard had lain in the whitewashed California springtime, and his mind had gone off into the autumn of Victorian England. Off into the haunted house with Neville and Quentin. Off to the abbey ruin, this very ruin, here. He had loved that story, loved it.

And it had never really occurred to him to wonder why. What was it about himself that was so willing to connect with a setting and a situation that were different from everything he actually knew? He had never produced a picture that wasn't full of the Gothic, the Victorian, the whole "Black Annie" aura. And why? He couldn't help but wonder about it now, now that he was standing here.

Because the rising medieval stone of the wall, the leaning graves—even the threatening weather—the whole classic ghost story scene—were truly as familiar to him as if he had been here a million times. They were as familiar to him as a celebrity's face, as if they slotted in—*thock*—to some archetypal jigsaw emptiness in his mind. They were that familiar—and, at the same time, he had never felt like such an alien, like such a stranger in a strange land.

What the hell was he doing here anyway, so far from home? Who were these people around him? Harper, Bernard, Sir Michael. Sophia. What the hell was he doing involved in all their lives? Making such a mess of them? He was dying, for Christ's sake. He should be with people he knew. With pals who would cluck over his predicament, and doctors who would tell him things that seemed to make sense. In a world he knew, really knew. Not like this one, which he'd only appropriated as a child, which he'd only spent his life reinventing.

He remembered this same strange feeling, this sense of being alien and apart—he remembered how it had overtaken him just before his attack of convulsions the month before. He felt a drifty, cold wisp of fear travel down from his chest to his groin. And he thought: *Not now. Not yet. Not again.*

But no, it wasn't that. It wasn't as easy as that. It was this place. This abbey. This ruined churchyard. This stately country house. This England. What had any of them to do with him? With the son of a cowboy star from the golden coast? They didn't want him here. He could feel that. They rejected him. They wanted him to go away and leave them alone. Hell, they'd murdered guys like him in this place once upon a time. Irritating, intrusive Jew-boys. They'd locked them up in the infirmary and just barbecued them. Yippee-aye-oh-kye-ay, babe. This place was not his place at all.

And if he didn't belong here, where did he belong? Who the hell was he anyway?

He snorted. It was a little goddamned late to ask.

The lightning flickered above him, crackled. And in seconds, the thunder boomed. The black clouds rolled and turned, and the wind walked among the graves. And Storm walked among them, his sad eyes moving on the speechless, haunted stones.

Who the hell was he? That was the question. Who the hell was he to come here and torture Sophia about her past?

Make her unhappy for his own selfish sake. She didn't want him here either. He was as alien to her as he was to this place. He only loused things up for her. Asking her to do this thing that was foreign to her nature. Because he was foreign to her nature. Because he didn't belong with her, in her world.

He had failed her, hadn't he? He would've killed to be her hero and he'd failed her, dead to rights.

He came to stand before the decaying crypt. A waist-high temple with pilasters worn to beaded strips, an iron door worn thin, broken through. He shook his head.

Haunted by whom? he thought.

Haunted by you, pal.

It was the scariest ghost story ever told. You just had to be there.

The rain began slowly. He felt a drop blown onto his cheek. He glanced up into a sky that seemed to hang not six feet above him. Another droplet fell, and more. He heard them patter on the tombstones. *Tip-tip. Tip-tip.*

Yeah. He smiled with one side of his mouth. *Tick-tick.* That's right. Time's running out on you, Jackson.

And then his smile faded. He looked down again at the crypt before him. At the rough crescent-shaped hole worn in the iron door. It went down into nothingness, down and down forever, for all he knew. And he raised his eyes to Belham Grange, to the wing of the house that extended beyond the double row of trees.

There were often, I knew, in abbeys and the neighbouring houses, secret chambers and hideaways . . . underground passages . . .

He remembered Sophia's story, the story she had told him about the noise in the house, about the night she had seen her father standing over her mother with a bloody knife. He had known at the time she told it to him that something had been left out of that story, that something had been missing. Now, as the rain grew steadier, stronger, he realized what it was.

The wind rose, cold, and the rain started slanting down. There was another snarl of thunder that seemed to come from deep in the belly of the sky.

Richard Storm turned up the collar of his trench coat. He turned away from the ruin, and headed back across the field to the house.

By the time Sophia reached the door, her father had withdrawn. The door stood open and she went in, closing it behind her.

"Daddy?"

"In the sitting room," he answered her.

But she stood in the foyer another moment, at the foot of the stairs.

"Right," she said in an undertone. She made a gesture with both hands. Held them open in front of her and pushed them down against the air: a calming gesture. She wanted to compose herself. She was agitated after her conversation with Storm. She was jittery, confused. Apprehensive. They were all feelings she disliked intensely. "Right," she said again.

She stripped off her overcoat, hung it on a peg by the door. Smoothed down her jumper as if to smooth down her inner self as well. She went along the corridor to the dining room, consciously trying to work her expression into one of cool irony. She did not feel she was succeeding very well at all—and then she was at the sitting-room doorway.

She stepped across the threshold. It was a long room, from the cold stone fireplace to the tall windows. And it was dark: the walls hung with dark, misty paintings, the windows with dark, heavy green drapes. Her father was at the far end, by the window that looked out across the field to the abbey. He faced her when she entered. He stood with the black clouds behind him. She saw the lightning flash down from the clouds, heard the thunder.

"Come in, come in, Sophia. We'd better talk," Sir Michael said.

She hesitated where she was. And it struck her for a moment: she was afraid; she was afraid of him. But she shook the thought off. It was ridiculous. He was her father. She approached slowly.

Much of the furniture was gathered in one half of the room, the near half. The sofa, table and chairs were arrayed together around the fireplace. She came around them, but then she paused again. She stood by the sofa, with her hand on the back of it. That left an open space of some distance— the length of the Persian carpet—between her and her father. She did not cross that distance, but confronted him from where she was. Landscapes of brown crags and fog covered the wall to her left.

"Yes, what is it?" she said.

She couldn't hold his gaze. Her eyes shifted away from him. To the window. Out to the abbey ruin. She could see Storm out there, afar off. He was moving beside the broken wall, walking among the gravestones. His coat was stirred by the wind. His hair was stirred by it. She wished he was here, in here, with her. What had he been about to tell her? Why was she so upset? She hated it.

Her father took a step towards her. Sophia felt her hand close more tightly on the wooden rail of the sofa back. Her father looked large, towering. His great head seemed hung bizarrely with loose flesh. His eyes were strange and quick and dangerous. With the black clouds rushing forward behind him, it seemed as if he himself were rushing at her.

"Why did you bring him here?" he asked her.

Sophia shook her head, confused. Tried to think of an answer.

"I don't like him," said Sir Michael. "I don't trust him. What is he here for?"

"Trust him . . . ?" said Sophia. She could not bring her thoughts to order. Why was she so afraid?

"Doesn't it even occur to you to ask yourself what he keeps hanging around for?"

And Sophia heard herself begin to answer as if she were listening to another person: "Well, doesn't it even occur to you that . . . ?" She pressed her lips together.

"What?" he said. "Go on."

"Well, he might be hanging around because he likes me? It might not have anything to do with you and this . . . anything to do with you."

Her father made an exasperated, dismissive noise. The clouds behind him flickered with unsteady light. The following thunder was loud.

"No," said Sophia, uncertainly. "I mean it. I don't know what the problem is . . ."

"For God's sake, Sophia, don't be childish."

"Am I supposed to run my friends by you for approval?"

At that, he took another step towards her. Large, unfamiliar. "Friends like that, yes. There are plenty of suitable men around."

Her hand moved nervously on the sofa back. She felt very small in front of him. And her knees were beginning to feel weak and shaky. "I don't know what you mean by *suitable*.

Richard is perfectly *suitable*..."

And again: that dimissive noise, like a whiplash. "He's ridiculous, if nothing else. And he's old enough . . . He must be forty, at least."

Sophia licked her lips. "Is that what's bothering you?"

"Are you playing some kind of game with me?"

"Well, what is all this? He says you threatened him."

"I'll do more than threaten him . . ." He came closer. She could see him more clearly. The quivering, pasty folds of skin, the skeletal outlines of his cheeks, the too-bright eyes. The sight made her faintly nauseous.

"I don't understand," she said. "I don't understand what's wrong. Why are you acting this way?"

"Sophia," he said. This was gentler, a tone she remembered, a voice she remembered. Her father's tone, his voice. The gesture he made with his hand was one she knew. But he seemed a different person. "I'm sure there are dozens of men who are interested in you," he went on, "who want to be with you. Half our clients are in love with you. That's not the point. The sad fact is, this . . . person is using you."

"Using me?"

"To get at me."

"Why on earth . . . ?"

"All right, if you're going to be purposely obtuse: to get at the Rhinehart."

"But you don't have the Rhinehart."

"Now you *are* being purposely obtuse."

"I'm not. I simply don't understand."

He shook his head at her sternly.

Sophia let go of the sofa back. She rubbed her hands fretfully together. Her mouth was dry and her stomach fluttery. "Daddy," she said. "Daddy, don't talk in riddles anymore.

Tell me what's happening."

"What do you mean? I just don't like my daughter being taken advantage of . . ."

"I mean all this about the Rhinehart," she said. "Why are you so upset about the Rhinehart? Whatever it is, if you explain it to me . . ."

Sir Michael eyed her as from a height. Through the window, under the gathering clouds, distant, she saw Storm pause before a low crypt. She wished he would come in.

"Did he tell you to ask me that?" Sir Michael said.

"What? Well . . . No. No, of course not, I—"

"What makes you think I'm upset?"

She laughed unhappily. "Look at you. You look awful."

"There's nothing wrong with me."

"You look positively ill. What is going on? Why are you acting all paranoid? What's frightening you?"

He reared—and Sophia quailed. There was another rumble from the rushing clouds. And then a soft patter on the tall pane between the drapes. It was beginning to rain. In another moment the water was washing hard against the glass. Sophia could see Storm moving away from the ruin, moving across the field out of sight, towards the house. She was desperate for him to come to her.

"Are you cross-questioning me?" Sir Michael said.

"Me?" Sophia's hand went to her middle. She was really beginning to feel sick. "Me, cross-questioning you? You called me in here—"

"I called you in here because you've allowed this unsavory man—"

"Oh, Daddy."

"—to push and wheedle his way into our house, to seduce you—he has seduced you, hasn't he?"

"What are you talking about? Seduced . . . That's insane. I'm a grown—"

"You've allowed him to seduce you and push his way into this house for the sole purpose of getting his hands on that triptych. If you're such a grown-up woman then you should've known better. You should've exercised a little judgement."

Sophia, practically cowering beside the sofa, practically cried out, "You're not making any sense. Why would Richard want to do something like that?"

"Oh, don't be ridiculous."

"I'm not—"

"Because he's a criminal."

"He is not."

"He's a sneaking, murdering—"

"Murdering?"

"—filthy bastard who doesn't care a damn about you."

"He does! Stop it! You're talking utter shit! Stop it!"

Quickly, Sophia pressed the back of her hand to her mouth. The wind blew the rain up hard against the window. A fork of lightning stabbed down into the hills, hurling the shadow of the abbey wall across the headstones. The sudden upsurge of rage had taken her completely by surprise, had left her feeling shaken and ill. She could not remember the last time she had spoken like that—had raised her voice at all—against her father.

He turned his shoulder to her. Lifted his chin. Frowned down across the room at her with his eyes hot and foreign and terrifying.

"I'm sorry, Sophia," he said. "I didn't realize he had got so far with you."

And, sick as she felt, she was angry again on the instant. Helplessly, she felt her eyes fill with tears. "Don't say that.

Don't say that to me. How dare you? I think Richard may be the single most decent and straightforward person I've ever met. What would he want with the Rhinehart triptych?"

Sir Michael waved her away.

"What do *you* want with it?" she said.

And with one more sharp glance, he showed her his back, faced the rain-scored window.

"Because it is you, really," she said to him, trembling. "You're the one who's been acting . . . dishonestly. I don't know what you're involved in. I've never known. You won't tell me. You don't tell me anything. You act as if I'm supposed to understand, as if it's a given between us. But I don't understand. Not really. I don't understand what's going on at all. How could I, Daddy? You don't explain anything. Everything between us depends on all these . . . secrets. Everything revolves around what you don't say, and what I'm not supposed to ask. It's always been like that. It's always . . ."

Weak and nauseated, she couldn't finish. One hand clutched at the sofa again, one went around her stomach. Sir Michael's powerful form was burned into silhouette by a lightning flash. The thunder was so loud this time it seemed to rumble through the flooring. The windows rattled with the wind.

And then the Great Man turned on her again. Turned where he was and looked across the room at his daughter with eyes that she could hardly recognize—they were so full of disdain for her, disgust and disdain.

"This is exactly the way it happened with your mother," he said.

There was a footstep at the threshold behind her. Dazed, Sophia glanced back and saw Storm walk in.

|12| "Get out of here," Sir Michael said. "Get out of my house, you son of a bitch."

The windows rattled again with another gust of wind, and the drapery stirred. And the old man seemed enormous and crackling with the tempest framing him. But Storm felt suddenly calm, suddenly clear and even in his mind.

She had done it. He could tell by the looks on their faces. Sophia had forced the issue out. The crisis had come.

He smiled, brushing the rain from his hair with one hand. Then he put his hands in the pockets of his slacks. He strolled slowly into the room.

"You know, I think you've got me all wrong," he said. He came up next to Sophia and paused. Felt her trembling there beside him, felt the agitation coming off her in waves. "I think you've got me figured for one of Iago's guys."

Sir Michael sniffed. "I suppose you're going to tell me you're not."

"Well, yeah. Since I'm not, I thought I would tell you." He strolled forward again, onto the rug. Moved towards Sir Michael until the two men were only a few steps apart. Storm wasn't much shorter than Sophia's father, but the old man was impressive all the same. And the rage and fear animating those dead, sunken features made him downright formidable. "I've got no stake in this," Storm went on. "Except your daughter. And as far as that goes, you're just gonna have to live with it. They don't let you shoot guys for that anymore."

Sir Michael seemed to grow in his place, seemed to rise up and up, ready to strike Storm to the floor with a single blow. In his pockets, Storm's hands balled into fists. He wondered whether Sir Michael was armed. The two men stood and faced one another, glared at one another.

"What did you mean about Mother?"

Sophia's voice came from behind him, cut through him. He'd never heard her sound like that before. He'd never heard anyone sound exactly that way. It was a rasping, feverish, desperate and terrible noise that squeezed his heart. He hadn't realized things had gone quite this far.

But Sir Michael's eyes glared into his and his own were locked in that glare, and he couldn't turn to her.

"You put her up to this, didn't you?" Sir Michael said.

"What did you mean, Daddy?" said Sophia.

She sounded as if she was going to cry too. And she was coming forward. Storm could see her in the corner of his eye, moving to stand beside them, between them. Stalking to stand there.

"You son of a bitch," said Sir Michael to Storm.

"Your daughter's talking to you, pal," Storm said.

"What did you mean that this is what happened with Mother?" said Sophia. Her voice was ragged with tears now. "What happened with her? What happened?"

Sir Michael didn't even look at her. His white mouth worked and his white eyes flashed. And the lightning flashed at the window, making the far-off ruin look close and dark. The thunder rolled right over them, right over the top of the house. And Storm thought: Nice effect. A little OTT, but nice.

"Look at me, Daddy," Sophia pleaded. "Tell me."

But Sir Michael didn't. "You're a dirty, low bastard," he said to Storm.

"Why don't you look at her, you jerk," Storm answered.

"Because you're the one controlling her."

Sophia was right beside them, almost directly between them. "Daddy," she said. "It's not him. It's me. Look at me. Tell me what happened to Mother."

"Using sex. Just like with Ann," said her father to Storm. "Did you think I was going to let it happen again?"

"You got it wrong, man. Talk to her. She's begging you."

"It's me, Daddy," said Sophia. And she *was* begging him. "Look at me. I'm not right. You never told me anything and now I'm not right. I almost died, Daddy. And I shouldn't have. I shouldn't be like this. I shouldn't be the way I am. Should I? Hurting myself?"

"Be quiet," Sir Michael barked without turning to her.

"I was trying to protect *you*," she said. "I've been trying to protect you and I don't even know why. Why is my mother dead, why am I like this, what's going on, tell me."

Storm had about had it with this staring contest. He could hear what was happening to Sophia, he could hear her voice, the pitch rising, hysteria near. And he could see her face straining forward, the tears coursing down it.

But Sir Michael wouldn't look at her, wouldn't release him, kept glowering at him like some living skull from one of his own movies.

"I swear to God you're a dead man," Sir Michael whispered.

And Storm smiled with one corner of his mouth. "Hey, guess what, babe. It doesn't matter. You're still gonna have to deal with her."

"Don't tell me how to deal with my daughter, you—"

And suddenly Sophia lost control. She started screaming in a wild, high-pitched, frantic babble that made Sir Michael start back, that scared Storm witless. Her fists flew up around her ears, her eyes squeezed shut, her hair flew back and forth across her face and she went on screaming:

"It's not him, it's not him, it's me, it's me dying it's like I'm dying Daddy listen look at me look at me tell me! Tell me! Tell me! Tell me! Tell me!"

"Jesus, Sophie," said Storm.

He put out a hand to her. She staggered back out of his reach. She clutched at her stomach. Flinched, bent over, gasped aloud. And then covered her open mouth with her hand so that her eyes peered over it, wide, shocked.

"Oh . . ." she said.

And before Storm could move to her, she stumbled away from him. She clutched at the sofa and pulled herself forward. Storm was afraid she was going to fall. But she started running. She ran out of the room.

Storm made to follow her. Sir Michael let out a rough growl and grabbed him by the arm. Storm tore free, spun, his fist cocked at his chin. Sir Michael recoiled, threw his arm up, expecting the punch.

They froze like that, with the wind beating at the window, with another burr of thunder, coming softer now, from farther away.

Sir Michael lowered his arm, his face reddening. "You . . ." he spluttered. "You filthy . . ."

Storm smiled. Let his fist open, let his hand drop to his side. He narrowed his eyes in a gunfighter squint.

"Jew," he drawled, "is the word you want."

And he turned his back on Sir Michael and went out after Sophia.

When Storm found his way to the foyer, he heard water rushing upstairs, a toilet flushing. He went up the steps quickly, two at a time.

He came into a long, lightless corridor with portraits staring down at him from the walls. A grandfather clock was ticking somewhere near him. And he thought, *Yeah, yeah, yeah. Tick-tick, tick-tick.*

Then, at the hall's far end, a door opened; a rectangle of yellow light. Sophia stood in it, bent, weary, braced against the frame.

Storm hurried down the corridor to her. She released the jamb and came forward, nearly fell forward into his arms.

"I've been sick," she said miserably.

"You're okay," he said. "You're gonna be fine. Is there somewhere you can lie down in this dump?"

She gestured at a door, and he helped her to it. They came through into a small bedroom, her bedroom. He didn't turn the light on. The windows were small and blurred with rain, the sky black outside. The room was full of shadows, and the shapes in it were obscure. Storm saw the canopied bed against one wall. He helped Sophia to it, helped her lie down. She rolled onto her side, facing away from him.

Storm sat beside her, on the edge of the duvet. He massaged her shoulder gently. After a while, he looked around the bedpost at the painting on the opposite wall. He could see it was the portrait of a woman. He could not make out her features in the shadows, but he felt her watching him. He went on massaging Sophia's shoulder.

"I don't know what just happened down there," she murmured.

Storm shrugged. "You blew a gasket, kid. It happens."

"Maybe in your family."

He laughed. "Hey, in my family, this was a good day. This was, like, the school picnic or something."

Sophia flumped over onto her back and laughed and started crying. "You're nice to me," she said through her tears.

He nodded. "You mean I'm nice to you and you're so horrible."

"Yes."

"What can I say? I'm a lousy judge of character."

She turned to press her face into his hip. He felt her begin to shiver under his hand. What a crazy dame, he thought. She really would've rather hanged herself again than let loose at the old buzzard like that. What a crazy country.

He reached across her, across the bed. Worked the duvet up out of its place and folded it over her, bundled her in it.

"What are you doing?" she said, her voice muffled. "You'll mess it up."

"Somehow, over time, I'll just have to learn to live with that."

She laughed again, and started to cry harder.

"Shh," he whispered. "Shh."

"But what's going to happen now?" she said.

He shifted to lift her head onto his thigh. He kissed her hair and stroked it. She shivered in his arms a long time, and the room slowly grew darker.

Finally, she began to be quiet. And after another while, as he held her, he heard her breathing grow deep and even.

He leaned down to press a kiss into her hair. He closed his eyes. He wondered if Sir Michael was heading upstairs with a gun.

And what, he wondered, is going to happen now?

 The long, slow hours brought the night down on all of them. On Sophia as she slept, and Storm as he held her. On Sir Michael, slumped in a chair in the sitting room below. On Bernard, shivering in his coffin. And on the mansion in World's End, where Harper Albright sat at the draftsman's table examining an obscure tome.

Over Belham and over London, the winter's day died.

✦

And after a time, Storm lay Sophia tenderly on her pillow and rose. He moved to the window. Looked out into the dark. The rain had passed on, and a mist was rising from the grass of the field, rising and twining around the abbey wall, around the headstones. Storm watched it rise, his own reflection faint upon the pane.

✦

Sir Michael climbed heavily to his feet. Moved, with his head bowed, across the room and out into the corridor. He went down the unlit passage into his study. He shut the door and moved to his desk. Sank into his leather chair. Pulled opened a drawer with one finger.

For a long time, he sat there, looking down at the studded leather box that held the Havana cigars and the sterling lighter, and the loaded .38.

✦

Bernard shivered and moaned. Murmured to himself, half-conscious. Roamed in his mind under blue skies, over green pastures. Wondered distantly if this was death, if he was dying.

✦

And Harper Albright sat and read, sat and read. The fire wasn't on and the office of *Bizarre!* grew cold, but she sat and read. Only the lamp clamped to the edge of the table was burning. It glared on the white pages and hurt her eyes, but she sat and read. Ten years ago, she reflected in frustration, ten or eleven years, she had decoded the Gothic runes scratched on a potsherd found near Avesbury. Her rendering— dismissed as occult guesswork by all accepted authorities— had inspired an entire offshoot of Wicca, centered on the incantation to the mother goddess she believed she had uncovered. The work had been slow, painstaking, back- breaking. It had taken her six months to complete the translation. It was nothing, she thought bitterly, on this.

She was reading the manual to Bernard's VCR. It was a European booklet in four languages. She had finally settled on the German version, the English being incomprehensible. She scanned the pages, page after page. Then finally— finally, finally—she rose up, weary, from the tall stool.

She grasped the videocassette that lay at the bottom of the slanted table, grasped it with exhausted, trembling fingers. This in itself had been no easy acquisition. Visits to three separate Prime Time rental locations. A long trek home to find some acceptable form of identification. A long search and the long trek back again. By day's end, the world was too much with her, but she had a copy of *Spectre* in her hands.

She carried it up the stairs. Mounting slowly, leaning hard on her dragon walking stick. She moved hunched through the shadows of the landing to Bernard's door. Entered his room, turned on the light.

The little space was as Bernard had left it, thoroughly out of order. The narrow bed was unmade. Jeans, shirts, under- wear were strewn over the stained carpet. Dishes with crumbs, glasses half full of gin, were stained brown with crushed stubs, or overflowing with ashes. The white shelves stacked high above the bed were stuffed with piles of books and magazines, the corners of torn pages sticking out of them. The piles of books and magazines on the bedside table rose up across from the shelves, the bed between. One book, called *The Origins of Consciousness in the Breakdown of the Bicameral Mind,* lay on the sheets near the grubby pillow. One journal, called *Raising Cane,* lay spread just beneath it. A pretty nun winked at Harper from the cover, caressing a ferule. *Sisters of Mercilessness.*

Harper frowned and shook her head. How long, she wondered, could the boy hold on? No, that wasn't what she wondered, not really, not all in all. She wondered, rather, whether she had given him the wherewithal to hold on long enough. Iago would be sure to find his weaknesses, but had she taught Bernard honestly enough to keep him from being taken by surprise? Had enough of the truth been understood between them, or had she only hoped it was, assumed it was to save herself the pain of speaking it?

She moved with shuffling steps to the television at the foot of the bed. Sometimes, she thought, it seemed the Catholics had it right: it seemed there was nothing that could not be forgiven except the failure to confess. The gods appeared to her just then to despise secrecy above all things. More than cruelty, more than theft, more than dishonor, they punished you for what you left unspoken—worse, they punished the ones you loved, the ones to whom you should have told all.

She worked the Prime Time case open and removed the cassette. She eyed the television on its stand, the long black box on the stand's lower shelf—eyed them with trepidation. She bent down. Pressed the TV button. The picture popped on instantly. This was encouraging. A commentator in a light blue suit started speaking to her about rugby. She pressed the channel selector. *Ein, zwei, drei, fier, funf.*

Funf—that's what the manual had recommended. But the commentator in the blue suit reappeared on the screen. Why should this be so? Whatever could it signify? She was filled with the familiar sense of misgiving she usually felt just before a machine did something really ghastly.

Nonetheless, grunting with the effort, she bent lower. Touched the cassette to the flap on the box.

To her alarm, the beast seemed to seize the thing right out of her hand and swallow it.

"Crikey," she said, straightening.

But the hours of study had not gone to waste. For the blue-suited rugby commentator now winked into jade nothingness.

And a moment later—as Harper lowered herself painfully onto the edge of Bernard's bed, as she propped her stick against the floor, as she folded her hands on top of the dragon, and rested her chin on the back of her hands—*Spectre* began to unroll on the screen before her.

15

Bernard, meanwhile, had begun to recite poetry. It was all that stood between him and the mouth of madness.

His progressive schoolmasters, in their enlightened kindliness, had never forced him to commit much verse to memory. You can always look it up, they told him—which shows how little they knew.

Harper, on the other hand, had drilled him with the stuff from his youngest years. "These are fragments," she had intoned, "which you may one day shore against your ruins." He had not really understood what she was telling him—till now.

Because in ruins he surely was. Convulsing in the blackness. Shivering against the confines of his stone enclosure. Vomit- and piss-covered. Feverish. Blind. Hour after hour after hour. Babbling insanely when his mind drifted. And when his mind cleared, inhabited by a horror that made him feel as if a bomb were going off inside him and he had no room to explode. Hour after hour.

Dying. He was sure he was dying now. He could not breathe. He felt as if his organs were mired in sludge. He was fading almost willfully from a consciousness that had become abhorrent to him. The invisible death's head beside him stared and grinned. Hour after hour.

And so, at last, with all the courage he had left, he began to recite.

It was one of those situations—it's remarkable how many of them there are, really—when only William Blake would do.

> To see a world in a grain of sand
> And a heaven in a wild flower,
> Hold infinity in the palm of your hand
> And eternity in an hour.

Yes, yes, that was a good one. You could work out the mysterious couplets of that one for hours. Weakly, Bernard licked his lips. He tasted something like decay. He went on.

> A robin redbreast in a cage
> Puts all heaven in a rage.

Oh, he knew a thing or two, did Crazy Bill.

He lay with his eyes closed, with his jaw slack, his mouth open. Every breath that left him came back again rancid. He was strangling on his own exhalations.

Every night and every morn
Some to misery are born,
Every morn and every night
Some are born to sweet delight.

He hugged himself, but not tightly. He hadn't the strength for that anymore. He simply held himself, cradled himself, rocked himself in clouds of debilitating nausea.

Some are born to sweet delight,
Some are born to endless night.
Some are red and some are blue,
And some are filled with sticky goo.

"I can't breathe," he whispered. And for he did not know how long, he was lost to himself. In a sunlit territory of emerald grass and rapeseed of a brilliant yellow. Of music and a river dappled with sunshine. And there, ranged everywhere along the lea, naked bodies, sweet, round, white, reclining. A vision of the sons and daughters of Albion . . .

And then the coffin lid clapped down over him and he was in the blackness again, with the smell of himself rotting alive. And he shook and cried, and whispered, "Mother."

And her voice answered him clearly: *We are led to believe a lie . . .*

Yes, yes, he thought, crushed under the sudden return of reality. Yes . . .

We are led to believe a lie
When we see not through the eye,
Which was born in a night to perish in a night,
Which doesn't scan,

But there it am,
Which doesn't rhyme,
But dying I'm,
So who gives a sod,
Which brings us to God,
And God appears, and God is light,
To those poor souls who dwell in night;
But does a human form display,
To those who dwell in realms of day.
For mercy has a human heart,
Pity, a human face . . .

But no, that was something else. Still Blake, but another poem.

Oh, what's the difference, Harper, he thought. Leave me alone, for Christ's sake. Let me go.

For Mercy has a human heart, she insisted to him,
Pity, a human face,
And Love, the human form divine,
And Peace, the human dress.

He hugged himself, rocked himself in the blackness. Don't tell me that, he thought. Don't tell me that, you pedantic bitch, and leave me here. I'm dying. And I'm scared.

Mercy has a human heart, Bernard. A human heart. And Pity, a human face. And Love, the human form divine. Trust me on this.

He raised his bloody fingers to his bloody brow. Dragged them down over his cheeks, smearing the blood. He groaned out, "Cruelty!"

And a spasm of nausea racked him. He clutched his stomach. Turned his head. Tried to retch, but couldn't. Sobbed.

Cruelty, he thought, *has a human heart,*
And Jealousy, a human face;
Terror, the human form divine,
And Secrecy, the human dress.

Well, yes, that too, Harper said.

"Secrecy," Bernard whispered.

Yes.

He lay back again, trying to breathe, trying to support the weight of darkness. All right, all right, he thought. Where was I? Secrecy . . . ?

Mercy, she said.

Right, right.

For Mercy has a human heart . . . Didn't we do this already?

No, no. It's still good. It's still right, Bernard.

And Pity—Pity, Pity—a human face. Pity.

And Love, she said. *Love has the human . . .*

"The human form divine," Bernard whispered, hugging himself, inhaling the stench of his offal, choking on the stench. *And Mercy . . .*

And Peace, she said.

Mercy, mercy.

These fragments . . .

Mercy.

These fragments you shall shore against your ruins.

"God!" Bernard screamed. Or tried to scream—it came out a rasping gasp.

These fragments . . . These fragments . . .

"God, father, father in Heaven. Help me!"

And then—as if in answer to his call—there came those sounds again. Did they? Did they come? He clutched himself. Opened his eyes—tried to—couldn't tell if they were open or not. Lay with his jaw dangling. Listened.

Yes. The clank of a lock. The rattle of a latch. The creak—oh, the creak of a door opening. The thud as it swung shut.

And footsteps. Footsteps on stone. Approaching.

Bernard peered up into nothingness. His entire body was a prayer.

There was a pause. And then the voice—the voice like smoke—swirled down coolly over him.

"Are you ready to listen now, Bernard?"

Pity has a human heart, a human heart, a human heart . . .

"Yes," he said, shuddering, crying. "Yes. Please. Please. I'm ready."

16

"By Jove, Prendergast," Hedley cried. "A stairway!"

Harper's eyes sank closed, her body leaned forward. She and her dragon stick seemed about to pitch off the edge of the bed to the floor.

But she jerked her head up, her eyes open. Forced herself to stare at the TV screen.

By Jove, she grumped. *Cobblers.*

She continued to watch Storm's movie as the appallingly ridiculous detectives descended into the vaults beneath the ruined church. Under jutting shadows, under skewed stone-work, under hanging arches, they went, following the repeated *clang-clang* rising from below.

Even now, she could barely remember that she had ever seen the thing before. Could not remember where she had watched it or when. Certainly not why. Which was not all that odd really, considering the quality of the piece.

Funny, Harper thought sleepily. Storm probably hadn't

even known that it was all run-of-the-mill German Express-ionism. She could see that he'd thought he was paying some sort of *hommage* to "Black Annie." There were the shape of the ruins, the repetition of the sound—*clang-clang*—the two men descending the stairs. But in fact, the look of the picture—the ambience of it—came directly from the old Universal Studio monster classics like *Frankenstein* and *Dracula.* And these had been fashioned by the German Jew Carl Laemmle along with his stable of emigré directors. Hollywood and his own inclinations, in other words, had somehow furnished Storm's mind with the German Romantic imagery of Rhinehart as it mutated into the pre-Fascist Expressionist celebration of Terror and Will. He too, in other words, was part of the story trail.

Which, so far, was about the only interesting thing she could think of to say about the film. The rest was cliché piled upon cliché.

She leaned on her stick and watched. Down and down, by roving torchlight, Prendergast and Hedley went. And now there was the body of poor, dear Sergeant What's-His-Name dangling from the wall.

"Poor devil," said Dr. Prendergast.

Poor devil, by Jove, thought Harper Albright.

The eerie music swelled—as eerie music will—and the two caped heroes moved out into a great underground chamber. There was Jacobus, the archvillain, bedecked in his penta-gram robe before the blanketed altar. And there was the heroine, of course, writhing on the wall in her seductively torn blouse. Her wrists chained, her mouth gagged—all very appealing, if you went in for that sort of thing. The poor girl did her level best to deliver the lines, "Mmf, mmf," with some sort of conviction. And her name, of course, was Annie.

And the villain was Jacobus. Harper lifted one gray eyebrow. Jacobus seeking immortality. Well, that was something anyway. If you thought of Iago watching the film twenty years before. You could imagine him—still reeling from the destruction of his cult, seeking desperately for a sign of his cherished destiny. You could imagine the hairs on the back of his neck bristling at even this minor coincidence.

But it was not enough. Not enough to draw him onto the trail. How could he have known to go from this ridiculous thing to "Black Annie" and the other stories?

Then the answer—a possible answer—began to take shape in her mind. *A spilled soda.* She had forgotten that. Hadn't Iago said something about a spilled soda, back in the church of the Templars? *A spilled soda, and the next stage was given to me.* Yes, that was it.

Harper felt a twinge of fear—her first real fear for the life of Richard Storm.

"Why, Dr. Prendergast, I'm so glad you could make it," Jacobus said from the TV.

And the doorbell rang.

Harper blinked, looked around her, momentarily confused by the intrusion of reality.

"You're just in time to bear witness to my final apotheosis," Jacobus said from the television.

The doorbell rang again.

Harper stood up in a flurry. The doorbell. It might be the police. It might be word of Bernard. It might be Bernard himself . . .

She dithered before the television, trying to decide what to do, how to proceed. If she turned the TV off, the tape might keep on playing and she would lose her place. If she tried to turn the tape off . . . well, she really hadn't the faintest notion of how to do that anyway.

The doorbell rang again. Reluctantly, Harper backed away from the set, edging around the bed.

The voice of Jacobus trailed after her, tinny from the set's small speaker.

"Poor Prendergast. That you ever thought to defeat me. Could you not see that I am the agent of an immortal power?"

The doorbell rang again, insistently. Harper knocked against the bedside table, the stack of books. She caught it before it toppled over, steadied it. Then, with a last glance at the show, she bustled towards the corridor.

"In such incarnations as this, I travel through the centuries," said Jacobus. "I feed on the marrow of time."

Harper stopped. She had her hand on the doorframe. She was about to leave the room. She looked back at the television set. *I feed on the marrow of time.* That was just what Iago had said to her in the Temple Church. And with a straight face too. She had thought at the time it was a little overwrought . . .

She stared at the screen. A close-up on the evil genius. A close-up on the grim detectives. The struggling girl: *mmf, mmf.* Jacobus.

"I was here before the oceans turned black with life . . ." he said.

"And when the deserts are white with death," Harper said along with him, "I will remain."

The doorbell again. Jacobus went on.

"The petty hindrances you have put in my way have only served to amuse me. But that's all over now . . ."

And with that, the cinema hunchback came chuckling forward. With a magician's yank, he pulled the blanket from the altar and there . . .

Harper felt cold sweat beading on her forehead. Felt all her fears—for Bernard, for Storm, for herself now too—coalesce into one churning anxiety. She stared at the TV screen.

And there, as she stared—there, of course, was the baby. Of course. The baby on the altar. Jacobus with his sword raised above it. The gagged woman screaming from the wall.

Good God, of course: it was all exactly as it had been in the jungle. Exactly what she had seen as she had peeked through the branches and seen the awful truth about the man she'd loved.

She had not forgotten it. Not really. She had repressed it, that was all. She had forcibly dismissed its possibilities and pushed them away, pushed them down—even after Storm's arrival. Even after he'd read that story at the party.

You suffer for what you fail to confess, she thought—even when you fail to confess it to yourself.

And she thought: A spilled soda. Yes. That makes it perfect.

She understood now. She understood everything that had happened. She even began to see, in her gathering terror, what was going to happen next.

The doorbell rang again. Again.

Harper hurried out of the room.

✦

By the time she opened the front door, Detective Inspector William Pullod had given up on her. He had gone back down the mansion's steps, was heading across the narrow street to where his Peugeot was parked before The Sign of the Crane. From the Peugeot's passenger seat, his assistant, PC Slade, watched him approaching.

But then Pullod heard the door open behind him. He turned around, saw Harper standing there. She looked down on him silently as he moved back towards her, back towards the curb at the foot of the steps.

She braced herself—physically braced herself, putting her full weight on her walking stick. The inspector, she saw, was arranging his features into a po-faced expression of official sympathy. She felt the chill night air blow over her, felt another chill answer it from within. Was it too late? Was it already too late?

Below her, the wiry weightlifter shifted uncomfortably in his overcoat. He squinted up at the old woman through one eye. In one hand, he tossed a ring of keys up and down, jingle-jangle.

"Miss Albright," he said. He looked away from her, along the dark street. But there was no traffic there, no one moving, nothing to see. He looked down at the keys in his hand instead. "I'm afraid . . ." he began.

Harper's fingers curled and recurled around the dragon's head. *I'm afraid,* she thought. There was a good English locution for you. *I'm afraid there's been a bit of a nuclear war.* The outer woman remained grimly firm but she could feel her framework wobbling. She hated that "I'm afraid."

"I'm afraid we've found young Bernard's car," said DI Pullod unhappily.

Harper lifted her chin. "I see. And where are you afraid it is?"

"I'm afraid," said the inspector, "it's right over there." And he gestured across the street towards the pub. "Right in front of mine." He held up the keys. "A constable found these in the ignition."

Harper only nodded.

"I don't suppose he's come home . . ." said Pullod.

"No," Harper said.

"And you're certain he hasn't just . . . run off?"

"Yes. I'm certain."

The inspector made a very close examination of the keys in his hand. His sharp, energetic features worked awkwardly. "Then I'm afraid . . ."

"The car might be meant as a message for me. Yes, I'm afraid so too," said Harper. A movement caught her attention. She raised her eyes to see Slade gazing at her from behind the Peugeot's window. She didn't know the man. Could she trust him? Could she trust Pullod?

There was a long silence as the DI resettled himself in his overcoat again.

"Inspector," Harper said slowly. "How many churches of St. James would you say there are in London?" That was the name of the church in Storm's film. St. James. Santiago.

The policeman's mouth pulled down, his hands went up on either side of him. "I . . . I don't know. Half a dozen at least, I should think."

"Yes," she murmured. "At least . . ." And she stood pondering. The speech from Storm's film had confirmed her instinct: Iago had found his destiny that day twenty years ago in the Edgware Road cinema. He had found it, and he wanted to cling to it. In some superstitious way, he was trying to inhabit the stories that had led him to the triptych. Perhaps trying to inhabit *Spectre* most of all. But then, when Storm had made the picture he was inventing an England he had never then seen. It raised certain logistical problems . . .

"Tell me this, then," she said finally. "Do you know of any St. James church that has been abandoned? Or even destroyed?"

Again, Pullod made that baffled gesture. But then, mid-gesture, he stopped. "Well, yes, as a matter of fact," he said.

"There was the bomb blast down in the Barbican. About six, eight months ago now, was it? Started a fire in a church down there. Might have been St. James. Yes, I think it was. I think I remember . . ."

But Harper was no longer there above him. The door to her mansion stood open, the entryway empty.

Pullod glanced back at Slade in the Peugeot. Both men shrugged.

And Harper returned. Slipping into her cape. Clapping her Borsalino down upon her gray bangs until the brim was just above her spectacles. She descended the stairs quickly.

"Uh . . ." said Pullod. "Miss Albright? What is it?"

"Don't be alarmed, Inspector," said Harper, walking right past him, walking towards the Peugeot. "It's only the Uncanny. But I believe I've caught the current of it," she called back over her shoulder to him. "Yes. I believe it's on our side now."

17 "You will live without pain, you will live without aging. You will live without the fear of death and above the laws of man."

Bernard lay like a broken toy, all the tension, all the life, gone from him. His arms hung dead on the coffin bottom, his legs lay dead, one bent, tilted against the sarcophagus wall. His head lay still on his flaccid neck, his eyes open, staring, his mouth open.

Love, he thought distantly. *Love has the human form divine.*

"You think now," Iago went on, "that you'll quail at the letting of blood, at the killing of your own children. But I promise you, you will not quail. More than that, I promise you the act will free you, will give you a power over your own life—and a joy in that power—you can't even imagine now. Any beast can give life to its offspring. But only we can give life to ourselves, over and over."

Bernard lay motionless, lay limp. Lay staring into nothing, seeing nothing. *The human form divine,* he thought.

"It will become your nature, Bernard, I swear. It is your nature now, if you would only confess it. You can't help but feel it as I speak. You can't help but imagine it: lifting the knife over the infant's body, unafraid of capture, unafraid of sin. Taking its blood for your own life. You can't help but imagine it and feel how exciting it is to you. It is exciting to you, isn't it, Bernard? Isn't it?"

Bernard lay barely breathing; staring. Arms dead, legs dead, eyes open. *Love has the human form divine.*

Then, slowly, as on a rusty hinge, his mouth moved.

"Yes," he said distinctly.

He thought he heard Iago sigh.

"You see, it can be done," came the smoke of the voice above. "We can be honest with each other about who we really are. Now," he went on, his tone growing more charged. "Now—will you let me release you? Will you let me free you from your coffin? Will you travel with me for a while—just a little while—and mix your life with mine, and give me my fair chance to prove my case to you?"

Love, thought Bernard senselessly. Lying, staring, not even aware of the tears that had started to run down his cheeks.

"Will you agree?" said Iago.

And Bernard, at last, said, "Yes."

At once there was a thick, scraping sound. Bernard's head remained where it was, but his eyes moved slightly. He looked upward. The deep grind of stone on stone came again.

He let out a silent sob of relief. The lid of the sarcophogus was shifting.

Now he heard other voices, murmuring. A grunt of effort. Another deep scrape. A long grating rumble.

Suddenly, a line of gray light slashed across his face like a sword. He shut his eyes, but the light throbbed red behind his lids. The cool air poured down over his cheeks, and his body seemed to seize it, drag it in.

"Oh," he whispered.

He stirred now, opened his eyes. Turned his head to look up as the line of light expanded. The light was not bright but it seemed to him a Niagara of blinding radiance. He squinted into it. Gasped the fresh air. A milkshake in the desert. He gasped and gasped it, his stomach rolling over with its unaccustomed richness. Exquisite. The pain in his head, the aching throughout his body: it was all exquisite, it was exquisite life, the promise of this exquisite life forever.

His shoulders began to shake as he started crying harder, with joy this time. He peered up into the cascade of light. It seemed to separate like swimmers in a water ballet, it seemed to bloom like flowers, changing from a downpour to a spreading canopy of streaming beams.

And there—at the center of those rays—there was Iago.

It was difficult for Bernard to distinguish between the surge of passionate pleasure that went through him at the opening of his tomb, and the powerful, bewildering warmth he felt upon finally seeing that face. The long, dark hair framed features chiseled in brutal planes and angles. But the eyes were as cool and smoky as the voice had been, relaxed, even witty. The smile was gently welcoming.

This was his father.

"Now you'll see," Iago said, the voice washing down with

the radiant light. "With me, above all else, you will never be ashamed of who you are."

Bernard tried to nod. "Love . . ." he almost whispered. But his eyes sank closed, and he fainted.

18

When Bernard looked again, Iago was gone. Another face had replaced his.

The scarred man leaned over the side of the sarcophagus. His piggy eyes were bright under the tawny, sharply cut hair. His disfigured mouth was disfigured even further by a grin. He wrinkled his nose comically.

"Phwor! Who's made a mess, then? All right, lad. Come on, up you go. Let's get you spruced and lovely for the road."

He reached down and grabbed Bernard's slack arm. Oofing and urring, he worked the young man's body up into a half-sitting position. With each fresh jolt of motion, Bernard felt a zig-zagging bolt of green lightning lance through him, nerve-end to nerve-end, top to toe. His head fell to one side, and he felt as if it had fallen on a bed of nails. He clutched at the scarred man's thick, muscular shoulders for support.

"There you go. Easy now," the scarred man said.

With his help, Bernard managed to roll one leg up over the sarcophogus wall. The scarred man was practically carrying him as he rose from the coffin's depths. He lifted Bernard easily, lowered him to the floor easily as if he were no weight at all. Bernard felt himself set down gently. He stood there, his back hunched, his mouth hanging open, his hand resting on the edge of the tomb. He stared down with glazed eyes, stared through the pools and puddles of bloody pain that kept spreading and evaporating just behind the screen of his vision.

"Now then, now then," the scarred man said. "You can't go anywhere looking like that, can you. We've got to get you out of those clothes."

Bernard waved him away at first, or tried to. He tried to undress himself. For a moment, his hand tugged ineffectively at the collar of his shirt. Then it fell to his side again. He stood still again, staring dully at the stones of the floor. The scarred man took hold of the shirt collar and worked it up over Bernard's head as if he were a child. He undid Bernard's belt and pulled his black pants down to his ankles.

Bernard swallowed, fighting off the nausea. When he managed to raise his eyes, he saw the dim recesses of an underground crypt tilting and turning around him. Columns and arches, spandrels and darkened niches rising and falling as if at sea. Stone tombs, carved effigies of the dead, plaques set in the wall and floor—they telescoped sickeningly in and back. It was all shadowy. It was all empty. It was all turning round and round.

Bernard licked his lips, swaying where he stood. He felt something damp in his hand, and closed his fingers around it. The scarred man had given him a sponge. He knew that he was naked now.

"Here, you do this," the man said gruffly. "Face too, there's blood all over it."

Bernard nodded. *Love has the human form divine,* he thought. And in loose, sloppy swipes, he began to sponge himself down.

"Put some grease into it," the scarred man muttered impatiently. "We haven't got all night."

Bernard nodded vaguely. Went on sponging himself the

same as before. And it was good to feel the warm rivulets running down his skin. He stood, bent and staring, thinking about that face, Iago's face.

With me, above all, you will never be ashamed.

Love, thought Bernard, *has the human form divine.*

"All right, that'll do," said the scarred man. He pried the sponge from Bernard's resistless fingers. "Here, put these on."

Bernard had to stare for a long moment at the folded clothes that were being held out to him. Gray sweatpants, white sweatshirt, white socks and tennis shoes on top. Drawing in a breath, he yanked at the shirt. He struggled to get his arms into the sleeves, wrestled the rest down over him. For the sweatpants, he had to hold on to the scarred man's shoulder. The pain pulsed in his head, as he bent down, as he went through the long, complex process of drawing his trousers on.

"All right. Here," said the scarred man, not unkindly. Bernard rested against his sarcophagus as the other knelt before him. The scarred man tugged one sock over Bernard's bare foot, then another over the other. He fitted on the tennis shoes as Bernard held weakly to the coffin's wall.

Love, thought Bernard. He tried to concentrate on that, tried to bring the full force of his focus to bear on it.

Then the scarred man stood up and the two men were face to face. The scarred man clapped Bernard on the shoulder. His pinkish eyes gleamed.

"There you are, bright as a button," he said. "And a face like an angel, haven't you?"

Bernard nodded and straightened from the coffin, still holding on to it, still holding on to the edge. He had to work his mouth open and closed a few moments before he could speak.

"Do you know . . ." he said thickly. "Do you know what I

kept . . . what I kept thinking all the while he was talking?"

The scarred man laughed once, his big body heaving up and down. "No. I give up. What was you thinking?"

Bernard licked his lips again. "Love," he said. "I kept thinking . . . Love has the human form divine. No matter what he told me. I just kept thinking that."

"Uh-huh," said the scarred man.

"That's what saved me," said Bernard.

And he hit the scarred man in the throat.

It wasn't a powerful strike. It didn't have to be: it took the scarred man so completely by surprise. The knife hand caught the thug in the Adam's apple. His mouth opened. His eyes widened. His tongue poked out. He gagged.

Bernard grabbed him by the testicles.

The scarred man's body bent violently. His butt went back, his torso jerked forward. Bernard staggered away a step. He clasped his hands together. He raised his two arms high. A great wave of pain broke over his head, and he cried out. Then he dropped his hands like an axe on the back of the scarred man's neck.

The blow drove the scarred man's face into the edge of the sarcophagus. Bernard saw blood spray out on either side of the thug's head.

Bernard reeled and dropped to his knees, retching a thin, black gruel. Still retching, he scrabbled at the floor, tried to stand again before the scarred man could recover, could attack.

Love . . . he thought.

The scarred man did not recover. He hung on the edge of the sarcophagus as if he were searching for something within. Then, slowly, he began to slide off it. Then more quickly. Then his big body dropped to the crypt's stone floor.

Bernard climbed to his feet. He stumbled to the coffin and grabbed hold of it before he fell again. He bent over the open tomb, his stomach convulsing.

The smell from within the coffin rose up to him. His own smell, the smell of his own death. And there, in the dust at the bottom of the thing, sat the human skull, its mandible missing, its eye sockets scored and broken. It looked bucktoothed and stupid there, staring blind.

Panting, Bernard reached down for it. The bone was rotten, it was soft and thin to the touch. As he clutched it, a circle of brain pan caved in under the pressure of his thumb. He lifted the skull and brought it up before him. Bernard, with his bald head, with his gray skin, his sunken cheeks, his deathlike grin, might have been looking at his own reflection.

He whispered to it almost sweetly, "Sell your soul to the devil, you bastard. Because your ass belongs to me."

And with a deep, animal growl, he hoisted his arm. Dashed the rotting thing back into the tomb. It crunched against the stone, spitting fragments, then fell broken on its side.

Bernard turned away from it, and his eyes were wild with fury. The scarred man lay curled and unconscious at his feet, the blood pooling on the floor around his head. Bernard pushed off the coffin and stepped around him.

He started staggering towards the stairs.

They were stone, the stairs, and winding. He mounted one by one. A rope run through a set of metal rings in the rock wall was the only banister and he clutched it in both his hands. Pulled on it. Lugged himself upward. The curving stairwell seemed to close and widen like an accordion around him. He began to feel sick again. His head felt as if a chisel were being pummeled through it from within. The blow fell repeatedly as he climbed. He gritted his teeth against it and went up, went on. The staircase grew blacker and blacker around him. The splashes of red grew brighter and brighter behind his eyes.

"Goddamn it," he gasped.

Bile bubbled up over his tongue to his grit teeth. He swallowed it back. Pulled himself up hand over hand, stair after stair.

And then he fell against the door. His shoulder hit the heavy wood. The jar of the collision seemed to drive a stake of pain straight down through the top of his skull. But under the pressure of his shoulder, the door was already swinging open. He was falling after it. Falling, for one wheeling second more. Then he stumbled into the church.

Dizzy, he looked around him. It was the same church. Where he had seen the men talking at the foot of the cross. Where he had witnessed the crucifixion. It was all over now, though. The place seemed deserted. A strange, false light hung behind the shapes on the stained-glass windows, but there was no light within. The aisles, the pews were dark. The altar to his right, the nave, the transept across from him: all were shadowy, dark.

Bernard snarled. "Come on. Come out," he whispered.

He staggered a step away from the crypt door. Staggered another step, and another, into the crossing where the transepts met the aisles. He looked around everywhere, his eyes so wide with anger he felt them bulging from his face. Everywhere, undelineated figures of stained glass gazed down at him dispassionately.

"*Come on!*" he screamed at them, at anyone. His voice seemed to tear out of his throat, to tear through his flesh, a killing pain. But the high church ceiling swallowed his shout without an echo. And there was no answer.

"Come out and fight," he shouted. *"Come out and fight like an immortal demon!"* He giggled. *"You cocksucker!"*

He giggled again. *Fight like an immortal demon*—that was a good one. He bent over helplessly, swaying where he stood, giggling until it hurt his lungs. His head was pounding. The stained-glass figures gazed down at him from their heights.

With a roar, he suddenly threw back his head. He howled, *"Come on, Daddy-o! It's Oedipus time!"*

He was laughing too hard to continue. He was crying too hard. He shook and tears poured down his cheeks. Snot dangled from one nostril, a white string. He wiped at his mouth and nose with a broad swipe of his palm. He staggered in a small circle, crying, laughing. Gripping his middle. Finally, he came to rest. Stood crouched and snarling like a wounded animal.

And it was only then that he realized he was surrounded.

Dark figures were moving in on him. Moving in stealthily from every side. From the deepest blackness against the walls, they came slowly into the grayer shadows. They converged upon him step by step.

Uh-oh, was his first thought. *Me and my big mouth.*

He turned to face them in one direction, then another, then another. The sturdy figures moved towards him. Down the aisles, out of the transepts. He spun again. Even from the altar, out of the penumbra of the ambulatory, they came. Tall, thick, husky figures, their arms ready at their sides.

Swallowing fear and nausea, Bernard kept swiveling, to one, another, another. He raised his hands, ready to defend himself and strike.

In the brief time he had left to reflect, he realized that he was not sorry it had come to this. They were going to kill him, he knew. But it didn't matter. He didn't mind. In point of fact, he wasn't even certain he wanted to live anymore anyway. Knowing what he knew. About his past. About himself. And this way, he reckoned, at least he might get to take one of them with him. To close with one of them, maybe even two. Rip a throat out, tear open a ribcage. It would feel good. It would send a message. A little E-mail to the old man . . .

"Come on," he muttered, swinging from one to the other as they kept moving in. "Come on." Swallowing his tears.

The circle was closing. The approaching shapes had come out of the aisles and the transepts. They had joined together and were all around him in the crossing where he stood. Any moment now, he expected them to rush in at him all at once.

But now they stopped.

Bernard spun, his knees bent, his knife-hands lifted, loose.

He cried out once more, loudly, despairingly. "Come on, will you!"

But only a single figure detached itself from the others, broke from the circle and came forward, towards him, down the center aisle.

Bernard faced that lone attacker, his breath scraping from his throat in feral growls. He waited, ferocious.

And yet, as he waited, some sound confused him. Some repeated sound. It reached him through the nimbus of his pain. He was flustered by it. Shook his head.

The figure came closer. Bernard blinked. He *knew* that sound. A steady, resolute, rhythmic clicking: the sound of a walking stick on stone.

He stared through the shadows. He made out, at last, the small, squat, waddling silhouette approaching. He made out the contours of the Borsalino. The line of the cane from hand to floor.

The figure stopped before him. Slowly, Bernard sank down onto his knees. He raised his arms. He waved them in front of him to cover his face.

"Don't look at me!" he cried out.

Harper lay a withered hand on his shoulder.

"It's all right, lad," she told him quietly. "You made it."

19 The body of Jervis Ramsbottom—the late Dr. Mormo—still hung from the cross. His arms had been released from the horizontal bar, but stout cord, wrapped around his throat, held him to the vertical. He hung there with his face purple, his eye sockets raw, his cheeks streaked with blood and jelly. His tongue protruded black under the light of PC Slade's torch.

"Poor bugger," the PC said.

"Poor bugger, by Jove," Harper murmured behind him.

"And look here." Slade lowered his torch a little. "That mark carved on his chest. The same as with that German antiques dealer who got killed around Christmas time."

Harper only nodded to herself, thinking. It bothered her, this. The dead Mormo, the tortured Mormo. What was Iago playing at, after all? The warlock had been a coward of the first water. He would have grassed on his mother at the slightest hint of a threat. What had Iago thought to get out of him this way?

The rays of police torches were arcing and crisscrossing all around the church interior now. Areas of char and ruin, piles of rubble, fallen beams stood out beneath their circles of illumination. The faces of saints and patrons frowned from the walls and windows as the light touched them, then slipped back into obscurity.

Beneath the swiftly sweeping shadows, Bernard sat in a front pew, his head hanging, his hands hanging down between his knees. A nurse sat beside him, washing the swollen bruise on his brow. DI Pullod stood over them both another moment. Then he moved away, and came to join Harper and Slade beneath the cross.

These three turned their backs as two crime scene men came forward to tend to Mormo's descent. They stopped by the chancel rail. Pullod glanced at Harper quickly, embarrassed. He looked only at Slade as he spoke, but Harper understood he was sharing the information with her.

"We've had a sighting of the black Mercedes," he said in a low tone. "One driver, it looks like. Your boy confirmed the license number." This with a half-nod towards Bernard, though he looked only at Slade. "They lost track of him in Morden, but it sounds like he's heading south along the A24. We've got roadblocks up. We're sure to find him." Now he did turn directly to Harper. "We'll run you and your lad over to hospital. I'll go down to Morden myself, see what's what. All right?"

Harper frowned, shook her head. "He won't go."

"He?"

"Bernard—to hospital. He won't go. He'll walk out, get in his car, and drive wherever he thinks he'll find Iago."

"He's in no fit state to drive."

"Yes," said Harper. "That's why I suggest you give us a lift." Pullod and Slade exchanged a glance. Slade rolled his eyes.

"You say he's headed south," said Harper thoughtfully.

Pullod nodded. "That's right."

The door to the crypt opened now. Lester Benbow—the scarred man—was led out between two large patrolmen. His wrists were pinned in cuffs behind his back. His face was smeared with blood. His eyes peered out of the mess, rolling, murderous.

When his gaze lit upon Bernard, the scarred man bared his teeth.

Bernard raised his head. Looked unsmiling at Benbow. Nodded.

Harper watched the scarred man being led away up the church aisle.

"I think, Inspector, we had better head north," said Harper Albright.

"North?" said Pullod with a laugh.

"Yes. I think we had better get out to Belham Grange as quickly as we can."

20 *I rose from the bed and moved across the room to stand before one of the windows on the far wall. Looking out between the curtains, I saw that night had now drawn down around the place completely. A gibbous moon, sporadically visible in the gaps between the racing clouds, served only to cast a pall of faltering and sickly light over the sere expanse of grassland to the east. In that field, now visible, now vanishing as the moon went once again behind its shifting cover, there stood an ominous and melancholy apparition: the ruins of Belham Abbey . . .*

Storm gazed sadly through Sophia's window into that misty, drifting night. What it is, old chap, old stick, he thought, what it is is time for The Reveal. That was the moment at the end of the second act of a film when the villain we thought was dead steps out of the shadows, or when the woman we thought we loved pockets the murder weapon—or when the hero we thought we admired is shown to be a dying louse without the courage to tell the truth. It was way past the end of the second act, thought Storm. It was way past time for The Reveal.

"What is it, Richard?" said Sophia softly.

He turned to find her awake, her eyes glinting in the room's darkness. She had pushed the duvet aside and risen on one elbow. He could make out the shape of her under the frilly canopy. And even now, he didn't know how he could ever tell her.

"You're up," he said.

Her shoulders rose and fell with a deep breath. "I've been awake for a while."

"Yeah?"

"I've been watching you. I've been thinking."

He didn't answer. He saw her shift a little. He thought she might have looked up a moment at the portrait hanging on the wall beside him.

"What was it you were going to tell me before?" she asked him. "Outside, before my father called me."

Storm still hesitated. He felt sick with sadness. "I don't . . . Look, maybe this isn't the time," he said—hating himself for it, hoping anyway she would let him off the hook. "With you so upset and all."

But she said, "I'm not upset. In fact, I feel very calm at the moment, strangely enough. I was just watching you. I was thinking about you, and I wondered."

Storm sat back against the window sill. He pinched the bridge of his nose, closed his eyes. "Oh, man," he said.

"Are you ill or something, Richard?"

He didn't move, didn't answer, couldn't. He kept his

fingers on the bridge of his nose, kept his eyes closed. If he could just sit here, he thought. If he could just sit here in the dark and listen to her voice, to the sound of her voice. He loved that sound. Mary Poppins.

"I thought—when you said you had something to tell me—I thought it might be that," she went on quietly. "I don't know why. It just came into my head. You look so tired sometimes. And your arm, you favor your left arm. And you just always look . . . so sad. Is that what it is? Are you ill? Is that why you always look like that?"

He smiled, his eyes still closed. Nodded. "Yeah," he just managed to say. "Yeah, that's why." And then, quickly: "It's bad, kid. It's what they politely call terminal."

She was quiet for several moments after that. Storm opened his hand now and covered his eyes with it. He felt the dampness against his palm. Shit, he thought. He didn't know what he had been expecting, but it wasn't this. This quiet from her. And when she spoke again, her voice was cool, even, politely curious.

"Does that . . . ? Does it frighten you? Are you frightened?"

He gave a short laugh. "Uh . . . well . . ." Lowered both his hands to his legs as he sat against the sill. He saw her watching him. "No," he said. "Since you ask. I'm not frightened. Not really. Sometimes at night when I'm alone, a little. But not much, even then."

"I didn't think so. I didn't think you would be."

"There aren't many symptoms—maybe the reality of it just hasn't hit me yet. I don't know." He sighed heavily. "I was . . . To be honest, I was afraid of the doctors more than anything. I think it makes them feel better if they can pretend they're in some kind of battle with it, even when the battle is really all over. I was afraid they'd cut me up, radiate me, poison me to death for no reason. That's why I blew town in the first place. But . . . no. Not this. This doesn't frighten me at all. It just makes me—it makes everything— really, really sad."

After a pause, she went on—went on in the same way, still cool, still curious. "It makes you sad because . . . ? Of regrets and that sort of thing?"

"Yeah. Yeah. Regrets." He wiped his eyes quickly, the corners of his mouth pulling down. "I got me a suitcase full of regrets, babe, believe me. The thing is, I just didn't . . . I didn't get it right, you know? I don't even think I got the rules of the game right. Not until you dropped your glass at the party. Until I looked up at you. And then I thought: Oh, yeah, I get it. I get it now. I mean, what a shmuck, right? Ach . . ." He looked up into an invisible corner of the ceiling above her bed. "Christ, kid, I should've stayed away from you. I knew that, damn it. I knew it. Or I should've told you right off. But I should've stayed away, that's the thing. What a jerk-o."

Sophia—with what seemed to him calm, unaffected movements in the dark—took the pillow from behind her and set it against the headboard. She sat up, patted it, propped herself on it, sitting quietly, regarding him quietly from under the canopy's fringe.

"I suppose you were pretending it wasn't true," she said after a while. "I suppose that's why you didn't tell me."

He smiled unhappily, his head going up and down. What a smart dame, he thought. What a champion dame. "Yeah, that's it," he said. "Not really pretending, you know—not like I believed it, but just . . . acting the part, sort of. Acting like we could be together. Like . . ."

He couldn't continue. He just went on nodding silently, biting his lip.

"Like we could go on to get married and have children and so on," she said.

He laughed, his heart in a vice. "And so on. Yeah."

"No," she said after a second or two. "No, I don't suppose we could do that now."

"No," said Richard Storm. "I don't suppose we could."

"Still," said Sophia, considering. "Still, if you had told me, I might well have stayed away from you."

"Well, that's it," said Storm. "That's what I should've done."

"No," she told him. "No. Because then I wouldn't have had the chance to realize that I love you."

Storm made a choked noise, covered his face with both hands.

"Which I did. Realize," Sophia said. "Just now. While you were standing there, while I was watching you at the window."

"I'm sorry, Sophie. I'm sorry."

"Don't be sorry." She ran her hand up through her hair. Slowly, once and then again. "Don't be foolish. Don't be sorry. I love you, Richard," she told him. "And at the end of the day . . ." But then her voice caught. Which surprised him. She had sounded so cool until then. But then her voice caught and she was silent for several moments, looking down thoughtfully.

"Well," she finished brusquely. "At the end of the day, I think you should come to bed."

21

Tick-tick. Tick-tick.

Sir Michael sat erect, motionless, in the high-backed leather chair behind his desk. The sound traveled to him through the walls.

Tick-tick. Tick-tick.

He gave no indication that he heard it, no visible sign. But he heard it. It completely occupied his attention. It sparked his imagination. He sat with his eyes open, gazing ahead. Imagining. The mahogany desk before him hunkered hugely in the unlighted room. The carved ram's heads on its pilasters stared as the Great Man stared.

Tick-tick. Tick-tick.

It was coming from the floor above him. From the room just above him, his daughter's room. He imagined that it was the frame of her bed, clicking as it strained at the pegs of its ancient joins.

He sat without moving, his lips slightly parted. Sat tall and precise. He had been sitting like that for over an hour now. In the study, with the door closed, the lights off, the room growing darker and darker. He had sat and sat like that as night had come.

He had removed the box from the bottom drawer, removed the pistol from the box. The box stood open on the desktop blotter, the tray with the cigars and the silver lighter lay next to it. Next to that lay the gun. And he supposed that was what he was gazing at—that he was gazing at the gun, but in truth he hardly saw it. He was just gazing, just listening, imagining, his hands folded in his lap, motionless.

Tick-tick. Tick-tick.

And there was another sound now, another sound above the sound of the straining bed. There was the sound of voices. His daughter's voice, her lover's. Their whispers, groans. Scrabbling in the wall like squirrels. Coming down to him.

Sir Michael did not move. Sat with his hands clasped. Gazed. Now he did see the gun on the blotter. He focused on it. The blunt gun.

Suddenly, Sophia cried out above him. It was an unmistakable noise. She cried out twice, once harshly as if in anguish and denial, once again as if in triumph and release.

Sir Michael sniffed. The ticking had stopped.

After that, it was quiet. It was quiet all over the house for a long time. Minute after minute passed, and Sir Michael didn't move and there was no sound in the house anywhere. Sir Michael didn't know how much time passed. Half an hour, an hour, he wasn't sure. He sat without moving. He thought about his wife, Ann. It was twenty years since she had died, but the thought of her was still wrenching to him.

After that long time, sitting like that, without thinking at all, he picked up the pistol. He slipped it into his jacket pocket.

Clearing his throat softly, Sir Michael swiveled in his chair and stood up. He moved around the edge of the desk, his fingertips trailing over the smooth border. He paused on the other side to button his jacket, pull the panels down. He felt the weight of the gun in his pocket. He went to the door and opened it.

It was so dark out in the corridor that he had begun to step forward before he realized that a man was standing there. Even then, he was so startled, he couldn't comprehend what it was he saw.

But it was a man. An enormous man who almost filled the doorway. With his vast shoulders and his heavy, cinder-block head, he looked like Frankenstein's monster. He towered even over Sir Michael. And he came slowly into the room.

Stupid with confusion, Sir Michael could only back away at first. Back away and watch the creature advance. His thoughts had all been on Storm, on Storm up in his daughter's room. He could not take this in.

Then he had a single moment of fear and half-understanding. He even had time to wonder if he had got it wrong, got it all wrong.

His hand flashed to his jacket pocket, to the gun. His mouth opened to shout, to warn Sophia.

Then the monster struck him unconscious to the floor.

22   A police car, with its siren blaring, is no good place for conversation. Pullod, driving, PC Slade beside him, Harper and Bernard in the backseat, all sat without speaking as the car laced through the evening traffic, as it plowed over the miles of the motorway.

Harper had her stick pressed against the floor, her hands folded on top of the dragon's head, her chin propped on her hands. Bernard leaned weakly against the door, his long legs stretched as far as they would go under the seat in front of him. His eyes were closed. His body looked limp and slender and frail in the white T-shirt and sweatpants, in the blue windbreaker one of the cops had loaned him.

The monotonous wail of the siren made it difficult for Harper even to think. It went on and on as the car's red lights flashed and faded over glimpses of night countryside. Car after car sank past the windows, sank back behind them. Harper leaned on her stick and stared at the seat in front of her, trying to string her ideas together. Now and then she glanced over at Bernard. He didn't move, didn't open his eyes.

After a while she leaned forward a little, towards the back of Pullod's head. She shouted to him over the racket.

"I wonder," she said, "if it might be possible to have

someone phone Belham Grange . . ."

It was Slade who half-turned to her. "Trouble with the line," he shouted. "They've had a storm up there."

"Perhaps, then," Harper shouted back, "you could radio and have a local officer drop by the place . . ."

"All taken care of, darling," Slade answered her abruptly. Then he looked out the window and muttered to himself, "Though why we should bother, I don't know."

Harper couldn't hear what he said, but she answered him anyway. "Because," she told him astringently, "Iago has been looking for the Rhinehart panels for twenty years. The only thing that's kept him from finding them is that, in all that time, they haven't changed hands. When Mormo got hold of the *Madonna,* it was reasonable for Iago to conclude that he might be able to get hold of the *Nativity* panel as well. Mormo was, after all, one of a few key fences of black-market art after the war. If the final panel had changed hands then, he might well have been aware of it. But if Mormo had had that knowledge, believe me, he would have told it at once. Since he didn't tell, it seems logical the panel must have been traded by one of the other key fences. And there's only one other such trader who's been involved in these events from the beginning—one other who bid at the *Magi* auction. And Iago knows who that is as well as we do."

She could not see Slade's face, but she understood he was rolling his eyes. She could not hear his voice, but she imagined that he muttered, "Iago!"

She did not answer him again. She sat brooding, leaning on her stick, trying to ignore the siren.

And there is also the fact, she went on silently, *that all this, all of it, must have begun with* Spectre.

What ill wind had blown Iago into that Edgware Road

cinema twenty years ago she would never know. It was his talent, perhaps—as it was hers—to ride the tide of the Uncanny. Perhaps she herself had been in the same cinema on the same day—she could not remember. She only knew that Iago had been there. Five years after she had ruined his cult scheme. He must have been feeling quite fragile, poor lamb. His sense of destiny must have been growing precarious as he scrabbled and seduced among the lost of the earth, desperate to produce the offspring whose blood he needed, all the while realizing that one day, one day the precious blue stone itself would dwindle to nothing.

How that thought must have plagued him. No matter how much blood he got his hands on, one day, one day, the stone itself would be gone. And then the discoloration on his wrists would begin. And then the living decay.

With these concerns, he had wandered into the cinema. He had sat and watched *Spectre*. And as the climax sent shivers of recognition through him . . . *a spilled soda*. Yes. Someone nearby him had dropped her drink in agitation and surprise. Oh yes, yes, it would have been the same. Exactly the same as at the Christmas party. The ghost story. The spilled drink. And Iago, looking up—as Storm had looked up—saw, for the first time, the beautiful Ann Endering, Sophia's mother.

She loved the cinema, loved American movies, and she had been there. And, startled by the film, she had spilled her soda, and Iago had looked up. Then, moved by the beauty of the mother as Storm had been moved by the daughter's beauty, he approached her.

Harper could imagine it. She knew Iago's mesmerizing attractions. Ann Endering—a kind, charitable, liberal woman—would have been his perfect target. If Sir Michael was any indication, she had a penchant for bold, energetic and somewhat dodgy men. And perhaps her idealism—her belief that the world could be made a better place—had softened her, as it did so many, to the beguiling logic of a powerful personality who saw himself as chosen for some great enterprise. In any case, she became his lover. Soon, he would have found out exactly why the film had disturbed her. She loved her house, her family history. She would have seen at once the connections between *Spectre* and the legend of the Belham Abbey Ghost. Perhaps she even recognized the debt the film owed to "Black Annie." Perhaps—knowing her history as well as she did—she knew more than that, much more.

As much as she knew, it was enough, finally, to fuel Iago's interest, to start him down the story trail. After that, the coincidences in the stories—the murdered children, the dream of immortality, the elixir of life in "The Alchemist's Castle," and finally the legends accruing round the Rhinehart triptych—would have led him on—on until, at last, "The Monk's Confession" fell into his hands and he understood everything. And he began his first abortive hunt for the triptych itself.

But by then—by then, Ann Endering understood as well. Too late, she realized who her lover was, and what he was doing to her. She would have been desperate then to keep the triptych out of Iago's hands. And, against all her social instincts, she would have seized on the final coincidence—the one coincidence that perhaps Iago didn't know: that one of the men most likely to be able to recover the Rhinehart panels was Sir Michael, was her own husband.

That was why the third panel had not surfaced, why Mormo didn't know where it was. Because twenty years

ago, before Iago's search had fairly started, Sir Michael—
without fully understanding why—secured the only one of the
panels that was in the west. At his wife's request, knowing only
that the man who wanted it had seduced her, knowing only
that this was his single avenue of revenge, he secured the
panel through his secret sources. And he hid it away.

Which left Ann to complete a task of her own: the task of
destroying herself. Because she would have been carrying his
baby, Iago's baby. He would have made sure of that. And she
would have known now what he was planning to do to it.
And she would have destroyed herself, and the child, rather
than let the infant fall into Iago's hands.

As well as she could with the siren blaring, Harper
brooded on these things in silence. And she brooded as well
on Richard Storm. She reproached herself for understanding
it all too late. She had sent Storm out to Belham to complete
her information. She had thought it a task of relative safety,
had thought it would keep him away from her dangerous
gambit with the *Madonna*. She had hoped he would be able
to help Sophia find the answers to her life, and would then
be able to retire from the fray in peace.

Instead, she had sent him right into the thick of it. And
Iago, as always, was one step ahead of her.

The car raced on and the four sat without speaking,
enveloped by the noise.

Then Bernard said, "Is it real, do you think?"

Harper glanced over to see him watching her. His eyes
half open, looking out through lowered lids. He hardly
raised his voice, but it reached her clearly.

"I would like to know, after all. It would help me to
know."

"What?" she said.

"Can he really . . . If he gets the third painting, if he has the triptych complete, will he really be able to re-create the crystal? Will he really be able to live forever on the blood of his own children?"

Harper extended a hand, patted the factotum on his knee. "Believe nothing," she told him. "It's the only defense."

The flasher's red glow slipped over his features. Harper saw him smiling bitterly. "If I believe nothing, darling," he said dryly, "then what will defend me against myself?"

Harper frowned, replaced her hand on the dragon's head, lowered her chin to the back of her hand.

"Believe nothing," she murmured again, "and trust to the Everlasting Thing."

Then the four sat silently, as the car raced on.

23 The gateway to Belham Grange was now huddled deep in mist. The local constable who had been sent out to investigate cruised by the entrance twice before he found it. Then he did not drive through, but only turned his car on the narrow country road, pointed his headlamps into the drive.

The mist curled in the headlamp beams, wreathed itself around them like a living thing. The local constable, a handsome blond youth with ladykilling blue eyes, leaned close to the windscreen and peered through it.

At first, there was nothing. Only the mist folding, falling, gathering over the first distances of the long front path between the overhanging trees.

Then something moved. A silhouette in the fog. Amorphous at first, then, slowly, defining itself as it approached the light. The figure of a man.

As the constable peered through the windscreen, his heart thudding, the figure moved into the scope of his headlamps. A tall man, with long black hair, with features cut in sharp, cruel angles. With deep, laughing, hypnotic eyes. He was wearing a white three-piece suit. He had green gloves on his hands.

He lifted one hand, one finger, and touched it to his eyebrow in a salute.

The local constable nodded, swallowing hard. He returned the salute to his master.

Then, quickly, he threw the police car into reverse. Spun back away from the Grange's drive. Stepped on the gas and roared off down the country lane, disappearing into the mist.

Iago put his hands behind his back and strolled casually down the drive towards the house.

24 Storm, then, was at the window again, looking out at the night, and wondering. He was buttoning his shirt, tucking it into his pants, and wondering about the reality of grace. Maybe, he thought, maybe this was it: the way he felt right now—hey, what did he know?—maybe this was grace, what religious people called grace. *I love you, Richard, come to bed.* I mean, was that a bolt from the blue, or what? It wasn't what he'd been expecting, that was for damn sure. It sure as hell wasn't what he thought he deserved.

Outside, through the window, the clouds, the moon, the drifting mist, threw their romantic, spectral shadows on the ruins of the abbey, on the wall, on the graves. A wonderful scene, he thought. A great setting for a movie, for a ghost story. And, hey, maybe there was still time for that. Maybe he could just zip a crew out here and shoot "Black Annie" straight off the page, a classy little one-hour job for Brit TV . . .

His gaze shifted. There, beside the outer scene, to the right of it, was Sophia's reflection, thrown by her bedside lamp. And she was buttoning her blouse, and looking down at the floor with her hair falling forward, and smiling to herself in a way that made his heart fill up with wine. He had the memory of her breasts on his lips, and the memory of her shudder in his fingertips, of her last cry, ecstatic and triumphant, in his ears.

And she said softly now, "Well," glancing up at him, "you've certainly got me in a complete fog, Mr. Storm. This day . . . you've got me so confused. I don't know where I am anymore. I hope you're happy."

A corner of his mouth lifted. Maybe he was. Happy. Maybe. He had his movie set, he had his girl, he had a feeling in his balls like hearthlight. Only a slight weakness in his left arm, only a suggestion of pain in the side of his head. Who knew? Maybe this was happy, happy enough. Maybe with this you could check out of the Life Motel and say hey, babe, enjoyed the stay—and then carry the grace out with you like a stolen towel. Who really knew? Maybe there was even more than this, more chances worth taking, some operation, some dread medieval torture of an experimental technique, that stuff they were doing in Baltimore, a one-percent chance of survival—hey, you could go for one percent, maybe, if you had grace on your side . . .

For a moment, a gray haze seemed to deepen before his eyes, the weakness in his arm seemed to threaten to spread through his whole body. But the sensation passed. It passed and, at the same time, his emotions overflowed. He was going to turn to Sophia, he was just about to turn, to turn maybe even with tears in his eyes, to tell her she was the world to him now, that she was the flavor of the world, and that he had forgotten—that he had never really known—how sweet it was, how incredibly sweet.

He was about to turn and say that when, looking dreamily out through the window, he saw something that baffled his imagination, that defied belief.

Storm's hands froze at the collar of his shirt. His lips parted, and he stared—stared through the glass as through a torn curtain at another world revealed.

He saw—did he? Yes—he saw a figure out there—a human figure draped in the mist, silhouetted by the moonlight, raven black, so black it seemed less a being than an absence of existence. It was tall. Its head was bent as if in prayer. Its profile was obscured either by a cowl or by flowing hair. And it was moving with slow and awful majesty among the churchyard stones.

Storm gaped. He pressed his nose to the glass. His sense of well-being deserted him on the instant. He felt woozy suddenly, paralyzed there, his marrow ice, his sinew water. It was real, he thought. He was really seeing it. He was seeing something anyway, a spectral something gliding through the mist, gliding steadily towards the fragment of the chapel wall.

He watched. He couldn't move or speak—couldn't breathe almost—but only gaped and gaped unblinking as if he were petrified on the spot.

"Holy shit," he whispered.

"What is it?" said Sophia behind him.

He didn't answer her. An hallucination, he thought. It must be an hallucination. But still it went on. And, as he peered into the night, the silent, mournful phantasm proceeded with its lifeless grace to the end of the churchyard, to all that remained of the chapel.

And there, beside that ruined wall—before the small crypt where Storm himself had stood—there, as he stood watching, frozen and amazed, the jet absence seemed to sink at the same stately pace, sink lower and lower into the hard earth, until only the head remained above the surface.

And then that too—all, all of it—had vanished.

Storm blinked. He felt very dizzy now, almost faint. He was sweating, cold. Hallucination. Definitely. That had to be what it was. And now, the massing mist, propelled before the wind, surged over the ruin, swept across the moon. In seconds, the torn curtain seemed to close. A steamy, roiling darkness pressed itself against the window.

Storm gave a whiffling laugh. "Nah," he said. "Nah."

But second after second passed, and he found he couldn't move. He could only gaze—gaze and gaze—at the invisible night as if that gliding figure were still before him.

Then Sophia broke his trance with a stifled cry. "Oh God," she said. "Oh, Richard—there it is."

"Huh?" said Storm thickly.

He had to tear himself from the night to turn to her. And when he saw her, even before she spoke again, the hairs on the back of his neck actually felt as if they were standing on end.

Sophia had risen from the bed. She was standing beside it, one hand thrown out to one of the posts. Her face was expressionless, her features cold, but there was a frightened, almost pleading look in her eyes.

And she said, "Listen. Can't you hear it? It's just the same. It's just the same." She turned to him. "Oh, Richard. Don't you hear it? What is it?"

Storm laughed uncertainly as she appealed to him. He had heard people say that they felt as if they were dreaming, but he'd never before experienced it himself. Now he did. Unclear in his mind, unsteady on his feet, he found himself once more in the grip of a sickening impression that his life was unreal.

And yes, he did hear it. He heard it too. In the walls, in the rafters, surrounding him, all over.

Tick-tick. Tick-tick.

He shook his head, trying to clear it. "That's what you never told me," he said dully—his voice came to him as if from the other end of a tunnel. "That's what was missing from your story. You never told me what was making that noise."

Sophia seemed not to hear him. "It's just the same," she repeated.

And the sound repeated: *Tick-tick. Tick-tick.*

Storm took a faltering step towards her. Maybe this was it, he thought. Maybe he was actually dying right this minute. Maybe he was slipping away from the real world into his own fantasies. Maybe that's what dying would be like: maybe only your dreams remained.

"What was it, Sophia?" he said again, forcing the words. "That night you saw your father fighting with your mother— the blood—what was it that was making that noise?"

Sophia made a quick gesture of denial, refusal. The fear in her eyes was turning to panic.

"Where's Daddy?" she said. "Where is he? Do you think he's all right?"

A noise broke from between Storm's teeth as a hot flash of pain went up one side of his head. He pressed the heels of his palms to his brow. He remembered that feeling of alienation out by the ruin, and he thought: Not now. He couldn't go under now. He had to hold on, by force of will.

He had to stay with her.

Tick-tick. Tick-tick.

"I'll find him," he said. He felt he almost had to shout over that quiet, rhythmic tapping. He felt sick. He felt the cold sweat breaking out all over him. "It's all right. I'll go find him."

He marched, with more boldness than he felt, across the room to the door. He threw it open. The action seemed to jar his mind clear, seemed to bring him back to himself a little. He stood confronting the dark of the hallway. Listening, waiting for the sound to repeat.

Sophia hurried to him, took his arm. "Is someone out there?"

He looked down at her. "It's all right," he said more firmly.

They stepped out into the hall together.

The sound seemed to have ceased. The hall was still. The whole house was still around them. Storm felt his way along the wall as they moved through the shadows, as they moved beneath the stares of the portraits hanging above them.

Trailing his hand above the dado, he found a light switch, flipped it. A row of lamps came on, throwing a musty glow over the long landing. Sophia hung close to him, clung to his arm, her face set forward, the taut expression of suspense on her features so perfect that it almost made him laugh. This old dark house, he thought, and the mysterious noise, and the stalwart hero, and the frightened girl: he could never have gotten this scene past the studios. He knew—he'd tried it— they'd thought it was too clichéd.

"I think it's stopped," Sophia murmured hopefully.

"What was it?" he asked her in the same low tone.

She pressed even closer to him, leaned against him. "I don't know."

"I mean that night, the last time you heard it. What was making that noise?"

She shook her head angrily. "I don't know, I don't know."

They went towards the stairway slowly, clinging to each other, Storm watching the corners, watching the shadows, catching the glimpses of the portraits as they watched him pass. He thought to call out, thought to shout for Sir Michael. But the house, the atmosphere of the house, seemed to press in on him like a threat. He was afraid to raise his voice, to bring the danger down on himself. They went on silently to the top of the stairs.

A switch there brought on the foyer chandelier. The base of the stairs became bright beneath them. The grandfather clock in the hall mimicked the ticking sounds they'd heard, but that was it, everything else was quiet. Storm's faintness, the aura of unreality was passing now. He was still sweaty, still a little sick, his brain still clouded and sluggish. But the worst of it was fading. He felt surer of himself, calmer. His step on the stairs was firm, swift. And he bore Sophia along with him.

They reached the bottom. Stood under the light with the coat rack and umbrella stand and gilded mirror all sedate and familiar in the small space. There was the front door just ahead of them, and to either side the dark, old wooden doors into the corridors, both now closed.

Storm didn't know which way to turn. And Sophia had stopped, had planted herself where she was.

And then she said softly: "Oh . . ."

And Storm heard it begin again.

Tick-tick. Tick-tick.

Seeming to vibrate in the fibers of the place so that he couldn't tell where it was coming from.

Tick-tick. Tick-tick.

"Which way?" he said—his voice was still slow and dull. "Which way do we go?"

She said nothing, and he moved instinctively towards the right, in the direction of the abbey ruin. But Sophia held him back.

"Let's . . . go back upstairs," she said. "Let's . . . I think we should just . . ."

Tick-tick. Tick-tick.

The sound sent a gout of juice through Storm—fear or excitement, he couldn't tell which. But it gave him energy. He made to move again. Sophia dug her heels into the floor.

"I just think . . ." she said. "I think we should just . . ."

"Shh," he said.

He slipped his arm free of her grasp. He went to the wooden door and opened it. Flipped on the light.

He stood looking down the empty corridor. The dusty runner under the yellow lampglow. The chairs and tables against the walls. The doors shut all along the way. And the arras with the many-headed dragon hanging against the wall at the far end.

Tick-tick.

It was louder now. Distinct, persistent, purposeful.

He stepped across the threshold.

"Richard . . ." Sophia rushed to him, clutched his arm again.

"This is the way you went, right?" he said.

She nodded, her face pale, the dancing sparks of panic still clear at the bottom of those pale brown eyes.

They moved along the corridor towards the sound.

"What was it?" he said. He felt the sweat roll down his temples, but his mind felt brighter by the moment. His blood was up. "What was it?"

She didn't answer. He could hear her breathing rapidly. Could feel her palm damp against his sleeve.

Tick-tick.

"Jesus!" said Storm. He searched for it. Over the runner, over the walls, over one closed door after another. Another staring portrait, a crumbling Roman temple in the mist. "Where did you go?" he whispered. "The last door, you said. Your father's study."

"I don't know."

"Yeah? Don't you?"

"Richard . . ."

Tick-tick. Tick-tick.

This time, she let out a noise at the sound, as if she'd been struck, as if it had pierced her.

They were nearing the end of the hallway and the many-headed dragon reared before them, all its mouths opened, all its teeth bared.

Storm tried to think. "They were fighting, right? And your mother was on the floor," he said. "And they were all covered with blood, and your father stood up and had something like a knife."

"Stop it, Richard. Stop."

"And what was making that noise, Sophia?"

She didn't answer. And then she said, "There was something," in a voice so small it was barely audible.

"What? What was it?"

Tick-tick. Tick-tick.

Her hand spasmed on his arm as the noise repeated. He felt it too, a double jolt of adrenaline. The last door was drawing close to them. He was almost dragging Sophia along. His free hand was rising, reaching for the knob.

"Something in the center of the room," she said quickly.

391

"That's right. You told me that. What was it?"

"It was a storeroom. There were just old things there."

"What was in the center of the room?"

He reached for the door to Sir Michael's study.

Tick-tick.

"Stop," said Sophia.

She pulled away from him violently. He turned, confused, to see her pressed against the wall. Pressed between a painting and the arras, the dragon to one side of her, a faded arcadia to the other. Her eyes were darting here and there as if looking for a way to escape. And she whispered quickly.

"Let's go back. It was nothing. They were fighting. For the knife. Whatever it was. I want to go." And then she blurted out, "It was a cradle, all right? All right? It was a cradle in the center of the room. I want to go."

He gazed at her blankly. "A cradle."

"An empty cradle, yes. Rocking on a floorboard. Because they were fighting. It kept rocking on the floorboard. Tick-tick."

Tick-tick.

The sound pulled Storm's attention from her. He looked up, down, everywhere for the source of it. And then he looked back at her where she was pressed to the wall, her eyes filling.

"Fighting for the knife?" he said. "You mean *she* had it? Your mother had it? Your father was taking it away from her."

Sophia's mouth went down and her tears spilled over. "She was hurting herself, Richard. There was so much blood. All this blood between her legs, pouring, pouring out between her legs. And she kept stabbing herself there . . ."

"Oh Christ."

"Stabbing and stabbing herself. And the blood kept

pouring, pouring out. And she just went on doing it, pushing the thing into herself. And the cradle kept rocking and it was empty, it was empty, because she kept doing that to herself . . . Oh God, I'm going to be sick again."

"No, you're not. No, you're not, it's all right."

He went to her. Peeled her out of the wallpaper. Wrapped his arm around her. Pressed her face into his shoulder.

"That's over," he whispered, drawing her to the door of her father's study. Reaching out for the knob again. "This is something else. That's over now."

"She hurt herself, Richard. She hurt herself so much."

"I know. But that's over. The past is past. Look."

Tick-tick.

He opened the door.

Sophia screamed.

25 By the light of the desk lamp, they saw Sir Michael stretched face down on the floor in a puddle of blood. There was a cord around his wrist but it trailed free, stained with red, as if he had worked his way out of it. There was a trail of red behind him, as if he had been crawling to the door.

Sophia clutched Storm's arm tightly. He had to yank himself free of her. Then he knelt beside the fallen man, knelt under the empty stares of the mahogany rams' heads carved into the enormous desk. He felt the blood seep warm through the knee of his trousers. He saw Sir Michael's back rise and fall on a shallow breath.

And even as he was kneeling, Sir Michael lifted his head. And Sophia screamed again.

The old man's face was the face of a dead man, the skin gray and thin as parchment. One side of it was smeared with gore. And his eyes bulged at them, round and white.

And his voice rasped faintly, "Get her out. They're in the house."

Tick-tick. Tick-tick.

But Storm was all energy now, beyond thought, his body white-hot with an electric fever. He was on his feet again, looking quickly over the book-lined walls, over the blood-streaked chair, the bloodstained desk blotter. There was the empty box, the silver lighter, the scattered cigars. And he was making sense of things without words, without thinking, connections leaping into his mind at every second. The crypt out by the ruin, the iron door into darkness, the way it led down beyond the end of the house, the way the phantom in the mist had vanished into it . . .

Sophia knelt by her father. She had pulled a cushion from a chair, was working it under his head to lift his face out of the blood.

"Lock the door," said Storm. "Call the cops."

He seized the silver lighter from the desktop.

"Richard?" Sophia said.

"Call an ambulance."

He was out of the room, out in the corridor, the excitement in him like fire.

He moved to the arras, faced the hydra-headed dragon.

Tick-tick.

"Oh yeah," he said.

He felt the rough fabric of the tapestry in his hand. He yanked down. The dragon collapsed before him. The arras collapsed to the floor. A paneled wall was behind it. Storm hit it with the heel of his palm.

There was a click. With a whining screak, the wall swung

towards him on a hidden hinge. The blackness was all beyond it.

Storm nearly laughed aloud. *Incredible!* he thought wildly. *An arras; a secret door; a haunted house! England! What a country!*

"Richard, the phone . . . !" Sophia cried out.

But Storm, unheeding, charged into the dark.

26 Tick-tick. Tick-tick.

The lighter flared, the flame rose high. Black shadows sprung up on every side of him. Black shapes arched and reared and danced under the fluttering light. The little hidden chamber was cluttered with old furniture and junk. Storm turned here and there quickly as the flame made first one object, then another, seem to stir around him. The fabric head of a horse, the glass eyes of a teddy bear stared at him from the corners.

He edged forward over naked floorboards. He could feel them give and sag under his weight. A single bulking thing stood in the center of the room before him. He held the lighter up for a better view, but the metal of it grew hot in his hand, seared his thumb. He saw the ancient wooden cradle for an instant, then shut the lighter's top. The flame went out.

In the pitch blackness, his shin touched the edge of the cradle and set it into motion. And the floor creaked underneath it.

Tick–tick.

And then an answer came from somewhere in the walls:
Tick–tick. Tick–tick.

Storm was pouring sweat now. The fever of excitement and the hectic vapor in his mind had become a single confusion, a lightning-tortured haze. He hardly knew what he was doing, what he was thinking—but he was shoving the cradle aside with his leg, kneeling unsteadily—almost dropping—to the floor.

He flipped the lighter open, spun the wheel again, set off the flame. He saw that the cradle had stood not on a loose floorboard but on a trap. A square door with an iron ring set into it. *Perfect!* he thought. *I love it.* He seized the ring and pulled the door up to reveal the narrow wooden staircase winding into the blackness below.

Tick-tick. Tick-tick.

Now, at last, as if drawn from the house's timbers, drawn from the air around him, from his own brain, the sound resolved itself upon a single center, a single source. It ascended in its unceasing, funereal tempo from the dark at the base of the stairs.

Tick-tick.

Storm started down to meet it.

"Richard! Richard!"

From somewhere above him, he heard Sophia's voice. It seemed muffled to him, far, far away.

He went down, kept going down. And as he descended, step by slow step, the damp wooden boards groaned thickly beneath his shoes, and the cry above him spiraled into a frantic skirl.

"Richard, be careful! Come back!"

His foot touched the bottom step, came off it onto a hard floor. He felt a clammy draft twine around his legs. The lighter's flame swelled and, in the broadening glow, he saw before him a long stone tunnel with rounded walls. His heart was thudding in his chest now and there was a thickness in his brain again, making him dizzy and ill. He wasn't even sure anymore if this was really happening.

But he moved forward slowly.

Tick-tick. Tick-tick.

Once more, the metal of the lighter burned his thumb. Once more, he covered the flame, put it out. But his feet kept sliding on over the stone floor, moving along the tunnel, deeper, deeper.

He held up the lighter. Cracked it. Spun the wheel. His own shadow dodged and capered in bizarre shapes on the stone walls around him.

And before him, he saw the tunnel widen into an irregular chamber. A crossroad. He had come to a crossroad. The passage went on ahead, another off to the left, another to the right. Storm moved into the broader opening at the center.

There, panting, dazed, he lifted the lighter. The flame-glow spread over the arches, over the vaults, over the entire space. His gaze fell at once on a small white mound of flakes and powder that had collected on the floor at the base of one wall. With another cognitive flash, he knew that the debris had fallen from one of the stones above it.

Looking up, blinking through his sweat, through the haze of his own mind, he could see the place. One of the stones in the wall had been chiseled. The mortar that held it was dug away, the block's edges frayed and chalky.

Before he had time to think, he was moving forward, one hand holding the lighter high, the other stretching towards the stone. His fingers were at the jagged edge of the rock. He gripped it, pulled. The stone shifted easily, wobbled, rolled free of its position. It slipped from his grasp and there was a loud crash as it dropped to the floor at his feet.

Storm hardly knew where he was, hardly knew if he was awake or asleep. He thrust the lighter forward into the opening. He felt as if the walls were shuddering around him, the whole house above him quaking to its foundations.

For there, in the niche revealed by the displacement of the stone—preserved in a clear plastic wrapping so covered with dust that the face underneath seemed transparent, distant, ghostly—there, before him, was the body of an infant.

Rhinehart's exquisite *Nativity*.

Storm stared at it a long moment, the lighter scorching his thumb, his free hand raised to his scorching brow.

And then they grabbed him.

27

"Why, Mr. Storm, I'm so glad you could make it. I left Sir Michael to show you the way. You're just in time to witness my final apotheosis."

The lighter had fallen from his hand, gone out. For a moment, the darkness was complete. But Storm heard that voice, heard those words, those half-familiar, half-remembered words. He felt as if he were sinking, sinking from the surface of the real into a whirlpool of his own imaginings.

And yet he couldn't sink. The grip that pinioned both his arms was so powerful, the form that hulked above him so enormous, that it was as if the walls themselves had come alive to take him prisoner. What felt like the muzzle of a gun was being jammed into his temple. It hurt. And then, a flame pierced his eyes, sent a blinding awl-point of pain straight into the middle of his forehead.

He looked away from the flame, looked up. Saw the face of Frankenstein's monster hanging somewhere above him. Well, why not? He would probably have Dracula and the Wolfman on him next. Maybe that's who was pressing the pistol—Sir Michael's pistol, it was—into his sideburn. No—he glanced over—it was a small, round thug with a crushed nose—the nose courtesy of Bernard, who had driven it into his face during the fight outside The Sign of the Crane.

Storm's head fell forward towards the bright flame again. The flame moved aside a little, so he could see more clearly. He saw a man standing in front of him, holding Sir Michael's lighter. It was the man he had seen at the auction. Tall and white-suited, with green gloves on his hands. With long sable hair framing an easy grin on a savagely angled face. And eyes—those eyes deepening and darkening in a way that captured Storm's gaze, that made him feel sicker, weaker, muzzier still. Murky eyes but blackly revealing: windows on a hellbound heart.

And Storm thought: Iago.

"Poor Storm," the man said. "That you ever thought to defeat me."

Storm shook his head weakly. The words were so familiar. "What?" he said. "What are you . . . ?"

Iago laughed. A good scary laugh. Better than Nicholson's in *Hellfire*. Why was it the bad guys always seemed so happy?

"Don't you recognize me?" Iago said. "You should do. You created me, man. I . . ." he pronounced, his eyes almost swallowing Storm. "I *am* Jacobus."

Storm nodded weakly. Now he understood. He remembered. Those words—they were his own words. From the script of *Spectre*. He grimaced, trying to draw back. Trying to fight against the seduction of Iago's stare. "Hey, babe," he said thickly. "Everybody wants to be in pictures."

Iago laughed again. He was moving the lighter now. Lowering it to a black candle in his other hand. He torched the wick. Clapped the lighter shut. Studied the candle quietly. "You know," he said. "This is great. Really. The two of us meeting here like this."

Storm tried to blink the sweat out of his eyes so he could look fiercely into that grinning, angular face. He tried to work his arms free from the grip that held them. The monster holding him jerked him back, tightened his hold. The pistol pressed harder against his aching head. He grunted with the pain.

Iago smiled. He was moving away, the candlelight receding into the shadows of the tunnel. He bent gracefully at the knees and lifted something that was leaning against the wall.

The panel. The *Nativity*. Iago kept moving away with it, along the wall of the tunnel across from Storm.

Iago set the panel down. He stood back and held up the candle. Storm, locked in the monster's grip, turned his head to look into the creeping glow.

He saw the Rhinehart triptych, complete at last.

The panels were leaning against the wall, resting on top of several sheets of brown wrapping paper that rose up behind them. *The Magi* was to Storm's left, the *Madonna* to his right. The *Nativity*—the beautiful Christ child—was set in the center. There were no frames to separate the pictures. They joined together into one flowing whole.

Iago passed the flame over the scene, smiling down at it.

"You know, I told my friends here to leave you alone," he murmured. He glanced up at Storm. "I did, truly. Well, I had my own reasons, but I am a fan of yours as well. I had them be as quiet as little mice just so as not to disturb you." He nodded thoughtfully, as if to himself. "Sir Michael gave up the location of the painting in return for his daughter's life," he said. "My gentlemen stabbed him to death with the softest touch imaginable. And off they crept to meet me here on little tippy-toes. You see? All to keep you out of it, Mr. Storm. Because I didn't want to hurt you if I didn't have to. Truly. And yet—and yet, all the while," he went on, in the same tone of reverie. "All the while, I had this suspicion, you know, that this was really our destiny. The moment I heard the sound of the pick on the stone, I thought, 'It'll travel. It'll travel through the walls of the house and he'll have to come to it.' Tick-tick, tick-tick. Isn't that remarkable? Destiny. Our destiny."

He looked down at the triptych again. Lovingly, Storm thought. He passed the candle back and forth over it.

Storm's own gaze was drawn by the shifting light. He looked at the panels too, from *The Magi* to the *Nativity* to the *Madonna*. And slowly—he thought—he could have sworn—slowly—he saw something in the paintings that almost seemed—what?—almost seemed to be coming to life. Changing. Metamorphosing as he watched. It must have been his own perception, but it really did seem that—there, where the triptychs joined—the scenes transformed themselves. No one image, but the very brushstrokes themselves seemed to come together into some sort of rune, some sort of mystic writing, that ran vertically along the lines of the joins.

Storm's lips parted. "Jesus," he whispered. "Jesus, it's really there."

Iago gave a little happy hum of laughter. "Destiny," he said again. "Beautiful."

Slowly, he began to stroll back from the panels, back towards Storm. Storm looked from the triptych to Iago's face. He felt fear rising from his stomach to his throat. Iago came nearer.

"The whole thing really is beautiful," Iago said. "Because,

in effect, you really did create me. Or re-create me, at any rate. Do you see? When I had lost my way, when I had lost my sense of identity, I saw your film and became again who I was meant to be. You made me, as they say, what I am. What you see before you, Mr. Storm, is a product of your own imagination. And that's beautiful. It's ironic, truly. A subtle mingling of the tragic and the burlesque. Because now, you know, you've seen me here and Sir Michael upstairs and all that—you've seen the triptych, what it is. And now, really, I simply have to kill you. So you invent me—and I murder you—which is rather lovely, I think."

Iago, smiling, holding up the candle, stepped up directly before Storm. Storm stared at him, thinking of Sophia. Wondering whether the bastard would hurt her too, or leave her be. Had she phoned the police? Were they coming? Had she left the house? He didn't even dare to plead for her, lest he remind the lunatic of her presence above.

Iago now shifted the candle into his left hand. The flame played over the stone walls, the outglow touched the paintings leaning on their paper against the wall.

With his free hand, Iago reached into his belt and withdrew a wicked-looking dagger. A curved blade, a bejeweled and golden handle.

"It's not exactly the Sword of the Serizzim," he said with a grin. "But it's all I could comfortably carry. And it'll do."

The candle flame shone on the blade and Storm could not take his eyes off it. The monster jerked him back again, lifted him off the ground. The pudgy thug with the gun grabbed his hair and yanked his head back.

Storm gasped, his mouth open. Iago, gripping the knife for a downward thrust, slowly lowered it until the point was hovering a centimeter from Storm's right eye. The burning blade filled Storm's vision. His throat felt as if it were filled with dust.

"Thanks for bringing a little touch of movie magic into my humdrum life, Mr. Storm," Iago said. "But what you've seen tonight is only for those who have eyes to see with."

And with a swift, vicious movement, he raised the knife up over his head, and plunged it down into Richard Storm's eyeball.

Or so he would have done—but the blade struck steel instead.

Harper Albright, rushing down the tunnel towards them, had drawn her sword. She brought it upward even as she ran, upward in a whistling backhanded slice. With a single echoless ring of collision, it caught the smaller blade in the center of its curve. The knife was flung from Iago's hand. It flew upward, spinning, sparking as the candle's gleam swung crazily over it, over the walls, over the startled faces.

And all Storm could think was, *Thank God I wrote a hero into this picture.*

And then there was no more time to think at all. He felt the giant being ripped away from him. He fell forward and saw the muzzle of the .38 drop across his eyeline as the pudgy thug swung around to take aim at Harper. Storm lunged back at the gun, grabbed the thug's wrist with both hands, wrenched his arm upward. There was a spurt of flame, a crash of thunder, the high whine of a ricochet as the weapon discharged.

Now there were curses and crashes and deep shouts all around him. Storm threw the whole weight of his big body against the pudgy thug, forced him against the wall of the tunnel as he kept the gun hand pinned high in the air. The thug tried to get his free fist up but couldn't, tried to knee Storm in the groin but had no room. Storm tried to pull the gun out of the thug's grasp. The violent lurch pulled them both off balance. They toppled down together to the floor, rolling over and over each other.

The shouts around him continued. Storm felt a blow to his ribs, but held fast to the thug's wrist, wrestling the gun muzzle high. He saw the pistol against a rising glow, then against a sudden sheet of light. He felt a searing wind blow over his face. For a second, he was blinded.

Fire! he thought.

The thug hit him again, then clawed at his face. Storm gasped as the flames rose over him, as the thug tried to shove his head down into them. The heat on his face grew. The smoke choked him. The flames seemed to lap at his cheeks.

Then Bernard was standing above them. He stooped beside them where they fought. He reached out silently with his long, delicate fingers and pinched the pudgy thug at the base of the neck.

The thug collapsed, unconscious, under Storm and Storm nearly fell off him into the crackling blaze.

Coughing, drawing his face away from the smoke, Storm held on to the thug's hand until he had pried the gun out of it.

Then he leapt up, away from the flames. Tumbled to the opposite wall and fell against it. He leaned there, with his hands on his knees, gasping for air.

He looked up at the young factotum, whose shaven head flickered orange with reflected firelight.

"Bernie. Babe. Nice move," he said, panting.

He straightened, turned. The flames were falling now, but he could still see clearly by their low light. He saw Frankenstein's monster face down on the tunnel floor. Two men were wrestling his great arms behind his back, were locking his thick wrists together with cuffs. Blood was burbling thickly out of a bullet hole in the giant's thigh.

Storm turned again, turned away. He turned to look down at the dying flames.

He saw at once what it was. He saw how Iago's candle had fallen, how the paper under the Rhinehart triptych had caught. The old wood of the panels had burned like tinder. It was burning still.

Storm moved heavily to stand over the triptych. He looked down into the face of Christ as the heat of the fire made the flesh of it split and curdle. The edges of the panels—the runes that he had seen there—were all in flames now, and settling into char.

Destiny, thought Richard Storm. *Yeah.*

The triptych settled with a cracking noise into the last of the blaze.

"Where's Harper?" Bernard said behind him.

Storm looked around blankly. He wiped the sweat from his face. "What?"

"Which tunnel did they go down?" Bernard had a flashlight now. He shone it quickly down one passage, then another, then another. "God damn it!" he shouted. He turned on the others—on Storm and the two men who were now standing away from the monster. The three of them looked back at Bernard blankly. And he cried out to them again:

"God damn it. Which tunnel did they go down?"

28 Harper hunted him through the blackness. Her stick rapped heavily against the stone in front of her. Her grim old face was set and savage. Her wheezing breath was rapid and harsh. Her footsteps pounded on the stone. Her heartbeat pounded in her ears. She could make out nothing ahead of her, nothing, and yet, beneath the brim of her Borsalino, behind the narrow lenses of her specs, her eyes were, as ever, quick and alive. She stalked through what she could not see into what she did not know. Which was her nature, after all.

Ahead of her, the tunnel curved gently. She felt the rising arc of the floor in the tip of her stick. She charged along the turning path, her quick steps sure, the steady rhythm of them rising into the rhythm of her pulse, her breath. The dizzying blackness rushed past her as she rushed on.

The air in the place was stony, cool and dry. It had no smell. It was the atmosphere of a cave. But now, as she pounded along, she sensed a change. In hints and wisps at first, a fresher breeze came down to her. A breeze more vivid with the moisture of mist, a trace of earth and winter in it. Her jaw tightened, her teeth gnashed together. She upped her pace, hobbling ferociously, the tempo of her stick on the stone increasing.

The air grew richer, damper, more alive. She felt the floor rising beneath her. She knew she was coming to the end of the trail.

But she was barreling along so swiftly by then that she almost walked into the dead end when she reached it. Her stick hit the wall in front of her. She pulled up short, her nose just inches from the flat stone.

Breathing hard, she turned. She edged backwards down the tunnel, one step, two, then three. There it was. A recess to one side. And it was faintly visible. The tremulous, intermittent silver light of the moon filtered down into it over the dim shape of a stairway.

Harper moved towards that light. Reaching out, she found

the banister, cold iron, crumbling with rust. The stairway was so steep it was nearly a ladder. She grimaced as she hoisted first one foot onto it, then another. Above her, she saw a broken outline of a hole, the fog beyond shot through with light.

And with the banister's rust flaking off under her palm, she drew herself up by the banister, up the stairs.

She was panting as she reached the top, as she extended her hand to the broken iron door. Already, she saw, it was ajar, the mist teasing at the edge, the fresh air washing into her through the gap. She had her stick and the railing in one hand; she pushed against the door with the other. The door complained and ground against the earth. But it swung steadily open.

Harper Albright climbed up the last steps, ducked her head beneath the stone architrave and rose out of the little crypt to emerge into the abbey's churchyard.

A plain of mist and moonglow. A field of graves. A dead elm hanging down as if in mourning. And the triangle of the shattered wall soaring black through the haze into the swirling sky.

Still breathless, Harper moved slowly away from the crypt. Scanning the ruined headstones, the changing shadows, peering eagerly through the mist, which gathered and thickened and dispersed again with each fresh rising of the wind. The lights of the Grange seemed far away behind her. The lights of a town shone distant in the hills. Here, the tendrils and sheets of fog closed and curled around her with their own strange glow and their own strange darkness. Harper moved through them cautiously, edged cautiously around the slanting stones. Scanning the churchyard, peering through the fog.

She flinched as the moisture gathered on her glasses.

Made a sound of exasperation. Looked through. There was no sign of him. Which frightened her. Because she could feel him there, watching her, watching her as she moved uncertainly among the graves.

And yet, except for the wind and the chatter of dead leaves against the stones, the place was still. So still, as she stepped closer and closer to the louring wall. So still she almost convinced herself that her sense of Iago's presence was imaginary. That he was there only within her mind, lodged there as he had been for ages, impossible to discover wholly, impossible to dispel.

A broken stele on the ground. She stepped over it. The moon went in behind a cloud, and the mist grew heavy and gray. The shadow of the chapel wall upon the earth faded into other shadows, which rushed and clustered to it like living things.

Harper moved closer to the wall, and closer. The wind whispered round her. She bent forward slightly, peering round the edge. There, too, the field seemed still and empty.

She straightened. She turned around. The wind rose with a hollow sigh. The clouds blew on.

The moonlight stabbed down into the earth and there stood Iago.

Harper let out a cry of surprise. He was standing a foot from her, towering over her. The smoky depths of his eyes had captured the silver light and gleamed with it, swirled with it. His grin showed gray in the swirling darkness.

She only had time to clutch the dragon's head tighter, to lift the end of the stick from the ground.

Then he pulled one green-gloved hand up across himself as if to slap her down. She jerked her head back instinctively, waiting for the blow.

But he held his hand there, there it hung. And slowly,

grinning, with the flourish of a conjurer, he lifted his other hand to it. He tugged at the fingers of his glove. Quickly, gracefully, he slipped the glove off.

Even as the clouds closed upon the moon again, Harper had light enough to see his naked hand. To see the thin, pulsing line of gangrenous decay that ran down from the base of his knuckles to his wrist.

She stared at it, fascinated. She was startled to hear his voice.

"Oh, Harper," he said sadly, grinning at her all the while. "Oh, Harper."

And the wind rose again, hard this time, moaning. The moon went out. The mist condensed between them. Harper saw Iago's figure obscured, almost spectral, as the fog gathered, as the wind blew and blew. In another moment, the thickening night, the thickening mist, cut her off from him completely. She could not see him, could not tell where he was. She raised her stick uncertainly in a feeble gesture of self-defense.

The wind blew on, and the mist blew on, and the moonlight shone down on her once more.

And Iago was gone.

EPILOGUE

Ah, love, let us be true
To one another! for the world, which seems
To lie before us like a land of dreams,
So various, so beautiful, so new,
Hath really neither joy, nor love, nor light,
Nor certitude, nor peace, nor help for pain;
And we are here as on a darkling plain
Swept with confused alarms of struggle
*   and flight,*
Where ignorant armies clash by night.

MATTHEW ARNOLD

Bernard leaned wearily against the corner of Belham Grange. He watched through hooded eyes as the stretcher-men carried Sir Michael's body out the front door and to the waiting ambulance. It was all red light before the house: police cars parked at odd angles, their red flashers whipping the thin mist. Constables and detectives moved about busily, their faces expressionless whenever the red beams crossed them.

A little way off the drive, on the grass, in the deeper darkness, Bernard could make out Storm and Sophia. They were standing together, his arm around her shoulder, and they watched the covered stretcher pass as well.

And Bernard watched it. Until it was slid into the back of the ambulance with a heavy metal bang. Until the stretcher-men climbed in after it. Until the doors were clapped shut, and locked.

The tires of the ambulance rattled on the drive's pebbles. The vehicle turned and headed away from the house, under the canopy of the double row of trees. Storm and Sophia turned too, Bernard saw. Turned and walked away, into the misty field, their heads held down.

Bernard heaved a sigh and shifted uncomfortably in the cool night air. He wondered bitterly if, by careful examination, he might discover some small part of his body that didn't hurt or throb or ache. He doubted it. He felt he could use a stretcher himself. And an ambulance. Maybe even a body bag. A body bag stuffed with a lot of recreational narcotics. It seemed to him just then a good place to spend the rest of one's semi-natural life.

He maneuvered his limbs to work the stiffness out of them, then leaned against the corner of the house again. Storm and Sophia were now walking away from him, over the field, towards the ruins of Belham Abbey. The gibbous moon hung bright out there above the wedge of wall. With only the last faint clouds wafting over it, it looked like a woman drawing a veil across her face.

Storm and Sophia stopped at the edge of the graveyard, and Bernard saw them close with each other. Saw Storm put his arms around the young woman, and she lean her head against his chest. He breathed the night in deeply and caught the sweet aroma of pipe smoke in the mist. The gruff voice sounded just behind him.

"Ah. Ha-ha."

Harper moved up to stand next to him. She had her pipe clamped in her teeth and was holding the skull-shaped bowl gingerly. She was following Bernard's gaze, looking off across the field at where the lovers in the graveyard embraced.

"Don't," Bernard said to her. "I mean it, Harper. Don't be pleased with yourself. I really think that would be one thing more than I could bear."

Harper tilted her head to one side, plucked the pipe from her mouth. Peered through her glasses at Storm and Sophia. "Well . . ." she said.

"Well, what?" Bernard crossed his arms on his chest and looked down at her, his shoulder still pressed to the wall. "Well, what? Is this your idea of a happy ending? Her father's dead, her lover's dying. They don't understand the half of what's happened here tonight. They probably never will. All they've got is this . . . this little space to hold on to each other in, all surrounded by a sea of confusion and grief. I mean, what the hell do you call that?"

"Life, Bernard," said Harper Albright quietly, watching Storm and Sophia still. She drew on her pipe again for a moment. The smoke filtered out of her mouth as she spoke. "I call it life."

"Life," Bernard mimicked her. "That's the best you can come up with when Iago's got dead away?"

Harper nodded thoughtfully for a long moment. "He works his work," she said again. "I mine."

After that, the two of them stood there for a while without speaking. Watching, as in the last of the mist, in the best of the moonlight, in the shadow of the abbey ruin, Storm lifted Sophia's face and kissed her gently.

Then Harper smiled. "In any case," she said. "Not dead away. He hasn't got dead away. Not quite. We have some of his men, who won't all be loyal to him. We have some allies on the police at last. The triptych has been destroyed and, if I'm not mistaken, there is a certain urgency to the business which will draw our quarry out into the open again before too long."

Bernard raised his eyes to heaven, shook his head.

Harper laughed. "Ha-ha." She reached up and clapped the young man on the shoulder. "Heart on a hill, lad," she told him. "The hunt is just beginning."

With which, she moved away. Walked away to the drive, to the deep shadows beneath the hanging beeches. She tapped her stick against the ground lightly as she walked. The smoke from her pipe trailed back over her shoulder.

After a moment, Bernard followed her.

✦

From the misty churchyard, Richard Storm looked up and saw them go.

He clasped Sophia against him, felt the warmth of her body there, drank the warmth of her body in with his. The wind lifted, and Sophia's hair stirred, and a trailing patch of mist rolled over the graves around him, rolled on before him. And through the gathering haze of it, Storm watched Harper's squat silhouette, moving away from him towards the trees. He watched the wedge of her cape and the outline of her hat and the swing of her stick on the earth. He watched Bernard's tall, willowy silhouette loping along beside her.

He held Sophia tightly, and watched his two friends moving away from him, moving and moving away until the mist closed over them, like a curtain.

ACKNOWLEDGMENTS

This is a work of fiction, and fiction of the most fantastical kind at that. Any mention of real names or places—John Wayne, Jack Nicholson, Sotheby's, etc.—is strictly for the purposes of verisimilitude. I've borrowed them as archetypes; neither they, nor anyone else alive or dead, has ever been involved in these events.

And as this is fiction, I won't waste the reader's time with a long list of living or printed sources of research information. But I must express special thanks to Dr. Jennifer Ellis and Dr. Richard Scofield for their medical expertise; to James Cohan for introducing me to the people and places of the art world; to Paul Sieveking of the wonderful *Fortean Times* for the lowdown on magazine work; and to Simon Brett for vetting my British culture and vocabulary.

Some authors also deserve special mention. Jennifer Westwood's *Albion: A Guide to Legendary Britain* is possibly the only encyclopedia I've ever read cover to cover with intense pleasure. Lynn H. Nicholas's *The Rape of Europa* provided a complete picture of the Nazi pillage of European art—which I then blithely changed to suit my purposes. And the books of Charles Walker provided a useful compendium of every possible paranormal conspiracy theory on the planet. I took the story of the Nazi witches from *The*

Demonic Connection by Walker, Toyne Newton and Alan Brown. I adapted Mormo's prayer from Francis King's *Sexuality, Magic and Perversion*, quoted in Walker.

Finally, my personal thanks to my agents, Barney Karpfinger—who provided immensely helpful suggestions for the book's third draft—and Frank Wuliger and his crew at Innovative Artists; to Ann Patty for her brilliant edit and advice; and, as always, to my wife, Ellen, for aid, comfort, support, patience, criticism and dinner.